The column of empty space churned violently, ripping apart the earth around it, sucking chunks of grass, of dirt, of rock, into its void. *No*, Michael realized. Not just earth. *Sky*. It was eating sky.

VOLUME 2: SARA'S SONG

GREG MITCHELL

Rift Jump Vol. 2: Sara's Song
Copyright 2015 Greg Mitchell
All rights reserved
ISBN: 9780692461808

Published by Genre Experience

Cover Art by Thomas Mason

Visit the author at
www.thecomingevil.blogspot.com

To Meghan, Jo Beth, and Dani,
who keep me coming back to reality.

TABLE OF CONTENTS

PREVIOUSLY...

Lurking in the dark void In-Between the worlds of the multiverse exists a being of pure evil known by many names—including "The Rage". This Great Beast exists because of Choice, and the Man in the Stetson who dwells in the White Place outside of time and space built the multiverse as a means of binding the Beast. This creature has only one goal: to escape Its imprisonment. To do that, It calls to those with the potential for great evil, promising power and fulfillment, seducing them into accomplishing Its dark will in seeking to destroy the various levels of parallel dimensions that make up the multiverse.

Among those chosen by the Rage is twelve-year-old Michael Morrison, an orphan striving to survive the crime-ridden streets of Los Angeles in the year 1991 with his brothers Edward and Seth. Guided by Rip, a conniving and cruel mentor, Michael is molded into a child soldier in a war between feuding gangs. A bloodlust grows within him until, by tragic accident, he murders a young girl at school: Sara Theresea, who rejected Michael's love. It is this one horrible instant that gives the Rage Its opportunity to sink Its claws into Michael's soul. Soon thereafter, Michael is gunned down by a rival gang and wakes up in the Desert of Choosing. Rip is there to guide him once more—this time into the employ of the Rage. But there is another presence there. The Man in the Stetson offers Michael redemption and a chance to travel the multiverse, combating evil. Overcome with guilt and grief, the young boy accepts the Man in the Stetson's offer and begins a violent campaign against the agents of the Dark—beginning with killing Rip. To aid in his quest, Michael is supernaturally granted invulnerability, as well as a sort of internal "radar" that guides him to the presence of evil. What follows are five brutal years of death-dealing that threaten to bury Michael's compassion and, perhaps, turn him to the Rage's will after all.

The key to Michael's salvation comes, quite unexpectedly, in the form of Sara Theresea, the girl he murdered as a frightened and confused boy. When he discovers her in a parallel dimension, seventeen years old and married to Charlie Bost—an abusive, cheating louse—Michael is moved to shake loose his apathy and rescue her. But not only that—he longs to spend the rest of his life with her, making up for his crimes. Aided by Johnny Frawl, a quirky young man and occult enthusiast, Michael breaches a dimensional wall and slips into the In-Between, seeking an audience with the Man in the Stetson. For a time, Michael considers leaving behind his mission to settle down with Sara, but comes to realize that his work is not yet finished. He manages to kill Charlie and deliver Sara, yet further endangers her when he asks her to join him on his inter-dimensional adventures. Desperate to flee her ordinary life, Sara readily agrees and soon the two teenagers become lovers and marry.

Over the next year, Sara accompanies Michael on his crusade to eradicate the Rage's agents, battling aliens, mutants, and monsters in the process. Together the two encounter a number of allies and adversaries, including alternate versions of Michael's brothers Edward and Seth, caught in a Civil War over alien technology; the costumed superhero Light Sphere; Michael's own tormented double, "The Hooded Man", who would turn him back to the path of evil; and Chris Thompson, a deadly servant of the Rage with the ability to create fire with his mind. All the while, Michael begins to question his own motives for serving the Light as he detects himself slipping further into darkness. Sara's love has reawakened within him a desire to do good, which suddenly seems at odds with his quest to administer judgment.

Sara is going through changes, as well. After spending her life thus far as a timid and shy girl—eventually victimized by Charlie—she is determined to become a stronger fighter, a goal about which Michael isn't too sure. While he works to quell his own violent impulses, Sara is discovering hers, slowly becoming a force to be reckoned with on the battlefield. Their marriage suffers as the two struggle to work together, but they must stand side-by-side when they arrive at their next world and meet eight-year-old Toby Jeffries, a boy ignored and unloved. Toby has a seed of the Rage within him that grants him the ability to generate ice, to devastating effects. Sara immediately connects to the boy, determined to protect him from those who would persecute or manipulate him because of his powers, and Michael, too, develops a fondness for Toby and wants to help him overcome the Rage so that he might not travel the same dark paths that Michael has.

It is on this world that the Rage's demonic representative, the Maestro, arrives with a company of firestarters led by Chris Thompson. For years, the Maestro has been tracking Michael across the multiverse, to "bring him to heel" and convince him to fulfill his dark destiny serving as a general to an army of grey-skinned, insect-like devils lying dormant on the war-torn world of Chelkan. At last Michael realizes the awful truth: While he's been serving the Man in the Stetson, the Rage inside his heart has insidiously been working to see Its will succeed nonetheless. Fearing what he might become, Michael wholly surrenders to the Light and expunges the Rage within, inadvertently creating a viscous and bizarre Behemoth in the process. In the ensuing battle, Chris and the other firestarters are killed, but the Maestro escapes into the night. At last, Michael defeats his deadliest opponent—his own dark nature personified.

With his heart finally free from the burden he's carried for so long, Michael is ready to begin anew, serving the Light and saving people, not simply destroying monsters. With Sara at his side, and young Toby as his apprentice, Michael sets off for new voyages.

Meanwhile, a sinister storm is brewing in the Void between the worlds…

ENTR'ACTE

The Glor stood impossibly huge. Towering at twenty feet tall, its lumbering pale yellow-green body was a mountain of muscle, clad in a simple loin cloth that must've cost the lives of a half-dozen yafleks, the buffalo-like creatures that raced along the grassy plains of the planet Yur. Michael Morrison liked the yafleks. They were affectionate, gentle creatures despite their burly size.

Michael did *not*, however, like the Glor.

"Run!"

Even as Michael shouted the command, eight-year-old Toby Jeffries was already hightailing across the leafy forest floor, hurling frozen projectiles behind him. The boy had only discovered his strange cryokinetic powers four months back, but was fast developing into an old pro. By the kid's side, Michael's wife Sara pumped her trim and muscular legs, her face dirtied and haggard, clutching the twin curved chukrahas daggers the Krinvox tribesmen had given her; the same tribesmen who had pleaded with the extra-dimensional strangers to rescue them from the semi-intelligent Glor in the first place. She launched herself over a downed tree, rolling her back along its bark, landing squarely on her feet and running still, just as the Glor set down one gigantic foot, splintering the trunk in a hail of wooden shrapnel.

Michael's heart dropped into his stomach, but Sara didn't spare him a second look. *She can take care of herself*, he was reminded once again.

As Sara maintained her pace downhill, half-sliding, half-tripping, Toby lost his footing entirely and fell backwards onto his seat. Michael pitched forward and cut a beeline in the bespectacled boy's direction, putting himself in the path of the deadly beast. In one motion, he hurried to the boy and scooped him up in his arms. Toby aimed both hands palm out at the ground and blasted a bridge of ice that carried them away from the monster. Enraged, the Glor bellowed and bashed at the ice slide with hairy fists, smashing aside chunks of frozen matter.

"Turn me around!" Michael shouted into Toby's ear over the clatter of falling trees and the Glor's thunderous roars.

"You're crazy!" the boy retorted.

"Just do it!" Michael said with a chuckle.

With a gentle twist of his wrists, Toby angled the ice snake to curve back around, putting it on a collision course with the giant.

"Higher!" Michael commanded, and Toby obeyed without further complaint.

The ice rose, the Glor barreling for it, spittle flying from its dull-toothed maw. "You're jumping, aren't you?" the kid asked, a sort of put-upon resignation in his voice.

Michael laughed and patted the boy's shoulder. "As soon as I'm clear, take off. Head back for Sara and get the speeder."

"She wanted us to do this together," Toby reminded him.

"Sara's got to learn her limits," Michael said, biting back his frustration. His guilt. He'd begun her training as a means of giving her the strength to protect herself when he wasn't around, but she was starting to carry her independence to dangerous proportions. She wasn't invincible.

Michael, on the other hand, *was*.

"Part of working as a team," Michael continued, the rush of the oncoming wind blowing back his chestnut-colored hair, "is using each member's strengths. This is mine."

Toby didn't object, though Michael knew the boy had a special fondness for Sara. He felt a small amount of disapproval at his *own* choice, but he had a responsibility to protect his wife and their young charge. It was Michael who had been given this mission by God, traveling the infinite multiverse, visiting alternate and parallel timelines to combat the dark workings of the mysterious beast known as "the Rage". Sara and Toby were along for the ride; a family he had selfishly taken on after years of doing his job solo. The loneliness had been excruciating, but having them to worry about seemed somehow worse.

Pushing aside his doubts, Michael leapt from the ice slide, stretching his arms wide, the wind tugging at his new hooded jacket. The Glor reached out for him with a hand the size of Michael's body, and he twisted in the air, slipping easily out of the giant's closing grasp, before catching the leather gauntlet on the creature's arm. At last Michael settled into the familiar routine that came with combat, shutting out his worries about his wife and surrogate little brother. He lost sight of them in his daring move, trusting Toby to head back to Sara and the speeder at the bottom of the hill.

Trusting Sara to go along with Toby was another matter. *Please, Sara, don't pick now to be stubborn.*

2

Sara dashed down the forested hill and felt her ankle twist. She let out a curse, but soldiered on. Ahead, she spotted Ak-Huel, the lanky Krinvox warrior in wraps of sand-colored garb, who waited by the parked hover speeder. They'd started this quest to vanquish the deadly Glor with a whole entourage of the tribe's best young men. Of them all, only Ak-Huel had survived. He was fearless and gifted and had proven himself well against the giant. Their desire to kill the behemoth was nothing personal—it was simply a matter of survival. A terrible viral outbreak had claimed innumerable lives, and the mythic Glor, thought lost for five generations on the planet Yur, possessed a rare blood that was essential to concocting a cure. Ak-Huel believed that the Glor was, perhaps, the last of its kind. Michael struggled with the morality of eradicating one species for the survival of another, but it seemed the only way, and Michael was the one with a direct line to God, or whatever. Sara supposed if God had wanted it differently, He would have sent some other options their way. Michael said they had to trust God's judgment. She didn't know about that, but she trusted *Michael.*

Mostly.

Ak-Huel waved her forward with his spear. "This way!" he shouted in broken English that he'd only recently learned from the "aliens".

Carried by her own momentum, Sara nearly collapsed on the thin, blue-skinned warrior, but he caught her and steadied her on her own feet. She stared up at his elongated face, his one blinking eye and a wide mouth filled with deadly needles. He would have been frightening to her a year ago, but after everything she'd seen on her travels, she brushed off his strangeness as easily as she would brush off this world when it was time to leave for the next.

"Thanks," she muttered, casting a look back to the hill.

Toby was on her in a second, riding some wild ice serpent. He was out of breath as he hopped off the cold platform and ran up to her, pushing his glasses back atop his button nose. "The Glor's coming! We have to go!"

Sara set her face, looking everywhere for her husband. When she did not immediately see him, she gritted her teeth. "Where's Michael?"

Toby blushed and averted her gaze.

Angry, she pounded the side of the speeder with a fist. "I told him we could do this together!"

Ak-Huel took gentle hold of her arm. "Mych-El very strong. Best obey."

Sara cooled at Ak-Huel's words, not wanting to give the impression of dissension in the chain of command. That the tribe hadn't handled the Glor on their own was testament to their fear and comparative weakness. But Michael had brought them courage. There was a time when he had done the same for Sara.

He's good at that, she mused, bittersweet.

Her anger toward her husband momentarily subsided. She nodded absently and turned to Toby. "Get in."

3

The Glor had one three-fingered fist wrapped around Michael's leg and hurled the flimsy human at a tree. Michael's back slapped against the rough wood and he flailed helplessly. Dazed but unhurt, Michael could only dangle as the beast slammed him on the dirt floor before releasing him. The Glor, perhaps believing his prey dead, continued down the hill after the others, giving Michael the chance to catch his breath before taking up pursuit. He scurried to his feet and raced after the monster, his fists clenched into balls of lead. Narrowing his gaze in concentration, Michael leapt onto the monster's calf and pulled himself up. The Glor paused in its march as Michael scrambled along its back. The beast thrashed and reached for him, but Michael dodged its gnarly hands, finally riding atop the creature's shoulders.

"I'm really sorry to have to do this!" Michael winced and raised his fists, bringing them down like hammers on the Glor's head.

The giant snorted and flinched under the barrage, but remained standing, listing from side to side, waving its monstrous arms, trying to dislodge the human. Surprise prickled Michael's mind, as he'd expected his attack to do *something* to the creature, but the thing was stronger than he'd anticipated. He bashed again with his tiny fists, rippling the supple flesh of the Glor's bald head. The beast stamped its feet on the ground, the whole hillside quaking in reply. Michael squeezed his legs against the monster's shoulders, trying to hang on, but it was obvious the Glor had endured enough. With renewed vigor it clawed for Michael relentlessly until its thick, dumb fingers found purchase. Michael gulped as he was effortlessly yanked free from his mount. He braced to be sent airborne, but the Glor wasn't through with him.

Using a hand that could flatten an average-sized home in one swipe, the Glor squished Michael tight. Even with his invulnerability, Michael felt his body constrict, heard his ribs grating against each other. He'd be a tube of ejected toothpaste by now were it not for the grace of God, and he did thank God in that moment. But the truth of the matter was that he was stuck until the Glor decided to release him, and no amount of bravado or strength was going to get him out.

He needed help.

The Glor, with its prize in tow, gave a good snort as if in satisfaction, then tromped down the hill.

4

Sara piloted the speeder back towards Ak-Huel's settlement, the wind pelting her face and ginger ponytail in the exposed cockpit. She squinted against the gusts, but steered straight. Glancing to the backseat, she saw Toby facing backward, keeping an eye out for Michael.

"See him?" she shouted over the wind.

He turned back, shielding his face. "No."

Ak-Huel rested in the passenger seat, his spear kept close, a look of apprehension frozen on his bizarre face. His was a primitive tribe, more accustomed to shamanism than technology, and the speeder was playing up on his superstitions. The speeder itself was, like the other odds and ends of tech back at camp, a gift from emissaries of the Empire, looking to adopt Ak-Huel's people into civilization. The Krinvox had resisted this long, determined to remain true to their heritage, but then the plague struck.

Sara wondered if that were more than a coincidence.

She faced Ak-Huel. "Don't worry. Michael will get your cure."

The alien nodded once. "Trust. Worry for Mych-El."

"Yeah. He's gone longer than usual." Sara chewed on her lip, glancing over her shoulder in the direction of the forested hill growing smaller over the horizon. What was taking him so long? A little concerned, she tried reaching out to him with her mind. Around the time they first met Toby, she and Michael had begun to develop a psychic link. They'd only had a little time to explore the possibilities before the link was apparently severed following Michael's fight with the Maestro and his subsequent regeneration, but Sara tried regardless.

Sara concentrated. {*Michael, can you hear me? Are you there?*}

Cold silence met her request, and she cursed. As she feared, it was the same as the last couple times she'd tried using their mental bond. It was like she could *feel* Michael still there, but his back was turned to her and she couldn't get his attention. His thoughts were closed off to her like a locked door and she pounded harder. {*Michael! Where are you?*}

No answer. She slewed the speeder.

Toby leaned forward into the cockpit. "What are you doing?"

"Going back for him."

Michael pushed with every ounce of divine strength he'd been imbued with, but could not pry loose the Glor's fingers. The monster trampled through the forest, no longer at a run, now just a swift walk. Michael had no idea where the Glor was taking him, and anxiety encircled him, as unmovable as the giant's grip. Though he felt no pain, he began to panic, desperate to get free and breathe fresh air into lungs that were dangerously close to flat. Nevertheless, all he could manage to do was steady himself and wait for the wild ride to end.

The Glor reached the bottom of the hill, but instead of heading east towards the direction of Ak-Huel's camp, it turned west and followed the foot of the forested mountain, pushing aside hanging branches and stepping over overgrown brush. At last, Michael glimpsed a nearly concealed cave opening. The cave mouth yawned open and the Glor had to duck to slip inside its jaws, into darkness. Michael relaxed only marginally, his curiosity overwhelming his despair. His captor slowed to a near crawl, edging deeper into the cave, turning down bends, its knuckles brushing against the rocky wall. Pebbles rained down on Michael's long sweaty hair. Around a corner, he detected the faint hint of fireglow. After a moment, they rounded the curve in the cavern and Michael saw lit candles, a huge oak table, and an equally enormous chair.

Stunned, he looked to the Glor. "Is this your home?"

Ak-Huel's people had told Michael that the Glor was simply an unthinking beast, driven mad by the smell of blood. But this was a domicile. Crude, maybe, but civilized nonetheless.

The Glor did not respond, except to hurl Michael against the nearby rock wall. Michael hit hard, but at last could breathe unrestricted again, and collapsed to the floor. He readied himself to stand, but the Glor was over him, jabbing a gigantic finger in his face. The beast did not press an attack, but gave a grunt, as if to say, "Stay". Michael remained on the floor, a warm peace soothing his soul.

When Michael had first started jumping the rifts, he experienced savage headaches or stomach cramps whenever he neared his assignment. But that was when he operated under the power of the Rage. On Toby's world, Michael managed to surrender that portion of himself to God—the Presence in the White Place—and he found that the old anger was gone. So were the headaches. Now, whenever his mission was in view, he felt only a calm assurance that he was doing the right thing.

He felt that now, and wondered what it could mean.

Once the Glor seemed satisfied that Michael would not move, the beast lumbered across the cozy den to a basin of water in the corner. Michael pressed himself to sit by the wall and watched in astonishment as the Glor gripped the basin and lifted it to its toothy mouth. It grumbled a series of growls and snorts into the bowl. The waters rippled and a soothing masculine voice emanated from the surface, speaking perfect English. "Why do you hunt me?"

Michael blinked in surprise and stood to a shaky stand. "Wha—? You talk?"

"Of course I do. I think, I dream. Is that so hard for you to understand?"

"I…" Michael looked to the exit of the cave, glanced around the home, then back to the Glor. "I don't understand."

"Exactly. Which is why I have the Waters of Truth."

"But how do you know English?"

"Is that your language? I don't. The Glor are ageless. We have seen the rise and fall of many societies, many cultures, many languages. The Waters of Truth speak all tongues."

"You…The Glor. Where are the others?"

The giant lowered the basin for a moment, his eyes dulling, his expression slackening. "I am the last. We have been hunted for sport for far too long. You would see the end of us?"

"N-No. That's not…" Michael blew out a breath and ran his hand through his damp hair, overwhelmed by this development. "Look, I don't want to hurt you. There's a plague killing the Krinvox tribe. Their legends say that only the blood of Glor can save their women and children."

The Glor nodded and breathed over the waters. "That is true. The plague struck once before, nearly three thousand generations ago on Yur. Back in a time when the Glor were welcomed at the table of nations."

Michael stepped forward, his spirit rising in excitement. "Then help us again."

"Why should I? I have remained safely hidden all these centuries, content in my reflections. The Krinvox know only tribal conflict with the Empire. I want nothing to do with either of them. We Glor are beyond war."

Michael chuckled, rubbing the back of his head. "I don't know. You seemed pretty good at it before."

"Fighting accomplishes nothing."

"Sometimes we *need* to fight. But I don't want to fight you. I'm just here to save the Krinvox."

The Glor gazed at Michael over the bubbling Waters of Truth, eyes narrowing in pause. "Perhaps your cause is noble. The Waters also allow me to see into your spirit. A warrior you are, shadowed by a great darkness. But I see you are a warrior with honor."

Michael nodded in appreciation. "Will you help me?"

"You need only a little of my life's blood for your cure. I will…make that sacrifice for you."

Michael released a long breath he hadn't realized he was holding in. "Thank you."

"In return, you must demand that the Krinvox leave me in peace. Or else I will once again adopt the ways of war. And there will be much blood."

Stepping up, Michael waved his hands. "No, we don't want that. Your generosity is really appreciated, and I'll make sure no one bothers you again."

The Glor's blistered lips parted into a warm—if not slightly unnerving—grin. "Then we are well met—AAACHH!"

Michael flinched in surprise as the Glor gnashed his teeth, roaring in pain. Glancing down, Michael spotted a Krinvox spear jutting out of the giant's leg.

"Hit him now!" Sara's voice echoed from deeper in the cavern.

A swelling blast of ice jetted across the empty space, crashing against the side of the Glor, causing him to knock over the basin. Next, Michael saw Toby rush in, hurling shard after shard of frosty rockets. Michael inched back as the Waters of Truth spread along the rocky floor, pooling at his feet. The Glor turned on his attackers, roaring and grunting, but without the Waters of Truth, his eloquence was lost. Ak-Huel was on the beast in a heartbeat, yanking out the spear and stabbing again.

"Wait!" Michael shouted, holding out his hands, but his voice was overpowered by the echoes of the Glor's outraged cries.

Then Michael saw Sara charge into the room, her blades at the ready, her face like impassive stone. With a shrill cry, she leapt forward and buried her curved chukrahas into the gentle monster, pulling herself up.

"*Sara!*" Michael pushed forward, trying to get to her, but the Glor spun about wildly, trying to displace the woman. In the process, a gargantuan backhand sent Michael sailing across the cave, smacking him hard against the rock wall. Invulnerable or not, he was dazed, and wobbled on his knees. Through blurry vision he watched Ak-Huel and Toby work to subdue the giant, bringing it to its knees. And Sara…

Michael's stomach soured at the sight of her cold, heartless face as she mounted the beast's shoulders and stabbed again and again, right into the base of the Glor's skull. Blackish blue blood sprayed everywhere, covering Sara in gore, but she would not relent. Her lips revealed strained teeth—and just the hint of a sneer—as she butchered the creature right before Michael's eyes.

At last, the Glor collapsed to the ground, its gaze locking on Michael. Michael felt his own eyes tearing up and reached a hand toward the monster, whispering, "I'm sorry." The Glor, however, grew pale as its eyes rolled into the back of its head, the light gone from them.

Ak-Huel lifted his spear and released a war-whoop in celebration. Toby took a seat across from him, out of breath, but looking pleased with his part in the battle. Sara wiped the blood off her daggers onto her dirtied jeans and sheathed them behind her back. Beaming with pride, she hopped down off the dead Glor and walked to Michael. She cocked her head, smirked, then held her hand out to him.

"Need a lift?"

Michael stared at the hand, suddenly scared to take it, but finally did. She led him to a stand and he looked at her askance, his sight listing to the defeated giant.

"You're welcome," Sara said with an offended laugh. Then she joined in Michael's observation of their fallen foe. "Not bad, huh?"

But Michael had no words.

6

Back at the Krinvox village, Michael sat by one of the small fire pits that dotted the camp, staring into the flame, his hood pulled over his head—partially for warmth, but mostly for privacy. Around him, the Krinvox danced in celebration. They had the Glor trussed up like wild game and some of the men were gutting it, disseminating all of the giant's parts to be used—not just for the cure to their plague, but for meat, clothing, tools. None of the ogre would be wasted and Michael supposed he was grateful for that, but to think of all that *was* lost… An entire species, wiped from existence. And for what? A few drops of blood that the beast was willing to offer in return for a little peace and quiet.

The electro-barriers around the perimeter of the village hummed, one of the few technological advances that the otherwise primitive tribe possessed. The force-field was there for protection against predators, but Michael wondered if maybe the real monsters were already inside the camp.

Ak-Huel approached, surrounded by a dozen screaming, laughing, rambunctious children. They clung to their papa, as did most of the tribe tonight. He was a hero, the only of their soldiers to return following the Glor hunt. Ak-Huel gave Michael's back a hard pat. "Happy! Glor dead! We saved!"

Michael nodded and forced a small smile. "Yeah, Ak-Huel. Your people will be okay."

Ak-Huel's kids tumbled around him like newborn pups, until the alien scooped up three of them in his elongated arms. He nuzzled their necks as they laughed, his expression softening. His one eye glistened with tears and he managed a small, meaningful nod. "Thank you, Mych-El. Thank you."

Once again Michael offered a half-hearted smile in response as the man of the hour and his joyful brood rejoined the festivities. Though Ak-Huel's fallen compatriots were mourned by family and friends, the general mood of the settlement was one of relief, a peaceful comfort resonating from the villagers who could now rest easy without fearing the plague. Looking deeper into the celebration, Michael saw Toby playing chase with the other kids and showing off some of his ice powers by creating snowballs for the children to pelt each other. Laughs were shared all around and the boy he'd adopted appeared happier than Michael had seen him in a while.

Michael hadn't told Toby about the Glor's true nature. The kid had a hard enough time adjusting to a life of rift jumping; he didn't need unnecessary guilt to compound all those confused feelings. He was only eight, for crying out loud.

Eight…

What have I done by bringing him into this?

Up ahead, Sara excused herself from her own warrior's welcome to approach Michael by the fire. She moved her lithe form like a cat. When he'd first met her, Sara had been a mousy girl, afraid of her own shadow. Now she was a fierce and powerful woman, confident and in full command of her body. She was undeniably gorgeous, but Michael was unsure about some aspects of her transformation. Confidence, he'd always wanted her to have. But she was prideful now. Arrogant.

Sara's broad smile glowed with excitement and accomplishment in the company of the villagers, but she visibly diffused as she neared him.

"Can I sit?" she asked, somber.

He nodded and she crouched beside him, hands draped over her knees. She stared into the fire as Michael studied her face, hoping to see remorse there. Instead, he saw nothing.

Nothing at all.

"You're upset about the Glor, aren't you?" she asked after a moment, tossing a small pebble into the fire.

Michael looked back to the crackling flames. "Yeah."

"I thought it was a threat. I thought I was rescuing you."

"I know."

"Had I known what you told me about it being a good guy, you know I wouldn't have hurt it."

Michael wasn't so sure. "I know."

She angled her blue eyes on him and he forced himself to hold her gaze. Her eyes used to sparkle. Like the clear blue waters of Dronaj in the Ufghar Galaxy. But now the shine had dulled. The waters were muddied. "Michael, we did what we had to do. We saved these people. That's what we do."

Was she trying to convince him or herself? He didn't offer a response either way. Just frowned and looked away.

Sara chuckled darkly. "Hit first and ask questions later, remember? That's how we've survived this long. *You* taught me that."

Michael stood, dusting off his jeans. "I know. That's the problem."

"Michael," Sara called after him, standing.

He stuffed his hands in his jeans pockets, lifted his eyes, and faced her more directly. She looked like she wanted to say something, to ask something, perhaps. Her face was marred by a concerned frown, that little knot forming on her brow just above her left eye. He wanted to say something, too, but wasn't sure what. Something *needed* to be said—maybe a thousand things. Apologies, confessions…the truth.

But the truth scared him, and he wasn't ready to face it just yet.

A tremor rumbled beneath his feet and Michael held out his hands to maintain his balance. Shrieks of surprise and worry erupted from the camp. Michael scanned their surroundings as Sara stepped to his side, searching as well.

"Are we being attacked?" she asked, drawing her chukrahas blades. "Do you think it's the Empire?"

Michael bit his lip. "Not sure."

Sara eyed him, alert. "Any headaches? Does your stomach hurt?"

"I told you, I don't get those anymore."

"But we need some kind of sign! How else are we supposed to know what we're supposed to do?"

"Faith," he said, saddened because he already knew from past experience that she would not accept that answer.

Sara's jaw tensed and she was careful not to look at him. "We need to rally the soldiers. Form a perimeter around the women and children."

"Sara." Michael gently took her arm, ignoring her instructions. She regarded him coolly, her eyes like slits. "Faith is all I have. This is who I am, now."

She nodded automatically, but her cold eyes did not thaw for him any longer. "I'll go find Toby."

The quake continued and the Krinvox ran haphazardly about, gathering children, spouses, weapons, items from their huts—anything they could get their hands on. Ak-Huel raced to Michael, a child in one arm, his spear in the other. His alien face was lit with terror. "Mych-El!"

The slender blue tribal warrior fumbled for his English, but Michael waved his hand, easing him. "I don't know what's happening."

One of the other Krinvox pointed a finger to the nighttime horizon, exclaiming something in her strange tongue. Michael looked to the skies and the camp followed suit, growing quiet.

Sara whispered, "What *is* that?"

Michael's heart thundered in his chest, his fingers growing numb. Across the prairie landscape, headed their way, was *black*. That was the first thought that entered Michael's mind. Examining it closer, trying not to hear the screams around him, he surmised that it was a cyclone made of solid black, flickering with purple lightning. The column of empty space churned violently, ripping apart the earth around it, sucking chunks of grass, of dirt, of rock, into its void.

No, Michael realized. Not just earth. *Sky.* It was eating sky. Snuffing out stars by the hundreds, devouring everything. Devouring reality itself.

Michael stared in dumb disbelief, watching the pillar of black as it erased the world, right before his eyes.

Headed his way.

The wind picked up, tugging at his hoodie, his long hair. Sara tucked a blade in her belt then pulled on his arm. He suddenly realized she was yelling at him. "Run! We have to run!"

Michael came to his senses, trying to tear his eyes away from the terrible empty void that sought to consume them. *It's the Rage*, he immediately knew, for he'd encountered the terrible consciousness in the dark spaces between the worlds. Was the Rage freed from Its prison to destroy reality as It saw fit?

But how? Why?

How would he ever stop it?

"*Come on!*" Sara shrieked in his ear, yanking on his arm.

He shook his head clear and turned back to the camp. The winds proved deadly, leveling the small hovels, then just as quickly sucking them into the sky— hurtling towards the vacuum. The Krinvox screeched, clawing at anything they believed might anchor them, but one by one were torn from loved ones' arms. They tumbled through the air, end over end, landing in the black space and disappearing forever. Wiped from existence.

Michael spotted Toby, lost in the crowd, frightened. The boy searched the faces of the tribe, his chocolate-colored eyes widening behind his glasses until they spilled over with tears when at last he glimpsed Michael. The boy raced for his caretaker and Michael hefted him up in his arms.

"What's happening?" Toby roared over the high winds, clutching Michael in a death-grip.

The cyclone was almost upon them now, swallowing earth and sky, flesh and blood, its hunger never satisfied.

"We have to get to the rift!" Sara yelled, her long red hair thrashing wildly, slapping her face. "If we don't, we'll die!"

Michael knew she was right. He handed Toby to her. "Go! I'll be behind you!"

Sara balked at him. "Where are you going?"

"We have to take them with us!"

"Who?"

"The Krinvox! They'll die here!"

"*Are you crazy?* How do you even know if that'll work? What if they can't breathe on the next world?"

"I have to try!"

Sara briefly considered, then nodded. She hurried to him and kissed him. "Come back to me."

He warmed inside. "I will. Promise. Now *go!*"

Sara fumbled and dropped the chukrahas still in her hand before tucking Toby close to her breast and racing through the camp, away from the ebon tornado, headed for where their rift first touched down. Michael surveyed the camp, saw bodies pinwheeling through the air, meeting their oblivion in the encroaching void.

"Follow me!" he shouted to the first Krinvox he saw—one of the men, shielding a female. "Come on! This way!"

The Krinvox couple nodded, then reached for him, but were both pulled off their feet and lost to the spreading darkness.

Michael gritted his teeth, and stepped away from the buffeting winds. He felt light on his feet, felt the draw to the Void, and could hear, once more, the voice of the beast In-Between.

The Rage.

{*You'll never outrun me, Michael...*}

For years, Michael had done just that, trying to escape the Rage, to break his own dark destiny. He struggled against his own wicked impulses, the urge within him to do terrible things. At last, he'd surrendered to the Being in the White Place. The Rage's hold on him was finally broken now.

It seemed, however, that the Rage was a sore loser.

Is it doing all of this just to get me? The entire planet—maybe even this entire galaxy—was being erased. *Is it my fault?*

"Mych-El!"

Michael turned at the sound of his name. Ak-Huel had one arm hooked to a post in the deactivated perimeter fence. In his other hand, one of his babies. Ak-Huel's gangly grip held tight to the little pup's arm, but the mewling babe was dangling in mid-air, drawn to the Void.

Michael shot forward, moving closer to the cyclone, his clothes whipping about, threatening to drag him into the black oblivion. Ak-Huel cried hysterically, something Michael had never seen the warrior do. The sight broke something inside of him.

"Where are your other kids?" Michael screamed.

Ak-Huel only wept, clutching onto his child. His last one, Michael feared.

Michael reached for Ak-Huel and pulled on the lanky figure, dragging him away from the abyss. "We have to get to my rift!" Michael said. "We have to get you out of here!"

"Daught-er! Save my daught-er!"

Michael extended his arm, trying to grab the child, but couldn't connect to her tiny frame. "I can't reach! Pull!"

Ak-Huel fought against the vacuum, but Michael felt his own feet beginning to lift off the ground, as though the planet's gravity was slowly being turned off.

"Can't!" Ak-Huel spoke. "I—"

The child slipped out of her father's grasp, crying as she fell into the Void.

Ak-Huel screamed a throaty rattle, tears spilling from his eye. Michael cried, too, shouting after the child, watching in horror as she simply plopped into the blackness, gone.

Michael yanked on his alien friend, but now Ak-Huel fought against him. "Let go! My daught-er!"

"You'll die!"

Ak-Huel pulled free from Michael's grasp and leapt forward, snatched out of the air and ripped through the black cyclone.

Michael stared at his empty hands, blinking back tears, then looked around. The Krinvox were gone. Only loose debris remained where homes once stood. A lone patch of Earth and sky surrounded Michael, and, at the edge of it, Sara, waving him forward.

Guilt churned his gut, and he felt like vomiting. *Everything's gone.*

Determination set in. Anger. Michael didn't know how this had happened or why. But he would find out and he would stop it from ever happening again, even if he had to punch his way through hell and damnation to do it.

Gritting his teeth, he took off for Sara, fleeing the whine of the cyclone barreling towards him. With every step he took, the ground he left behind was pulverized and consumed in the abyss. Stars blotted out overhead, and endless darkness dogged him. Sara came closer into view, but he couldn't see Toby. The boy must have already stepped onto the sheet of paper at his wife's feet that served as their vehicle to travel the multiverse. At least he prayed Toby was safely through. If he lost the boy or Sara in all of this—

A terrible scream shook the space behind him, a banshee's wail that sent a shiver into his soul. He reached Sara and instinctively faced the whirlwind once more. The scream persisted, and there, suspended in the air by the purple lightning but unaffected by the pull of the cyclone, was a lean shadowed figure, its fingers splayed, reaching out for him. By the frame and by the cry, he judged it to be a woman. Gaunt and clad all in black, the short-haired woman leveled her hands at him and screamed, a shrill, frightening sound.

Sara hollered, "*No!*" then grabbed Michael by the shoulders and threw him into the rift.

Michael was blinded by white, then his vision returned. New information from this latest world assaulted his mind: *Daylight. Hot. Desert. Mountain. Cliff!*

Michael's Converse sneakers slid in loose gravel, undoing him. At once, his ankle buckled and he lost his balance, tumbling down a steep embankment. With each roll, he slapped up more dust, and his fingers desperately sought purchase. He dug them deep into the loose topsoil, finally slowing his descent. Suddenly exhausted and disorientated, he momentarily lay his head in the dirt, catching his breath.

After a moment's pause, a tiny cry carried over the still, empty air and Michael's head jerked upright. "Toby?"

Only a terrified shriek answered him. Michael scrambled to his feet and turned about. For the first time, he realized how high off the ground they were, as a breathtaking and empty desert stretched out to the horizon. High winds pushed against him, and Michael stumbled about, shouting "Toby! Toby, where—"

He saw the tops of little digits clutching the edge of the sheer cliff. Michael hurried and slid to his knees, peering over. Toby dangled helplessly over a wide chasm, the color gone from his face. Tears were frozen in his wide, petrified eyes, his cracked lips trembling. "I-I fell," he sobbed.

Michael lay flat on his stomach, grappling for the child. "Hang on, man. I got you."

As soon as Michael's arms were extended, Toby latched onto them, frantically pulling himself up. Michael took firm hold and brought the kid to safety, even as vertigo distorted his vision. In no time, both of them were sitting, turned away from the ravine. Toby continued to shake, his teeth chattering, and violently hugged Michael. The boy buried his face in Michael's shoulder, and Michael gave the kid a dusty pat. "It's okay. We're okay."

A dazzling burst of rainbow-colored light exploded from the piece of paper that served as their doorway to other worlds. Sara emerged from the quickly fading light, dazed-looking and pale. Michael eased Toby off of him and stood fast. "Sara, watch your step."

She managed to maintain her balance, but her eyes were distant. Glassy. She looked like she'd been crying.

Michael nodded to Toby. "Wait here."

The boy returned the gesture, finally laying on his back and heaving a great sigh of relief over his ordeal. Michael climbed up the slope and held out his hand for Sara to use as a guide. She took it, but did not face him.

"What is it?" he asked her, searching her for injury.

"Did you see her?" Sara asked, her body trembling. "Hanging in the sky?"

Finally her eyes locked on his, relaying stark terror. Michael nodded. "Yeah. I don't know who she is or why she did this, but we'll find her. We'll figure this out. We'll make her pay. For Ak-Huel, his family, *all* of them."

"No." Sara slowly shook her head. "That's not... I don't mean that..."

Michael frowned. "What?"

Sara fixed him with a wide-eyed gaze, a mad glint in her eye.

"The witch," Sara said, shaking. "It was *me*."

PART SIX: A GIRL NAMED SARA

1

THREE YEARS EARLIER

The transport from Bevenshire was a half hour late. Charlie Bost huddled by the door to the station, watching the tracks, blowing warmth into his cold hands. Climate was closely monitored and controlled beneath the domes that protected the small townships from the radioactive Earth, keeping the temperature at a perfectly comfortable setting. During his tenure in City Maintenance, Charlie had been tasked with repairing the automated generators a time or two, himself. Today, however, his cold came from within. His nerves shivered, his stomach trembled. A frigid sweat had developed on his sloping forehead, icy drops trickling down his temple. He did his best to wipe the moisture away discreetly, careful not to draw the attention of the two patrollers making the rounds.

Traffic was momentarily light at the station, but Charlie knew as soon as the Bevenshire transport arrived, the boardwalk would be bombarded by commuters returning home from work. It'd be a madhouse for about forty minutes, with everyone pressed together in a jumble of limbs and noise.

A perfect time for a robbery.

Charlie flexed his fingers, loosening up the stiffness in his fat knuckles, painfully aware of his limitations. As pickpockets went, he was neither the most cunning nor the swiftest. He stood at over six feet, lugging around an incredible gut that slowed his uneven gait. His hair was unwashed, his dark mustache and beard scraggly and grown-in. Today he wore a ratty old coat over his stained T-shirt, his pants and work boots scraped, scratched, and dirty. He looked homeless, which, as of last week, wasn't too far from reality. He'd come home from a night drinking with the boys to find an eviction notice stuck to his door. The landlord had been lenient on him after Charlie lost his repair job—another

31

result of one too many nights "drinking with the boys"—but now the old goat was getting impatient. Charlie had been sort of asking around for work, all the while blowing the last of his severance pay on booze and smokes. He was sure that his big break was just around the corner, but that didn't seem to convince the landlord. Charlie had a week to come up with the money for rent or he'd be out on the streets.

He narrowed his eyes as the Bevenshire transport passed through the clearing gates that kept the poisonous outside at bay, and slewed into the station. Charlie seized a deep breath, rubbed the feeling back into his anxious hands, then stuffed them in his pockets. He did his best to quell the urge for a cigarette and started for the stalled transport at a slow, casual pace. He passed behind one of the armed patrollers and held his breath for the duration. The cop, however, seemed too distracted by the transport's shutdown routine of hissing exhaust and flashing lights to notice the lurking would-be thief.

Charlie grinned at his wonderful luck and moved closer to the doors that would soon open and spew forth passengers. And, with them, the jackpot.

Something flickered in his peripheral, like a bright reflection. He glanced that way and just made out the shape of a tall, thin man, strangely dressed in a top hat and an ill-fitting tuxedo with long coattails. The gaunt figure removed his hat in a grand gesture, revealing the wildest white mane, styled back as though blown by a perpetual fierce gale. As soon as the image registered in Charlie's mind, the glint of the sun through the domed skylight dazzled his eyes and the man was suddenly gone. Charlie frowned, but pushed the odd appearance out of his mind. He had to stay focused on the task.

A green light blinked on above the sliding hydraulic doors. They parted with a gust of pressurized air and Charlie's eyes widened at the sight of impatient and tired workers looking to retire for the evening. He knew that look all too well, and a part of him was actually glad to be unemployed. With work came responsibilities, and with responsibilities came imprisonment. Now he was free to do what he wished, with whomever he wished.

Only freedom, it seemed, didn't pay the bills.

The throng filed out of the transport in a semi-organized flow of traffic. Charlie swam upstream, his eyes roving over each face, looking for a worthy mark. Better to find people who looked like they had money to spare. What right did the rich have hoarding their fortunes while the Charlie Bosts of the world languished in poverty? They owed it to him to help a guy out in his time of need.

He started zeroing in on the folks in nicer clothes manicured to perfection. Those cats with the designer brands, their hair styled and not a strand out of place. They were the good-looking of the world, the affluent. It was guys like them who stepped on the working class. It was guys like them who had kept

Charlie down his whole life, he suddenly realized. There was always someone smarter, better looking—sober—to take his job away from him. So what if he liked to drink a little to take the edge off? The world was a rough place. A guy needed a little escape, especially being trapped underneath this blasted bubble, forever closed off from the world. It was suffocating! Didn't they see that?

No, of course, they didn't. They'd built kingdoms for themselves.

Well, it was time for Charlie to finally build his own kingdom.

Greed wrapped spindly steel fingers around his heart and squeezed, and Charlie seethed against his oppressors. They deserved to be robbed. It was high time someone brought them low.

His eyes locked on a young man—probably late twenties, early thirties—headed his way at a brisk pace. The guy wore the look of middle management, dressed to impress. Pressed to his ear was a flip-com, and he barked orders into it, to one of his lackeys no doubt. So focused was he with asserting his authority, he didn't see Charlie aimed in his direction. Charlie threw his shoulder into the man, fumbling to take advantage of the encounter and rifle through the man's coat pockets.

"Watch where you're going, idiot!" the put-upon man spat angrily, his lip curled in disgust.

Charlie mumbled a curse under his breath, but dipped a nod regardless and disappeared into the crowd.

"Yeah, some jerk just walked right into me," Charlie could hear the young exec saying into the flip-com.

Charlie took his hands out of his pockets and admired the wallet he now held. He grinned and quickly thumbed through to find a couple creds. Not a whole lot, certainly not as much as he'd hoped to discover, but enough to—

"Hey! You!"

Charlie recognized the man's voice and froze. Turned. Saw the young exec pointing in his direction, wagging his flip-com at him and shouting to the patrollers. "That guy just stole my wallet!"

Charlie spotted the patrollers perking up at the accusation. Saw them leveling their black visors on him.

He spat a curse as patrollers scampered his way, urgently pushing aside the commuters. Charlie spun about and slipped to the ground in his haste, dazed. A man walked by and hooked an arm under him. "Hey, man, you all right?"

"Move!" Charlie bellowed and shoved his rescuer to the ground before taking off at a mad run. He wheezed as he hurried down the main thoroughfare moving away from the station. For once in his life, he wished he'd laid off the greasy foods and pack of smokes a day, as he huffed with each laborious step. A stitch in his side threatened to sabotage him as he carried his tremendous bulk on sore knees. Sweating profusely, he cast wild glances behind him. The patrollers were still on his trail.

"Stop!" they commanded, but he sneered and pressed on.

Charlie pushed his way through the crowd amidst hollers and curses. "Outtathaway!" he shrieked, panting terribly. He toppled one young woman and her little girl, but refused to stop.

Until, that is, he felt—first—a painful prick in his back fat, and then the searing jolt of electricity. His right leg seized and he tripped forward, scraping his chin on the concrete. He did his best to move, but his muscles were stiff and uncooperative.

"Don't move!" The patroller with the spent Taser stepped into view. "Or you'll get it again!"

Charlie growled and reached behind his back, searching desperately for the Taser's prongs. He grit his teeth, letting out a sharp squeal of pain as the cop pumped him full of another dose of electric current. Still, he groped along his jacket, feeling underneath it to where his back was exposed. Taking hold of the metal prong, he withstood the agony and pulled it from his flabby flesh.

The patroller fumbled for him, trying to cuff his arms, but Charlie swung meaty fists in every direction, pummeling the cop even as another one neared. Through blind luck, Charlie landed a heavy blow to the side of the patroller's helmet and sent the man tumbling sideways.

Gasping for breath, Charlie pushed to his feet, dropping the wallet in the process.

"Freeze!" the second patroller shouted, gloved hands tugging at the Taser on his utility belt.

Charlie eyed the money longingly, but left it behind. Eyes tearing up in frustration and defeat, he shoved and swore and shouldered everything in his path. It wasn't fair. He just needed a break. Why wasn't anyone ever there to help him when he needed a hand? He wasn't a bad guy! He just needed a chance.

The cops were closing in and Charlie's heart plummeted when he saw two more enter the fray, flanking him on either side. He felt sick inside, and thought to stop and crumple into a weeping mess right there, but no. They wouldn't break him. He had his pride to think of. He just needed to get out.

Charlie rounded a corner and slid to a halt, realizing he'd just taken a wrong turn down a dead end, with only a trash bin waiting for him. *Taunting* him.

"Dammit!" he roared, the word breaking into a sob, and he kicked the can for good measure.

"Interesting choice of words," a melodious, cultured voice rumbled in smooth tones.

Charlie jumped and wheeled about, gaping into the face of the strange man with the shock white hair he thought he'd seen earlier.

"You," he gasped. "Who are you?"

The man regarded him through eyelids half-closed, giving him a haughty appearance as he looked down his hooked nose at Charlie from beneath the brim of his outlandish top hat. Thin lips barely parted into a smile—more of a leer— as he said, "Oh, that's not the question you want to ask."

Charlie blinked, put off by the remark.

The tall man in the ill-fitting suit bent over like a drinking straw and said, "The question you want to ask is 'What do I want'?"

Charlie's blood turned thick and frosty. "Wh-What do you want?"

"He went down here!" Charlie heard patrollers shouting.

He panicked and paced, tangling his pudgy fingers in unwashed hair. "What am I gonna do?" he muttered.

"Charlie, Charlie," the gaunt figure groaned.

Charlie stopped. "How do you know my name?"

"I can see right into the heart of you, my friend. All of your desires."

Shuffling footsteps sounded closer. Charlie held his breath and waited for the cops to appear at any moment.

Speaking rapidly, the tall figure hissed, "All your life, you've always wanted *more*. You have an insatiable thirst, Charlie. More money, more friends, more power, more women, more pleasure. More! *Lust* is your god."

"Shut up, will ya, and help me get out of this!"

"Oh, I can help you. Yes, because you see, Lust is your god…and he has heard your prayers."

Charlie eyed him, slowly beginning to calm. "Who are— What do you want?"

The man cocked an eyebrow, bemused. "For you to trust me. Do you trust me, Charlie?"

"*Down here!*"

Charlie balked in horror as the patrollers emerged around the corner, staring down the barrels of their Tasers. His heart thundered painfully, and he feared he'd drop dead of a heart attack right there.

Then a white-gloved hand casually extended in front of him.

Charlie eyed the hand, then the man who offered it.

"Do you trust me, Charlie?" the tall man repeated.

"Not seeing I got much of a choice," he said in heavy breaths.

The skeletal figure remained emotionless. "We always have a choice."

Charlie winced and took the gloved hand. Immediately, the patrollers—seven in total now—swarmed the alley. But, instead of firing, they merely looked around in anger. Bewilderment.

"I thought you said he went this way!" one shouted.

"He did! I watched him!"

"Where is he?"

Charlie opened one eye fully, then two, standing perfectly still as the cops buzzed about him, checking every crevice, aiming their Tasers in every direction.

But no one moved to apprehend him.

Despite his own fear, Charlie laughed. Looked to the white-maned man and guffawed. "No way! No freakin' way!"

Having lost their prey, the cops retreated, still bickering back and forth, finding other places to look further down the station. Once they were safely gone, Charlie took his hand from the man and danced about, mouth open in a wide grin. "That was some trick! Why didn't they see us? You like some kind of magician, or something?"

"No," the man said, clasping his hands behind his back. "I am the Maestro."

Charlie paused, a bit deflated. "Okay, sure. Whatever you say. How'd you do that?"

"Oh, that was just the *beginning* of what I'm capable of."

Charlie's euphoria slowly faded and he caught his breath. "All right, now. What's the gag? What do you want from me?"

"Only to give you the desires of your heart."

"Heh." Charlie watched him, just to make sure he was serious. When the creep didn't crack a smile or anything, Charlie relaxed. "Okay, sure. Whatever I want. Money, food, chicks."

At this, the Maestro brightened. "Indeed. One 'chick' in particular. A very, *very* important chick."

Charlie slapped his hands together, realizing he was close to cackling. "This is rich. When do I meet her?"

2

She was blonde, green-eyed, and had a perfect hourglass figure. Her strong, well-toned thighs jutted out from beneath her short, short skirt, her perfect golden artificial tan making mouths water wherever she passed. Her abundant bosom nearly broke free of her tank top as she leaned over the tables on her shift, offering drinks and meals. Her nametag read: NICOLE, and more than one guy came to the Courtyard just to check her out.

Charlie Bost being chief among them.

He watched her predatorily, dragging her into his basest fantasies. For a moment, he'd nearly forgotten the lean figure that towered over his shoulder like a scarecrow. It'd been a day since the Maestro had rescued him from the patrollers. Since that time, not one cop had come knocking at his door. The creep was a weirdo, but seemed good for his word. The Maestro had been dodgy on what it was he wanted Charlie to do, exactly, but that didn't stop Charlie from imagining his abundant rewards.

"Her," Charlie whispered hoarsely, eyeing Nicole as she bent low over a table to wipe it down. "I want her."

The Maestro sighed, as if bored. "Not yet. She's not the one we have for you."

Charlie had no idea who this guy meant when he said "we". He looked sharp to the Maestro. "What do you mean? That wasn't what we agreed to."

A passing customer eyed him strangely and Charlie remembered that no one could see the Maestro but him. Flushing with embarrassment, he huddled by the drink dispenser and poured himself a mega-sized soda, mumbling into his chest. "What's the deal, huh?"

The Maestro stood there, the picture of refined patience, unbothered by Charlie's protests. "Trust. Remember, Charlie."

"But-but," Charlie stammered, then looked down when he saw an elderly lady quizzically ogling him. "But you said I could have whoever I wanted."

"You *can* have her. Later. You can have all the women you want. But first, you've got to marry a very—"

"Whoa, whoa!" Charlie nearly dropped his drink, but quickly recovered lest the other patrons notice his hysterics. "Who said anything about *marry*? I'm just lookin' to score."

"Ah, the consummate gentleman," the Maestro groaned without humor. "You can have your many lady friends, but you've got to court one girl, in particular, first."

"Who?" Charlie asked, sipping his soda.

The Maestro placed a strong, ice-cold hand on Charlie's broad shoulders and turned him around, facing the end of the Courtyard where a young girl, no more than sixteen, sat. She was petite, with long, straight red hair, her bright blue eyes scanning the pages of a thick book. With her nose buried in the text and her slight frame swallowed by a baggy flannel shirt and jeans, she was Nicole's perfect opposite.

"*Her?*" Charlie choked. "She doesn't even have a body!"

"Late bloomer," the Maestro suggested. "I know she's not much to look at, but *that's* the girl you're destined to woo, Charlie. You marry her, then we'll give you riches, security, and any girl you want to entertain yourself with on the side."

"Really? No take-backs?"

The Maestro held up two fingers. "Scout's honor."

Charlie considered, finally conceding. "Fine. What do I gotta do?"

3

Sara Theresea brushed a few wayward strands of bright red hair out of her face, tucking them behind her ear in one fluid motion, while her crystal blue eyes remained fixed on the pages before her. She loved the feel of flipping through actual paper. It felt like a connection to a distant past. She wasn't old enough to remember the world before the Wars, before the atmosphere was ruined by chemical weapons and turned toxic. Back then, trees were everywhere and paper was commonplace. Once the skies were poisoned, though, the trees withered and died, never to be reborn again, and paper became a thing of the past. Everything was digital now, but Sara frequented the back room of her high school library, digging around in the musty old paperbacks of yesteryear.

Presently, Sara read the adventures of *Alan Worth: Space Explorer*. There were a number of books in the *Alan Worth* series and Sara had made a point to read every one she could find, even ordering some of the rarer editions through libraries in other townships. She absolutely loved reading about alien worlds and parallel dimensions. Exploring her world was impossible; she couldn't even step outside of the protective glass dome that separated her from the noxious landscape. She was confined to her township, with its own school, its own government, and totally cut off from the rest of the world. And while the city was big, it had an end, and Sara always found it.

She gazed through the skylight of her enclosed township, staring into the deceptively charming cerulean sky above, knowing that to move past the emergency doors without the proper protection would kill her in a matter of minutes. Even *with* the proper protection, there was nothing to see out there and the next township was a hundred miles away.

No, she was stuck here in her small little world, dreaming of adventures in other dimensions where there were no boundaries.

Sara shook off her wistful daydreaming, re-focusing on the book. She realized she'd completely skimmed over the last page of her novel and hadn't grasped a single word. Preparing to pull herself out of the clouds and put herself back in the cockpit with courageous Captain Worth, Sara flipped back a page.

Suddenly, she heard a familiar, "Hey, Sara," over her shoulder and turned to see the boyish face of Johnny Frawl. He shook his shaggy blonde hair in an attempt to banish his bangs from his round cherub face, and took a seat across the table from her in the Courtyard, giving his long black coat a flourish to avoid sitting on it. "What's going on?"

Sara held up her book. "New one just came in from Haverstack."

Johnny's tiny eyes enlarged at the sight. "Wow! You've got to let me borrow that when you're done!"

Sara giggled. "Don't worry."

Johnny Frawl was Sara's only friend, she admitted without shame. The boy was rather odd, always working in his father's occult bookstore. He was interested in strange things that earned him many unjust labels from their high school peers, such as "witch" or "Devilist". But Johnny was simply curious, just like Sara. And he too loved books with real paper in them. In fact, the two of them first met in that back room of the school library, delving into the old boxes trying to find hidden treasures.

"Is it good so far?" Johnny leaned over the table to sneak a peek.

Sara flipped to the back and held it up for him to see. "Even has a map of Venus in the Appendix."

"Finally!"

"It's pretty detailed, too."

"Cool."

Johnny reached out for the musty old novel, but Sara yanked it back, her smile widening. "Wait your turn."

"Awww…"

"I thought you were working today, anyway."

"Ah, my dad gave me the afternoon off. I was on my way to see if the new games came in when I saw you sitting here. It's been forever since we've had a shipment, you know?" Johnny scratched at the tabletop with his fingernail, moping. "I hate living here. I hear that the townships closer to Centric get everything a month after it comes out."

Sara frowned for her friend's sake, though she didn't enjoy vid games as much as he did. "Our grandparents didn't know how good they had it," she offered. "Being able to take walks under open air. Go wherever they wanted."

Johnny crossed his arms, looking a little like a pouty toddler, and Sara bit her lip to hold back a grin. "It's not fair," he sighed. "I'm ready to get out of this place."

Sara almost laughed. "Where are you going to go?"

"I could always get a loading job. Townships gotta get supplies somehow. I could leave this place. See the world."

"Or what's left of it."

"Beats staring at these four walls."

"I hear Haulers hardly ever get to stay home. Demands are too high. I'd never see you."

Johnny's peach-fuzzed cheeks flushed crimson and he grinned suddenly. "I guess we could leave together. I could get my license and we could get our own transport. You could be my co-pilot and we could travel the world just like—"

"Alan Worth!" Sara finished for him, bursting into giggles. Her smile gradually faded, giving way to a sad, dreamy sigh. "I *wish*. Right now, I'd just be lucky to pass Coach Seevers' history class." Her grades were failing, a constant source of contention between her and her parents, who couldn't understand why she didn't study instead of "filling her head with fantasy stories". But what did they know? It was their generation that destroyed the world in the first place, and now they were going to yell at her about how to cope with it? *Maybe Johnny's right. Maybe we should run away.*

Johnny seemed about to comment on his own feelings about the gruff Coach Seevers when he spotted something over Sara's shoulder. He darkened.

"Uh…" the boy began. "I think someone's coming over here."

Sara looked up from her book and spotted a burly, older man—mid-twenties by the looks of him—towering over her and slurping a large drink through a tiny straw.

"Hey," he huffed.

Sara blushed, looked once to Johnny, then said, "Uh…hi."

"I'm Charlie," he said, though did not offer his hand to shake.

For reasons she didn't entirely understand, Sara beamed and grinned uncontrollably. "I'm Sara."

"Thought you might like to go out sometime," he said, a bit awkwardly. Then, as if just spotting Johnny, he stammered. "Um, is this your boyfriend or something?"

Johnny frowned. "Smooth."

Sara choked back a chuckle. "No, no. He's just a friend."

"Oh," Charlie shrugged it off, reverting back to his straight-faced delivery. "So, anyway. Wanna go out? I'll pay for it."

"Um…"

"Dude," Johnny began. "How old are you?"

"I'm twenty-four," Charlie responded, his large frame expanding as if threatened.

"She's only sixteen," Johnny said, and Sara immediately kicked his shin under the table. "Ow!"

"Johnny!"

"What? You're jailbait!"

Sara momentarily hid her face in her open book.

Charlie ground his teeth, then offered one anxious look over his shoulder across the Courtyard. Stiffening, he turned back to Sara. "It's just dinner. That's not against the law, is it?"

Sara shook her head, almost in tears at her embarrassment. "No."

"So, you want to or what?"

The corners of Sara's mouth turned up without her permission. "Sure. Sure, that'd be fine."

"I'll meet you here tomorrow night. Seven o'clock. Wear something nice." Without giving Sara a chance to respond, Charlie sipped on his huge drink, turned around, and meandered away, his head hung low in a mope.

Despite the rather bizarre proposal, Sara grinned after her would-be suitor, knowing her eyes were sparkling. Finally, Johnny barked, "Hey!"

Sara jumped with a start and faced her friend, who appeared outraged. "*What?*" she snapped back.

"What was *that?*"

"He asked me out."

"Yeah, I saw that! That guy's a creep. I don't trust him."

Sara's face felt hot and she averted her eyes. Sure, it was a weird way to get a date, she could see that. But still, he had *noticed* her. "No one's ever asked me out before, Johnny. Why'd you have to try and ruin it?"

Johnny stood, teeth gritted and fists clenched. "I was just trying to do you a favor. You're better off without him."

"Maybe I just want to give him a chance, all right?" Sara shouted back, slamming her book on the table. "Maybe I don't want to be dateless for the rest of high school like *you.*"

Johnny froze, as if slapped, and the color drained from his face. Sara's stern expression broke. "Oh, Johnny, I'm sorry. I didn't mean it."

"Sure you did," he said. "Fine. You want to jump on the first guy who asks you out, be my guest. But don't expect me to like it."

Johnny stormed off and Sara watched him go, helpless. Finally, she gathered her novel into her bookbag and sadly headed home.

4

Johnny doesn't understand, Sara thought as she arrived to her front door and turned the handle. He enjoyed being the social outcast, deriving some sort of sick pleasure from being ostracized by the kids at school. It made him feel superior, perhaps, but Sara wanted nothing more than to be normal. Accepted. Loved.

Okay, Sara had to admit that Charlie wasn't exactly the Prince Charming she had always envisioned. Had this been a fairy tale, he would more likely have played the part of the troll with his pronounced brow, crooked discolored teeth, and breath that smelled like an ashtray.

But he asked me out. He must see something in me. Something worthy...

She smiled again, unable to contain her excitement.

Sara quietly shut the door behind her, entering the dark and cramped apartment. Years of accumulated junk lined every wall, threatening to spill on top of her whenever she returned home. Being surrounded by clutter was one of many byproducts of living in this domed mall—everyone had more frivolous possessions than they could possibly have room for. In her life, Sara had rarely visited a home that wasn't just as overstuffed with needless things. Rich or poor, it didn't matter, there were endless stores that catered to both. Everyone spent, everyone hoarded—some just had more expensive junk than others. With nothing left to conquer in the outside world, folks seemed to fill their need for adventure with gratuitous shopping. With ceaseless *getting*. But spending money had never made Sara especially happy, unless of course, she was buying a book. It would take more than gaudy purchases to bring her fulfillment. She was ready for a life of adventure, not content to sit and accumulate things, like her parents.

As usual, Sara found Dad in his recliner, kicked back with socked feet pointed to the ceiling. He had one arm tucked under his head like a pillow, his lightless eyes zeroed in on the big screen television, watching the news. Her dad was dressed down from his hard day at work that ended only a half hour ago, his jeans and undershirt still smelling of the waste recycling plant. Mom always kept an incense burner near his chair to ward off the odd odors he brought with him, but his pungent fragrance was never entirely banished from their home.

Sara leaned against the doorframe to the living room, watching her father. "Hey, Dad," she greeted, but he did not stir, his attention firmly fixed on his program.

Billy Theresea resembled his daughter with similar firebrand hair, though his remained wild and uncombed, its shine long since dulled as it turned to grey at the temples and down into his scruffy beard. He was a joyless man, Sara often reflected, rarely moving from this recliner and this TV. Her mother always apologized for the man's aloofness, citing he was simply tired from working so hard, but Billy, himself, never offered an explanation for his behavior. Didn't feel that he had to, Sara supposed. He worked, he paid the bills; to her father, that was all that was required of him as the man of the family.

Sara frowned and crossed his eyeline, hoping to draw his notice, but he simply stared through her, mumbling, "Move." She did and sat on the couch beside him, praying he'd break routine and maybe ask her about her day. About school.

"Mom was looking for you," he said, eyes never straying from the television.

"I got caught up," she said, suddenly beaming at the thought of Charlie and her impending date. She almost thought to tell her dad, but stopped just short.

Dad didn't probe any further, only offered a non-committal grunt. Sara nestled in the tattered couch and joined him in watching the screen. She took comfort in his presence. He lifted one freckled arm from its position draped over his plump belly and moved it to the arm of the chair. Sara studied his impassive face, his bright blue eyes that never rested on her, and surreptitiously reached over and gently lay her hand on his. He made no move to return the gesture, but also didn't spurn her affection.

That was enough to elicit a smile out of her, and while he watched television, she watched him, noting the wrinkles in his face, the hard set in his eyes. She wondered what he thought about, what he *cared* about. Buried somewhere in the piles of papers and trinkets in this old house was a single picture from his time in the War, his arms around his buddies, grinning for the camera. It was Sara's favorite picture of her father, a mystery begging to be unraveled. Over the years, she'd often dug it up and studied it. When she was younger, she used to ask her father about it, but Dad refused to talk about that part of his life, except to say "That was a long time ago".

In that photo, Billy Theresea's smile was infectious and youthful. Sara had never known him to smile like that in her entire childhood, though her mother swore that he used to smile all the time when he played with Sara as a baby. Her father never spoke about the War that ruined the Earth. Never talked about those men in the photo and how alive they all seemed to have been together. Nor why he seemed so dead now.

In the darkest parts of her heart, Sara feared that she'd killed her father's delight. Her parents had been in their late forties when she was born, an unexpected interruption on their happy life together. Reproduction was strictly regulated in the domes, as there just wasn't room to house a very large population. Sara's birth had been unplanned—and un-cleared through the proper channels. Because she was a First Birth, her parents were simply slapped with a hefty fine. Had she been an unlawful Second Birth, well…there were far more barbaric penalties.

The circumstances of her entry into this world left Sara with a lot of questions, but she'd never ask her dad because, when he did speak, he only spoke the truth. Sara considered that the truth might be that he never wanted her, never loved her.

So she would never ask the question, for fear of the answer.

Instead, she kept her slender and soft hand on her father's rough one, hoping to prove her worth to him, to earn his love. They sat there like that for a time, watching TV together as an anchorman made a follow-up report of yesterday's attempted theft at the transport station. The culprit had disappeared without a trace. Sara's mind wandered during the report, drifting back to Charlie and his offer to buy her dinner. Already she worried over what to wear, knowing she didn't have much in the way of nice things. Her parents had never prided themselves on appearances, content to a simple life. The two of them rarely took special excursions and didn't seem to have any aspirations about anything. One day simply bled into the next. Sara worried the same fate awaited her.

But maybe Charlie would change that. She hoped so.

"*Sara*," her mother's sharp voice cut through the quiet.

Startled, Sara looked over the couch to see Mom standing in the kitchen, wiping her hands on a dish towel. Kaye Theresea watched her expectantly, placing her hands on her wide hips, shaking her dirty-blonde curls with consternation. Mom wore the scornful, disapproving look that rarely left her face these days. Sara rolled her eyes, dreading the lecture to come.

"Where were you? I had supper ready a half hour ago."

"I'm sorry," Sara sighed. "I got distracted. I was reading and—"

Her mother huffed and popped the towel before disappearing back into the kitchen. "I *swear*, Sara. You'd lose your dumb head in a book if it wasn't attached to your shoulders."

Sara flushed with sudden anger. She turned back to the TV, but could still hear her mother hollering from the other room. "Well we didn't wait for you," Mom said in a rush, sounding wounded and dramatic, as usual. "I just wrapped up your food and put it in the refrigerator. You'll just have to eat it cold or make something else if you don't like it."

"It's okay, Mom," Sara drawled, her heart picking up, and tightened a fist. *Just let it go.*

"Maybe that'll teach you to be on time," her mother was still nagging.

Sara clenched her jaw, working hard to tune out her mother. Then she glanced over and caught her dad eyeing her with a sly grin. At first, she felt a flare of anger, but then he muttered with a mischievous wink, "Welcome to *my* world."

She giggled unexpectedly, warmed by the chance to share the misery with her father, but was cut short when Mom popped her head back in. "Something funny, young lady?"

Sara growled and stood. "I'm going to my room."

"Fine," Mom spat. "Starve yourself. See if I care. It's not like I had anything better to do than make you food you don't eat."

Sara groaned, louder than perhaps necessary, and made a show of storming off, clomping up the stairs to her room. Behind her, she heard her mother turning her wrath on Dad, snipping, "You're no better. She gets this from you, I hope you know. One of these days, I'm going to be dead and gone and you'll all realize how much you needed me."

It was a tired rant that Sara could repeat from memory, but Billy Theresea never took the bait, never argued back, never raised his voice. Just once, Sara wished he'd shout back. Give Mom hell and put her in her place. Anything to show that he was still alive. That he still cared. But the fight was long gone from her father, left behind in the War.

Sara entered her room and turned up the radio, drowning out her mother's thunderous complaints with some Fluber Pixie. The pan flute kicked in, accompanied by a thumping synth-bass line and Sara fell back on her bed, determined not to let her mother's hurtful words sting her this time. This had been a good day. She wouldn't let that woman ruin it. Sara desperately wanted to tell her mom about Charlie, to prove to the hateful hag that she wasn't worthless, after all. But once her parents found out that Charlie was twenty-four, that'd be the end of that romance. No, she'd have to keep it a secret…which, she had to admit, made their date seem all the more romantic. Keeping secrets was so *adult*. She'd have to get dressed up, sneak down the balcony in her room, and slip across town by moonlight.

It would be an adventure.

Sara's life suddenly didn't seem so confined anymore. She smiled wide, losing herself in daydreams. Suddenly, the world seemed to open up, just for her, and she would meet it unafraid.

5

Charlie's world grew smaller.

He sulked in a less-traveled corner of the indoor city, his humorless friend soothing him from the shadows.

"She's a skank," Charlie muttered, sucking out the last of his soda before chunking it into a trash bin. He sidestepped the pedestrian traffic, every once in a while casting a glance over his shoulders. He was still a bit fearful that the authorities would catch up to him, no matter how much his new benefactor tried to convince him to the contrary.

The Maestro conceded, "She's not much to look at, I'll grant you."

"Then why do I have to date her? What was wrong with Nicole?"

"Nicole's not in the plans, Charlie. We've been through this."

Plans. Charlie had no idea what he'd stumbled into, but if he didn't start seeing some returns soon, he was prepared to ditch this lunatic and all his talk about "gods". The last thing he needed was to get mixed up with some religious nut. His father had been a zealot, banging his fist on the Book of Revealing Mysteries, shoving that authoritative finger in Charlie's face and going on about sin and darkness. Charlie never had much use for his old man and had written him off years before the coot shouted himself into a heart attack, but from time to time the late Reverend Bost's proclamations of doom reverberated in his ears. *"Your sin will follow you home, son,"* his father had always warned.

The Maestro lingered just behind him and Charlie wondered about his father's words.

Shaking off the chill in his bones, he grumbled, "This is going to be the worst night of my life."

The Maestro considered before replying, "I doubt that." He paused then began again, "You've done the hard part. She's already hooked. You just have to keep her trailing along."

Charlie thought to ask more questions, but the Maestro had made it clear that he wasn't ready to reveal his "plans". Instead, Charlie kicked at the ground, a bit sheepish. "Look, I hate to break this to you, pal, but I'm not really boyfriend material."

The Maestro cocked an eyebrow dryly. "I would never have guessed."

"I mean, if I was, I wouldn't need *you*, right? I was just looking to score with some hot action. This whole commitment thing…I'm not really good at that."

Expressionless, the Maestro placed an encouraging hand on Charlie's meaty shoulder. At the strange man's touch, Charlie felt sick inside. "I'm *counting* on that."

6

The following night, Sara sat nervously in the Courtyard, her hair pulled up, revealing a face accentuated by makeup. She'd never worn makeup before and was absolutely petrified that she'd done it wrong. That was a thing a mother was meant to teach her daughter, but sadly that relationship was long since broken. The woman infuriated Sara, belittling her to the point she feared she'd eventually disappear, but she did wish things were different. Sara still had memories of baking with her mother when she was a little girl. Kaye had been so patient back then, gently instructing, raising a daughter to care for a home. Sara often wondered what had changed. What she'd done to disappoint her mother so.

Maybe Charlie wouldn't notice her clumsy attempt at making herself pretty. Or, if he did, maybe he'd be too much of a gentleman to say anything.

She worried over her dress too. It was yellow and she always thought she looked dreadful in yellow. Lavender was her favorite color, while yellow, she believed, made her look like a giant sunflower she'd seen in old books. But, without a job, she wasn't able to buy a new dress on her own, and she certainly wasn't asking her parents for money to buy a new outfit to go on a date with a much older guy. The only dress she owned was this yellow one, which her mother had bought her a year ago when they'd made plans to leave the city and visit Sara's grandmother over in Haverstack.

Sara watched the shoppers passing by, large bags full of useless things clutched in their manicured hands. Life was always so commercial here, and Sara was sick of it. She yearned for the world before the War, back when people still traveled, back when there were still things to see. Most folks were content to bury their boredom and loneliness in their shopping, but Sara wanted more for her life. Johnny felt the same.

Her spirits momentarily dimmed at the thought of her friend. He'd been by her side since the third grade, and she regretted how she'd snapped at him yesterday. She'd have to mend things with the big lug. She missed him already.

"Hey," a brusque voice called, and for a brief, fantastic moment, Sara dreamed it was Johnny, come to make amends.

She turned, all smiles, then saw it was Charlie. Her smile dwindled, but she did her best to turn it back on. "Hi."

Charlie eyed her up and down, his gaze seeming to hover on how the dress hung loosely just off her shoulder. "You look okay."

Sara bit her lip, furrowing her brow. "Um…thanks?"

Charlie took a seat and snapped his fingers, catching the annoyed attention of a server. Sara noticed that while she had struggled to look her best this evening, Charlie wore a T-shirt decorated in small burn marks from dropped cigarette ash, a pair of shorts, and flip-flops.

Her heart sank, but she remained hopeful.

Charlie faced her again, his face impassive. "What was your name again?"

Sara dipped her chin, shyly. "It's…it's Sara. Sara Theresea."

"Right, right. Sara."

"I never got your last name."

"It's Bost," Charlie responded before snapping his fingers again, leveling an impatient stare at the nearby server. "You hungry?"

Sara brightened at Charlie's meager gesture of concern for her. "Uh, actually, yeah. I skipped supper. Told my parents I wasn't feeling good. I had to sneak out to come here tonight." She finished that last part with impish glee.

Charlie grunted in acknowledgement, watching as the waitress made her way across the court. She looked steamed. "Your dad ain't gonna call the cops or nothing, right?" Charlie blurted, suddenly wary.

Sara waved her hands nervously. "No, no! No, it's cool. They'll be all right."

"Oh." Charlie nodded.

The waitress approached, her eyes daggers of hatred. "Can I help you, *sir*?"

Charlie loudly proclaimed, "I need a Centric Cheese Steak Sandwich with extra fries. Don't get stingy on the ketchup. And a soda. Biggest one you got."

Charlie finished off, looking pleased, then noticed Sara, as if just remembering she was there. "Did you want something?"

Sara blinked rapidly. "I—I…just a water. And…"

"A water?" Charlie spat, laughing. "That it? You need to eat more than that if you plan on putting any meat on. You're skin and bones as it is!"

The waitress scowled at the loud man, and Sara lowered her chin. "I'll have a grilled chicken sandwich."

"Well, that's a little better," Charlie guffawed and the waitress left, grumbling under her breath.

"You sure are a cheap date," Charlie said aloud, nothing on his face suggesting that he realized or cared that he was being rude.

Sara tried to grin in spite of the evening's rocky beginning.

It can only get better from here, right?

7

Charlie flicked on the light switch, revealing his apartment. Sara stood tentatively in the hallway, clutching her purse and staring down the room as if it were a lion, poised for attack.

Charlie entered, belching loudly, and tossed his empty soda cup toward a nearby trashcan, missing it by feet. Noticing Sara still stood at the threshold, he waved her in. "Come on. It ain't gonna bite."

"I've…I've never been in a man's house before."

"Well," Charlie started, flopping down on his couch, "here it is. The king's castle."

The "king's castle", in this case, was littered with trash and dirty laundry. Like her home, it had that cluttered effect, but Mom had at least tried to keep the junk organized, shoved into neat stacks or packed in boxes along the edges of the rooms. Here, it was like a living trash bin. The familiar cliché "Could use a woman's care" immediately sprang to Sara's mind and she found herself able to look past her disgust. Charlie obviously needed her.

That made her feel kind of good.

She entered the apartment with trepidation, and Charlie bellowed. "Close the door behind you, will ya?"

Sara did, hearing it shut tight, and felt like she was a million miles from anyone. Uncomfortable, she remained close to the door.

Charlie slapped the couch cushion beside him, sending plumes of dust swirling about the cigarette-flavored air. "Come on over. I can't talk to you all the way over there."

Sara grinned, embarrassed, and scooted closer to the couch. Slowly, she lowered herself to a sit, but kept her knees pressed together and her hands nervously in her lap.

Charlie laughed. "Loosen up, why don't you? What's the matter? You don't trust me?"

"No, no!" Sara interjected, afraid she'd hurt his feelings. "That's not it at all! I just…this is really new for me."

Grinning, Charlie replied, "It's new for me too, Sara."

Sara's heart warmed. He'd used her name. "Really?"

The dark shadows under his eyes receded momentarily, revealing a sincerity she'd not seen in him before. "Yeah. I haven't had too many girlfriends."

Sara's doubts and fears fluttered away. *Of course!* That was why he'd been acting so strange—he was just as awkward as she was. She quickly forgave his off-putting behavior. Charlie was a kindred spirit, just another lost soul in this crummy town trying to find something real.

She giggled, as if sharing a private joke. "We're a pair, aren't we?"

He faced her, his eyes locked on hers, and Sara's heart thundered. Charlie bit at his lip, as if deciding on what to say—what to do. Finally, and much to Sara's shock, he leaned in for a kiss. It was wet and sloppy; his breath was atrocious and his mustache whiskers were coarse…but Sara did not fight. This was her first kiss and she didn't want to ruin it by focusing on how it might have been better.

This is good enough, she decided, disappointed.

She kissed back as best she could, but felt uncertain when Charlie's tongue pressed between her teeth, probing for her own. She pulled back at first, but his large hairy hands were immediately around her small waist, urging her onward. Giving in, she let him kiss her however he wished, just thankful that someone found her kissable at all.

When his hands moved from her waist to reach higher, however, Sara froze. *Is this what a first date is supposed to be like? He just said dinner. I didn't know I'd have to…*

"Hey," she quietly said, prying his hands off of her. "Slow down."

Charlie continued to kiss and grope. "It's okay, Sara. I'll make it nice."

"No, wait," Sara struggled as Charlie's grip tightened. "I'm not ready. This is too fast."

"You don't want to be alone, do you? I don't either," he said. "Come on. It's okay."

Finally, Sara kicked out with her legs, propelling herself to a stand. "*No*, Charlie!"

Charlie groaned, Sara's pink lipstick smeared all over his mouth. "What's your problem?"

"I…I have to go. I have to go home."

"Sara," he whined. "Come on, things were just starting to get good."

Sara did not stay to argue. Instead, she grabbed her purse, raced out the door, and cried all the way home.

8

Sara returned home that night, sneaking into her bedroom, undetected. Slipping into her pajamas, she padded downstairs to find Dad snoring in his recliner, the TV still on. Mom was long in bed, and Sara felt cold and alone in the house, agonizing over the hurtful turn in her evening. She sat on the couch, near to her snoozing father, and once tried to stir him, thinking she might say something about Charlie, even though the thought of it made her nauseous. Yet her father slept on and Sara relaxed in that. She curled up on the couch under an old blanket and slept at his side that night. But when she awoke in the morning, Dad's chair was empty and he was already off to work.

Sara withstood the usual grilling from her mother on eating a better breakfast and doing better at school and being a better daughter and living a better life. Arriving at school, Sara kept to herself, paranoid now that others somehow knew about how she'd acted the night before. She still wasn't convinced she'd done the right thing. Was she wrong to leave Charlie, or wrong not to allow things to get physical? What was expected of her? What was normal?

Finding her locker, she dialed the combination and relished the quiet space inside, however limited it was. She felt safe and secluded as she gathered her breath and collected her books for the morning's classes. *Get a grip*, she told herself. Nodding in self-affirmation, she slammed the locker closed, prepared to face the day, then shrieked at the sight of Johnny Frawl waiting for her.

"Sorry," he muttered with a shrug.

"You scared the crap out of me!" She huffed, clutched her books, and headed on her way to class.

"So, how was your date?" he asked, keeping step with her in the crowded halls, pressed on all sides by a current of rowdy students.

"It was…different than I expected," Sara said, pulling her books closer to her breast, almost protectively.

"Was he a perv?"

"*No*," she stopped in her tracks and quickly defended, unsure if she were trying to convince Johnny or herself. "He was just…he was a little backwards." She resumed her walk, Johnny at her side. "He's never had a girlfriend before. But," she continued, more confidently, "it's not like *I'm* an expert, either. So I'd say we're a good match."

It was Johnny's turn to stop, his face grim. "Waitaminute. You're not thinking of going out with that Neanderthal again, are you?"

"I don't know," she admitted. "I might. If he asks."

"Sara," Johnny exhaled sharply. "Why are you doing this?"

"What do you mean?"

"Face it, you're just going out with him because you don't think you can *get* anyone else. You're too good for that."

"Am I?" Sara bit back. "What's so special about me, anyway? Oh, forget it."

She marched past him, but he shouted after her, "You're smart, for starters. Smarter than most of the losers around this dump."

She slowed and looked to him. "Stop it, Johnny."

"And you're pretty, too. Sure, you've got the chest of a twelve-year old boy, but those things can grow in."

"I said 'stop it'!" Sara shouted, angry at first, but catching herself in a laugh halfway through. She didn't know whether to punch him or hug him. Finally, she settled for smacking him on the arm of his dark coat. "Who asked you anyway, stupid-head?"

"I'm just saying. There's plenty of guys around here who would kill to go on a date with you."

"Name one." Sara put her hand on her hip and cocked an eyebrow, mindful in one horrifying moment how much she must look like her mother.

Johnny blushed. "Well…me."

Sara halted in shock. Then, without a word, she turned tail and walked off.

"What?" Johnny called after her. "What did I say?"

That's all I need! Sara fumed, leaving her friend behind. One day she was the quiet girl in the corner, nose-deep in a book, and the next day she had not one, but *two* guys throwing themselves at her?

This is too much.

Frustrated, she pushed open the doors to the auditorium, where the drama class rehearsed the school play, and nearly plowed down some tall, gangly blond-headed boy in jeans and a too-large olive denim jacket in the process. He stopped just short of getting smacked in the face by the door and slipped off one ear of his headphones, giving Sara a brief listen to the aggressive electric guitar blaring from the speaker. "Watch it," he muttered, his dark eyes piercing and mysterious.

Sara thought his name was Michael something-or-other. He had a bad reputation, but Sara wasn't in the mood to tangle with a high school tough guy. She balled up her fist and snarled. "Watch it yourself, *jerk*!" she said, and shoved past. The aloof boy regarded her for a moment, then shook his head, readjusted his headphones, and took his leave out into the hallway.

Sara dropped into one of the numerous empty chairs, staring ahead as the class took instructions from the drama teacher on the stage. Her world seemed to be expanding beyond her expectations, opening the floodgates of uncertainty and conflicting emotions. Johnny was such a good friend and she felt she could

51

tell him anything.

Well…almost anything. She wouldn't dare tell him about how she and Charlie's date ended last night. *That was…it was just a misunderstanding,* she reasoned. *I was sending out the wrong signals and things just got carried away. It won't happen again.*

It was true, she had so much more in common with Johnny than she did with Charlie, but Charlie had asked first. If Johnny liked her so much, he should have been a man about it and made a move. He only wanted her now because he couldn't have her.

Despite her anger towards her friend for pulling such a stunt at a time like this, Sara had never felt so alive. So powerful. Men were vying for her attention. She was *desirable.*

A sly grin formed on her lips.

9

Charlie awoke on the couch, the Maestro looming over him.

"Shyeah!" the large man bellowed, swinging until he fell to the filthy floor. "Don't *do* that, man!"

"Wake up," the Maestro uttered, his voice hollow.

Rubbing the fresh sore spot on the back of his head, Charlie said, "What do you want?"

The Maestro watched as Charlie picked himself up and moved into the kitchen, digging around in his refrigerator for a mid-morning beer. "How did the date go?" the strange man casually asked, removing his top hat to smooth his untamed mane.

"We didn't do nothing," Charlie grumbled, popping the top on his brew. "Not for lack of trying."

"Ask her out again. *Try* it again."

"I don't know, man," Charlie began. "She's…she's really nice, you know? She's not that kind of girl."

"Yes, but, see, that's your part in this arrangement, Charlie. *Make* her that kind of girl."

Charlie shrugged, taking a long swig as a distraction. The Maestro took note of his hesitation and stepped closer. "Don't tell me you actually…favor her?"

"She's just a kid, all right?" Charlie replied. "I didn't sign up for corrupting high school girls, okay?"

"That's where you're wrong," the Maestro threatened, his cold, dark shadow swallowing Charlie. "You signed up for whatever my Master has planned. That's what happens when you sell your soul. It doesn't belong to you anymore; it belongs to us."

The gaunt man bent forward, pressing Charlie's back to the wall with his sickening, unblinking stare. The room seemed to darken, except for those eyes, lit like tiny, flickering flames of hellfire. Charlie nearly dropped his can of beer and gulped hard. For the briefest of moments, he was a young man again, shrinking in terror before his demanding father, shriveling under the holy man's stern glare. With nothing but a glance, Charlie was stripped bare by this creature that lurked in his kitchen, exposed like raw muscle.

"F-Fine," he gasped. "What do I have to do to get what I want?"

"Now there's the Charlie Bost I've come to depend on." The Maestro returned his hat to its perch, then clasped his hands behind his back, standing erect, skulking about the room in a bit of a march. "We have to step up the game a notch. Consummate your relationship with the girl and she'll feel obligated to stick with you. But we need to do something to drive her towards you. The crescendo will be so much sweeter if she feels protected by you. Like she can trust you."

"I don't get it," Charlie said.

"Of course you don't. Let me spell it out for you." The Maestro paused, then finished, his back to Charlie. "A girl like that…she'd be devastated if something were to happen to her parents. Losing them at her young age would most certainly hasten her transformation."

The bottom dropped out of Charlie's stomach. "Wait, what? No. No way." Setting down his beer with a shaky hand, Charlie moved for the monster. "Are you out of your mind? I'll get caught! There's no way! Besides, I… I mean… You're talking about killing? I didn't want this!"

The Maestro remained unblinking, his eyes half-closed in his usual arrogant expression. His lips dripped into a slight snarl of disgust. "As long as they're around, she'll always have a life to go back to. We have to take that life away. With them gone, she'll have no one to turn to *but* you."

Charlie grew quiet. Sickened. "You're evil."

The Maestro remained stoic. "At last you understand."

10

Sara sat on Charlie's couch with him nearly on top of her, smothering her in kisses. She did her best to return his affections, though she could barely breathe. At just the moment she thought he'd suffocate her, he pulled away unexpectedly and stood. He began to pace.

She caught her breath, her hair a mess, her cheeks hot. "What? What is it?"

He shook his head and bit a knuckle. "Nothing."

She huffed a laugh. "Well, it's obviously *something*."

Charlie took a seat on the opposite end of the couch, wringing his meaty hands, a terrible brooding expression absorbing his haggard face.

The last month had often seen Sara sneaking out of her parents' house at night to spend time with Charlie. They stayed inside his apartment most times, careful to be seen in public as little as possible so that Sara's parents would not catch them. Their conversations were still a little awkward, but their evenings were more dominated by other pursuits, anyway. She and Charlie would neck and she'd let him feel her body, but they hadn't yet taken things all the way. She was slowly warming up to the idea, for fear that she'd be a bad girlfriend if she didn't. Yet, strangely, it was Charlie who pulled back now.

"Are you okay?" she ventured quietly, worried that maybe he didn't find her desirable anymore. "Is it... is it me?"

He waved her off, wincing. "No. I got a lot of stuff on my mind. You...wouldn't understand."

She inched closer to him, hugging his arm. "I'd like to. If you'd let me."

Charlie remained distant from her, watching some dark corner of the room as though he expected something to emerge from the shadows. "I don't want to bring you into it," he muttered.

She leaned her head against his shoulder, feeling him tense at her touch. "Charlie, I appreciate you trying to protect me, but I can help you. Let me take care of you. You don't have to do anything alone anymore." She took his hand and softly kissed it. "Neither of us do."

He was quiet for a long time, lost in some unspoken sorrow, sniffling just a bit. She glanced at him, seeing tears form at the corners of his beady eyes. Her heart broke for him, whatever he was battling, and she wondered what she would have to do to prove herself to him. For weeks now, late nights had been spent with Sara trying to soothe Charlie's heartache, hoping her touch and their physical connection would brighten his spirits. During the days, Sara wrote long love letters to Charlie during class, promising that she'd be there for him whenever he needed her and that he could trust her with all of his secret fears.

But he always refused to open up to her. She loved him for that, she thought. It was heroic in a way, wanting to shield her from his pain, but ultimately foolish. He had made her strong by giving her confidence, and now she wanted to return his kindness by helping shoulder his burden.

"You'd better get home," he grumbled, hanging his head.

Sara nodded, disappointed that she'd failed again to reach him. She collected her things and smoothed out her hair. "I'll always be here for you," she spoke into the silence. "You know that, right?"

He offered no reply and Sara quietly let herself out of the apartment.

Once Sara was gone and safely out of earshot, Charlie jumped to his feet and let fly a curse he'd been holding in all night. He ran plump fingers through his tangled hair, beginning to sweat. Beginning to panic.

"Charlie…" the darkness whispered to him.

He spun, already knowing the Maestro would be there. "I get it, all right? I know!"

The devil was closer than Charlie had anticipated, his chest puffed out, white-gloved hands grasped behind his back, wearing that unwavering look, with his pupils like tiny pinpricks of black on white. "We have been patient with you. But my kind is not known for our grace."

Charlie nearly stumbled back at the ghastly visage, recalling that the Maestro looked more unnatural with each appearance. He was changing, or perhaps, shedding the illusion of the frazzled conductor of some hellish orchestra. The lights in the apartment dimmed and bent, casting macabre shapes along the wall and the Maestro's shadow grew sharp talons and stretched to every corner, blocking Charlie in.

Crippled under the weight of his master's unblinking vindictive glance, Charlie choked back a desperate sob. "I *can't*. I've tried to do what you want, but I just can't." He paced back and forth, wringing his trembling hands. "I c-can't eat or sleep… It's killing me inside, man! I didn't want this! I-I appreciate what you've done for me, but…I'm out. I can't do this no more."

Fearfully he regarded the Maestro, bracing himself for the worst. Instead, the demon only stood there, perfectly still, chin lifted slightly, peering down at Charlie over his sharp nose. "I understand."

Charlie gulped. "Y-You do?"

The Maestro spread his arms and Charlie flinched and yelped. The straw man grinned, relishing Charlie's terror, then spoke evenly. "You lack inspiration."

Charlie screwed up his brow. "Whattya mean?"

"I was like you once. When I first heard the Song, I was frightened, as well. But you have to listen, Charlie. Let it move through you. Feel it. Let it guide you."

"I don't know what—"

The Maestro flexed his fingers, splaying them wide, then snarled in pointy-toothed joy. Instantly, Charlie's blood hit a high boil and he felt as though his head had exploded, though he still saw, still heard, still screamed. He clutched at his ears, shrieking, and doubled over onto the floor. Still screeching, now weeping, he looked up to see the Maestro twirling about the room, extending his arms in graceful lines as he conducted his latest composition.

"Please…" Charlie wheezed, coughing up phlegm and black blood.

"Listen to the music, Charlie," the Maestro sang, his eyes closed in euphoria. "Do you hear it? Do you hear the melody? We are all measures and motifs. We serve the Song. And what a Song! The Song that darkens souls, that devours the worlds, that will tear down the walls of heaven! Hear it, Charlie! Hear it!"

Charlie touched his head to the stained carpet, weeping in scratchy sobs. His body quaked in pain, his vision beginning to blur and play strange tricks on his mind. At the corners of his line of sight, he detected alien colors, twisting and folding in the space before him, enveloping him like silk ribbons of unspeakable pleasures. His eyes followed the magnificent rainbow-colored light as it danced and twirled about him, beckoning him. A terrible crack formed beneath him, splitting his apartment and revealing a great chasm of unending darkness. The starless black void opened up to him, but it was not empty. Things lurked in the space In-Between the worlds, snickering at him, seducing him with profane tongues, promising him every base and cruel and degrading desire he'd ever dared to imagine.

He teetered on the edge of that Void, beginning to giggle and slobber into its waiting jaws. Hot, foul breath blasted across his face as a rumbling voice like a thousand chariots addressed him.

Charlie…

"Yes," he whimpered, terrified and yet somewhat honored that something so hideous knew him by name. "I'm here… Tell me what to do…" He held his hands to the heavens, closing his eyes in ecstasy as the rainbow wrapped tighter around him, filling his mind with its will. "Tell me what to do…"

12

Sara climbed the trellis to her bedroom window and slipped into the inky blackness. She was quick to take off her shoes and tiptoe in her socked feet, lest she wake her parents in the other room.

"Don't bother being quiet about it," her father's voice boomed at her side, and the light of her lamp clicked on.

Sara's body tensed and she jumped, her heart fluttering like a bird in a cage. "Dad!"

He sat in the chair at her vanity, reclining like he'd been there for a while. Mom was in the doorway, leaned against it, her arms folded and her scowling face red with tears. Comparatively, Dad looked unbothered, except perhaps a bit tired. "We need to have a talk, Sunshine," he said evenly, but patiently, calling her by a name he'd not used since she was ten.

"Where were you?" Mom cut in so fast the question came out as a single word.

"I…" Sara's face grew hot and her eyes darted everywhere but on the expectant faces of her parents.

"Don't lie to us," Mom snapped. "You've lied long enough."

Sara looked between the two of them, uncertain of what they knew or, at least, what they *thought* they knew. "I don't—"

Sniffling, Mom said, "I came in here looking for you tonight. When you weren't here, I thought… I don't know *what* I thought. I was terrified and we called your friend Johnny."

"We know about Charlie," Dad gently added.

Immediately Sara's heart burned with hatred towards Johnny and she tightened a fist.

I'll never speak to him again.

"Johnny told us you've been seeing him," Mom said with a huff. "An *older* man, Sara."

"Johnny's just jealous!" Sara shouted instinctively.

"He's worried about you," Dad said, still even. Still controlled. "So are we."

Despite her hurt feelings and Johnny's betrayal, Sara warmed at her father's concern. For so long she'd wished he'd turn off the TV and look at her. Now he had. She felt like crying. Like falling into his arms and telling him how much she loved him and how she only wanted to make him proud.

But, no. He'd waited too long. She had Charlie now. *Charlie* told her she was special. Charlie had been there for her when no one else had. She wouldn't betray him.

Her father should've come around sooner.

Mom cried, "I don't understand how you could keep this from us. This man's too old for you. Whatever he's doing…whatever you're doing…it's illegal. It's wrong."

"We're not *doing* anything," Sara defended, letting go hot and angry tears. "He loves me and I love him. He *needs* me."

"I know it feels like that now, Sunshine," Dad said. "You're going through a lot of changes and everything feels different, we get that. But you've got to pull away and get a clear head about this."

"I am thinking clearly," Sara argued. "I'm not a little girl anymore!"

"Are you…" Mom weakly attempted, "Have you slept together?"

"What? No! And even if we had, that's none of your business. That's between me and Charlie!"

Dad stood now, his perpetual apathy starting to crack, revealing perhaps the younger man he'd once been, back in the War when he still smiled, still fought for something. "You watch your tone. You're not an adult yet. You live here, you live by our rules."

"I'll leave then! I'll move in with Charlie!"

"Sara!" Mom gasped, breaking out in fresh tears.

Dad backed down in his wrath, his face hard but calm. "Don't do something you'll regret, Sara. Your mom and I love you. Always have."

"Then show it!" Sara screamed at the top of her lungs. After all this time, why did they pick now to tell her these things? Why did they suddenly care? *You're too late*, she thought.

"We want what's best for you," Mom implored, sounding like a different woman. No longer the critical judge, but a sympathetic protector. "If you think so much of this Charlie, why haven't you brought him here? Why haven't you given me and Dad a chance to get to know him? You've shut us out."

"Because you wouldn't listen! I knew you'd say he was too old and you'd never give him a chance!"

"Sara…" Dad began, hurt furrowing his brow. "When have we ever not listened to you? Sunshine, we've always been here for you."

"No!" she finally roared, years of neglect and built-up rage billowing out beyond her control. "You haven't!"

Dad flinched, his eyes watering as he looked back at her, suffering the brunt of her rejection. He looked completely deflated, humiliated. Sara realized how deeply she'd cut him and she sobbed louder.

"Dad…"

He turned his back to her, stone still. Was he crying?

"Dad?"

Mom was a mess now, weeping into a crumpled tissue. Her eyes were so puffy that they'd almost swollen shut. Oddly, she gathered herself and spoke with compassion, "What do you want us to say?" she said without hate, without condemnation. "You were a surprise to us, Sara. We weren't ready for you. We had no idea what to do." Mom stepped forward, pressing a caring hand to Sara's wet cheek. "But we always loved you. We made a lot of mistakes and we know it hasn't been easy, but we did our best. We gave you all we could. One day, when you have a child, you'll understand that."

Sara hung her head, unsure what to do now. There had been more honesty between her and her parents in the last five minutes than the last five years. For the first time in so long, Sara felt like she could talk to them. Maybe more importantly, she felt like they were ready to listen.

But the truth of the matter was, through Charlie, she had realized she didn't need them anymore. She'd found her worth somewhere else and she was ready to stand on her own—with Charlie. In the pale moonlight shining in through the domed skylight that kept them confined, her parents suddenly seemed very old and very small. They meant well, she understood that now. But they would never be able to give her what she needed. She would have to find that on her own, out from under their care.

Maybe this is what growing up is like.

Mom said, "The very fact that you kept all this a secret proves that you knew it was wrong. You've got to stop this, Sara," she pleaded. Pausing, Mom looked to Dad, who still hadn't faced his daughter. "Or, at least, wait a few years, until you're old enough. If it's really meant to be, then he'll still be there for you, and Dad and I…won't hold any objections."

Sara considered it all too briefly, but shook her head defiantly. She was a woman now, with some difficult choices ahead. Facing her father's back, wishing he'd look at her, she shook her head sympathetically. "You don't understand. He needs me. And I need him. We just fit, like you always said you and Dad did. He's the one, Mom. I've never been more sure of anything in my life."

"Sara, please," Dad said, finally turning around. His face showed no sign of tears, but his eyes were sad. Defeated.

And Sara knew she'd won. Trying to hide a smile she felt bubbling forth, she backed away from them, leaving their embrace, reaching for the trellis behind her, beckoning her to a new life of romance and intrigue.

"You can't stop me, Dad," she said softly. "I love you, but…this is my decision."

Not pausing to give her parents time to react, Sara quickly threw one leg over the balcony, then the other, and hurried down the lattice. Dad and Mom both shouted after her, running to the balcony, but she did not reply. Sara landed on the ground, looked back in one last, silent good-bye to her parents, and ran down the darkened corridor.

She was on her own now, and no longer tried to contain the exhilarated smile that spread across her face.

13

Charlie waited just around the corner and caught his breath as Sara passed just inches from the shadows where he hid. He closed his eyes, struggling to steady himself. He'd been sweating profusely since he left his apartment, and his hair was now soaked and matted to his sloping brow. His numb fingers loosely clutched the shotgun, his heart pounding an erratic rhythm. He remained in the dark recesses of the narrow alley, but peered around the corner just enough to see Sara hurry into the distance. She seemed different tonight. More sure of herself. Powerful. He wondered what had changed or where she was going. Was she on her way to see him?

He gripped the gun tighter, wringing his hands around it until his black leather gloves creaked. With chattering teeth, he faced the dome's glass ceiling, staring into the moonlight. Tears threatened to emerge, but he willed them back, reminding himself of that terrible presence in the Void between worlds and Its insatiable hunger. Charlie understood that hunger, for he felt it, too, a common bond that tethered him to his new Master.

A dull boom-boom-boom throbbed in his mind, just behind his eyes, and he saw those same awful and captivating rainbow-colored lights creeping into his vision. The lights danced for him, swirling, beckoning, and twirled like a peaceful stream to Sara's front door. That light promised him things— wealth and women and all the things he'd been denied in his life. But he could have it all in abundant supply.

"*Kill for me,*" the rainbow said.

Voracious lust drove Charlie forward. He licked his lips, resisting a nervous chuckle, and slipped a black stocking mask over his grizzled features. He walked the path laid before him, helpless now to change his fate. In fact, he was now happy about it. Happy that he'd finally found his place in the cosmos. Some were meant to be light, while others—he now knew—were destined to darkness. The Maestro had opened his mind to the symphony.

We all have our parts to play.

Without even thinking, Charlie heaved his massive boot through the front door, breaking it open. Immediately he heard a woman's shrill, startled cry and saw the older, blonde-haired woman before him. He pulled the trigger, silencing her cries and sending her stumbling back. Another shout—this one from a man with Sara's eyes and firebrand hair—and Charlie whirled and fired twice more, filling the house with thunder, smoke, and death.

There, he thought. Just as quickly as it had started, it was over.

14

Sara walked homeward, bracing herself for the worst.

She'd gone back to Charlie's apartment and banged on his door a good ten minutes, but there had been no answer. She had no idea where he'd gone, but it didn't matter. All that mattered right now was that she was going to have to return home and face her parents and the wrath that was sure to come.

"Sara?"

She stopped underneath the sign that flickered SUPERNATURAL SURPLUS, and realized she had inadvertently walked right into the path of her *former* best friend.

Johnny had the door half-closed behind him and was in the process of turning off the sign and closing down the shop for the night. Seeing Sara, he quickly locked up and approached. "Hey."

"I don't have anything to say to you," she told him, her voice cold.

"Sara, I *had* to tell your parents. That Charlie guy is dangerous. I just…I can feel it."

"You're just jealous," she repeated what she'd told her folks.

"That hurts, Sara. I thought you knew me better than that."

Sara faltered. "I…I don't know anyone as well as I thought I did. Not you, not my parents—"

"What about Charlie? You know *him*?"

Sara glared at him. "One day you're going to meet somebody and you'll understand what it's like to be in love. I hope you do, Johnny. I really do."

Satisfied with voicing that self-righteous condemnation, Sara held her head high and headed home, leaving Johnny's broken heart in her wake.

"I already do," she heard him softly mutter after her, but she no longer cared.

15

Sara arrived home to find the local constables surrounding her building. Barriers had been erected, their blinking red lights disorientating her. A crowd of neighbors pressed against the barricades, quiet and tearful.

What's going on? Sara thought, curious and growing alarmed. She searched the faces, looking for Dad, but didn't immediately see him. Couldn't find Mom, either. The door to the apartment was wide open and a swarm of officers trafficked inside and out. Some took pictures, while others talked to those standing about.

"Dad?" Sara called in a tremble.

Anxiously she shoved through the crowd until an officer stopped her. "Stand back. Get back."

"That's my house!" she screamed, trying to look over his shoulder. Trying to see inside. In the midst of the men, she glimpsed a splatter of maroon paint on the walls. "Why is there paint on the walls?" she asked, breathless. "Who— Someone painted on our walls!"

The man's eyes grew hooded and his jaw tensed. "Miss, you know that's not—"

"Dad!" she shouted, trying to push the officer away. Unable to shake him, she screamed frantically into his face. "Where's my Dad? Where's my Mom?"

She was suddenly aware of the eyes on her, as neighbors sobbed and some even reached for her, touching her shoulder, her back, for support.

"Get off of me! Where are my parents?"

But she already knew.

"I'm sorry, miss," the officer said heavily.

Sara collapsed to her knees, shuddering in her grief. "No-no-no…"

"There was a robbery. Your parents must've put up a fight. We've been looking for you. We're just glad you're okay."

Sara wrapped her arms around her stomach, gagging. The constable knelt before her, touching her knee. "I'm so sorry, Miss Theresea. They're gone."

16

Charlie Bost sat in the quiet of his darkened apartment. He'd rearranged the furniture so that his chair faced the front door. He sat in that chair, staring at the door, the shotgun secure in his grip.

Let 'em come, he dared the police nervously. *I'll be ready for them.*

Since leaving Sara's, his giddy euphoria had evaporated. The rainbow lights had left him, the insistent voice of his Master grown silent. He felt alone now, and very afraid. He'd done his best at the crime scene not to leave any tracks. Per the Maestro's instructions, he'd taken some worthless trinkets to make it look like a botched robbery—a music box, some cheap jewelry, as much as he could carry alongside his shotgun—but promptly discarded them in an alleyway dumpster. Soon, he would have no need for such things. He was going to be rich beyond measure. He'd have everything he needed. Everything he *wanted*.

And all it cost were two lives.

Guilt churned his stomach, undeniable and persistent. For the hundredth time, he ran his fingers through his sweaty hair, once more slipping into blind panic. All he'd wanted was to pay the rent. Maybe have some pretty girls like him. He never meant for it to go this far. But it had and now he was stuck. He'd marry Sara—as the Maestro had ordained that Sara *would* marry him—and, in return, he would get to keep his freedom as well as the fulfillment of all his hedonistic fantasies.

In between sobs, a manic grin split his scruffy face and he giggled to himself. "Yeah…yeah, almost there now. Almost there."

A knock at the door.

Charlie sprang to his feet, kicking over the chair in the process, and aimed the shotgun at the door. "Who's there?" he bellowed.

A feeble cry emanated from the other side. "Charlie? It's me…I know it's late but…I've got nowhere else to go…"

Of course, Charlie realized. *Of course it's her.*

"Uh…yeah. Sure. Hold up a sec."

Fumbling in the dark, Charlie stashed the shotgun in the closet—as if, at the sight of it, Sara would know that it was the same weapon that killed her parents—

and turned on a light. He smoothed down his dark, shaggy hair, trying to look presentable. He unlocked the door, stammering, "You caught me—ah—asleep. I was asleep."

He opened the door to see her there, a hastily packed suitcase in her hand, her face a mask of crimson anguish. Shame stabbed Charlie in the gut, but he managed to ask, "What's wrong?"

Sara paled and fainted in the hallway.

Charlie shot fearful looks down the hall, then promptly dragged her inside. He brought in the girl's luggage, too, and secured the door behind him. As Sara lay unconscious on the floor, Charlie paced about, watching her and biting his brittle nails anxiously.

"Relax," a dark voice soothed from behind.

Charlie did not have to turn around. He knew his guardian demon had returned. "This is too much."

"Everything's under control. You've done well, Charlie. This is where you and I part company."

Charlie spun to the haunting figure, wide-eyed. "But what about our deal?"

"Don't worry. Everything is in place. You'll have wealth and women beyond your dreams. But keep the girl close to you. Watch over her until my Master has need for her."

Charlie paused in his pacing and bent over the young girl, studying her sleeping face. With a trembling hand, he brushed her cheek, marveling at how such a common, unimportant teenager had so drastically changed his life. Finally, he looked to the devil. "What's so special about her, anyway?"

"To tell the truth," the Maestro began, crooking his body to join Charlie in observing the sleeping girl, "I have no idea." He shrugged. "I never thought to ask."

17

The following year blurred by. Sara and Charlie married almost immediately after her parents' death, more for financial security than love. Indeed, even on their honeymoon, Sara spent the whole night crying in Charlie's arms, still mourning the loss of her parents. Charlie held her and stroked her hair, though he seemed strangely distant and even shed a few tears of his own. Sara imagined that it hurt him to watch her suffer, and forgave his blank expression and distracted words, though she felt starved for true affection.

When the couple finally did make love for the first time a few days later, it was cold and meaningless, and Sara immediately feared that she had made a horrible mistake in marrying Charlie. But she was determined to stick by his side, chalking up their empty lovemaking to the fact that the two of them were new at love and had little experience.

Sara became the dutiful wife, learning to cook and clean, praying that her obedience would bring about passion in their marriage. Housework gave her something to focus on, as she dropped out of school at Charlie's insistence that she had no reason to return.

"You go to school to get a good job, right?" he said. "Well, I've got all the money we'll ever need."

And it was true. As far as she knew, the man never worked, but they always seemed to have enough money. Without school or a job of her own, Sara remained bound in Charlie's apartment, doing chores and preparing his meals, all while he disappeared for hours on end. When he returned home, he smelled like cheap perfume, and sometimes Sara found makeup on his shirts when she did the laundry, which was odd since she never wore any herself.

She chose to overlook the signs of infidelity and never pressed the issue with Charlie, who slowly spiraled into alcoholism. It seemed her husband was carrying around an immense burden and found his only solace in booze. *That* was something Sara tried to address. Just like in the poetic letters she wrote during their courtship, she voiced to him that he could trust her. Could open up to her.

He responded by slapping her across the face. For her part, Sara did not cry at that initial attack. She was utterly stunned to earn such a rebuke when all she'd wanted to do was help the man she married. But it seemed that, with that one slap, the floodgates were opened. Charlie began to take out his frustrations on her more frequently, hitting her and crying as did so.

"It's your fault!" he'd sometimes blubber in his drunken rages. "I didn't mean for any of this…"

Soon, his fists became less than adequate to communicate his anger, and that's when Charlie moved on to the shotgun. For their entire married life, Charlie had kept a shotgun by his side of the bed and would often jump out of a sound sleep and reach for it, aiming at shadows. He never told Sara what he feared was coming for him, but whatever it was, he felt he needed the shotgun close by. Eventually, he brought the shotgun into their marital disputes, using the butt of it against Sara's face. Obvious bruises kept Sara in the house, away from questioning glances, and she became a prisoner in her own home.

When Charlie was away on his mysterious adventures, Sara leaned against the balcony and watched the happy shoppers below, unable to ever join them. She often thought of her old life—her parents, Johnny, and reading about faraway adventures—and realized that was all lost to her now. Charlie, her own grand adventure, had become her final trap.

Weeping, Sara would stare into the skydome at the blue sky beyond and pray that whatever god could hear her would see her turmoil and deliver her from her folly.

But she didn't get her hopes up. Sara wasn't much for believing in gods.

Nevertheless, someone *had* heard her: A boy named Michael.

PART SEVEN: FRACTURED

1

NOW

By nightfall, the desert winds had turned icy. Of course young Toby, being cryokinetic, was unaffected by the harsh climate, but Sara Morrison shivered down to her bones. The three of them had spent the entire day wandering across the barren landscape, spotting no sign of life. No roads, no settlements, no *anything*. An endless vista of red-sand mesas stretched before them, offering only the occasional cactus for milk. Were it not for Toby's generated ice cubes for Sara to suck on, she imagined she would have dehydrated hours ago under the brutal, unflinching glare of the bright white sun overhead. Now the sun had long since set, but without its presence, the cold night had crept in, proving to be just as blistering and cruel as the day had been, in its own way.

Before the darkness completely overtook them, Michael and Sara had managed to find some scrub to bundle together, and Michael used Toby's glasses to beam the last of the sun's rays onto the pile of grass to begin a fire, but the warmth of the small flame did little now to deter the chill in the small camp. Sara scooted closer to the heat, warming her hands against it, her knees pulled up to her chest. At her side, on the ground, Toby slept soundly, mouth slightly agape. Sara watched him with a sad smile. It was easy to forget that Toby was only eight. In battle, he was a tremendous asset to the team. He did whatever was asked of him without question, and his powers were blossoming more each day. He was a soldier now.

But when he slept, Sara no longer saw the warrior, but just a little boy far from home.

We took him from his home, she thought, as he let out a short snore. It was no home, not really. Just a mother who neglected him, a father who abandoned him, and alien overseers who would keep all humans confined to a chained-in ghetto. *But we saved him from that.* Together, she and Michael had given Toby a purpose, a chance to use his unique skills for a cause that mattered.

Tenderly, she stroked his temple, momentarily forgetting her own discomfort. "We'll take care of you," she whispered to him. "We'll be good parents. You'll see."

He snorted once and stirred, then rested. Sara grinned, brushing back his uncombed hair.

Calmer now, Sara clutched her knees and craned her neck to behold the starry heavens. Without the artificial glow of cities, she gazed on the galaxy in its natural glory. She'd been to a number of those worlds, she surmised. Seen exotic aliens and set foot on planets that most humans could never dream of visiting. At Michael's side, she'd been a part of shaping the histories of those worlds, and even their parallel selves. She'd routed kingdoms, healed the afflicted, and rescued the defenseless. In just over a year, she'd lived a thousand lives—a thousand adventures—and transformed into someone so completely different from that timid girl with her nose buried in *Alan Worth* stories. If only Johnny could see her.

She smirked, her heart heavy. She missed her friend. Wondered what he was doing now.

Home seemed so far away. That old Sara—with Johnny, her parents, Charlie—that wasn't her anymore. Some days she wondered if it had *ever* been her, or if she'd just dreamt it all. Only now was she beginning to wake up. Funny that it had taken exploring the multiverse in its richness and mystery to fully discover everything she could be. But wasn't that the point of the multiverse? A realm of infinite possibility?

Sara was the master of her fate now. Not her friends, or her family—or even her husband.

Souring slightly, Sara turned to the distance and stared at the nearby mountaintop. She squinted against the pale glow of moonlight, but could no longer make out Michael's shape atop the flat rock. *Maybe he's finally given up*, she thought. She hoped so, for his sake. He'd been up there for over an hour, trying to get a line through to God.

When she'd first met him, Michael had been so focused and sure of himself. His invulnerability had given him a confidence and recklessness that had wonderfully shattered Sara's miserable and predictable life. He'd rescued her from Charlie and whisked her away on his marvelous exploits. With the help of his painful premonitions, he'd been her guide across the cosmos, battling Evil. It was terrifying at first, but Sara eventually got the hang of their whirlwind combative lifestyle. She'd even grown comfortable in it.

Michael, though… These days he was different. After he died on Toby's world, after he spent eons in hell—in the blink of an eye—he returned to her a changed man, both inside and out. His eyes, the ones she always loved, were no longer black. Now they were bright blue. His face was changing too. Subtly, in ways perhaps imperceptible to everyone else, but not to Sara. She knew his face, had studied it every time they talked, asking herself how she came to be so blessed to have this powerful man take her as his wife. But that face wasn't hardened anymore, and the bitterness there that she used to take strength from had softened. *Michael* had softened. His "danger sense" had vanished, and now he was as lost as she, beseeching the heavens for some new direction. They needed that direction now, more than ever.

Finally, she could push the memory away no longer, and her thoughts turned dark, returning to the Krinvox and the terrible ebon cyclone that had erased their world. Worse, she recalled the sight of herself at the forefront of that maelstrom, screeching and stretching her arms forward.

That was me…

Sara shut her eyes, trying to block out the haunting figure, but couldn't. She'd thought of little else all day, wondering what it meant. Michael, too, had remained quiet on the subject, choosing to hold his own counsel—as usual. What was he thinking? She knew he already had reservations about the more assertive attitude she'd been displaying lately. Was this revelation a new reason to distrust her?

That was me, she thought again, struggling to understand.

"No," she muttered aloud on accident. No, that banshee looked like her, but it couldn't be her. *Just a double*, she reminded herself, hoping to quell the doubts in her heart. During their honeymoon, she and Michael had faced off against the Hooded Man—some darker version of Michael that had given in to the Rage rather than rebelled. That's all this witch was. Just Sara's dark self.

"That's all," she whispered, willing herself to relax.

A shuffle in the night broke Sara from her troubling thoughts. She whipped about, startled, as her eyes worked to adjust to the darkness past the fire's dim light. Leaning into the shadows, she squinted and searched, feeling her hackles rise. She couldn't see anything, but rather sensed something out there, in the black. Circling. Watching. Instinctively, her hand eased around her back and gripped the handle of the Krinvox chukrahas blade she had stashed there. She'd lost the blade's twin back at Ak-Huel's camp during the devastation, but was thankful she at least had one of the curved daggers for protection.

Something shimmered in the night, a pair of eyes catching the faint moonlight. Sara's breath caught in her throat and she slowly brought her knees down to the sand, preparing to jump to her feet.

"Hey," a voice called from behind.

Sara scrambled in the dust, getting to her boots, the curved blade raised and poised to chop. She turned about, snarling in fright and rage, then saw it was only Michael. He had his hands in his pockets, his hood drawn, his face downcast and brooding. He glanced up, seeing her tense, and his newly blue eyes came alive.

"What is it?" he asked in a hurry, making his own scan of the desert.

She turned back to where she'd spotted the shape—the eyes—but the glimmer was gone, as well as the anxiety that seeing it had dredged up in her. Sara heaved a sigh through her nostrils and lowered the dagger, her muscles still tingly and nervous. "I saw something, but it's gone now. Just an animal."

Michael regarded the dying fire's light and frowned. "Too bad. We could've used the food."

Sara handled the blade and sat cross-legged in the sand, absently stabbing the chukrahas into the hard-packed earth. Michael calmed, his shoulders slumping, but he didn't sit. Instead, he paced about, removing his hood and rubbing the back of his neck. She recalled when she'd first laid eyes on him over a year ago. He was powerful and majestic, then. Wild and savage and bigger than any problem she'd ever had.

Now, he was just… Just a man. A boy, really. Only eighteen.

We were just kids. What were we thinking running away together?

"Well?" Sara asked hopefully. "Did you get through?"

Michael shook his head without a word.

Sara's heart settled a little further into despair, and she muttered, "Great." Furious now, she plucked the blade out of the dirt and stuck it back in. Again and again, creating a thumping rhythm.

"How are you holding up?" he spoke into the quiet.

She shook her head, slowly blinking. "It was me," she whispered. "How could it…?"

"It couldn't," he blurted all too quickly. "It was just a *parallel* you—from a different reality within the multiverse. We had to run into one eventually. We've already seen one of me. It was only a matter of time."

Sara huffed a tired laugh, plunging the blade into the dirt again. "So she's like my evil twin?"

Michael looked out over the desert, quiet, sullen. "I don't know what she was. We'll figure it out. We knew the Maestro would come after us, after what I did. But we defeated him before. We can do it again. We just have to stay focused, together, and trust God—"

Sara blew out a long sigh, yanking the knife out and burying it again. "Yeah…"

"What's wrong?"

She took a deep breath and faced him, searching his unfamiliar face. "Nothing," she said, at last. He frowned, obviously not buying it, but Sara quickly changed the subject. "How are *you* holding up?"

Michael shrugged and surveyed the lonely night once more. "Still trying to sort through it all. It happened so fast. Losing Ak-Huel…all of them." He shook his head, knelt, and threw another handful of twigs onto the fire. "I don't know. I don't know what to do. Except pray."

Sara sighed. "Michael, I—Look, about this whole God thing."

"I know you don't get it," he grumbled.

"I *get* it," she replied softly. Leaning closer, she locked eyes with him, wanting him to know that she still loved him, she was just—getting to know him again. "I can't begin to imagine what you went through when the Maestro sent you to the In-Between. The things you must have seen there…" She went back to stabbing the blade in the earth. "That shook you. You say you saw God—maybe you did! I'm not doubting that God's out there somewhere in all of this mess."

He faced her, his expression pained. "What *do* you doubt?"

She held his gaze for an uncomfortable moment, then answered, "For months now you've prayed to him, but you haven't seen him, right? I mean, you tell me that you completely turned your life over to God, and the Rage's hold over you is broken and now you're one hundred percent on God's team… But where is he? Where was he when the Krinvox needed him? Why didn't he stop that witch?" Sara glanced to the ground, her heart breaking. "We're supposed to be working for God, but he never shows himself. How do you know…?" She fondled the chukrahas handle, taking a breath, not wanting to start a fight, but desperate to be heard. "How do you know God is who he says he is? How do you know he's telling you the truth about *everything*?"

Michael looked away without a reply.

Sara said, "For five years you thought you were serving him, killing the Rage's agents. Then you find out you were being played by the Rage that whole time. How can you trust that you're not being played *now*? Maybe all of this is just some elaborate setup that the Maestro is using to—"

"Sara, stop," he softly cut in, standing to his sneakers. He exhaled, sounding tired. "Just stop."

She eyed him, worried. "You don't, do you? You don't really know if you can trust him."

"I trust him," he snapped. "He has his reasons for the radio silence. Usually he's trying to teach me something. But I've been there, to the White Place. I've *seen* him. In that Place, I get it. Somehow I get everything. I understand what he's doing, what he's trying to show me. I might've forgotten what that was, but I haven't forgotten that it's still there, all the same. There's still a purpose. He's still with us. I just…I have to be patient."

Sara watched as Michael visibly wrestled with uncertainty. He pursed his lips in concentration and paced about the fire again, the flickering light casting shadows across his deep-set eyes. Sara sensed his pain, his loss. He was trying to keep it together—to be the strong leader he'd always been—but the rules of the game had changed and he was worried. He wouldn't say it of course, but still she knew.

To see Michael searching for a God who never revealed himself was heartbreaking. Michael deserved better than that for all that he'd been through in the name of his God.

With his back to her, Michael said, "I think…maybe it's time we talked about getting Toby somewhere safe."

Sara gaped at him, horrified. "You mean leave him? After we took him away from his home? You were the one who was all wanting to raise him—to teach him to use his powers!"

Michael whirled on her unexpectedly. "Sara, he's eight years old! You saw what that witch did! She destroyed an entire world! It's not safe—"

Toby stirred in his sleep and Sara hurried to her feet, moving away from the boy. Doing her best to keep her voice down, she hissed, "Rift jumping has never been safe. Toby is a lot tougher than you give him credit for." Her heart thundered powerfully, and she spat, "We both are, for that matter."

"What are you saying?" Michael retorted, brow furrowed.

Sara caught herself, unsure of where the outburst had come from.

No, on second thought, she knew. She'd never allowed herself to feel it— had never dared express to Michael all the frustration she felt, how being the useless dead weight in every fight had clawed at her soul until she felt like she'd explode if she couldn't *do* something, *be* something. But it was time now. Her jaw set, she spoke in an even, cold tone. "You know what I mean. Back at that fight with the Glor, you ditched us and went solo. You have to stop doing that. When will you ever trust us?"

Michael's mouth drooped slightly, his focus wavering. He turned away sharply, mumbling, "I can't believe you." Before she had a chance to respond, he faced her again, angry. "All right, you wanna talk about the Glor? Let's talk about the Glor. You charged in like some wild woman and killed that thing—"

"I told you I was *sorry!*"

Michael shouted over her. "Worse, Toby was right there with you!"

She set her shoulders. "He thought he was helping you!"

"Look at what this life is doing to him." Quieting, he snarled at her, hurt. "Look at what it's done to *you.*"

Sara scowled, tears stinging her sinuses. He did not back down, though, and the silence that grew between them nearly suffocated her.

"Why are you fighting?" Toby whined. Sara broke eye contact with Michael and saw the little boy sitting up, rubbing at his bleary eyes before slipping his glasses back on.

She softened. "We're not fighting, baby. Go back to sleep."

Michael ran his fingers through his hair and walked off. Sara watched after him a moment before going to tuck Toby back in, worried that she was more alone than ever.

2

The three of them got an early start the next morning. Before the sun had even finished breaking free of the horizon, Michael quietly stomped out the last of the smoking brush from their fire. Sara gathered what few belongings they'd managed to grab before fleeing Yur's destruction, while Toby just sat on the ground, aimless and waiting. They walked in silence until midday. Toby kept them in steady supply of ice chips to stay hydrated, but Michael knew that if they didn't come upon food soon, his two companions would starve. He knew from being trapped in another desert long ago—the one in between the worlds where Rip had tempted him to join the Rage—that he could survive without food thanks to his invulnerability. Despite the tedium of trekking through this no man's land, Michael reasoned he wasn't too terribly uncomfortable. But as he chanced brief sidelong glances at Sara and Toby, he saw them weakening by the hour; their flesh paling, their steps slowing more and more. He keenly felt the burden to provide for them, but seemed increasingly useless in that regard. That feeling of uselessness was becoming common to him. Sara was sensing it, he knew. That was why she was growing more headstrong.

She doesn't believe in me anymore.

If *she* was frustrated by the changes in him, he was doubly so. He'd died back on Toby's world, but God had regenerated him, changed him somehow. Now the face that met him in the mirror wasn't entirely his own. Even more than that, that cold, churning rage that had propelled him like a speeding train through every obstacle was simply gone, like it'd been scooped right out of him. Sure, he still felt angry when provoked, but it was nothing like it had been before. For as long as he could remember, that single-minded wrath had taken over for him, giving him the strength to accomplish impossible feats. The Man in the Stetson—God—had once told Michael that he would keep him from harm, but it had been the Rage that was at the core of his superhuman strength. And now…now it was gone. Not just the power to fight, but the will, too. His headaches and stomach cramps—his "danger radar" that guided him from mission to mission—was absent, as well, leaving him directionless in a multiverse of infinite threat, infinite peril.

We're lost at sea here, he prayed to God. *What am I supposed to do?*

Who am I supposed to be *now?*

He groaned under the weight of his questions, and soldiered on through the desert, knowing nothing else to do.

Sara kept her distance from him, walking on the other side of Toby. Michael watched her, careful not to let on that he was staring. Scariest of all developments since his regeneration was the separation from Sara. Since the day he took her from her world and her old life, they'd been through everything together, and always as a team. Somewhere along the way, most inexplicably, they'd even developed a strange psychic link. By the time they'd run afoul of the Maestro in Toby's dimension, they'd been able to communicate telepathically. Now that link was severed, even before they'd fully begun to understand it—another casualty of his rebirth.

Sara had once occupied the space inside his mind, as well as his heart, a constant and comfortable part of him. But now that level of intimacy was gone from their marriage, and he felt lonely and distant from her.

He missed her terribly.

Worse, he began to doubt her resolve. The witch who destroyed the Krinvox bore her face. And, as much as he wanted to believe it was an evil doppelgänger, Michael feared a more sinister possibility. Sara *was* changing. Whatever violence had dwelt deep in his heart seemed to have relocated to Sara's. She was more aggressive than ever and constantly questioning his reliance on God. A year ago, he would have said that there was no way Sara was capable of conjuring something like that unspeakable Black Pillar, but after seeing what she'd done to the Glor without hesitation… He just wasn't so sure anymore. The thought sickened him and he hated himself for even considering it.

Please, God, tell me what to do.

Frowning, he crossed the short distance to his wife and brushed against her hand. "Hey," he began, quiet, trying to maintain a level of privacy, though Toby walked nearby.

Her blue eyes remained fixed on an indistinguishable point up ahead as they walked. "Hey."

Michael searched her eyes, trying to peer into her mind like before. To prove to himself that she was still his Sara. But that door was closed to him now. "About last night, I wanted to apologize. I said some things that I shouldn't have."

"But you meant them," she said quickly, as though she had already imagined they'd be having this conversation and had already rehearsed her responses. "You *do* think that I'm different now."

"I think we're both different, yeah. We've changed."

"We've done what we had to, to survive," she said automatically.

He looked down at the sand as his worn Converse sneakers trudged through it. "Yeah…"

Now she faced him, her stare hard and piercing. "Can I ask you a question?"

His stomach rumbled with nerves, tensing for an attack.

She continued, "If you had it to do over again, would you take me with you? And I want you to be honest."

Michael averted her demanding gaze, his heart thumping painfully. He thought of all they'd seen together, the laughter, the quiet talks, the times they made love. Before he met her, he'd been little more than a dead man, kept alive only by his hate. But she'd breathed life and color into him. How could he regret that?

Yet, whenever he shut his eyes he could see only the Black Pillar. What if he were responsible for turning shy, daydreaming Sara into a monster on a quest to destroy worlds? It couldn't be possible; that witch couldn't really be her, not *his* Sara. Or could it? Quiet, he mumbled, "I…don't know."

She huffed and resumed marching, quickening her pace. He kept up with her, wanting to finish his thought.

"Being with you all this time…" Michael shook his head, struggling with the words. "This has been the greatest year of my life. And…I thought I had saved you, but the truth of it is, you saved *me*."

Sara slowed just a bit and offered him her attention.

He finished, "But I look at what rift jumping has done to you. What it's already starting to do to Toby. I thought I was giving you a better life by bringing you with me—"

"You did," she breathed softly, her eyes finally filled with a spark that wasn't anger. "That's what I'm trying to get you to see. You gave us *hope*. Don't take that away from us now. Let us in. Let us do this with you."

He shut his mouth and nodded, his brow still knotted in consternation. "I *am* trying," he finally confessed, and left it at that. For as long as they had been married, eventually they always found themselves right back in this spot—Sara yearning for independence and Michael too afraid to let her go. In the beginning, the reasons had been simple to Michael. He was indestructible, and Sara was so fragile. It made sense to protect her, to keep her locked away like a valuable treasure. But Sara had more than proven herself capable. She didn't need him anymore, not in the same ways she used to.

As if detecting his worry, she hooked a finger in his and gave a little squeeze.

They shared a small, sad smile, and for the first time in a while, Michael felt like they were on the path to discovering each other again.

"What's that?" Toby piped up, jogging ahead a few steps.

Michael and Sara followed, and Michael saw a dark shape in the distance. He had to shield his eyes from the glaring sun, but thought he spotted—

"It's a house!" Sara exclaimed, tugging on Michael's arm. "Is it?"

A warm grin spread across his gloomy features. "Yeah. Yeah, I think it is."

Toby was already running for it. "Come on! Let's go!"

Michael laughed, then caught Sara smiling. She paused for a moment and took Michael's hands. "We're going to be okay," she whispered.

He leaned down and touched his forehead to hers. "I think we are."

3

Sara raced after Toby across the rocky terrain. The boy gabbed excitedly to no one in particular, waving his arms. She chuckled, too, as she ran with Michael at her side.

"Toby, slow down!" she giggled.

He carried on, whirling his hands in the air, nearly tripping over himself as they began a small ascent to the house. From here, Sara could make out the details more clearly. The house was just an old shack atop a tiny hill. The boards were grey and warped and the roof had caved in on the left side. One lone twisted tree reached out to scratch at the eaves with its leafless branches. Already, Sara's heart began to sink. "The place looks abandoned," she said to Michael. "Probably not going to be any food."

"At least it'll get you guys out of the heat until we figure out our next move."

Toby disappeared over the top of the mound and the sound of his giggles faded.

"Toby, wait!" Michael hollered, mid-laugh, climbing after him. "Hold up!"

Sara scraped her hands against the craggy surface, her pace slowing as she clambered up the knoll. At last, she and Michael reached the crest and the house—

And froze.

Toby stood there in the yard, stone still. In a fraction of a second, Sara feared maybe he'd stumbled upon a rattlesnake, but then her eyes drifted to the bodies…

She caught her breath.

Strewn about the hard-packed earth, Sara saw the gory remains of whom she assumed to be the house's original occupants. Intestines had been thrown about and now she noticed dried bits of entrails hanging from the gnarled tree. A couple of the bodies were missing arms or legs, but soon she spotted them, discarded like trash. Human men and women lay at her feet—maybe five in all, though in such a condition it was hard to be sure—all of their ribcages pried open, their internal organs removed.

Or devoured.

Large, black, scaly birds, the size of storks she'd seen on other worlds, pecked at the rancid flesh of the rotting bodies. One bird lifted its head, blinked six reptilian eyes at her, and squawked in a low, croaking bass that made her queasy.

Toby trembled in his spot and Sara cupped his shoulder and steered him to face her stomach. "Don't look, Toby," she said, realizing the damage had already been done.

She shot eyes at Michael, who met her expression. He grimaced, all business, and kicked at one of the alien predators. The beast opened its beak, hissed, then hopped to another meal. Michael stooped in the dust next to a woman's body.

"What did this?" Sara asked. "You think it was that animal I saw last night?"

He scratched his chin, looking over the corpse. "Could be. Probably, I guess. The blood's dried up. They've been here a while."

Sara edged closer, still pressing Toby against her, and got a better look at one of the cadavers—this one a male. His mouth was twisted in horror, eyes milky and staring at the skies. The man's face was oddly painted—half-white, half-black. He was clothed in dark patchwork clothes. Animal skins, she recognized. Glancing to the other victims, she saw they all bore the same war paint.

"Part of a tribe," she muttered, mostly to herself, but Michael nodded.

"Looks like." Michael's eyes fell on Toby and he tipped his chin to the shack. "Why don't you get him inside?"

Sara nodded and guided the little boy. "Come on, Toby."

She stepped over a torn leg, holding her breath to keep her disgust in check, trying her best not to disturb the dangerous-looking scavengers, and crossed the threshold of the house. Still shielding the child, she quickly scanned the first room and saw signs of a struggle. There wasn't much in the way of furniture or belongings—just crude handmade chairs, a ratty hammock, a table, and clay pots—but what little these people had possessed, it had all been trashed. Blankets were shredded and jars had been smashed to the clapboard floor.

Sara righted a chair that was mostly intact and scooted Toby towards it. "Stay here," she whispered, and drew her chukrahas. Gripping it with the tip raised high, Sara eased throughout the remaining three cramped rooms in the shack. More signs of struggle, more damage. Thankfully, though, no more bodies. And no sign of whatever thing had butchered these people.

When she returned to the main room, Michael entered, his face stern.

She tucked the blade back in its sheath and sighed. "What now?"

He glanced once more to the bodies outside. "We need to bury them."

"Burning would be quicker," she offered.

He faced Toby. The boy just stared at his hands in his lap, unblinking. Michael took a breath and said, "We should—"

The loud grinding of gears interrupted Michael's sentence. The roar of an engine grew closer. No, she realized, multiple engines. Michael and Sara hunkered low and slipped beneath the front window opening. Outside, the large reptilian birds whooped in protest and flapped away, their leathery wings beating powerfully against the air. Sara watched as three busted-looking motorcycles and one rickety truck—all adorned in spikes and skulls—came into view.

Headed right for the house.

She whispered to Michael, even though she knew the vehicles and their occupants were too far away to hear. "We have to move. We can't be here."

"There's nowhere to run. It's flat land as far as I could tell. They'd see us. Better just to face them. They could be why we're on this world. Maybe they're friendly, like the Krinvox."

Sara cast another glance to the three human skulls chained to the front grill of the truck. "Mm, thinking not." She spoke over her shoulder. "Toby, we've got company. You good?"

He lifted his head and nodded once, drying his eyes. "I'm good."

The vehicles slowed to a halt and the driver of the truck hurried out, leaving the door standing open. He was wild-eyed and fat, his naked flabby arms covered in a thick carpet of curly black hair. On his bulbous head, his hair was shorter on the sides, parted down the middle by a thick green-dyed mane that trailed all the way down to the small of his back. The bikers joined the troll-like human and removed crude metal helmets and goggles, revealing their faces. Sara saw that all of them were dressed like the bodies they'd found. All wore dark animal furs and their faces were painted that same curious half-white, half-black.

And they all bore rifles or shotguns.

She and Michael stayed out of sight, but she just managed to peek out of the side of the window opening. The new arrivals stumbled about the remains. She couldn't make out their words, but heard the emotion in their voices. Rage, terror, confusion. They shouted at each other in a bizarre clucking language, kneeling over some of the bodies, gnashing their teeth, gesturing wildly. Sara closed her eyes for a moment, taking a deep, steadying breath. She eased out her chukrahas and clutched it close to her chest. "This is bad," she whispered to Michael.

He remained focused on the scene out front, lips tight. Suddenly he said, "I'm going to go talk to them."

Toby crawled over to Sara, his face open. "What do you want *me* to do?"

Michael and Sara traded a look. "Stay here," Michael said. "If it goes bad, you two sneak out the back. I'll keep them distracted."

"Are you going to hurt them?" Toby asked, fearful.

Sara watched her husband expectantly. Michael shook his head, then smirked. "Nah." He ruffled the boy's messy hair. "Remember, Toby. Just because you have the power to hurt someone, doesn't mean you *should*."

Michael eased out of his hiding spot and lifted his hands in surrender. Sara patted Toby's knee, keeping patient watch on her husband. He exited the shack to the indignant and startled shouts of the tribe out front. Instantly, they had their guns on him, issuing commands and protests in a series of barks and clicks.

"We're not here to hurt you," Michael announced loudly and slowly. "We want to help you."

The hairy leader with the green mohawk hollered to his men, pointing with his sawed-off shotgun and shouting in his indecipherable tongue.

Toby inched closer to Sara's ear. "What are they saying? What do we do?"

Sara ignored the boy, narrowing her eyes as Michael slowly lowered his arms, relaxing. Mohawk stomped and shouted, his long unwashed locks lashing about. Though Michael seemed calm, Sara could tell the situation was building to a breaking point—only she didn't know which side would break first.

"Do we need to hide?" Toby hissed, edgy.

"No. Sneak outside. We'll circle around them. You go right, I'll go left."

"But Michael said—"

Sara turned to the child, sharp. "I know what Michael said, but—"

The crack of a shotgun caused Sara to jump, and she wheeled about to the window. Michael was laid out on the ground, writhing in the dust. In Mohawk's hands, the recently fired sawed-off shotgun exhaled smoke.

Sara snarled in rage and shouted, "Toby, hit them!"

Without waiting for the boy, Sara jumped to her feet and charged into the open air. Mohawk took one startled step back, pointing at Sara and garbling the word, "*Her!*" He fumbled and leveled his gun again, firing another round of buckshot. Sara was already out of the way, circling to the left and swinging a leg that hooked Mohawk in the double-chin and hurled him to the ground. She finished him off, bringing her blade down right into his doughy gut. He gasped, the last of his life leaving him, and Sara leveled her glare on the nearest biker as he raced for her, screaming a high-pitched warble and waving a chain. Before he reached her, though, a battering ram of solid ice slammed into him, catapulting him over the edge of the dirty embankment.

Toby rode in on his ice slide, hurling sharpened icicles at the other tribesmen. They dodged and hid behind the truck for cover, returning fire with dinged-up rifles. One bullet whizzed within an inch of Toby's foot, shattering the ice beneath him, and the boy fell with a small cry. Wrath lit up in Sara like hot fire and she pushed ahead, sliding along the hood of the truck and squarely kicking the rifleman in the face, dislocating his jaw with a solid *pop*. He gargled in pain and doubled over, while Sara went to work dispatching the others, kicking, ducking their desperate, untrained swings, and slashing and hacking with her curved blade. She made short work of them, leaving them to groan and twist in the dirt before the survivors piled into their vehicles and sped away in retreat.

Once they were gone, she called over her shoulder, "Toby, you still good?"

"Still good," he coughed, rubbing the arm where he had landed.

Sara wiped her chukrahas clean on her jeans, a pleased smile worming its way to her hard face. She laughed and turned back to Michael. "See? I told you we could take care of ourselves."

But Michael wasn't moving. He lay still on the ground, splayed out painfully—a bright red blossom of blood over his right shoulder.

Sara's eyes widened in horror. "Michael!"

She scrambled over the loose topsoil, kneeling at his side. Her hands roved wildly about him, trembling in panic. Toby was at her side an instant later, shouting, "What's wrong with him?"

"No," she gasped. "No, no, *no*...Michael! Michael, *wake up!*"

The blood continued to spread, ruining his shirt, his jacket. Sara pulled back a quaking hand, her fingers drenched in red. "He's hurt," she gasped, her mind struggling to process the impossible notion. "This isn't supposed...this isn't possible..." Crying now, she flung herself over him, screaming into his paling face, "*Michael, wake up!*"

4

In his dreams, he sees the Black Pillar devouring the Krinvox. Sees Ak-Huel reaching for his daughter, pleading that she be restored to him. He sees the witch, suspended in the air by the storm, howling after him. Stretching for him. It's Sara. With black eyes and a wide hungry mouth, ready to swallow him into oblivion—

Michael bolted awake, wheezing for life, his heart racing like a prize stallion. His mind told him to escape, but he couldn't move, the last throes of sleep binding him in paralysis. After seconds that seemed like an eternity, his breathing slowed and his muscles eased. Calmer now, he blinked sight back into his eyes, disorientated as though he'd just been ripped from one world to the next. Once his blurry vision righted, he realized he was staring through a hole in a tattered ceiling, watching starry lights twinkling back at him. He tried to lift his head, but rasped in pain—

Pain. He felt *pain.*

It started in his chest, a numb sort of weight that spread to his shoulders, his arms, his neck. His fingers tingled with raw sensation and he curled them, feeling them stiffen against his command. His head hurt too much to turn, but he scanned the room with his eyes. It was the shack from before, dimly lit by a single candle he couldn't quite see. Shapes moved in the shadows and he tensed, suddenly terrified and vulnerable.

"Help!" he cried. "Where am I—"

Sara entered his field of vision, and for a flash of time he was back in his nightmare, the witch stretching her arms to encircle him. He flinched in involuntary revulsion, but cooled just as quickly. It was his Sara, her eyes still blue, her long, ginger locks lightly kissing his face. The sight refreshed him and his eyes stung with tears. Sara had already been crying, dried dirty paths streaking her face. She tenderly touched his cheek, her caring eyes widening. "I'm here, sweetie."

He tightened his shoulders—still trying to move—only to jerk under the assault of sharp, needle-like pricks beneath his flesh. "I'm...what happened...what..."

"You've been shot," she said, under control, but obviously frightened.

"Shot?" he asked, bewildered. "Shot..."

He looked to her, uncertain, but glimpsed Toby standing off to the side, away from the action, looking worried and oddly out of place.

"Toby," Michael breathed, glad to see the kid okay.

Toby stayed back, watching intently but not venturing any closer.

Sara gently turned Michael's head to face her. "I fixed you up as best I could. You had some shot buried in your shoulder, but I pried it out. I cleaned the wound and bandaged it with some of the sheets I found. I don't know how clean they are, but it's the best I could do."

Michael swallowed hard, his throat dry. "Thank you..."

"Found food, too," Sara blurted anxiously, nodding towards the other room. "Odds and ends of canned food. I don't know where they came from, but they were there."

Resting his head back, Michael felt a few scant tears escaping. "I don't understand. This doesn't—" He willed the pain away and forced himself to rise to a sitting position in the hammock where Sara had placed him. As he did so, he cried out unexpectedly, stung by an excruciating pain in his chest and shoulder.

Sara shot out her hands, steadying him. "Stop."

He grimaced, squinting through miserable tears, and snarled, "I have to try and get a line through. I have to talk to him. I have to find out why this is happening."

"What makes you think he'll even answer? It's not exactly like he's been forthcoming with the info up until now."

"He *has* to answer!" Michael spat, petrified and lost. His body began to shake uncontrollably and he ran the only hand that would obey him across his face. Taking deep breaths did little to expel the feeling that he might vomit. He gathered himself and half-turned to Sara. "I'm sorry."

She rested her hand on his shoulder in a careful way, as if she were afraid she might break him. Along with the pain, Michael felt a deep shame. He'd lost his ability to detect danger, lost the strength that the Rage provided...

Now this...

He couldn't lead his family. Couldn't protect them. *Not like this.*

He retracted from her gentle touch and stood, though his head throbbed and every movement took incredible effort. "I...need to go. I need to figure this out."

"Michael—"

A cry threatened to escape, but he stemmed his humiliated tears, clenching his jaw. "Don't."

She held his gaze a moment more, then nodded and looked away. He glanced at Toby, and the boy watched him steadily. Like a stranger.

Michael pressed his lips and left the shack behind, venturing into the desert.

5

Sara sat propped up in the hammock, Toby resting across her lap. She absently stroked his unruly hair, but her eyes—and her mind—were fixed through the window opening into the darkened terrain. Michael was still out there, his face lifted to the heavens. Like the night before, he'd been waiting for God to answer him for nearly two hours. He had stood tall for a long time, then bowed for a while. Even from inside, Sara had heard his sobs. His desperate pleas. By now, a sort of resignation had set in, and Michael merely sat cross-legged in the desert, shoulders slumped and back arched. Waiting.

In Sara's heart, hate grew. Hate for Michael's "Man in the Stetson". What kind of cruel trick was he playing, that he'd take away Michael's powers *now*, of all times? Now, when some witch with her face was out there in the multiverse, devouring worlds?

She cursed the Man in her heart, her eyes narrowing in anger.

"Sara?" Toby mumbled, half-asleep, startling her from her rage-filled thoughts.

Still brushing his unwashed hair back from his soft, smudged face, she forced a smile for his sake. "What's wrong, baby?"

84

"Are we safe?" he asked, and her heart broke, for it was the same question he asked every night. It'd been four months since Toby started jumping the rifts with them, but the boy was still adjusting to life without a home. Without a mother. His own mother had been a miserable one, but he still missed her. Still felt the sting of her betrayal when she turned him away once she discovered his abilities. He was just a little boy, Sara was reminded, lost in the multiverse. Most nights he couldn't get to sleep unless Sara held him, and *every* night, before he finally drifted off, he asked the same question, as though he were asking for permission to sleep.

He felt so small in her arms, so unlike the fighter he had been earlier in the day, flinging ice at their attackers with wild abandon. Now he looked like any kid, on any world. She bent down and kissed his cheek. "Of course, baby. You're always safe with us. We won't let anything happen to you."

"But Michael doesn't have powers anymore," he spoke, his voice small and timid. He sounded like he might cry.

Sara hesitated to answer, understanding his fears all too well. She wasn't sure how they were going to survive the situations they constantly found themselves facing without Michael's strength.

But I'm strong now, she reckoned.

"We'll figure it out," she finally said, maintaining confidence in her voice. "Besides, we'll look out for each other, won't we?"

He nodded minutely, his body growing warm—a sure sign that he was about to fall asleep. "Will you sing to me?"

"Sure." She grinned at him, still stroking his twisted locks, as she began to softly sing him a lullaby that her father used to sing for her. The same song Toby requested every night. Michael said once he'd heard the song on his world, only the lyrics had been different.

"My darling sunshine, my little sunshine
You send the rainy clouds away
Don't ever leave me, my little sunshine
And make my world so sad and gray…"

"I love you, Mommy…" he whispered in a daze, and Sara paused, caught off guard. Then the boy snored, totally out.

Her heart tittered as she speculated on whether Toby's words were meant for her, or if he was caught in some memory from his past. Regardless, she brushed her lips against his ear. "I love you, too, Toby."

With the boy asleep at last, Sara leaned back and resumed her watch out the window. Enough time had passed, and she reasoned it was time to go out there and bring Michael back inside. He needed sleep. Besides, she couldn't shake the worry that those tribal warriors might return for payback.

A shuffle outside, and a black shape passed by one of the other windows. Sara stiffened in alarm, her breath catching in her throat. She looked closer, but saw nothing. Still, the back of her neck broke out in gooseflesh and she eased Toby's slumbering form off her and onto the hammock, drawing her curved dagger. Sara crouched low and crossed the room to the window, placing her back to the wall and carefully peeking outside.

She gasped.

There, a dark shape—darker than the night—stood out from the starry sky, low to the ground and on all fours. The same creature from the camp last night.

Twin glowing eyes stared back at her. Watching her. Waiting for her.

{*Sara*}

She balked in surprise, the voice loud and clear in her mind, just like it had been when she and Michael communicated in their nascent telepathic bond. But it wasn't Michael's voice in her thoughts, rather a stranger's, penetrating her mental defenses. Violating her.

{*Sara*}

The animal's eyes glowered in the moonlight, brightening each time the voice pulsed in her thoughts. With sickening revelation, Sara realized the animal was in her mind, sharing the space with her. She shivered in its psychic presence. {*Get out. Who are you? What do you want?*}

The creature bowed its snout. {*Come out and see.*}

Then the four-legged animal turned and loped off, disappearing down the backside of the small hill, beckoning Sara to follow. Sweat dotted her brow, and her breathing became hurried. Damp fingers flexed around the chukrahas handle. Sara looked back to Toby. The boy slept on, none the wiser, peacefully resting in the quiet. Sara turned back to the window to see Michael still seated on the desert floor, showing no sign that he was ready to give up on his futile prayers.

What am I doing? she asked herself, now worried that the animal had heard her tussling with indecision. At last, she drew a steady breath and slipped out into the night, jogging in increasing anticipation. She came to the crest and looked out, the pale silver moonlight guiding her path. Down in a ravine, she spotted the small lumbering beast. Was it a dog? A wolf?

Checking one last time to be sure that Michael hadn't taken notice of her late night exploit, Sara climbed down into the narrow valley, loose rock sifting under her boots. By time she touched the bottom, the path was clear and the animal was gone. Dark rock walls flanked her on either side, all but concealing the moon. She eased her way down the corridor, her chukrahas at the ready, keen eyes cutting back and forth.

{*Where are you?*} she thought to her passenger. {*No tricks.*}

In the shadow of the rock, two yellow orbs peered back at her. A third light, lower than the pair, flickered bright, then was immediately snuffed out. She heard a sharp intake of breath, then watched as a plume of smoke curled into the open air. Out of the black, a man—not a wolf—strode forward. He was barefoot, and had on a pair of old dusty jeans. The man was of a lean build, his tightly muscled core shrouded in a leather jacket that immediately struck Sara as achingly familiar. It had fewer tears and holes since she'd last seen it, but it was impossibly *Michael's* jacket; the one he'd had when he found her on her world. As for the man's face, it was haggard and tanned, evidence of too much time exposed to the elements. Crow's feet reached out from wise and cunning eyes, and the stranger's long, silvery hair was braided like his beard, parted down the middle, and pulled back by a tie-dyed bandana.

He puffed on a joint and removed it, then grinned to reveal an extended canine. "Hey, Red," he casually greeted, sounding just like the wolf in her mind.

She inched back a step, poising her blade to strike.

"Been waitin' a long time to talk to you."

Her brow creased, no doubt creating that little knot above her left eyebrow that Michael always found so endearing. She hated that knot.

"The Rage has got plans for you, little darlin', and that right there is the understatement of alllll tiiiime." He drew a long drag on the smoke.

Sara hardened her face, yet felt the tiniest flutter of excitement. What could the Rage want with a regular person like her? "Who are you?"

"Just a man who's touched the darkness in between worlds. Name's Rip."

Sara's mind whirled. She instantly knew this man. He was the one who had convinced Michael, at twelve years old, to kill a man in cold blood. Rip had been the one waiting for Michael after his death, trying to recruit him to join the Rage.

As far as Michael was concerned, Rip was the devil himself.

She eyed him with suspicion, acutely aware of how far away Michael was. "You said you've been waiting to talk to me. Why?"

"Your destiny," Rip said, without any hint of irony. "I'm just a signpost to help guide people like you along the path."

"What are you talking about?"

He raised the joint to his lips, but hesitated. Confused, he said, "I thought that would be obvious. We're at the End Game, darlin'. You've already seen it." Frowning in concern, he added, "You *have* seen it, haven't you? Big ole tower of black, eating up every blasted thing?"

Sara paled and feared she'd gasped aloud.

He grinned, looking relieved. "You *have* seen it then. Whew. Had me worried for a second there, Red." He touched his scrawny chest, taking a breath. "Time's a wonky thing when you walk in and out of it. That's good, though. That's real good. That means it works. Ha ha, we did it! Or, at least, we *will*."

"Wait," she panted. "The Black Pillar. The witch. My double."

Rip's eyes widened and he stifled a laugh. "*Double?* Oh, no, darlin'." He inhaled on his smoke, then let out a slow breath. "Deep down, you know better than that."

The dagger in her hand faltered, her heart growing faint. "I don't believe you."

He shrugged, indifferent. "Not yet. But you will. I mean, that's a done deal, right? You've already seen it."

"What is it?" she demanded. "What's happening to the multiverse?"

"It's breaking down. We're shattering the mirrors and you're gonna be the one holding the sledgehammer. Everything we've been planning, it's all come to this. You can't imagine how long my Master has been waiting for this moment."

"The Maestro," she spoke the word like an incantation, fearing that just saying the demon's name would summon him.

Rip waved her off, blowing smoke out his nostrils. "Oh, Aztaroth? *That* weirdo? Nah."

She blinked in surprise, unaware that the Maestro had a proper name, and wondered what other secrets Rip knew. "But I thought you were working for him?"

"*For* him? *With* him, maybe. For a while, but he was too caught up with getting your runaway husband back in the game to lead that monster army on Chelkan or whatever. Awfully complicated plan, wasn't it, especially after he brought in all those firestarters. But I guess that's how them creative types are. So wrapped up in their clever thinking." Once more he faced her, just a hint of yellow shimmering in his eyes. "That's all in the past, now. Aztaroth had his chance to find what he was looking for on all those worlds. My Master, though, he's getting impatient. The Maestro's out. Now we've got a new plan…" He trailed off, laughing. Nodding to her, he took a hit off his smoke. "And it all starts with you."

Sara considered how to respond. She thought to run, even to kill this man who would say such things to her. Who would even suggest that she would ever have a part to play in the Rage's schemes. Yet, she couldn't deny what she saw destroying the Krinvox. *It was me.* What was she capable of? How could she do such a thing?

Panting heavy, her knife hand still raised, she declared, "Tell me everything."

Rip nodded over his shoulder. "Follow me."

Sara lowered her blade, never taking her eyes off the strange man. Rip turned his back to her, walking on, leading her deeper into the narrow ravine. Sara made to follow but paused, fearful. She looked back to the cliff above, thinking of the shack. Her family.

"I-I can't," she said. "I can't leave Toby for long. He's sleeping."

"The boy won't know you're gone," Rip drawled. "'Sides, it'll only take a minute to tell you what I got to say. Just want to make sure it's in private." He gestured to the skies. "Away from prying ears, you know?"

Sara frowned, but followed after him, deeper into the twisting chasm, where none but the faintest sliver of light remained. They were practically subterranean, with the topside world fading fast behind her. With each step, her heart padded faster, her nerves on edge with equal parts curiosity and fear.

"H-How does it happen?" she asked, desperate to know, but worried that she had left Toby alone for too long. Or that Michael had discovered her absence. "*How* does it start?"

Rip bobbed his head from side to side, in thought. "Hmm, couldn't say, really. Hasn't happened yet, from my perspective in the timeline. You could say the future destination is already written, but how we get there—well, that can change."

"What is the Rage?" Sara posed, terrified of the truth, but hungry for it all the same. "*Really?*"

"No one's ever seen it—not up close. I s'pose the best way to think of it, is like this…alien force. Some kind of intelligence, greater than people."

"Like God?"

Rip chuckled. "Not exactly. Maybe like an anti-God. See, it's been pinned up, behind the walls of reality, in the darkness, In-Between. But it's trying to get out of the cage."

Sara's stomach rumbled with excitement and revulsion. "Why?"

"Why *else*? To be free, Red! Ain't that all any of us wants? To be free?"

Sara lowered her head, contemplating.

"The multiverse is like one big prison. We gotta unlock the cage, bring back the Chaos. But that God your hubby's so fond of answering to, he don't like things bein' free. He likes 'em right underneath his thumb. Just like he's got Michael. Just like Michael's got you."

"I'm not under anyone's thumb," Sara blurted in hot-faced defiance.

"Whoa," Rip chuckled, holding out his rough hands, as if to stay the tide of her fury. "Got some fire there, don't'cha?"

Sara chewed on her lip, her jaw tensing. "But…what does this have to do with me?"

"The Rage picked you out a long time ago, sweetheart. You were meant to be its greatest asset against Michael. A little back-up, to keep Michael on the path. Ensure that he kept feeding that hate in his belly so he'd be ready to lead the army one day."

Sara blanched and stopped dead in her steps. "What?"

Rip saw she was no longer moving, and he halted as well. After taking one last pull off the joint, he finally flicked the remaining stub into the night. "Think about it, Red. Every moment of your life—meeting Charlie, your parents' death, joining up with Michael on his inter-dimensional road trip…all a part of the Big Plan."

Sara blinked rapidly, her stomach churning. She recalled that the Maestro had said the same thing to her only a few months ago. "The Maestro," she began. "He said that my pain was like a song."

Rip nodded with a fanged grin. "That was the Maestro's part of the Big Plan. To forge you into a weapon. Something strong and unbreakable. A killer."

"I'm not a killer," Sara defended, though she knew that wasn't entirely true.

"Everyone's a killer, if you put 'em in the right situation," Rip darkly replied. "Just need a little push, that's all."

"And that's what you're here to do?"

"I'm here to…let's say, *show you the light.*" He snickered at his own lame joke, and continued, "Anyway, the original plan was to have Michael lead the Chelkan army, right? Well, somewhere along the way, your little hubby started thinking he had a choice in the matter. Aztaroth was brought in to turn you into one of us. He started messing with Charlie's head and convinced him to kill your folks—"

Sara's mouth went dry, and her eyes simultaneously filled with tears. "That was *Charlie?*"

Rip nodded casually. "Of course it was, Red. He was in on it from the beginning. And the idea was, once you were good and ready, the Maestro would slip you into Mike's life. You'd get close, win his heart—whatever—and then, if he still wouldn't own up to what he was meant to do, you were gonna turn on him."

"Then what?"

He shrugged. "Then you'd kill him, if he wasn't worthy to lead. Or, Chaos-willing, he would've killed *you* in self-defense and lost his soul in the process. After that, I'm betting the fight woulda been knocked out of him and he'd be back on *our* team." Rip considered. "It would've been pretty epic, really. Would've loved to have seen the look on his face when the trap was sprung."

Sara shook her head, overcome with so much emotion she felt numb. "Y-You're telling me that everything…" She trembled with fury. "Everything I went through—that was all you guys?"

Rip held his hands up in surrender. "The Maestro, if you wanna be technical."

Tears blurred her sight. "You were just screwing with me to...to use me against *Michael?*"

"Hey, hey, easy, Red. That's all in the past, like I said. Mike changed the game when he killed the Maestro's firestarters and slew that black goop brewing in his belly. Aztaroth's plot was foiled, as they say, and that dumb army is *still* trapped on Chelkan." Rip leaned in closer as Sara tightened her fist around the chukrahas, squeezing until it hurt. "But, hey, it turns out it wasn't all in vain. We underestimated you, ya know? You got a lot more potential than we *ever* thought. And...if you've seen the Black Pillar, then you know you're gonna more than live up to that potential."

Sara resisted every urge to cry. To run into the darkness and shout and curse and beg that it wasn't true. She thought of Mom and Dad and how they'd finally come around, there at the end. They were finally ready to be there for her, and they could've been a family, but she'd left them to die for Charlie. Charlie!

She thought of Charlie's fear of the dark and the things he'd scream in his nightmares. He'd been used, too, manipulated to ruin her life just so she'd be the ace up the Maestro's sleeve if Michael refused to lead that cursed army!

Everything... Everything... She'd been doomed from the start...

Growling, her voice breaking, she demanded, "Why? The Rage wants to destroy the multiverse. *Then* what? What would be left?"

Rip pursed his lips and shrugged. "Damned if I know. Eternal darkness. Chaos in the wild black of the In-Between. Hell, maybe we could take that dark matter and make a new reality. Make it any way we wanted to."

"You're crazy. You're following some weird alien thing on, what? Faith?"

"In the end, ain't that all any of us has?" He leaned over her, but not to threaten. "The Rage is trying to set you free, little darlin'. That Big Old God up there is just a dictator, trying to make us bow down to his will. But you don't need him. You're *special*, sis. You've got power inside you, growing every day. It's the Rage. It'll never leave you, never let you down. You'll have the strength to shape *your own* destiny. Make it whatever you want it to be. But first..." Rip's eyes dimmed, and in the shadows they flickered just like the eyes of the wolf. "...you've *still* got to take out God's little errand boy. That part of the plan hasn't changed."

"I won't kill Michael," Sara vowed, though felt a tinge of doubt somewhere deep inside, in the dark places of her soul that she tried to ignore.

Rip grinned, his canine gleaming. "We'll see about that." Stepping away, he watched her with amusement. "You think you really know him? You think all this time he's been the good guy?" He huffed a snort-like laugh. "He ain't told you yet, has he?"

"Told me what?" she asked, confused.

He smiled and glanced into the darkness. "Yeah, there's a lot I'd reckon he's not told you. Can't say that I blame him. Some things a man's too ashamed to admit, but believe me when I tell you, he's got his fair share of secrets. Even from you, pretty darlin'."

Sara narrowed her eyes at the man, seething. "You don't know him."

"Don't know him?" He threw his head back in a fit of unexpected laughter. "Sis, I *made* him. Oh, I know him, all right. I know what he's capable of. What he *really* is."

Sara maintained her cool, but Rip continued, "Though I guess these days he says that's all part of his 'holy mission', right? Wise up, Red. You really believe that? The guy's a sociopath. You can't trust him, you know? Not really. And as long as you and that little boy of yours stay with him, you'll never be safe."

Rip's words sparked a recent memory and Sara suddenly remembered Toby, sleeping sound, confident that she was watching over him. Protecting him. Her heart hurt, knowing he'd been abandoned his whole life. *I can't put him through that again*, she reflected, then turned to head back topside. "I'm leaving."

"Go ahead," Rip called after her, conversationally. "I played my part for now. I set you on the path. But you'll be back. I'll be right here when you're ready!"

Sara marched faster, nearly running now, trying to escape, but Rip yelled, "You can't trust him, Red! Ask him about the girl with the trumpet case! Ask him!"

6

Sara didn't get much sleep that night. Michael eventually came in from the cold, but was sullen and aloof. He lay down in one of the beds in another room, with no announcement, and slept fitfully. After a while, Sara went in and lay next to him, watching him toss and turn, and listened to his deep breathing. She wished he'd talked to her, but Michael was never much for sharing his feelings. He felt so *much*, she knew. She saw it every time she looked deep in his eyes. A constant storm surged within him, but he rarely shared that with her, determined to stand on his own. He was indestructible, after all, God-like in his power. And who could relate to a god?

Only now he was just a mere mortal. For the first time in their marriage, it seemed they were finally on an even playing field. She had always envied his gifts, but seeing him without them now…it wasn't the way she'd expected it to be. She had imagined she'd feel closer to him. Instead, he was more distant than ever. Strange as it was, Michael seemed weak.

Rip's words taunted her through the night. What was Michael keeping from her? He didn't like to talk about his past, owning to the fact that he hadn't always been a good guy. There were ghosts in his attic, and she'd always been respectful not to press him on it, trusting that he was changed. But what was this terrible secret? Would knowing it really turn her against him? More and more, she felt like she was back in Charlie's apartment, a silly young girl begging her man to share his fears with her. And now that she knew the real reasons behind Charlie's silence, the way he had been manipulated and had manipulated her in turn, her desire to know more about Michael's past suddenly seemed to take on a sense of urgency. She trusted him and felt certain he couldn't hold secrets as filled with betrayal as Charlie had. But there must be something. Would it really be enough to set her on the path to becoming that witch who rode the Black Pillar?

According to Rip, it was a foregone conclusion. She'd seen the witch with her own eyes; she *would* turn. Somehow, some way, it would happen, and she could never escape it. Just pondering it shot a burst of panic and dread through her, keeping her eyes open when she should've been asleep. She wept for periods throughout the night, and had even tried stirring Michael, hoping to talk to him about it. She quickly thought better of that, and was grateful he slept on. What would Michael do if he discovered her destiny? Surely he'd try and kill her. He'd have to. No doubt his God would even command it, to spare the multiverse.

And wasn't that what was best? After seeing how beautiful the multiverse was—after saving it countless times with Michael—how could she turn her back on it and destroy it?

When dawn broke, she still had no answers, but had tired out from the asking and finally collapsed to sleep. When at last she woke, the space beside her was vacant. Immediately she sat up, her heart thumping at a quickened pace. She stood from the thin mattress, feeling the stiffness in her neck and back. She heard a clatter from the other room. The chukrahas waited for her underneath the bed and she took it, stealthily easing into the shack's main room. Toby was there, awake and already busy. He held a pillowcase, stuffed to bulging with the canned foods they'd found yesterday. Sara frowned, quizzical, and tucked the blade in its sheath behind her back.

"Hey," she called, curious. "What are you doing?"

Toby looked up quickly, then went back to his task, somber. "Michael told me to pack. We're leaving."

"Leaving?" she laughed, flabbergasted. "And go where?"

The boy shrugged, keeping his head down. Sara knelt to pluck a scrap of shredded cloth from the floor, and used it to tie back her long hair to get it out of her face. Looking about, she sighed, "Where is he?"

"Outside."

Sara passed the child, giving his back a pat and a quick affectionate rub. She exited the domicile to find Michael seated on a rock outside. In his hand, a crude spear that he'd apparently pried off of the twisted tree in the yard. He had a knife—judging by its design, it came from the shack's kitchen area—and used it to hone the point of his homemade weapon. Slung across his shoulders by a leather strap, Michael wore the sawed-off shotgun that had inflicted his wound yesterday. Michael never carried guns; he simply never needed to. To see him with one was strange. He wore a grimy undershirt, stained by blood and dirt. His eyes were set on the blade as he cut a sharper edge into the spear; his expression acerbic.

Sara hesitated at the sight of him, surprised by his behavior. "What are you doing?"

"Preparing."

She approached cautiously and stood over him, watching him for a time. When he didn't bother to look up, she ventured, "Did you sleep at all?"

"Not really."

She stuck her hands in her back pockets, sagging. "Yeah. Me, neither."

"We need to get moving."

Sara brightened. "Did you hear something from the Man in the Stetson?"

Sharpening his stick, Michael grimaced. "No."

"Then…?"

At last he paused long enough to face her. Shadows pooled under his blue eyes, and for just the briefest moment, Sara saw some of the old Michael there— mean and ready to explode.

She missed him so much.

"We still have a job to do. God still has us on this world for a reason. I don't know why he's not talking, but it doesn't matter. We're just spinning our wheels out here. So we're moving. We'll see where he leads."

Sara slipped her hands out of her pockets and set them on her hips. "Are you kidding me? We're not even going to *talk* about this?"

He raised the spear to his lips and blew off the wood shavings in a frustrated huff. "What's there to talk about? It's not like the mission's changed. This is what we do." Glumly, he added, "This is who we are."

"The mission hasn't changed? *Everything* has changed! You don't have your powers, we've got…*someone* out there with the ability to destroy a whole world, and your fancy spirit guide is nowhere to be found. All of that, and you're just going to pretend like it's business as usual?"

"What do you *want* me to do?" he said loudly, propping his hands on his knees where he sat. "You just want to quit?"

"No, of course not," she said, surprising herself by how much she meant it. She recalled the beauty in the worlds. *How could I ever destroy all of that?* "But you're not strong anymore."

He snorted a sigh out of his nostrils and looked to the ground. "Yes, let's please keep talking about that."

She flinched. "I'm sorry. I didn't mean—"

"Of course you did," he said, finally standing, and looking terribly tired and lonely. "It's what you've been thinking since Toby's world when I came back from the In-Between. I'm 'different', right?"

"You are," she said, not bothering to deny it. Averting her eyes, she finished, "It scares me."

He nodded, staring blankly at the ground. "Me, too."

Now Sara sat on the rock Michael had previously occupied, draping her arms over her knees. "Maybe…I don't know. Maybe God doesn't need you anymore."

Michael turned to her, sharp. "What?"

"Maybe that's why he's not answering. Why you're not 'mystically protected' or whatever. I mean, we defeated Az—the Maestro's army, right? You avoided your destiny and *didn't* become some Rage-fueled monster like the Hooded Man and all those other Michaels. Maybe he's finally finished with you."

Michael blinked rapidly, then turned away. He took a couple of breaths, his eyes softening. He looked happy. Relieved. "I guess I never thought of that." Sara hadn't seen him so excited in a long time, and it was as though his secret heart had been revealed to her.

Does he want to quit? But if they did quit, then what? Could she ever go back to being a simple housewife again after everything she'd done? Even if they settled on a fantastic world, even if she pursued a challenging career, how could it ever compare to literally saving all of existence, nearly every day? No. No they couldn't quit. *This is who I am now. Who I want to be.*

Sara brightened and stood again, energetic, hoping to dissuade him from getting too comfortable with ending the adventure. "But if that's true, then we're on our own. *We* can decide what we want to do now. We can explore the multiverse and help people *our* way. In *our* time. We don't have to worry about rules and waiting for orders."

He stared into the distance, saddening. "I…don't know. Right now, it doesn't matter. That witch is still out there and I've got to stop her first. After that," a glimmer of hope shone in his eye, like he was seeing a light at the end of a very long tunnel, "…after we deal with the witch, we'll see what happens."

Sara shuddered at the menace in his tone, ashamed of things she hadn't even done yet. For a split second she thought to confess her late night talk with Rip, but stammered, "W-We'll figure all of that out. But let's figure it out together. As a family. No more Man in the Stetson."

Yes, Sara reasoned. Yes, this was what she needed. Freedom. Rip was right. God was all about keeping them under his control. Michael had become completely subservient to him, and she saw now that her anger wasn't with Michael for changing, but with the Man in the Stetson for keeping him in this grip of fear and approval. She could have her Michael back. They could be a team again, on their own. She didn't have to do things Rip's way. She didn't have to kill Michael. *If I can just convince him, instead...*

Michael frowned, wringing his hands on the spear, suddenly disappointed again. "No. Even if... I can't control where the rifts take us, Sara. I never could. Even if we played it your way and we went off the grid and did things on our own, we're still relying on God to take us where he wants us. That means he still has things for me to do."

Sara blushed, her forehead breaking out in perspiration. She hadn't considered that. But Rip had said she was special. She had access to the Rage, now, like Michael once had. There was power there. She'd seen it in her husband, even though Michael had never truly tapped into it. A dark, but enticing, thought formed in her mind and she bit her lip to pin it in a nervous smile. "We could find *another* way. We've met other Jumpers, you know? Like the Hooded Man. Chris? And they *could* direct the rifts wherever they wanted to go."

He rolled his eyes and laughed. "Yeah, and they were all working for the Rage."

She didn't return his laugh. Only stood there, quietly expectant. Finally, he eyed her, horror dawning on his face.

"No," he said, walking past her.

She shot out and took hold of his arm, not realizing she gripped the wounded one. He winced and hissed through his teeth in pain. *I caused him pain.* As horrible as it was, she felt a surge of strength. Sara instantly released him, but instead of apologizing for hurting him, she said, "How much do we really know about the rifts or where they come from? About your powers? Look at what Toby can already do, and he's not even really trying. Think about what Chris and the other firestarters could do. We have no idea all that's out there. All that we could be accessing—"

Michael shook his head, firm. "No way. You're wrong, Sara. You don't know what it was like living like that. Yeah, okay, so I *do* miss being able to take down a spaceship with my bare hands, but the things the Rage makes you do... The voices you hear...the thoughts..." He closed his mouth, calming. "I don't want to teach Toby how to use his powers. I want to help him see that he can live *without* them. They're a curse."

Silence lingered after his proclamation, but Sara's mind was already working. A sickening feeling stung her heart, bringing to mind a question that she didn't really want answered, but she probed him anyway. "Is it that...or do you not trust me?"

His back remained to her long enough that Sara recognized he was avoiding her. He rubbed a knuckle and hung his head. "Sara, I… I can't help but think… That witch—"

"You think it's me," she accused him, though didn't know why. It *was* her. Why would she hate him for thinking what was already true?

He exhaled and faced her, his eyes red with tears. "I don't know. I don't want to think it is. But maybe it *could* be. You know how many Michaels were out there, and all the awful things they did. I could just as easily have been one of them—"

"But you weren't," she snapped, stepping closer. "You fought it. I can, too."

"Not by using the Rage, you can't," he said, his jaw clenched. "It'll trick you. That's what it does."

As he spoke, he seemed haunted, and Sara remembered what Rip yelled after her as she hurried back last night. Her stomach trembled, but she quietly asked, "Michael… who was the girl with the trumpet case?"

He sucked in a sharp gasp, his eyes widening for just a fraction of a second. "W-What?"

"You said the Rage tricked you and made you do things. You told me once that you killed a lot of bad guys—but you also killed one good person. Was…was that the girl with the trumpet case?"

He blinked tears out of his eyes. "Where did you hear that?"

Sara's breath caught in her throat. "Uh…you…mumbled it in your sleep when you were hurt." Eyeing him closer, she said, "But it *is* true. Isn't it? Who was she?"

Toby exited the shack, their bag of foodstuff dragging behind. The kid huffed and rolled his eyes. "You could help a little, you know?"

Michael absently wiped at stray tears on his high cheekbones and moved to Toby's side, scooping up the bag over his shoulder. Sara watched him evade her question and knew that Rip was right. Michael had been lying to her all along. Keeping things from her.

Just like Charlie had.

What else was he not telling her? Did she really know her husband at all?

The rumble of faraway engines startled Sara out of her suspicions. At once she looked to the horizon and saw a cloud of dust swirling their way in the distance. Michael was at her side, lips firmly together.

"It's them," he growled. "They're back."

Sara squinted against the early morning sun and saw the glint of metal. She detected dirt bikes, like yesterday. A truck. And—

"Oh no," she breathed, her heart sinking. "They've got a tank."

Michael slipped off his shotgun and tossed it to Sara, then gripped his spear and shouldered the bag of food. "Toby, we're moving. Go."

The boy scanned to either side in wide-eyed terror. "Where do we go?"

"We run," Michael said, already crossing the yard in great strides. He pointed down to the ravine below with his spear, where Sara had her rendezvous with Rip the night before. Where he'd filled her head with blasphemous considerations. "Down there. We'll cut through there. Hurry!"

7

Michael panted under the weight of the bag of food, nearly stumbling as he crossed the ravine's rocky terrain. He was flushed, his long sweaty hair dangling in his vision, and his lungs burning with exertion. Not to mention, his wounded shoulder screamed at him in agony. The last time he'd sustained such an injury was when he'd temporarily turned his back on the Man in the Stetson to go rescue Sara from Charlie. He'd fought most of that battle without his powers and would have died were it not for his eventual surrender to the White. As soon as his powers had been reinstated, though, Michael had forgotten all about those pinpricking sensations of pain, but now the memory, mixed with the feeling of fresh, present hurt, came rushing back to him in an unrelenting wave of misery. It was as though he were aging with every passing second, his body beginning to tear and break, piece by piece, bit by bit.

He grunted and fell forward, catching himself on a jagged rock and nicking a bloody scratch across his knuckle. Growling under his breath, he pushed himself up. Sara was there, hooking one arm under him.

"You okay?" she asked, that worried knot forming above her left eye.

He jerked away from her, humiliated and angry. "I'm fine."

"You need to stop," she told him without the least bit of sympathy, holding her place as he marched a few paces ahead. "Your arm's bleeding again. You've probably torn your stitches."

He huffed, utterly spent and ready to pass out. "Keep moving."

"*Michael*," she snapped, frustrated.

Glancing to his side, Michael spotted Toby. The boy, too, was red-faced from the heat, his lips parched. Still the kid kept his distance, as though expecting Michael to explode into flames or something. He desperately wanted to talk to Toby, to calm him, but he hadn't the words to say. How could he assuage the kid's fears when his own were prevalent and unmoving in his mind?

Michael sucked in a lungful of air and it felt like sharpened glass grating against the inside of his chest. He turned to Sara, about to retort, and saw her as if for the first time. She stood facing him, her toned limbs not drooping, her head held high. Like Toby, she was flushed, but there was a definite toughness about her. She seemed totally unbothered by the heat or the hike over uneven ground. Instead, she was only focused on him. On *his* weakness. She was strong, he now saw for certain. Stronger than he'd ever given her credit for. What was she becoming? Every time he closed his eyes, Michael saw that witch, stretching her nails for his face, shrieking her banshee's cry. If they carried on, would that be Sara's fate? If so, it was a fate he'd doomed her to by bringing her with him. Regret and shame bore down on him and he suffered their weight. There was so much he had to repent for, concerning Sara.

Now she was asking about the girl with the trumpet case…

How could he tell Sara that it had been *her*? A parallel her, sure, but he'd murdered Sara all the same. It had been that one hateful act, however accidental, that had opened him up to the Rage for the first time, and locked him into this horrible life of jumping from one dimension to the next, fighting the worst beings in Creation. Nothing but war, nothing but death.

I can't do this anymore, he finally declared in his heart, voicing a decision he'd felt coming since the Glor's death. Perhaps even longer. He met Sara's eyes, seemingly across a wide chasm. Sara, smudged and dirty, with a weapon perpetually in her hand. Such a far cry from the shy, insecure girl he'd rescued from her tower. How was it that she had changed so much in just a little over a year? But he was different as well, and not just since he'd lost his powers. She knew it, too.

There, in that ravine, looking from his wife to his adopted son, Michael felt an undefinable sense of sadness, as though he'd just stepped into someone else's life. A life he no longer fit into. A life that had moved on without him. Maybe Sara was right. Maybe his powers were fading because God was preparing him for retirement. Could he really quit after all this time?

Despite his newfound physical pain, Michael's soul was refreshed by the thought of leaving rift jumping behind and settling down. He'd never had a real home before. He'd been running and fighting his whole life—and rift jumping since he was twelve. He was good at it, and found some sense of comfort in the job. But it wasn't who he wanted to be forever. How many times had he begged God to let him quit? Was God finally giving him his wish?

A peace settled over him like an answer and he relaxed. It would be good to quit. Not just for him, but for his family. It was time—

A thunderclap caused him to flinch, and Michael's eyes cut from Sara to the hill in the distance over her shoulder, where the shack they'd just left had suddenly been reduced to a flaming husk. Sara turned and stared, too. The tank had arrived at their momentary home and now blasted again, finally obliterating the hovel. The devastating *thwoom* reached Michael's ear three heartbeats later.

"Keep going," he hurried, urging Toby along.

A startling blast detonated overhead and red rock rained down on them, pelting their heads and shoulders. Michael awkwardly grappled Toby, doing his best to shield the boy from the debris, and hugged closer to the ravine wall. Sara staggered about and turned towards the ruined shack. Michael's eyes followed and he sighted the dirt bikes getting closer, and the tank's cannon now aimed in their direction.

"They spotted us!" Sara said.

"Run!" Michael ditched the bag of food and took his spear in both hands.

The war-whoop of the raiders drew near, echoing through the ravine like the yipping cackle of a pack of demonic jackals. Another deep bass thumped in Michael's chest and more of the gulch tumbled, large boulders crashing into the hard-packed earth all around. Sara dodged the downpour, only to stumble over a rock outcropping. She went down with a yelp, landing hard on her side. Michael turned to Toby, trying to tuck him away. "Stay here," he hollered over the rumble of another mortar shell. Toby nodded, petrified with shock, and Michael crossed to Sara, gravel and dirt splashing against him. He hefted Sara to her feet, and she faced him with terror.

"What do we do?" she said, her voice like a whisper almost drowned out by the cacophony of exploding cliffs.

A rider gunned his engine and a dusty motorcycle adorned in skulls and black crow feathers catapulted off the cliff above and landed with a hard bounce behind Sara. The rider—some maniacal thin, shirtless man with his face painted in black and white halves—hefted up a tomahawk-like axe and shrilled as he bore down on them. Michael put himself between Sara and the Rider, bringing his spear to bear. More dirt bikes flanked them overhead, cheering on their wild comrade, raising their shotguns and crude javelins in rowdy support. Even the tank seemed to park in expectation. Michael felt their eyes upon him, heard their taunts.

He gritted his teeth, fingers flexing around the spear. The bike ramped off a boulder and the Rider flipped backwards off of it as the machine twirled two rotations in the air, hurtling straight for Michael. He threw himself out of its path and heard it smashing against the rock wall. By time he recovered, the Rider was already on him, howling in mad delight, a mouth filled with misshapen, discolored teeth opening into a grotesque smile. The tomahawk came down like a lightning strike and Michael barely had time to raise the spear in defense. The blade bit into the wood and Michael rolled back onto the hard ground, taking the Rider with him.

Releasing the tomahawk, the maniac became a blur of punches, beating at Michael's head, face, arms, chest. Michael blocked as best he could, his vision clouded by red stars. At one point, Sara came to his aid, yanking the raving thing from behind, but the man cackled and sprang up in an uppercut, laying out Sara in a single punch before falling upon Michael with his fists. Michael tugged at the Rider's filthy spiky hair, but the scrawny raider only yipped and giggled, punching, punching, punching. Michael felt *black* creeping into his consciousness and saw the witch again in his mind. He fought to cling on to lucidity, for he was sure that if he gave in and passed out, he'd never awaken again.

On the ridge up above, a piercing whistle sounded and the Rider instantly retracted, like a pet brought under the control of its master. Something like clarity crossed his expression and he stiffened, plucked Michael's discarded spear from the dirt ground, and stalked for Sara.

"*Her!*" he growled, a strange alien dialect garbling the familiar word. He hefted the spear high and Sara shielded herself as best she could before—

Michael heard a sharp gurgle, and blinked one puffy eye open. Through a haze, he saw the maniac still looming over Sara, the spear no longer in hand, as he clutched at something protruding from his chest. A spear?

No, Michael realized with heartrending understanding. It was a shard of solid ice.

The Rider shivered, eyes fixed on the projectile that had impaled him. Then the man's eyes rolled into the back of his head and he collapsed sideways to the dust, dead. Michael rolled over, fatigued, his face throbbing in a dozen places, and saw the boy standing like a statue.

"Toby," he coughed, but the boy's eyes would not meet his. Instead, they remained on the dead biker.

Michael pushed up with his aching arms and wobbled to a stand. "It's okay, Toby," he muttered, his mouth numb, his teeth loose. He reached out with swollen fingers, and the boy's eyes flicked to him. Then the child backed away.

Michael paused, unsure what to do next. "Toby."

Through tiny quivering lips, the child uttered, "Do *I* have to protect us now?"

Michael retracted his hand, his one good eye beginning to water. "I…I—"

"*Yes*," Sara hissed at Michael's side, stepping forward. She shot Michael a scornful, condemning look, then turned back to the boy. Michael could only gape at Sara, his jaw hanging loose in shock and horror.

Toby sniffled, an adult's burdens settling on his delicate shoulders.

"Toby, no," Michael quickly countered, but the damage had been done. Up above, the raiders regarded the grisly fate that had befallen their comrade and screamed in primal savagery. They began to hurl their sharpened instruments down and fire their weapons. Sara flinched and raced for cover, but Michael stood fixed to the spot, his hands still forward, beckoning Toby to him. The boy ignored him, however, his face hardening as he lifted angry eyes to the sky. Toby held his hands to his side, fingers splayed, and the skies darkened, a terrible chill blowing through the narrow ravine. Michael withstood the powerful gales, pushing his heels into the packed dirt with all his might. Above them, the raiders halted their attack, watching the blackening skies in astonishment.

"Toby, don't," Michael spoke louder. "You have to control it, Toby. Don't let the power get to you. That's what the Rage wants."

Beneath Michael's sneakers, the ground growled. He reeled, as pieces of the surrounding cliffs broke off and slid down into the gulley. Through it all, Toby remained perfectly still, tightening his fists. At once, a giant serpent of ice broke through the earth and coiled about, shooting for the sky. Similar to Toby's ice slides, it grew and contorted, yet unlike the slides, this new creation became a profane, misshapen mutation of ice, spikes, and teeth. Michael fell backward onto his seat, watching in alarm as the leviathan took shape.

Toby cut hard eyes on the tank, and in an instant, the ice dragon slammed down into it, pulverizing the machine in a brilliant explosion. The raiders wailed and shrieked, revving their engines and preparing to retreat, but Toby didn't allow them to leave. His serpent churned in the air and dove for them, gobbling them up in bloody sprays or slapping them away with concentrated malice. Broken bodies rained from the heavens, along with flaming shards of splintered dirt bikes.

Michael was unable to turn away as the scene unfolded, the screams of the dying filling the world. At last, tears frozen in his eyes, he looked to the boy. Toby stood in the midst of the carnage he wrought, his young face paling until it was almost solid white, with purple veins crawling like circuitry beneath his skin.

Michael jumped to his feet, ignoring the pain. "Toby! Stop!"

But the boy would not. Michael pushed ahead, the wintry winds slapping his face. "*Toby!*"

Even Sara screamed from the edge of his vision. "Toby, that's enough! It's over!"

A viscous obsidian clouded Toby's eyes at the corners, slowly swallowing the whites of his eyes, then his natural light brown irises.

Michael's stomach lurched. *It's the Rage. It's taking hold.*

When at last the child's eyes became solid black, Michael tightened a fist and socked him across the jaw. Toby blacked out and collapsed, the storm blowing away even more quickly than it had come, the grotesque ice dragon pausing, then disseminating into a torrential downpour.

Michael stood over the unconscious child, holding his trembling fist, feeling disgust roil his gut. Sara hobbled over to join him, bracing herself on a rock. Without acknowledging her presence, Michael knelt down and scooped the boy in his arms, clutching him close. "I'm sorry," he whispered into the kid's ear, then softly cupped his head and held it to his chest in a tender embrace. He silently held the boy near him for a moment, his mind filled with a ping-ponging of emotions, before gently laying him back on the earth.

Finally, rising to a difficult stand, Michael leveled an accusing glare at Sara. "*Now* do you see?"

8

Sara sat at their campfire that night, while Toby used her lap for a pillow once again. Though Toby's storm had passed, the darkness he wrought remained throughout the day, disorienting Sara's sense of the passage of time. An arctic pall clung to every breath, the lasting effects of Toby's wrath, and she wondered when it would finally pass. Was the boy still controlling the weather subconsciously, even as he slept, or had he created something with a mind of its own now? For the part she had played in Toby's attack today, Sara felt awful. She and Michael hadn't spoken since, save for quick words on where to set up camp for the evening. Once the fire had been built, Michael took off again, though whether to look for his God, or just to get away from her, Sara wasn't sure. Left alone with Toby, she simply soothed his ruffled hair, tenderly humming her lullaby.

Seemingly from nowhere, Michael returned, surprising her. Her hand was halfway to the chukrahas on the ground before she realized it was him. In his arms, he carried a bundle of dry twigs. Bearing an unreadable expression, he simply dumped the sticks by the fire, dusted off his hands, and took a seat opposite Sara. Their eyes met through the flames and a soft, familiar silence warmed Sara's blood. Though they did not smile, she sensed just the faintest hint of the bond they once shared prior to Michael's regeneration.

"Hey," he spoke after a time.

"Hi."

She briefly thought to ask him if he'd heard from the Man in the Stetson, but decided against it.

"I've been thinking," Michael began, those new-blue eyes of his focused and sharp.

She nodded, her heart picking up an anxious rhythm. "Me, too."

"It's something you said earlier. That maybe God didn't need me anymore to fight his battles." He smirked, chuckling sadly. "I guess he never really needed me. He just let me come along for the ride. To *teach* me something, if I know him." Michael directly faced her, his handsome face strong and bold. "If that's so, I think I've learned the lesson."

His declaration surprised her, and Sara found herself leaning closer. "What is it?"

"When I was in the White Place, he told me that the mission wasn't about fighting. It was about living. About loving in spite of all the evil in the worlds. I'm tired of being out here, constantly fighting. I… It's time, Sara."

"You *do* want to quit," she answered, forlorn.

He only nodded.

She sat staring into nothing for a few moments, letting the reality of Michael's decision soak in, then glanced to the child in her arms. "Is this because of what happened today? With Toby?"

"Yes," he replied automatically. "A part of it, anyway. Truth is, I wanted to quit from the moment I met you."

She frowned. "You never told me that."

He smiled. "I lived for the fighting for years, but you showed me there was something else to live for. Family. *You* are my family. Toby, too. This… He can't be doing this. I don't want this life for him. Or you. Today just proved it to me."

Sara rubbed her forehead wearily. "Today was scary. I didn't know he had that much anger inside him." She gazed once more upon Toby's sleeping form, now peaceful, bearing no hint of the terrible force he had been earlier. Sighing, she turned back to Michael. "He deserves a better life than this."

"He does," Michael said. "It's too dangerous. The temptation to use his powers will be too strong for him if we're constantly fighting one alien threat or another. Especially now that I don't have *my* powers."

"He shouldn't have to protect us," Sara agreed with a measure of guilt. Carefully, she eased Toby off her lap and gently laid him on the desert floor. "We should be the ones protecting him."

"Then we agree?" Michael asked, his words thoughtfully measured.

She nodded and stood. Though quitting wasn't what she had thought she wanted, Sara had to admit to herself now that Michael had argued his case well. A life of danger was exciting, but how long until someone got hurt? Irreparably hurt, whether physically or emotionally? She couldn't look at Toby's innocent face and not consider that continuing on their current path might destroy him.

"Yeah. What about the witch?" she asked with trepidation. After what had happened to Toby, she felt ridiculous to think that she had even remotely considered tapping into the Rage. Michael was right. It was a wild beast that could never be domesticated and would surely devour her in the end. Her husband was right about everything, and recognizing it didn't anger her anymore.

Michael rose to his feet and brushed off the seat of his jeans. "I don't know, yet. The Man in the Stetson's still not showing up, but I feel right about this— in my heart. We need to get out. This is what's best for us." He edged closer to her. "For our family."

Sara watched the firelight dancing across his smooth features. He reached out for her, gingerly touching her waist.

"I still want to be a family," he said, his voice cracking.

"I do, too," she whispered, then found her place in his arms. "I'm sorry. About everything."

"Me, too," he exhaled, squeezing tighter. "We're going to get through this. We're going to figure this out."

She nodded quickly, her face buried in his chest. Tears burned in her sinuses, but she felt something like laughter, delightful and free, bubbling deep inside. Whether she would laugh or cry, she wasn't sure, but she was happy. Happier than she'd been in a long while.

Sara parted from Michael, exploring his eyes, about to tell him she loved him. Just over his shoulder, though, a wolf's eyes glinted in the gloom, and Sara's heart stopped. Michael's smile faltered just slightly as he raised a curious brow.

"What's wrong?" he asked.

{*Sara*} The wolf's voice invaded her thoughts.

She pulled away from Michael, absently looking to the ground. "…Nothing. Just tired."

He brushed a stray strand of hair away from her face. "Why don't you lay down. Try and get some sleep—"

"No." She faced him in a hurry. "I'll be all right. I just need to move around. *You* sleep. I'll take first watch."

"You sure?" he asked lightly.

She nodded, looking down again to avoid his gaze. "Mm-hmm. I can handle it."

He grinned, relaxed. "Okay." He fixed her with meaningful and earnest eyes. "I *do* trust you, you know. I feel good about this. Like everything's going to work out."

His words pricked something in her and she frowned. "I'll be back."

Then Sara headed off into the night to meet the wolf.

9

Sara clutched the chukrahas and trod across the darkened desert landscape. By now, the firelight of their camp was merely a flickering spot on the horizon at her back, and she hoped that Michael was soundly asleep. A weak glow of moonlight guided her rocky path as she rounded a knoll and descended into its cold shadow where twin orbs met her in the black.

She did not start at the sight, but simply stared through her brow, intense and threatening. "You can come out. I'm alone."

The four-legged shape in the shadows crept closer, rising to stand on its hind legs before donning the shape of a man as it entered the pale moonlight. Rip stood before her in boots, jeans, and the leather jacket Michael would one day inherit. Sara rubbed at the abrupt chill in her arms, her back arched defensively. "What do you want?"

He chuckled through a fanged grin. "Gettin' awful cozy with the enemy there, ain't ya, sis?"

"Michael's not my enemy," she spat, determined. "He's my husband. I love him. I don't care what you think my destiny is, I'm not going to hurt him. I'm not going to hurt anybody."

"Aw, you two kissed and made up, is that it? You think it's as simple as that?" He sighed and shook his head. "He tell you about the girl with the trumpet case yet?"

Sara's cheeks flushed.

Rip snickered. "Thought so. Still holdin' out on you, huh?"

"It doesn't matter what he did. He's different."

Rip's wolfish eyes lit up. "I'll say. I've been watching him. His strength has faded, hasn't it? Don't you get it? The Rage has left him—now he's vulnerable. It's *your* time, now, Red. The Rage is giving you a chance to strike at Michael's heart. Take him out, just like you were created to do. Then we can *really* get started."

"Stop it," she hissed. "You don't own me. You don't control my destiny. *I* do."

He folded his arms, raising a mocking eyebrow. "Then why are you out here?"

She faltered under the question, then tightened her jaw. "I..."

Rip stepped forward and she flinched, bringing up her blade in defense. He halted, lifting his hands as if in surrender, grinning. "Whoa, easy, sis. I don't mean no harm. I'm on *your* side, remember?" He paused, then clapped his hands once together. "Look, we can stay out here all night going back and forth and wasting each other's time. Let's make a deal."

She eyed him suspiciously. "What kind of deal?"

"Come with me. Let me show you what Michael won't. Let me take you to that moment—the darkest secret of his life. You see what I gotta show you and you decide then. I'm willing to bet that, after you see it, you're gonna sign on the dotted line, but if you see it and you'd rather just kill me instead..." He trailed off, smirking. "Well, we'll settle things that way, if you'd prefer."

Rip took another step towards her, but this time Sara stood her ground. "Come on, Sara. It's time you finally learned the truth about that boyfriend of yours."

He extended a leathery hand. Sara considered it. If she went with him, would that start her down the path to her damnation? *No. I can control this. I just have to look. Once I know whatever this secret of Michael's is, this crazy werewolf will leave me alone. I just have to show him that it doesn't matter.*

She took his hand.

"Sara?" Toby's voice cut through the dark.

Sara yanked away from Rip and spun on the boy, caught. The child stood frowning, serious eyes darting between her and Rip. "Toby!" She quickly holstered her weapon and hurried to him, taking his shoulders with both hands and bringing him into the shadows with her. Panicked, she peeked back in the direction of their camp, but saw no sign of Michael. Bending over, she put her face mere inches from the boy's and snapped, "What are you doing here? Where's Michael?"

Did he see everything?

Toby's lip quivered, his eyes widening in fear. "Michael's already asleep. You weren't there when I woke up and I was scared. I went looking for you."

She closed her eyes and touched her head to the boy's, inhaling through her nostrils. "Toby," she breathed after a moment, calmer now. "You shouldn't have come out here."

Toby pulled from her, snarling at Rip. "Who is this?"

Rip smirked, hiked up his britches, and hunkered down on his haunches. He smiled at the boy like a kindly grandpa. "Well, hey there, little brother. The name's Rip. I'm an old friend of Mike's."

Toby's brow crinkled and he watched Sara closely. She nodded at length, then looked away. Toby turned back to Rip. "How did you get out here?"

Rip laughed and glanced up to Sara. Facing Toby, he clapped a sinewy hand on the boy's shoulder, instantly revolting Sara. "I'm a traveler of the worlds." He pointed at the boy's tummy, giving it a playful poke. "Just like you, dude."

Toby stood still, his eyes searching and distrustful. "You work for God? Like Michael?"

Rip sniggered and faced the dirt, scratching his bearded chin. "Heh. Not quite."

Toby took a step back, paling in trepidation. "T-The Maestro?"

The wolf in man's clothing stood now, his good mood darkening. Sara feared him in that moment, and guided Toby behind her. "Toby," she spoke to the boy, though her eyes were locked on Rip's, "go back to the camp. Go back to sleep."

"No," Toby declared, slipping out from underneath her touch to stand on his own. He closed his tiny fists so tightly that Sara worried he was about to conjure another storm. "This doesn't feel right. I don't like him." He glared at Rip, but the old man just chuckled. "We need to go back to Michael. *Both* of us."

Rip crossed his arms, regarding Sara with a lifted grin. "Well, Sara? What's it going to be?"

Sara bit her lip anxiously. Gnashing her teeth, she knelt before Toby again, rubbing his arms. "Toby, this is important, okay? I... I can't explain it. I just... When you're older, you'll realize that there are some things you just have to do."

Toby narrowed his eyes at her. "Then I'm coming, too."

"*No*," Sara cut in.

Rip chirped, "Bring the kid. This is something he should see, too."

Sara weighed her options. She was fairly sure that whatever Rip had to show her wasn't something Toby should ever see. But if she insisted the boy go back, he would no doubt wake Michael...

I can't let him see me like this.

Sighing in defeat, she faced the boy squarely. "Okay," she said, ashamed. She stood and took Toby's icy hand in hers, then presented herself to Rip. Regretting the words almost as she spoke them, she said, "Let's go."

Rip inclined his head in a slight bow, then uncrossed his arms. Digging around in his back jeans pocket, he procured a worn and creased notebook. Sara watched in confusion as he flipped through its lined pages, finally settling on a single sheet. With little fanfare, he tore the paper from its brothers and released it from his hand, where it gently settled on the rocky soil. He gave a wink and a snap of his fingers, and the paper came to life, glowing with a soft rainbow-colored light.

"A rift," Sara gasped. Looking to Rip, she asked, "Is that where the rifts come from? H-How did you do that? Where did you get that book?"

"My gramma."

Sara balked. "Your *gramma*?"

He nodded, a wistful pride in his glimmering eyes. "She was a powerful witch who used charms and incantations to prolong her life to a ripe old age of a hundred and twenty-five." His face shining with a mixture of nostalgia and reverence, Rip continued, "The night she died, meteors rained down from the sky, lightin' the heavens on fire."

Suddenly Sara's mind was filled with a thousand questions, but the only one she could voice was, "Where does it go?"

"Don't worry, Red. We'll be back in a jiff." He smiled and gestured to the rift. "Ladies and kiddos first."

Sara shared an expectant look with Toby and squeezed his hand. "It's going to be okay," she muttered to him, her voice shaky. "I won't let anything happen to you."

The boy's face was stiff with fear, but his eyes were trusting.

What am I doing? Sara chided herself, but she'd come too far to quit now.

Together with Toby, she stepped into the rift, disappearing in a blast of light.

10

"Michael."

Michael stirred under the hooded jacket he'd been using as a blanket and slowly attempted to pry his eyes open, but only one would cooperate. On his left side, the world was visible only through a tiny slit, as the swelling had yet to go down on that side of his face. As soon as he returned to consciousness, he was reminded of a thousand different aches he'd forgotten in restless slumber. Now his body was against him once more, stiff and creaky, his gunshot wound burning with fever. He saw that it was still dark out, with the campfire going strong.

"Michael," someone called his name once more, urging him to awaken.

He glanced to his right, looking for Toby, but the boy was gone. Michael sat up, wincing in misery, and looked to his left. No sign of the kid. Or Sara.

Instead, he saw a man seated on the other side of the fire. Kind and wizened blue eyes watched Michael from behind bifocals that rested on the man's aged and open face. A duster and red scarf protected him from the cold, though Michael knew the man wore such garments whenever he assumed corporeal form to visit him, no matter the weather. The man's gaze was intense, peering out from beneath the worn brim of his Stetson hat.

Michael grinned wide. "*You*. I knew you'd come." He worked with difficulty to slip his jacket on. "Where's Sara and Toby?"

The Man in the Stetson shouldered the brunt of Michael's question. His gentle expression did not falter, but there was a hint of sadness in his eyes. Something was wrong. Michael felt it deep in his gut, and worry squeezed his stomach. "What?" he asked hoarsely. "What is it?"

"Do not resist," the Man in the Stetson said, a simple statement unrushed, but spoken with an air of great importance.

Michael was about to ask what he wasn't supposed to resist when headlights blinded him from the side. A loud truck's roar bore down on him and Michael heard the nearby and familiar *whoop* of raiders. He cut hard to his right to see that a band of armed men—still in their mismatched fur and feathers, but now also wearing armor, their faces painted black-and-white—hustled upon him. The raiders hefted spears and guns and danced around him, yipping and snarling and laughing and cursing.

Real fear took hold and Michael swiveled back to the Man in the Stetson, only to see that he was gone. His hope bottomed-out as shadows moved in the firelight.

Do not resist, the Man had said.

A giant of a creature strode amidst the hobbling, cackling lunatics, casting a wide stretch of black across Michael. He looked up from his place in the dirt and beheld a lanky giant—its skin bright pink save for the uniform black-and-white face paint, with two eyes on stalks protruding from the creature's head. The sight took Michael by surprise, for he'd assumed the raider band was all human. Curious now, he took a closer look at the figures closing in on him. Most were human, yes, but there was a smattering of aliens in the band, as well. One green-skinned and reptilian, another a diminutive squirrel-looking creature with a spiked tail. But all of them, alien *and* human, displayed the trademark dual facial painting. They were a tribe, but what had united them?

What planet am I on?

Eye-Stalk raised his muscular arms and his giant three-fingered hands, bringing the revelry to a dull chatter around him. The alien's eyes narrowed, but somehow flared as well, and he pointed a gnarled finger in Michael's direction.

"What do you want?" Michael asked. He'd tried communicating with the raiders before, but had simply gotten a round of buckshot for his diplomacy efforts. He worried he'd not fare better a second time, but if the Man in the Stetson had shown up, then perhaps these were more than simple bandits. Maybe they were his assignment on this world, after all. "I don't want to fight," he said.

Eye-Stalk remained with his finger leveled at Michael, then barked a series of rolling clicks. The quieted marauders erupted anew in hollers and yelps, and fell on Michael with kicks and punches. He threw up his hands to block their blows and did his best to twist out of the way to protect his face, but the band swarmed him on all sides, taking turns stomping on him or poking him with the blunt ends of their spears.

Michael could make no protest, coughing up air and blood, before finally collapsing on the dirt. At last, Eye-Stalk issued another command of clucks and the mob dispersed. Michael sucked in oxygen, burning his lungs, then felt himself being lifted as two raiders—one of them that reptile alien he'd spotted—hoisted him up. They forced his hands behind his back and tied them there, then hurried him to his feet, and slipped something over his head that smelled like wet dog.

He instinctively gagged against the smothering odor, but hadn't time to dwell on it long when something hard smacked against the back of his head, knocking him out.

11

The rift brought Sara, Toby, and Rip to a city at night, where they were surrounded by towering skyscrapers that emitted a muted yellow-orange glow against the dark skies. Sara and Toby followed along behind Rip as they traveled down a trash-laden street, passing by decaying buildings and lopsided houses. While the neighborhood was largely abandoned, groups of shabbily dressed strangers—mostly males, Sara recognized—clustered in whispering groups, leering at Sara as she walked by. The sounds of faraway shouts carried like a rotting stench on the air as a trail of police cars, their sirens and lights blazing, sped by her and squalled around a corner.

Up ahead, Rip casually strolled, unaffected by the noise, the pungent stink of smoke and motor oil, or the curious onlookers they attracted. He had his hands in his jeans pockets, walking with a definite sense of direction. Sara and Toby followed at a distance, as Sara knew beyond a shadow of doubt that she couldn't trust this man. Toby kept an eye out around them, anticipating trouble, but Sara's attention remained on the weird man who would be her dark mentor. Rip evoked the same aura as Michael had when she first met him, intense and clad in tough-guy bravado, with a sense of the mysterious cosmos in his eyes. She knew the moment she first saw Michael, as well as Rip, that these men had walked in worlds, lived lives that she had only read about in *Alan Worth* novels. Michael had come to rescue her from her suffocating life with Charlie. Now Rip sought to liberate her from Michael and lead her on her next great adventure. The only question was, did she still feel the pull of the unknown?

"Where are we?" Sara said, hoping to distract herself from her conflicting emotions. She still clutched Toby's hand tightly. The kid's eyes darted from side to side, tracking those who sipped from bottles wrapped in brown paper or traded tokes.

Rip pushed on, talking over his shoulder. "Los Angeles, California, Red. The year is 1991. Ole Mike is twelve years old this year."

Sara glanced at hungry-eyed predators congregating on dilapidated front porches. She was reminded of the poverty that had plagued Toby's home, and felt a pang of guilt that Michael had grown up in similar circumstances, while she had lived in a nice apartment, well-fed and spoiled.

And I threw it all away for Charlie.

Souring, she shook aside her regrets. "This was his home?"

Rip nodded, his back to her. "Both of ours. We grew up on these streets, me and Mike. I taught him everything I knew. I took care of him—his brothers, too. Eddie and Seth. They were like sons to me. Mike most of all, and I loved him as best I could."

Toby's hand grew colder within Sara's and she looked down, remembering the destruction he had caused earlier. A gang of youths was circling them, hollering and pointing and laughing, puffing up their chests and showing off. Sara could easily ignore them, but Toby was only a little kid, and his fear showed as his teeth began to chatter and his flesh took on a frosty pallor.

"It's okay," she whispered to him, trying to calm him down lest his fear lead him to create another devastating storm. "Just keep moving. They won't hurt us."

"Reminds me of home," he said softly. After a moment, he finished, "I hate home. People were mean there."

Sara squeezed his hand and smiled, trying to detract from his nerves. "Come on, it couldn't have *all* been bad. Wasn't there anything you liked about home?"

Toby considered, taking his attention off the rough crowd around them. In a moment, his eyes darkened. "Not really. I mean, I liked playing my video games and drawing, but…all I really wanted was a family."

She tugged on his hand, smiling wide. "*We're* your family. Yeah?"

Excited, he beamed. "Yeah."

"Up here," Rip called to them, turning down a street lined with overgrown trees.

Sara followed, pushing through low-hanging branches before glimpsing a sprawling two-story complex ahead in a clearing. The place was well-lit and perhaps the nicest structure she'd seen in this neighborhood, though that wasn't saying much. The place still seemed to be about fifty years old, with graffiti tags along the surrounding brick wall. A rusted chain link fence hemmed in faded and outdated playground equipment, but the second story balcony made her think of home and how much she'd always loved gazing out over the balcony at the town below.

Sara regarded the place. "Is this a school?"

"It's *his* school," Rip grinned, regarding the building like an old friend. "And class is in session."

"I don't understand."

He faced her, animated. "Legend tells that, on the patch of earth where that school now stands, there once stood a church. A *Christian* church, back then, and my Gramma Moore sang in the choir." The man closed his eyes in remembrance. "Growing up, she used to tell me that when she was younger, she had the voice of an angel, and I could believe it from hearing her sing when she'd putter around the kitchen, baking cookies and homemade bread." He paused for a moment and breathed deep, as though he expected to smell her baked goodies again, but no delicious aromas materialized. Shaking loose from the memory, he carried on. "Came a time when Gramma heard the Song of a New God in that ole church building."

Sara pursed her lips. "The Rage. Yeah, I get it."

He winked. "It whispered to her, saw something special in her. Soon after that, the church folk threw out their crosses and Bibles and started praying in Its name, beckoning It out of the Void with sacrifices of blood. Folks around town didn't take kindly to that, as you can probably imagine, and burnt that old black church down, but Gramma escaped and sold her soul to be Chaos' wanton bride. That's when the haints came to her, spirits that moved in and out of the worlds."

Sara listened intently, fascinated but repulsed.

"Aztaroth showed up, too. Taught her things, like how to travel the dimensional planes like the angels did. She learned all kind of secrets that she wrote down in her old notebook." He tapped his back pocket. "The book I got now. 'Words are magick,' Gramma always told me. She was right. It was those potent words that made the rifts in the first place."

Sara heard voices and Rip hissed, "*Quiet!*", before dropping to his haunches, hiding in the brush. Sara and Toby followed suit, watching as a pair of teachers walked past, papers in hand, talking as they approached their respective cars in the thinned-out parking lot.

Rip turned to Sara and put a finger to his nose, winking. "Best not to get spotted." He jerked his bearded chin to the balcony. "You head on up. Me and the little brother, here, will wait for you. Give you a chance to see it."

"See *what?*" she barked, frustrated and angry.

He scowled, his eyes shimmering in the moonlight. "Second story. Take off for that balcony up there. Hurry. It's time you knew the truth."

Sara looked to the school, her heart pounding. Toby stood up, moving closer to her. "What do we do?"

Sara put a hand on the boy's shoulder and glared at Rip ferociously before again facing the boy's trusting eyes. "I don't know what's up there. I…Stay here."

Toby snarled. "*What?*"

"I'll be right back." Bringing the child closer, she whispered to his ear. "Make sure he doesn't try anything, okay? If he does—"

"I'll blast 'im," he said, rubbing his knuckles for effect.

Sara tried to smile, but failed. She kissed Toby on the cheek, causing him to blush, and ran for the school. Consumed with steely determination, she climbed the fence and crossed the playground, heading for the campus.

Headed for her fate.

12

When Michael finally came to, he sat in the corner of a darkened clay hut. Straw and raggedy cloth had been spread beneath him—a sort of mattress—and a bench adorned in mismatched candles brought warmth and dull light to the single room. Surprisingly, his hands weren't in shackles, and Michael made avail of that freedom, massaging the back of his head to feel a risen lump where someone had knocked him unconscious.

Something moved just past the corner of his eye and Michael jerked with a wince, spotting Eye-Stalk standing guard over him, tightly gripping a gnarly spear made of jagged scraps of metal. The alien regarded Michael, its chin lifted high in arrogance or authority. The creature took in a breath through tiny nostrils and harrumphed, then crossed the room and disappeared through a tattered burlap curtain—the only entrance or exit in the room. Now Michael spotted tiny square holes cut out of the adobe wall.

He crawled to one of the shoebox-sized windows and glimpsed a camp. Similar huts dotted a flat terrain and a series of bonfires lit up at intersections like street lights. Raiders—much more subdued than Michael had ever seen them—milled about like the residents of any other village, talking, trading. Like before, he noticed a motley assortment of humans and aliens, but all of them sported the same dual colors on their faces.

The curtain swooshed open and Eye-Stalk stepped in, uttering another rumbling series of clicks and barks. Michael blinked back in confusion. "I-I don't understand."

Eye-Stalk prattled off again, raising his voice, then appeared to grow frustrated and stormed about the hut. He hurried to Michael and roughly stood him to his feet, then clucked his tongue once more in quick succession, his face inches away from Michael's, like he was trying to explain a word. Michael couldn't understand the strange clicking ramble, let alone repeat it, and simply stared back at the alien. Exasperated, Eye-Stalk now used the blunt end of his spear to force Michael down on one knee.

"Okay," Michael huffed. "Kneel. I got it. Are we about to meet your chief or something?"

Eye-Stalk gruffly replied and forced Michael's head into a bow, woofing.

"Okay, okay!" Michael growled.

When at last Eye-Stalk seemed satisfied with the level of Michael's humility, he gave a snort and stood stiffly beside him as a sentinel. Not wanting to suffer Eye-Stalk's ire once more, Michael kept his head down, but couldn't help but lift his eyes to peek at the curtain, waiting to see who was so important.

At last, a slender pale hand reached in and pushed the burlap aside, and a huddled figure in a long cloak of black fur entered. Michael squinted against the low light in the room, but couldn't make out more than the bent-over shape of the new character, as well as a wild shock of white hair. The mysterious creature hobbled to the candlelit altar, lifting his withered hand in the air. He emitted a high-pitched string of rolls and clicks.

Eye-Stalk started in place, as if in surprise, and returned with excited chatter of his own. The straw man patiently rebuked his faithful guard and, after eyeing

Michael in anger, Eye-Stalk finally snorted in derision and stomped out of the hut.

Michael remained silent and kneeling as the creature—the leader of this tribe, he assumed—still faced the candles, slowly running his hands along the tops of the flames. The leader moved trance-like, in a kind of dance that only seemed to involve the upper half of the creature's body. Or...no. There was a kind of rhythm to his hand movements. Michael had seen it before, in a concert hall.

It couldn't be...

"You'll forgive my friends," the hunched-over man said, his dry, bored voice instantly recognizable. The sound of it sent a wave of despairing fear through Michael's soul. "I've done my best to civilize them, but old habits and all. After you destroyed my firestarters, I was forced to collect for myself *new* followers. What good is a conductor without an orchestra?"

"No," Michael muttered under his breath, lifting his head, beginning to stand.

The misshapen creature turned to face him. With the candles illuminating his profile, Michael saw him clearly at last. A long, gaunt face stretched beneath that untamed mane of snow white hair, eyes half-lidded and dark. A long, hooked nose stretched over a drooping mouth that parted into a toothy leer.

"No!" Michael bolted to his feet, his hands tightening into fists.

"Hello, Michael," the Maestro said, unbothered by the show of aggression. "It's been an age."

13

The door to the school was unlocked. A few teachers milled about in classrooms, talking to one another or doing after-hours paperwork. Only the rare student roamed the halls, coming from football practice or a school club meeting.

Sara moved past them all, wasting no time. She tried to hurry without *looking* like she was hurrying, for fear that her strange presence—and stranger, her dirtied, militaristic attire—would draw attention if she lingered longer than a moment. She took the steps to the second story, sweating with anxiety.

Finally, she hit the second level and pushed through the door, entering the small outdoor area. On the balcony, alone and obviously nervous, a young boy paced. His face was sullen and pensive. He struck her as oddly familiar, but Sara ignored him, searching the courtyard for...Well, she didn't know what she was supposed to be finding. Rip hadn't told her that much.

The door on the other end of the balcony opened, and Sara's heart stopped. She was staring at herself.

A young girl, no more than twelve or thirteen, tall and thin with long red hair—even longer than Sara wore it now—exited the building, carrying a case…

A trumpet case, Sara realized with sickening dread.

Her heart quieted to a dull throb, and now her mind worked in overdrive.

"Hey, Sara," the somber boy greeted.

Sara tore her eyes away from her younger self to the boy, startled.

"Hey…Michael." Young Sara returned the greeting, taking one step back while her lip curled ever so slightly in apprehension.

Michael?

14

Michael put his back to the wall of the clay hut, his fight or flight trigger going haywire. Blind panic assaulted all his senses, even as the Maestro moved sluggishly away from the altar, rubbing his gnarled hands together in something like impatience.

At last, the crooked demon—once tall and elegant, Michael remembered, but now twisted and decrepit—lifted a long finger. He wagged it thoughtfully, a crooked smile forming on his drawn face as he spoke, song-like, in delicate resonances, "We have much to discuss, you and I. I suppose I should start at the beginning, seeing as how we are at the end."

"The end?" Michael blurted. "Of what?"

He jostled his finger once more, sniggering. "This will go much faster if you let me finish uninterrupted, as we haven't a moment to waste." The Maestro paused in his shuffling and straightened out the front of his cloak, as if to make himself more presentable. "Who am I? Every one of God's creatures must ask that at some point, is that not true? We all want to know our purpose. My purpose was simple in the beginning. I composed beautiful masterpieces to praise Our Glorious King at His Eternal Throne. The halls of heaven were filled with my concertos. I suppose I could have taken credit for such brilliant work, but at the time, I wanted no part in the accolades of my angel kin. I lived simply to honor Him, and…" He smiled, somewhat saddened. "I was fulfilled. For a while."

He paced, sloth-like, rubbing at his pale, swollen knuckles, and his tone became suddenly manic. "Then, ha ha. Then one day, I heard a *new* Song. It was unlike anything I had ever heard. Unlike anything in all of Creation. It was strange and alluring and I listened to it. *Followed* it. Out of nothing, Our Maker made Light, but with the first dawn, there also came Shadow. And it was there *in* that Black that I heard a song that harkened back to an age before Time and Space. Before Order."

Fixing a pointed look at Michael, the Maestro paused, wearing in his bulging eye a crazy glint that Michael had never seen before. In times past, the demon composer had always been poised, immovable, and haughty, as though he were above all things, but now he seemed unhinged. "Have you ever stopped to consider what existed before Time? Before *us*?" the monster asked. "Even we angels have a beginning. But not God. God has always existed, beyond ages and epochs. Can you fathom that? Of course you can't, because we are creatures of Time and Space, bound by form and structure. God is…ha ha. He simply Is." Sighing whimsically, the mad Maestro continued, "I heard Chaos, singing to me. Had it always been there, with God? I suppose so, in a way. It hadn't possessed any shape, I'm sure, but God is Order. By its very definition, how can there be Order without Chaos? But, see—" The Maestro lunged for Michael, clinging to his hooded jacket with desperate, trembling fingers. "See, see, see," the Maestro raved. "It *wanted* shape! That's what the Song was telling me! And *I* was chosen to give It shape! Me! The least of all angels!"

"The Rage," Michael said in a reverent hush.

"To you, yes. To others, no. Not to me. *Never* Rage." The Maestro pulled away, rubbing his hands together, sneering at them. "Never, never, never. To me, it came as Pride. Yes, Pride. I could write Its song. I was more special than the other angels—even more special than those clods of dirt that God had directed His sympathy towards." Pointing a crooked finger, the Maestro hissed, "*Humans*. Others were jealous of you. We praised God and He ignored us. You ignored Him and He lavished His grace upon you. But I wasn't jealous. Not like Calico, he who was splendidly adorned in color. Oh, *that* angel has an axe to grind against humans." The Maestro looked up at Michael, his haunted eyes now glistening with the hint of tears. "But not me," he gasped, imploring sympathy. "You must believe that. I was never jealous of you. I only wanted to compose my opus. But not for Him, any longer. For me. All for me." Moving about the room, growing agitated and twitchy, the Maestro continued, "So I wrote as my sacrilegious muse instructed and I showed my music to the choir leader of the host, proud of my accomplishment. So, so proud." Huddling over, the creature sobbed for a moment, the sound of his weeping strangely human.

Michael watched him, struck with pity despite his fear of the demon. He took a step forward, his heart burdened with questions. "What's *happened* to you?"

The Maestro snapped and straightened. Donning once more his mask of impassive nobility, he carried on, "Little did I know how my music might affect my friend. Little did I know that Pride would corrupt *him*, as well, and lead him to rebel against Our Maker with a third of the host of the angels."

Michael paused in thought. "You mean, the Devil?"

"He has many names now. Even I have forgotten his true one. He is much like Chaos, in that respect. So many faces. So many names. A different temptation for every man. Chaos became his father, and the Devil, in turn, became the father of lies. So full of lies is he, I worry he has trouble remembering the truth. He's come to think that *he* is the Chaos, or that Chaos came from him. But the Chaos was already there… And I heard it before all the others."

"You started the war in heaven," Michael said, the truth slipping through his trembling lips.

"Once the rebellion began, Chaos was loosed. It had shape. But It was not merely content to destroy our angelic fellowship. No, no, no. It turned Its attention to Earth. To what God treasured most. It slithered as a serpent and tempted the Woman, first, then her mate. Pride infected them, as well, and Creation was ruined. A new plan was in order, one that God had already devised in His infinite wisdom."

Michael nodded, for the Man in the Stetson had already told him this before. "That's when he created the multiverse. To contain the Rage. To give people a choice."

The Maestro nodded, tears streaming down his sallow cheeks. "And then there came perpetual battle: The moral struggle to decide good from evil." He lifted his hands to the heavens, weeping now. "And the Song came *alive*! Such wonderful agony as the Light and Dark warred for dominion in the hearts of Men! There was pain and war and temptation and resistance! There was *drama* in the worlds, exquisite tragedy, and it sang to me! On one world, a man finds true love and raises a family—in another that same man rapes and murders and steals, and it's all hinged on a choice! *On a choice!*"

Michael attempted to cut through the Maestro's dramatics, "What do you want with me?"

The demon quieted, his tears drying, and grew forlorn once again. "I continued to follow the Song. I wrote my masterpieces in the blood of my victims, using the broken shards of their shattered dreams as my quill. I followed Chaos wherever it led. I was obedient to my Master… But that's all changed. I didn't know…" The fractured creature held his face in his hands and whimpered. "I didn't know."

"What didn't you know?"

The Maestro peeked through his steepled fingers, one eye glowing. "You've seen it, haven't you? A pillar of black night, carried by purple lightning as it devours the worlds."

Michael's breath caught. "Yes."

"The Chaos is rattling the bars of Its cage. It has found a new servant, one who can do what I could not. I gave Chaos form, but this new servant will set It free. And now…" Crying, the Maestro waddled to Michael, pulling at his shirt and jacket. "I didn't know! There was beauty in the tension, don't you see? There

118

was wonderful music in misery and suffering, but only when there was hope for good! I was so wrong! The *balance* made the music beautiful! Now the multiverse is breaking down, and there's only clashing, clanging, banging!"

The Maestro pulled away and clutched his ears as he swirled about the room in a tottering, haphazard mess that brought him dangerously close to the flickering candles. "It's all noise now!" he shrieked at the top of his lungs. "The Song is over and now there's just damnable *noise*! I've been tricked!"

Michael unconsciously extended his hands, hoping to steady the raving monster. The Maestro came to a stop, his eyes engorged with madness. "That's why I've brought you here," he moaned. "You have to save us, Michael. You have to stop the Chaos before It escapes and destroys the Song forever."

Spent, the Maestro collapsed to the straw floor, touching his face to the ground and shaking with sobs. Michael stood over the demon, numb by all that had transpired. To think he'd spent so long running from the Maestro, seeing him as some sort of bogeyman. But to see him like this, now…

His forehead still pressed to the ground, the Maestro coughed and wheezed, desperate to calm himself long enough to catch a breath. Michael bent to one knee, his voice turning sympathetic. "How? How can I stop it?"

The Maestro's cries silenced and he lifted his ashen face. "The Order is breaking down… The mirrors are shattering. He's fumbling for the lock. Past, present, future—it all runs together. I see it all now. I fear it has made me quite mad…" Through quavering lips, he croaked, "So much noise. So much noise…" His eyes cleared, and a bit of the monster's sanity seemed to be restored. "It's Sara, Michael. It begins with her."

Michael retracted, growing sick. "When I saw the Black Pillar, there was… There was a witch."

"Yes."

He shook his head, defiant. "But it was her double. Some other Sara from some other—"

"No," the demon said quietly. "It's *your* Sara."

Michael stood now, furious. "No. You're lying."

The Maestro slowly rose, as well, holding his hands out in a silent plea. "I have no reason to lie anymore. My Master had plans for her. After you went rogue, I was meant to fashion a weapon that would not only kill you, but *destroy* you in the deepest part of your heart. So I visited upon Sara any number of cruelties. I manipulated Charlie—leading him by his own carnal lusts—and used him as my instrument. I tortured her mind, heaping misery on misery." He closed his eyes and breathed deeply, as if savoring a comforting aroma. "Sara's song was exquisite. Her tears made such a sweet melody…" When he opened his eyes again, they faintly glowed, lit by a hellfire within. "But just like before, my pride was used against me. I gave the Chaos Its first shape, and so I did with Sara. I see now that Chaos was using her against *me*, as well. It was raising up my replacement all this time."

Michael briefly considered whether this might all be a trick or a lie. Over the years, the Maestro had worked deep behind the scenes, crafting machinations within machinations. It had been a labyrinth trying to sort through it all, trying to discover the truth. Maybe this was only another scheme designed to confuse him and lead him off track, keeping him busy while the Rage carried on the campaign to destroy Its multiverse prison.

Yet, the Man in the Stetson had *wanted* Michael here. Presumably to hear the Maestro's confession.

Could this all be true?

The Maestro implored, "You must kill her, just as she would kill you."

"She wouldn't kill me. She's nothing like me," he seethed. "When the Rage found me, I was hateful and cold, but she's kind and *good* and pure."

The demon chuckled. "Is she still?"

"Of course—"

"No, no, no. The Rage is already building in her. Has been for some time—since long before she met you. Being with you only watered the seed I already planted in her heart years ago. When I last encountered the pair of you, you could speak to each other's minds, am I right? I thought I saw something there."

"Yeah."

He grinned. "A psychic bridge made possible by the Rage in you both. A bridge that you severed when you fully rejected the Dark and chose the Light."

Michael blinked slowly, unable to deny the logic in such a claim. The Maestro veered towards him. "Do you see now? The Change has already started. And, look! You're both here, where it all began!"

Michael screwed up his brow, perplexed. "Where?"

"This desert! Don't you recognize it? You've been here once before! This is where the Chaos brought you! Where Chaos brings all Its children!"

Michael's breathing hitched. That's what Rip had said, when he'd first landed in that desert long ago— "In between the worlds," he mumbled.

"Yes! This is the Desert of Choosing!" The Maestro hurried to one of the small windows and pointed out. "Look! Look at my followers! They were all chosen, too. Chosen by the Dark. And they were brought here to decide who they would serve—the Light or the Dark. But they rejected both—and went mad because of it, ha ha! That's why they paint their faces as they do. They are trapped here in this non-place because they rejected both sides. They're caught *in between*, just like I am now." The Maestro calmed and drew close to Michael. "It's Sara's time to decide, as well. Rip has already been speaking to her—"

120

Michael lashed out and gripped the folds of the Maestro's cloak, bringing him close. "*Rip?* When?"

The demon chuckled. "You should have paid your darling wife more attention, Michael. Surely you've seen it over the last year. How she's envied you, competed against you, resented you for your incredible gifts. Haven't you seen it?"

Doubt ran through Michael's mind as he shuffled through dozens of different memories from his time with Sara. *Had* she been resentful since the beginning? *How could I have missed it?*

Dumbly, he loosed his hold on the demon. "I…"

The Maestro smoothed out his cloak. "The Dark is strong in her. I sensed it, but I didn't see the extent of her capabilities. *Rip*, however, has." Snarling, he spat, "That mangy cur has sought to curry favor with the Master for too long. I brought Rip into the orchestra simply to tune the Rage's instruments, but now Rip fancies himself a conductor in his own right. I only wanted to obey the music, but Rip… He wants the worlds to burn." The demon gestured to the window and the raiders beyond. "He's been seeking to thin out my followers. To cripple my stronghold! You've already seen what he's done!"

Michael frowned. "That shack, when we first got here. There were bodies. Torn apart…by an animal."

"Rip's work. And now he's seeking to lure Sara to his side." Sighing, the demon relented. "And it will work… He will find the lock, and the Chaos *will* be loosed."

Michael paced, running a shaky hand through his sweaty hair. "There's got to be a way to stop her."

"Kill her," the creature whispered.

"*No.* I can talk to her. If she knew what she was doing, she would stop."

"But she won't! You've already seen the Black Pillar! The witch! The future has already been written."

Michael turned on the monster, gritting his teeth. "You said the same thing about me, remember? You, Rip—you all told me I had some dark destiny or whatever, but I stopped it from happening! I made a choice, didn't I? I made a *different* choice! Sara can make a choice, too. We're in the Desert of Choosing, right? Isn't that what this place is for?"

The Maestro stared at Michael, his face darkening and his eyes seeming to focus on an object far in the distance, as though he were looking through the worlds. "Yes. And… she's already made her choice. She's not in the desert anymore. She's already started down the path." He straightened in a hurry. "The time for talking is done. I've seen how it begins, but not how it will end. You must *kill* her, before the entire multiverse is destroyed."

Michael braced himself against the wall, glaring out the window, burdened. He struggled to breathe under the weight of the decisions that plagued him.

Please, God, I can't kill her. Not again…

"You're a hero, boy," the Maestro implored, his voice a dry, hollow rattle. "Will you not save us all?"

Michael shut his eyes against the demon's question, willing this moment to pass. He never should have taken Sara with him. And now he'd done the same to Toby—

He halted. Turned to the deformed creature. "Where's Toby?"

"With her," the demon said without pause. "Your family is falling apart, Michael. What will you do?"

Michael leaned his head on the wall, breathing deep. At last, he stood tall, beyond sorrow and despair. Beyond decisions. He just had to see his family. "Can you take me to them?"

The Maestro nodded quickly and, with extended nails, seemingly sliced through the veil of reality. A rip opened up in the fabric of space, bleeding crackling black energy. "Here!"

Michael gaped at it, spellbound. "You don't need a rift?"

"I was an angel, boy. I walk the worlds at will. Now, come! We must hurry!"

15

Thirteen-year-old Sara Theresea put her head down and started walking faster, doing her best to sidestep the boy in her path. Michael Morrison was only twelve years old, but already had the reputation of a man twice his age. Everyone at school knew he was a troublemaker, always back-talking teachers and getting into fights with the more popular kids. She supposed beneath that cloud of anger and those shabby clothes he was kinda cute in a mysterious way. He had silky blond hair that hung longer than most boys wore theirs at her school, and glittering, menacing dark eyes, but Sara knew better than to get mixed up with him. Her parents would have a *fit*.

But Michael slid off the railing, blocking her path of escape. "Where are you going?"

"Home." She eyed either side of her, made uncomfortable by the boy's unexpected confrontation. "My dad's waiting for me outside."

She tried to squeeze by, but Michael scurried to make eye contact with her. "I need to, uh, ask you something."

"What?" she asked, coming to a full stop, frowning, and pretty sure she was blushing.

"I was wanting to know if you would want to…uh…go out?"

Sara's throat went dry. "Like on a date?"

"Um..." Michael's pale cheeks turned pink. "Yeah."

A sudden outburst of laughter broke forth from her throat without her permission. She didn't mean to be rude, but she couldn't help feeling put on the spot. She'd never been asked out before, and she certainly didn't fancy her first offer coming from *Michael Morrison*, of all people.

But Michael looked ready to throw up, waiting for her decision. His jaw clenched. "Stop it," he blurted.

"Stop what?" She tucked her firebrand hair behind her ears, nervous and ready to get home and write this whole bizarre encounter in her diary.

He glowered at her, eyes narrowing. Through strained teeth, he said, "Don't laugh at me."

Sara felt real fear in that moment, remembering what her friends had told her about Michael and his brothers. They were orphans, street kids who were in a gang or something. What would a boy like that see in her, anyway? Maybe he was joking. Of course. That had to be it. "You're not serious, are you, Michael?" She chuckled, trying to rise above the awkwardness. Yes, he must be teasing her. "I mean, don't take this the wrong way or anything, but I don't want to go out with *you*." That came out meaner than she'd expected, and she scolded herself for not being better at talking to boys, but it was the truth. He was a criminal, headed for a life of juvenile detention, probably even prison. She was a good girl from a good family. She *had* a future. They were from two different worlds. Even he had to see that.

"Stop laughing at me," he growled, his whole body taut with rage, his fingernails digging into his palms.

Wow, he's really upset, Sara marveled, disappointed with herself for being so cruel. Michael didn't have any friends that she knew of, though she'd seen him with that weirdo Johnny Frawl yesterday after school. But mostly Michael just skulked about, listening to heavy metal on his headphones, sporting the long hair and black clothes that made respectable parents shake their heads in disapproval. No one liked him, and Sara, herself, had never given him a second thought until tonight. But she didn't want him to feel bad.

"Oh, stop being so dramatic," she teased, realizing she sounded just like her mother. She just wanted to lighten the situation. To make him see that it wasn't that big of a deal. "Don't be a baby."

She laughed again, a nervous chortle designed to break the tension. She waited for him to join in the laughter, to see how funny this was. Even if she ignored his reputation and chose to go out with him, it would never work. And it would just be a pity date. They were too young for that kind of relationship, anyway. But maybe after this, she'd talk to him a little more in the hallway. Let him know that there were no hard feelings. That her rejection of him wasn't personal, just pragmatic.

Yet she would never get that chance. Michael roared in red-faced anger and shoved her. Sara gasped for air, feeling herself tumbling over the balcony's ledge.

Then young Sara Theresea felt nothing at all.

16

Sara Morrison, eighteen years old, watched as her pre-teen self plummeted over the school's second story balcony. She clamped a hand over her mouth, muffling a scream, as tears spilled down her face. Her mind told her to run—to save the girl—but the moment passed before she had a chance to act.

The young boy Michael—*her* Michael, six years younger—clutched his stomach as if struck and dropped to his knees. He screamed a throaty growl, sobbing uncontrollably, pulling at his hair and smacking his head on the stone railing in self-inflicted punishment.

"What's going on out here?" a woman's voice startled Sara back to the moment. She withdrew into the folds of the building as a dumpy female teacher emerged. Still holding his stomach, Michael picked himself up, and ran right by Sara's hiding place.

The teacher hurried to the railing and looked down, then burst into breathless hysterics. "9-1-1!" she shrieked, sobbing loudly as she raced into the school, begging for help.

Sara watched the woman for a moment more through the glass doors, horrified and stiff. At last the teacher fainted from shock as the sparse remaining faculty and students rushed to her aid.

Trembling, Sara came out of the shadows and approached the ledge. With numb fingertips, she touched the stone, leaned over the edge, and saw herself at twelve or thirteen, broken and bent unnaturally. Dead on the steps below, bleeding out. Sara's vision blurred with tears, a sob caught in her throat. She wanted to retch.

Michael had killed her. *Her* Michael. That was his secret. That was his past that he would never tell her. Now she knew…

"Sara! Sara!"

Hearing her name, she turned and saw Michael—grown now, just as she'd left him in the desert—running out onto the upper courtyard towards her, covered in sweat and dirt. Out of breath, he stumbled to the edge beside her and looked down at the broken form of the young girl on the steps. A cry escaped him, and he clutched the stone, his breathing hitching. "No…not again…"

Sara just stared at him, open-mouthed, as he wept over her doppelgänger below.

Suddenly, he looked up at her, as though suddenly remembering that she was there. His face twisted in pain. "I tried…I tried to get here in time…" Michael pounded the railing, weeping. "I tried!"

"You…"

Michael shut his eyes, wiping the tears that soaked his dirtied face. "Sara—"

Sara inched away. As if fearful of losing her, Michael reached for her, his hands trembling. "Sara…oh, Sara, I—" He went to hold her, to love her, but she shoved him back.

"*Get away from me!*" she screeched hysterically, and ran.

"Sara!" Michael cried anew, chasing after her.

With her own tears rendering her path fuzzy and smeared, Sara hurried down the stone steps, two at a time, wailing. At last she touched down on the lawn, desperate to find Toby and get out of there. She rounded the school and hastened across the darkened playground when Michael finally caught up to her. He gripped her arm, mid-chase, and spun her around so fast she nearly lost her footing.

"You…you…" Sara whimpered, trying to voice her thoughts, holding her stomach as she backpedaled. "You *killed* me…you killed me…"

"No," Michael shook his head, quick and defiant. Desperate. "Not you. *Her.*"

"*As if that makes it any better!* She was just a child and you *murdered her!*"

"*I* was just a child, Sara!" Michael pleaded. "I didn't mean for this to happen! I didn't want any of this to happen!"

Sara shook her head. "Stay away from me."

"Sara…"

Terrible understanding overtook her. She paused, feeling ready to throw up. "Is *that* why you took me with you? Was I just some sick fantasy to make you feel *better* about yourself?"

He slumped, weeping, stripped bare before her. "I…I don't know. Maybe it started out that way, but—"

Sara shook her head at him, eyes wide in horror and barked a defeated laugh. "So this… this was all a lie… Everything we had…" She gnashed her teeth. "I am such an *idiot!*"

"No! Sara, I—"

Toby came up from behind, red-faced from running, his eyes frightened behind his glasses. "Did you scream? Why was there screaming? What's happening? Michael!"

Sara spun to the little boy. "Toby, stay back! Get away from him!"

"What's wrong, Sara? Why are you crying? What's wrong with Michael?"

Sara grabbed Toby, pulling him to her, as she backed away from her husband.

Michael's face broke with misery and he lifted his hands once more to touch her, but Sara jerked away and slapped him across the face.

"*Don't touch me!*"

"Sara, you know me!" he shouted at her, his voice cracking. "You know I would never do anything to hurt you! I love you!"

He's just like Charlie, Sara. Voices, strong voices, pounded in her mind. *He lies to you. Your feelings tell you that. You're scared. You don't trust him. Trust your feelings. Trust your instincts. Michael's a liar. He'll hurt you unless you stop him. Defend yourself and the little boy! Michael will take it all away! He killed you once, he'll do it again!*

The voices in Sara's mind pressed against her thoughts, slowly shrouding them like a thick fog, accompanied by a throbbing boom-boom-boom. She released Toby and gripped her head, dropping to the grass. She moaned, trying to shake off the psychic onslaught. Michael touched her shoulders, bracing her. "Sara, don't listen to it! I know what you're feeling. I felt it too, that night! It's the Rage. I know it's telling you to give in, but you *can't!* Do you hear me? You have to fight it, Sara. You have to be strong!"

Sara screamed again, her hands cupped to her ears, but the voices only grew in intensity. *You can't trust him. He's trying to trick you, to keep you weak. You have the power inside you, Sara. All the strength you'll ever need. Show him, Sara. Prove to Michael that you are the strong one.*

Michael knelt before her, gripping her, trying to shake her out of it. "Sara, come on! Fight it! Be strong!"

At once, Sara's twisting stopped. She looked up and faced her husband. "I *am* strong."

He fell back onto the seat of his jeans, his face aghast. "Sara..."

When Toby looked up at her, he jumped back, startled. "Sara...your eyes. They're black."

But Sara no longer cared.

She stood, at last freed from the shackles of fear and doubt. She felt incredible, like a current of cold electricity surged through her, filling her with power and hate. Flexing her fingers, she tested the strength in them. Strength to bend steel, to punch through concrete, to rend flesh if she chose.

Michael slowly rose, watching her carefully. His face was puffy and streaked with tears, but he appeared resilient. "Sara," he said, with iron in his voice. "You don't have to do this."

She eyed him with black orbs. "But I do. It's who I am. Who I've always been. My parents never understood my power. Charlie tried to keep me weak. *You* tried to keep me weak. You've been using me this whole time to ease your conscience. You never knew *me*. The real me."

He tightened his teeth, quivering with emotion. "If you do this... I...I can't let you leave, Sara. I can't let you start that Black Pillar." His eyes were full of love for her, but his hands formed fists. "You know that. Please…" His voice broke. "Please don't make me do this."

"Stop me," she dared him, "if you can."

He shook, face reddening, then shouted and charged, swinging his good fist. Sara felt as though she'd fallen beneath a cold flood. It consumed her, rendering her weightless. The feeling was magical, ethereal. She simply sidestepped the punch and he swung again, desperate. She blocked this one with one hand, the other relaxed behind her back. Michael charged again, but he was feeble. Sara saw that now. Stripped of his powers, he was nothing to her. She gripped his throwing arm and tugged him off-balance, then kicked him across the gut. He heaved and doubled over, but was on his feet just as fast. Despite his weakness, he remained stubborn, swinging wildly, kicking out, leaping.

But Sara was already ahead of him, laughing as the intoxicating Rage pushed through her. Now she understood what Michael had felt all those years. The thrill of the fight. She grabbed his outstretched arm and punched him hard in his shotgun wound. He cried out in pain, but she silenced him with a direct hit across the face that toppled him to the grass.

"You can't win," she declared, as the wind began to stir all around her. "I'm stronger than you now."

Michael righted himself, his face twisted in anger. "Sara, *stop* it!"

Her laughter carried on, something like electricity flickering against every nerve ending inside. It built within her, lifting her to heights of ecstasy she'd never known. At last, she flung her head back, an enraptured sigh escaping into the blackened night. At that moment, with her eyes directed upward, she saw it.

Storm clouds circled about her, a deep disturbance in the sky's belly rumbling like an angry god's growl. She moaned in elation and looked to her hands, sensing them tingling. When she beheld them, purple lightning danced between her fingers. She laughed anew, delighted at the sight, and rolled the electricity over her knuckles. "Look!" she panted. "Look what I can do!"

Michael staggered towards her, clutching his wound. It pumped blood, and he looked drained. So frail. So mortal.

"Sara…" he called to her. "Don't—"

"Ha!" she barked and thrust her hand forward, baking him in lightning. He screamed and fell back flat, squirming on the ground as his body sizzled under her attack. His hooded jacket started to smoke as he raged against her.

"No!" a tiny voice broke her merriment.

Sara relented and turned slightly. Toby stood there, shaking and weeping.

"Sara!" he sobbed. "Why are you doing this?"

Sara considered him as Toby scurried over to Michael and braced him as he stood. The boys, *her* boys, huddled close, in awe of her terrible majesty. She gazed at her hands, still burning with raw energy, then once more regarded the circling storm above. She felt the Rage within her, scraping against her insides, clawing to escape.

Yes, It hissed, using her own voice. *You're growing stronger. Almost strong enough to unlock my cage. But not yet. Your hate must yet grow.*

The storm dissipated, Sara's rage unable to keep it together. *Soon, though,* the Rage whispered with glee. *So soon…*

"Sara," Toby bawled like the child he was. "Y-You're scaring me."

"Good," she said, looking on him in disdain. "You *should* be afraid."

A few isolated claps of applause sounded behind the scene and the trio turned to see Rip, exiting the shadows. "Whew! 'Bout time. I was afraid Sis wouldn't go through with it."

"Rip! What did you do to her?" Michael cried, holding Toby to him protectively.

"Not me, Mike. *You.* You did *all* of this, with your lies and your secrets. Really, did you think you could keep her under you forever?"

Rip rounded Michael and the boy, taking his place at Sara's side.

Michael pleaded, "He's a liar, Sara. He lied to me, and he's lying to you."

"I know," Sara answered, and Rip started slightly in surprise. "I didn't do this for Rip. I did this for *me*."

Rip chuckled, a bit anxiously. "Well, whatever gets you there."

Sara turned her black eyes on the old drifter of worlds. "I hate you for what you've shown me. But you'll get yours. Michael already killed you, when you first tried to recruit him."

"She's right," Michael said, sneering through bitter tears. "She's right."

Rip turned to each Morrison, fearful and confused.

"I killed you," Michael told him, vengeful. "Six years ago. With your own knife. You'll see."

"You think you're the first Michael I've trained?" Rip snarled, his canine prominent. "You're all punks. All talk."

"But he's different," Sara said, her words cold and menacing. "He was invincible. He can't die. And *you* can't win."

Rip's usual calm seemed cracked. He turned to Sara, nearly gulping, trying to regain the upper hand. "Well, Red, you and I got work to do. The Rage beckons."

"Sara…" Michael began again, focusing on his wife.

There was a flutter on the wind and Sara looked up to see a single sheet of paper riding the breeze—the rift that had brought her here to her destiny. It seemed to have flickering images on it—like a movie being played on a sheet hanging from a clothesline—and it was coming for her.

"That's our ride," Rip said, waiting for the rift's approach.

"Sara, don't go," Michael begged, still holding Toby to his side.

"She's got to work to do." Rip leered. "Gotta set the Master free!"

Michael stepped forward, indifferent to Rip's gloating. He stood before his wife, vulnerable. "Don't let it end like this. We can work it out."

But Sara was beyond talking with him. She felt wholly different, a machine, devoid of compassion for this man who used to be her husband. He was a liar, a killer. Let him cling to his God if that made him feel better, but he would meet justice for what he'd done. Perhaps Sara was meant to give it to him, but not yet. She wasn't ready. Now was the time of her independence, to finally be free and to discover her path. Her true path. She didn't need Rip's help, or his plans for her. He'd shown her the way, but she was her own woman now. And with the Rage as her Master and tutor, she would learn to harness all the unspeakable gifts she had earned tonight in pain and tears.

"Good-bye, Michael," she told him, with no warmth in her voice.

"Sara!" Toby ran up to her, tears threatening to spill out from behind his glasses. "Don't leave…"

His plea was almost enough to make her reconsider. She had made him such earnest, tender promises, but she knew, now, that she was never meant to keep them. The Rage was already telling her that the boy was of no consequence. He might always be special to her, but right now, he was dead weight. They had survived their war with the firestarter army, but Sara had a *new* war to begin. Family would only get in the way. Slow her down.

The rift landed on the upper courtyard, just as the cries from the school reached their ears. Faculty had discovered young Sara's body on the grounds. The cops would be here soon to investigate. Michael looked trapped, caught between the need to flee with Toby, and the urge to stay and rescue his wife.

But Sara was beyond rescue now. She was in command of her destiny. *At last.*

Rip stepped up to the rift. "Come on, Red. Time to go. You'll see ole Mike again. The Rage is just starting up all the good things it's got planned for you."

Sara moved for the rift, turning her back on her family, feeling waves of hellish power emanating from her. Michael called after her, "I love you."

She turned on him, slow and deliberate. Her face like a stone, her eyes jet black and soulless, she replied, "I don't care."

Then she stepped into the rift, and, in a brilliant explosion of rainbow light, she and Rip were gone, drifting away into the ebon, starless sky.

PART EIGHT: BORN TO RUN

1

TWO YEARS LATER

On the distant world of Devar, airspeeders of varying sizes, shapes, and colors zoomed past each other at high speeds, hurrying about on their nightly routines.

Meanwhile, Sara Morrison fell.

The speeders blurred by as she spread her arms out like wings and plummeted downward. Her dark jacket billowed behind her, the velocity rippling the hem, and the wind slapped against the dark visor of her red helmet. She worked hard to keep her eyes open against the onslaught of air, knowing the visor was protecting her, but dumb human instinct prompted her to flinch when she should have kept her eyes open.

"Oof!" Sara's thin frame connected with a flying semi and she rebounded with a startled gasp. The initial contact threw her off balance and left her confused, creating a domino effect as she crashed and bounced off other motorists as if she were in a high-flying game of rush hour pinball.

Finally she landed hard on the top of a shorter building that reached to the 165th level in Vertical City. Sara groaned, catching her breath, feeling fresh bruises swelling up on her sore body. Standing to shaky legs, she dusted off her jeans and readjusted her helmet. Fearing she'd broken a rib, Sara seethed in pain, but pushed it aside for now and crouched on the edge of the rooftop, overlooking the sea of lights and zipping hover vehicles below her. Her eyes told her nothing, as it seemed she'd lost her quarry, yet her senses remained attuned.

"Come on, come on," she muttered, struggling to focus with her wounds screaming at her.

At last, she spotted the oblong black box traveling towards the west.

There!

With a cavalier shout Sara dove, headfirst, over the edge of the rooftop, resuming her plunge through the skyline levels. This time she prevailed against her instinct and did not close her eyes. Remembering a trick she'd seen Michael employ on her first rift jump with him, she gripped the flapping edges of her jacket and felt the coat balloon, catching the powerful gale. Grinning with rebellious confidence, she zipped through the lanes, cutting a path through the violent winds.

Below, she spotted the black box that held her target, growing larger and larger in her field of vision. Its details became clearer, and she identified it as the armored transport she'd encountered earlier. She'd initially planned to lift her prize before it made it on board, but there had been more opposition than she accounted for. Which meant, as usual, she had to do things the hard way.

Almost, now…

Sara braced herself as she haphazardly glided through the chaotic lanes of Devarii hover-traffic, finally angling on the transport. Extending her fingers in anticipation, she concentrated until she was in reach. As soon as she touched metal, she clamped down. Summoning an ounce of Rage, dredging it up and into her muscles, she felt It empower her with augmented strength. Her body swung wide and slapped painfully against the broad face of the transport, but her grip held. She clenched her teeth, heaving deep breaths. Step one was complete.

White-knuckling the railing with one hand, Sara reached beneath her jacket and retrieved the circular device that Wurgyl had given her for this job. She could only hope that it worked better than Wurgyl's usual trinkets.

"Here goes nothing," she said behind her helmet and smacked the device against the van. It magnetically locked into place and immediately began drilling into the tough transport hide, spitting flickering sparks. As though it had a mind of its own, the "cutter bug"—as Wurgyl had called it—skittered in a rough circle-like pattern. Sara waited impatiently, counting down each second until the bug finished its task. Once the hole had been cut, the slab of metal peeled away and blasted off. Sara hugged close to the transport, saving herself a painful dislodging, then swung around and poked her head inside the opened can—

To immediately meet the barrel of a rifle.

She yelped and ducked out of the way, as a crackling round bolt of energy sailed past and struck a nearby motorist. The innocent bystander's hover car immediately buckled and careened off course. Sara watched it crash-land into a penthouse suite, a twinge of guilt flaring in her heart for the fate that had befallen its unlucky driver, but her sorrow did not last long.

Settling her resolve, she made another pass and grabbed the edge of the rifle. She gave a good yank, ripping it and the security guard out of the car. As they fell below her, she climbed inside the armored transport to find that Rifle Man had been its only guard. Gleefully, she slid off her helmet and shook free her short, spiky red hair, a few sweaty strands dangling in her eyes. She brushed them aside with her forearm, then pressed her ear to the wall of deposit boxes. Wurgyl had said the thing would give off a hum, and she hoped he was being literal for once.

Up and down she moved, beginning to doubt Wurgyl's reliability yet again when, at last, she heard a bass rippling through the metal. Grinning, she set her helmet down on the speeding transport's rumbling floor and retrieved a lockpicking kit from her back pocket. She activated the penlight torch and began to cut through the box.

"Hurry," she whispered to the tool, her teeth on edge. "Come on."

The laser easily slid through all resistance, creating an opening just large enough for Sara to stick her hand inside and acquire the relic. She held the pulsating rock in her hand and smiled. It didn't look like much on the surface— just another hunk of rock. But deep within its pores, it emitted a faint and beautiful glow.

The Grell Stone. Yes, this would do nicely.

Then the door to the cabin slid open abruptly and two Devarii guards entered, roaring in disbelief. Without warning they aimed their rifles and fired, and Sara dropped the Stone as she slid out of the way. The first guard charged after her, looking to bash her with the butt end of his rifle. Sara dipped beneath him, feigned to the side, then came up with a hard cross to his jaw.

The purple-skinned Devarii people had hard shells like armadillos to protect their three strong hearts. Even *her* strength was no match against that stone-like husk, but she unsheathed her chukrahas and stabbed the alien in the thigh. It shrieked in surprise and clutched at the wound as Sara yanked her blade free of its torn meat.

The second guard trained his weapon on her, but she wove around the staggering first guard, doing her best to use him as a shield. All the while, the Grell Stone remained on the ground. She slipped by the guard and reached out for the relic, but the second Devarii opened fire, nearly taking her hand off at the wrist. She jumped to the side and kicked the second guard in the ankle, upsetting his balance for a tiny space of time. Seeing her moment, she sheathed her blade, wrapped slender fingers around the rock, then dove out the opening she'd created, entering freefall.

It was in that moment that she realized she'd forgotten her helmet.

Wind punched at her face, ripping against the folds of her coat and turning her end over end. She tumbled through the air, completely blind and disorientated until—

"Ack!"

She landed on her hip, crumpling the hood of a passing speeder. Still she held the Stone. Dazed and in incredible pain, she glanced up and beheld the bright red sports-speeder that had broken her fall. The frightened Devarii driver—Sara thought it might be a female of the species—balked in horror.

Sara glanced up and saw the armored transport angling back for her, the guards poised out of the opening, firing down.

She wasted no time in climbing up the hood of the speeding vehicle, smiling pleasantly at the driver. "'Scuse me." The driver scooted to the side and Sara hopped behind the throttle, yanking hard on the joystick and pivoting the car away from the transport, placing her into oncoming traffic.

Speeders screamed by at high speeds. Sara gritted her teeth and piloted the craft while the vehicle's alien owner howled in fear. Sara drowned out her cries and barreled on through approaching traffic, as rippling rings of kinetic energy raced by close enough to ruffle her choppy locks.

"Hang on!" she shouted, yanking the mechanical beast to the right and avoiding a head-on collision by millimeters. As it was, the crossing vehicle scraped against Sara's speeder, kicking up sparks and shooting the shriek of grinding metal into her ears. She did not flinch, but kept driving.

Checking her rear display, she saw the transport bearing down on her bumper. "This is going to be close," she panted.

Leveling a determined glare up ahead, Sara spotted her salvation with great relief. Not far away, carelessly caressed by the wind, a glittering sheet of paper that would be her ticket out of here.

Jerking to the female Devarii, frozen by fright in the passenger seat, she roared, "Keep it steady!"

Without waiting for her to acknowledge one way or the other, Sara climbed over the lowered windshield of the car and scurried across the ruined hood. To her credit, the female Devarii did as she was told, once more taking the reins of her speeder, and maintaining an even speed. Sara stood up, nearly surfing on the racing vehicle, and bided her time.

Another blistering blast of energy rocketed by, and she whipped her head to see the transport charging for a rear-end crash that would surely dislodge her. She ground her teeth, gripped the Grell Stone tight, and waited. Waited. *Waited.*

Then, just as the transport surged forward with a throaty roar, Sara leapt off the speeder, aimed for the paper.

In the blink of an eye, the rift received her and she vanished.

"There," Sara announced, plopping the Grell Stone on the counter without fanfare. "Pay up."

Wurgyl nearly jumped in astonishment and leaned forward, studying the rock. His long ears flapped with excitement. "Wow, Red! You actually pulled it off! I can't believe it!"

She leaned on the counter, nodding her head humorlessly. "Yeah. Turned out to be a lot tougher than you said."

He gaped at her, his pointy buck teeth comically protruding from his pouty mouth. "Wha? I gave you the security code."

"Didn't work. They must've already changed them. I had to get this one on the go."

The bald-headed alien snapped his finger and pointed wildly at her. "But the cutter bug—"

She grinned. "That worked. Lost it, though."

He frowned, still unable to hide his teeth. "Oh. That'll come out of your cut."

She sighed and held out her hand, palm up. "Let's move this along, shall we? I've got places to be."

Wurgyl shrugged and dug around underneath the counter. "Always straight to business with you, Red. You know, if you hung around long enough, we might accidentally become friends."

She groaned in good humor. "See, that's the thing, Wurgyl. I'm not looking for friends. Just money. A girl's gotta eat."

He shrugged with a chuckle. "Fair enough." He retrieved a scanner and held it to her palm, dialing in the correct amount before activating the laser, transferring her funds straight to her DNA. Once he finished, he retracted with a smile. "There you go. Anything else?" His eyes lighting up in sudden excitement, he snapped his fingers and dug around beneath the counter again to reveal a shoebox-sized container that held two wraparound strips of metal. He placed the box on the counter, his eyebrows raised. Wurgyl then held one of the items up and slipped his hand inside—like brass knuckles, Sara realized. "Howabout these? Just got a pair in! Arkonian Power Bands! Grants the wearer the strength of *ten Xylocks*! The might to knock a small moon out of orbit!" He paused, his ears drooping. "Well, at least that's what the brochure said…"

"No thanks," she said, already turning around and heading out the door, in no mood today for one of Wurgyl's pitches.

He called after her in a shaky, almost apologetic tone, "Well, uh, thanks again, Red. Howabout next time we find you a simpler job?"

She laughed, amused by the troll. "Yeah. Sure thing."

He waved goodbye, and Sara left his shop, stepping out into the carnival that was Supernova.

Supernova was the hottest social spot in Bakellian Space—provided one could find it. The famed millionaire—and reported hedonist—Orgynamus Bor originally built the ring-shaped space station as a dock and casino for weary freighters, out past the Luvell Rim. Anything could be found on Supernova for the right price. Drugs, prostitution, gambling, extortion, murder, and sundry forms of debauchery soon put the sin palace on the radar of every intergalactic police agency, and Supernova took to flight. For the last thirty years, the station had retained its freedom by remaining elusive, constantly moving from system to system with no warning or advertisement.

Sara could relate to that kind of constant motion.

Many a band of young and reckless ne'er-do-wells were reportedly lost in space while looking for the legendary station, as Supernova's reputation grew to almost mythic proportions. The saying soon became, "No one finds Supernova: it finds you." Unless, of course, one were to have a personal, mystical rift in their possession. *In that case*, Sara mused, *you can go anywhere you want.*

Sara passed by the seemingly insignificant sheet of paper lying in the darkened alley beside Wurgyl's shop, not yet ready to leave this world. Instead, she waited for a gargantuan Hurk bounty hunter to pass, then looked up to behold Supernova's busy thoroughfare, nearly blinded by the overabundance of neon lights. Ill-tempered and smelly spacers of all species pushed together in the cramped space, cursing and shoving their way down the boardwalk to the black heart of the station. At the sight of all the activity, a glowing smile spread on Sara's face. Assaulted by the sights and sounds of the garish station and its abundant supply of vendors hawking their wares, her body buzzed with excitement, her heart kicking up in anticipation.

She loved it here.

Straightening her dark jacket over the chukrahas blade still tucked against the small of her back, she effortlessly merged with the foot traffic, immediately lost in the crowd. An especially foul-tempered rhino-faced alien in dingy pilot overalls—Sara believed that, in this reality, this species was known as a Dun—snorted once at her and grumbled before carrying his back-breaking girth on its way. Sara ignored the rude look, her eyes fixed to the billboards and video advertisements, newly intrigued by each catchy brand of pop music and flickering light. On Supernova, ads also spritzed specific scents in the direction of their would-be customers, leading their marks by the nose. Sara breathed in the aromas, instantly remembering her favorites and keeping a mental tally of which stores she'd visited and which ones remained.

She had stumbled upon Supernova quite by accident last year, but made a point to return here often to revisit the spectacle. The multiverse could be so lonely, but here, with all the people, the entertainment, and the stores—it reminded her a bit of home, really. Silly that, after all she'd seen and done, she still reflected sometimes on that domed village in some insignificant backwater dimension. She'd been miserable there her entire life, but Time, it seemed, had a way of rewriting memories, provided enough of It passed. For the briefest sliver of a moment, her mind flashed to Michael, but she was quick to push away the warm feelings threatening to stir, focusing her attention ahead.

Pressed on all sides by the throng of aliens, she dodged tentacles, talons, beaks, and pincers as she made her way to the beating heart of Supernova. A vaulted doorway waited at the top of a small flight of wide steps, beckoning wayward souls inside. On either side of the brightly lit entrance, two tubes pumped sparkling bubbles into the air. Once burst, the bubbles drizzled a grimy ichor that instantly soaked into the skin and afforded passersby a small rush. The bubbles were, of course, designed only as a sample, and the euphoric high quickly evaporated, leaving people wanting more. The drug was, not-so-cleverly, called TranSINdence and could be purchased for dirt cheap inside.

Sara climbed the steps, feeling a jolt as TranSINdence bubbles sprinkled on her short hair and into her scalp. She laughed despite herself, her worries instantly dissolving while the momentary high rushed through her system. By the time she entered the club, she'd come down, but her mood remained bright. Crowded around the entrance were the junkies who couldn't wait, sprawled out on lounge cushions, blowing TranSINdence bubbles into the air and laughing in delirium as the drug soaked their flesh and muddled their minds. Sara didn't mind a chemical-induced mental vacation now and again, but by and large she needed to remain alert. Devar was on the other side of the galaxy, but she'd still made off with the Grell Stone. It wouldn't be long before the media took the story and spread it out to the far corners of known space. Soon, her face would be plastered on the wire and she'd have to leave this dimension for a time.

Still, she had bigger problems than the Devarii Home Council: namely Rip.

So far she'd managed to evade her pursuer across the worlds, but the Old Dog was relentless. She'd had a close call only yesterday—the first in months. She'd been surfing the waves on some uncharted prehistoric planet in another dimension, looking to clear her head, until he showed up. Fortunately the local wildlife, reptilian spider-snakes, had gotten stirred up, allowing her the opportunity to make a mad dash back to her rift, and she lost Rip in the frenzy. After that little escapade, Sara figured she'd earned a little R&R on Supernova, but the glamorous life didn't come cheap. Traveling with Michael all that time— and his unlimited cashflow—Sara had taken for granted how hard it was to make a living in the multiverse. Stealing was fast, and if she did her job right, no one was seriously injured. She had contacts like Wrugyl spread all over the multiverse, who could hook her up with a little errand here or there that required her rather unique skillset, keeping her in a steady supply of spending cash. And while she pulled her heists mainly for the money, she couldn't deny that a part of her just did it for the thrill.

Just to keep things interesting, she thought, smiling. Thanks to the Grell Stone job, she had enough for a really good time tonight. Maybe it'd be enough to keep Rip out of her thoughts.

She sidled up to the clear plastic bar amidst a cacophony of booming sonics and swirling laser lights. Aliens gyrated against each other on the dance floor, making advances with their scaly, feathered, and amorphous bodies that they furthered in private booths outlining the club. As soon as her fingertips came to rest on the bar's surface, a blue light scanned her prints for identification, while also reading her musical tastes and choosing a private selection for her pleasure. Her personal soundtrack at the bar was dulled by the cacophonous music coming from the center stage, but she appreciated the sentiment all the same.

"Hey, Red!" the bartender bellowed, wobbling his way over to her.

She smiled and rested her chin in her hand. "Hey, Trax. How's business?"

Trax, a midnight blue mass of tentacles with no eyes that she could see and a creepy, large, gap-toothed grin where most beings' stomachs were, shrugged four of his eight roaming appendages with a chortle. "Can't you tell?"

She laughed. "Yeah."

He reached to the glowing orbs behind the bar without looking. "Usual?"

A nod. "Please."

"You got it, Red." Trax produced a clear globe illuminated from within by a swirling pink mist. He set it on the bar with a flourish. "There you go."

Sara pressed her palm flat to the bar to place her payment, then scooped up the globe.

"Let me know if you need anything." Trax moved on to his other clamoring customers.

Sara only smiled in response, cradling the globe in front of her face. She tilted the orb from side to side, studying the azalea smoke inside. A strange sense of awareness washed over her as the bass buffeted her back and the lights danced across her eyes. She reflected over the long journey that had led her here and saw, in her mind, the faces of those she'd left behind. She took firm hold of that mental image and gripped it tight, keeping it at the forefront of her consciousness. Then, giving the globe a twist, she sighed. "Bottom's up." The orb popped open like a plastic Easter egg and the pink fog coiled about her head like a wreath, filling her nostrils. She shut her eyes and inhaled deep, the smoke burning her sinuses, then turning pleasantly warm.

When at last she opened her eyes, Michael and Toby stood there, looking just as she'd left them two years ago. The two of them waited before her, all smiles and forgiveness.

"Hey, you," Michael breathed, the pink fog moving about him like a forcefield.

Tears welled in Sara's eyes, but she barely managed a smile. "Hey."

Quickly, knowing the fog's spell was short-lived, Sara knelt down to Toby and tousled his unruly hair like she used to. "I miss you guys."

"We miss you," Toby said, bright and happy and no longer terrified of her. "We love you."

"I love you," she wept and stood. Already Michael's face was evaporating in the rosy fog, but Sara reached out and caressed his chin before he faded. "And I'm sorry…"

The vision dissipated and the noise and lights of the club returned, harsh and cold. Sara frowned and took her seat at the bar again, waving Trax down for another round of ReMemory.

3

Three hours later, Sara lounged in one of the club's private booths, alone, bleary-eyed and numb. After a couple orbs of ReMemory, she'd settled on a bottle of Jamari Brandy that now neared its last drop. Despite her best efforts to remain sober, the lure of Supernova had gotten to her, and now she was drunk and in no mood to run anymore. But that was fine, right? *Don't I deserve a break?* Of course she did. Just one night. She'd finish off the brandy and then she'd jump right out of here. Go back home, sleep it off, and start tomorrow with a clean slate. Maybe she'd visit the Living Rocks on Eox again. That was on the far end of the multiverse, and the scenery was breathtaking and sure to lift her spirits.

Having chosen her course of action, Sara depleted the brandy and set the bottle down with a loud clank. She stood to her feet, ready to bid Trax farewell, when a sharp whine split through her senses.

"Ack!" She touched her temple, wincing against the unbearable pain.

The high-pitched shriek drowned out everything else, scraping across her mind with cold fingers. What was happening to her? If she didn't know better, she would've sworn she was suffering one of Michael's terrible migraines—his danger sense. Was *that* what this was?

Why is it happening to me?

Then—

"Well, well," a casual voice intoned, instantly silencing the earsplitting ring.

141

"Look who I found."

Sara opened her eyes to a squint, her muscles still tense, as her migraine began to fade. "Rip," she croaked.

The Old Dog, with his silver braided locks, still in his dusty apparel—including the leather jacket that would one day belong to Michael—sauntered into her booth. "Hey, there, sis." He drew her attention to a bottle he dangled casually from one hand. "Want to help me drink this?"

It wasn't a question. Sara huffed, her brain still a bit sore, and flopped down on the couch. This time, though, she refused to get comfortable. Instead she leaned forward, bouncing the balls of her feet, trying to sober herself up as quickly as possible. Rip, on the other hand, leaned back at ease in the chair across from her and propped his boots on the clear table. He screwed the cap off the drink and downed a few greedy gulps before offering it to her.

She refused and he shrugged. He took another swig then tucked the bottle in his lap. "So," he began after a deep breath, "how ya been?" Rip smirked, revealing his extended canine. Pointing at her, he chuckled, "You know, I almost had you last week until those blasted spider-snakes came at us."

Sara knew that "last week" to Rip was "yesterday" to her, but she'd grown accustomed to Time being subjective when one was a rift jumper. "Yeah," she forced a dark sneer. "You came close."

"How'd you get out of that, anyway? I saw you fall in that pit."

"Trade secret," she quickly countered.

"Fair enough, Red." He scratched his nose, a warm smile lingering on his whiskered face. "*Red*. I hear you're calling yourself that these days. Gotta say, I'm a little flattered."

"Don't be."

He paid no attention to her remark, interlacing his nicotine-stained fingers and stretching his arms behind his back. His leather jacket parted, exposing his naked torso, and Sara glimpsed a myriad of tribal tattoos darkening his flesh. In the light of the club, the ink seemed to twist into nauseating shapes and patterns.

She forced herself to look away, disgusted.

He sighed. "As far as aliases go, it's not bad. Sure took me a while to catch on, to realize I wasn't looking for 'Sara Morrison' anymore. It's good, though, that you're putting distance between the new you and that old identity—that old life. That ain't who you are anymore, little darlin'. I'm glad you're finally starting to recognize that." Rip stood with a tired groan. "Well, come on. Let's get going."

"Where?" she snapped.

"Back home. Back to the desert to finish your training. Come on, sis, I told you we had things to do. When I said that, I didn't mean for you to stick around for a week and a half, long enough for me to teach you how to control the rifts, then run out on me while I was sleeping. You've got a lot left to learn, and the Rage is tired of waiting for you to 'find yourself.'"

"Whatever happened to 'freedom'? Isn't that what you were selling me? The freedom to follow my own rules for once?"

He gestured to her posh surroundings. "Look, I think I've been real understanding about your little adventure. You got your first taste of freedom and it went to your head. Happens to the best of us. But we didn't wake you up so you could make the multiverse your own personal playground. At least, not yet. We've got work to do first, starting with taking out that boyfriend of yours."

Rip made to leave, as though that settled it, but Sara remained seated, snarling. She thought back to that horrible night two years ago, when she'd first succumbed to the Rage. She'd always expected It to give her power, but It had completely taken her over, pushing out her thoughts—her very will—to make room for Its own. She could've killed Michael that night. Toby, too. She'd actually begun the process of summoning the Black Pillar and then—

No. It'd been too close. She wasn't ready to be a monster. There had to be another way.

"I'm not going," she stated.

The Old Dog paused and turned to her. His wolf eyes flickered golden. "Kid, don't push me. While you've been on your extended vacation, the Rage has been taking out Its frustrations on *me*."

"Then find someone else!" she blurted, wringing her hands in anger and worry.

Rip growled and slammed his hands on the table, knocking her empty bottle to its side. She watched it roll onto the floor and come to rest by her boot, knowing the exchange was about to grow much more heated. "Listen here, little darlin'," Rip spat. "There *ain't* no one else. You've seen that witch with the Black Pillar. That's *you*."

Shame punched Sara in the heart and she flinched. "Not yet."

"But it will be. Sure as I'm standing here in front of you. All this that you see? All these new friends you've made? It's your destiny to destroy all of it. That's who you *are*. You can't run from that."

"Michael ran," she said between gnashed teeth, glaring at him through her brow. "Right after he kills *you*."

Rip shut his mouth and blew steam out his nostrils, straightening. She could tell that the thought of his eventual death haunted the Old Dog, and took great joy in reminding him of it whenever she got the chance. "*Now* who wants to outrun fate?"

He looked away, hands on his hips, taking deep breaths. His body trembled with unspent rage, and, with his back turned to her, Sara again eyed the empty bottle against her foot. *It'd make a good weapon.* Rip faced her once more, and she quickly cut her eyes back to him. "Where do you think you're going to go, anyway? Where you do you think you're going to hide?"

Dropping back into his seat, he gestured wildly with his hands, tossing his braids about. "Let me clue you in on something your boyfriend never quite got when *he* tried running. You ever stop long enough to think about why you appear where you do when you go to a new dimension? I mean, take this place here. Nice club. Cute dancing girls. But in this dimension alone there's no less than twenty-five thousand known inhabited planets, and yet you landed *here.* Why? Also, how was it that no matter when you guys dropped in somewhere, it always seemed you were right in the middle of a war or something? Did you think that was all coincidence? Or maybe trouble just followed you around?"

He leaned forward, his eyes glimmering in the laser light show. A grin parted, revealing his fangs. "See, the multiverse is this cage, right? But every cage—it's got its structural weak points. You've got the walls of the multiverse keeping Chaos held prisoner, but there are fault lines in every dimension of Creation where the wall's thin. Sometimes, *real* thin. That school where you turned? Michael, too, right? The Rage is strong there. That's where It called to my gramma, remember? The fabric's worn thin in these patches, you get it? The Rage has a stronger influence there, and a greater chance of whispering to someone through the bars of Its cage, to find someone to set It free. Places like that, they're like a supernatural magnet, drawing all types of bad—just like Supernova, here. Places like that, there's always some war or crisis or some monster or some…" He trailed off, drawing her gaze to him, then grinned. "Or some drunk husband who needs killing, right?"

She fumed.

Rip continued, "All these times that you've been rift jumping, you've been slipping in through these cracks in the wall." He leaned back, slowing his speech, a bit of mystery in his tone. "My gramma was the one who taught me about the cracks and how you can navigate them if you're clever. But that's not all. See, Aztaroth told her that out there in the multiverse somewhere, there's an Origin Point for all the cracks. Like a hub."

Sara considered this development as Rip continued, "He called it 'The Gateworld'. It's like when your windshield gets hit by a rock. The glass may spiderweb, makin' the whole thing weak—but it all came from one point." He brought his fingers together into a tight point, then splayed them outward suddenly, pantomiming an explosion. "Someone must've thrown a big rock at the multiverse to make it crack like *that.* That's why we've got the rifts. Me and Azzy, we've been slipping in and out of those cracks, trying to follow the faultlines to the Gateworld. We find *that* place? Then we give it a good tap and shatter all the glass—and our Master gets free. That's where *you* come in."

Why hadn't Rip said anything about this before? The man had a soft spot for his Gramma Moore, no doubt about that. Had his nostalgia for her teachings lowered his guard momentarily, or was he purposefully baiting her? If *she* found the Gateworld first, could she seal the cracks for good? Close the rifts? Stop the Rage?

Rip gave a dismissive wave of his hand. "Aztaroth had that stupid army of his, traipsing all over Creation, trying to find the Gateworld, but we've got you now." He clapped his hands and leaned back. "So, you know, jumpstart that Black Pillar thing and let's smash some worlds. We'll find the Gateworld eventually."

Shaking her head, Sara objected, secretly testing Rip's story, "God already told Michael that you can't destroy the multiverse. He'd never allow it. It's pointless to even try."

The Old Dog leaned forward, pointing a knotted finger in her face. "We'll see about that, sis, but you're coming whether you like it or not. *That* was the deal. Where you gonna run, Red? Because everywhere you go, the Rage is still there. Still whispering. Yeah, you might outrun ole Rip now and again, but you'll never escape *It*. You think the Rage is just going to keep letting you tap into Its power without making sure you fulfill your end of the bargain? My Master always gets paid in the end. No matter what. Just ask Charlie."

Rip perked up, jerking his head towards the dance floor as though someone had just called his name. Simultaneously, an incredible pain seized upon Sara. She screamed involuntarily and doubled over, clutching at her stomach. It felt as though someone were slowly dragging a serrated blade along her abdomen.

"*Aah!*" she shrieked, struggling to breathe now. Her eyes watered and bile rose in the back of her throat. "Help me," she choked, clutching for Rip's leather jacket.

He regarded her curiously, then frowned. "Oh, man," he groaned as though he'd simply knocked over a glass of milk. "How long has *this* been going on?" He sighed and hunkered down to her spot on the floor. "Not good, sis." He lifted her head and pulled down her lower eyelids, checking her real close. "Not good at all."

"What's happening?" she wept, but knew. She'd seen Michael suffer these attacks too, along with the headaches. It was what he'd felt each time he came upon his "big mission"—that is, whatever it was the Man in the Stetson had for him to do on any given world. But now she wondered how her husband could stand it all those years. How could he think straight and push past the pain to do *anything*?

Rip shook his head in pity. "You're being pulled in two different directions, little darlin'. Remember, I told you that every dimension you jump to, you're smack in the middle of a cosmic hotspot? The battle of Good and Evil is strongest there. You feeling like this means that something's coming—some Big Fight, and you're gonna have to choose a side to fight for. Feel all that churning in your gut? Like hot coals? The Light's pulling you one way and Dark the other."

Despite her torture, clarity came to Sara's mind as she finally understood so much more of Michael's journey through the multiverse.

"Happens to one of us every now and again. The *uncommitted* ones. But once you make your choice—now, I mean your *once-and-for-all* choice, sis—the pain goes away easy enough."

That's why Michael stopped getting the headaches and the stomach cramps, she realized. *He chose the Light, once and for all.*

Rip scratched his bearded chin, sizing her up with a beady glare. "You feeling the tug like that? It means God still thinks there's some good left in you. Yeah, Red, that ole boy's got his hooks in you still. You should be beyond this by now. You lack conviction for our Master." He stood over her, threatening. "You've been running too long, girl. It's high time you dance or get off the floor."

In a flash, he reached down with one hand and took firm hold of her head. She winced as he turned her face to stare across the dance floor. He leaned closer and pointed, directing her focus. Through a blurry haze she spotted that rhino-faced Dun from earlier, when she'd first arrived. A table was overturned beside the brute and a crowd had begun to form. The stocky alien bullied one of the lissome dancing girls. She twisted in his vice-like grip, weeping for mercy, but the Dun backhanded her, eliciting a startled cry.

Sara seethed at the sight, the pain in her stomach subsiding in an instant.

Rip spoke into her ear. "There. It's a flashpoint, Sara. A crossroads, even. You feel the tug and it's directing you to that creep. Looks like every dimension has a Charlie, doesn't it? So now you've got a choice to make. How are you going to handle it? Which master will you choose to serve, once and for all?"

She rose to her feet, balling her hands to fists. Rip backed away, grinning with fangs exposed. "Kill him, sis. Feed that Rage in ya. You'll feel better."

Sara clenched her teeth until they hurt and strolled out of her booth. A steady boom-boom-boom sounded deep in her gut, like tribal drums. Blood thundered in her ears, and she closed her eyes, relishing the beat. It steadied her, commanded her, and propelled her forward. The Rage was seeking an opportunity, trying to slither into her mind, to control her, just as it had before. Her arms and shoulders remained stiff as she lowered her chin to glower at the Dun. Around her the thumping club seemed to dull, to slow, as the crowds parted to allow her room. She closed a fist, the skin over her knuckles stretching and turning white. With her other hand, she eased behind her back, beneath her jacket, and gripped the handle of the chukrahas.

She swiveled her head and spared one last look behind her. Rip stood there, back at the entrance of her booth, raising his bottle in a toast to her. In her mind, the Rage whispered to her dark promises, beckoning her to open herself up to It—to receive the fullness of Its power and blessings. She'd danced with the Rage every time she went out on a job for someone like Wurgyl, but always kept It at bay—just siphoning enough of It to get her through. But the Rage wanted so much more for her. From her. *Let me in*, the Rage hissed, and she sensed Its aggravation. *Let me work through you. Be my vessel, and we will devour the worlds together.*

Ahead, the dancing girl attempted to climb back to her bare feet, but the Dun shoved her to the floor once more, cursing and bellowing at her, splashing his drink in her face. The woman wept and the Rage roared in Sara's heart. *Join with me and we shall make him suffer. Discover who you were truly meant to be. Stop resisting me.*

The Dun reared back to strike, but Sara caught his burly arm one-handed, stopping him in place. He turned to her, sharp, his jowls jiggling in contempt. He burbled something at her in his alien language, and Sara detected the threat in his tone. The Dun tried to twist free, cocking his fist to punch her, but Sara had her blade under his flabby chin in a fraction of a second. The rhino alien paused, eyes widening.

Sara kept the blade to his throat, pressing him to his knees, subjecting him to the same humiliation he'd visited on his female escort. Sara tilted her head to behold him, blinking blackness into her eyes. The alien recoiled in fright, but was helpless to escape. She clamped down on his wrist, hearing bone snap. The brute yelped in excruciating pain, tears welling.

Kill him, Sara. Make him suffer, just as you have suffered. Join with me at last. Come home.

"Yes," Sara muttered, seeing Charlie in the rhino's face. Hate encircled her heart with icy talons and clutched, squeezing out all warmth and compassion.

Don't, another voice whispered to her, cutting through the maelstrom like a bolt of lightning.

She faltered, her grip loosening, the inky black waning from her eyes to reveal the blue once more. Startled, she scanned the room, but saw no one speaking to her. Instead, she met the shocked reactions of the entire club. Trax watched her from his place behind the bar, his large mouth turned down into a disappointed frown. Even the dancer that Sara had sought to save stared at her as though she were some awful monster birthed from nightmares.

Just like Michael and Toby did…

Sara shook free from the Rage's influence, feeling sick inside. She'd done it again. Let *It* get too close. Her knife hand quavered and she eased it off of the Dun's throat. The alien fell back on his abundant backside and scrambled away, huffing laboriously. Sara stumbled back into the crowd, disorientated. "Get away from me!" she roared at the clubgoers, and they hurried off, fearful of her wrath.

She touched a hand to her head, dizzy and ready to go home. Ready to get away. Ready to—

Rip stood before her, arms crossed. His brow was creased and his wolf's eyes blazed golden. "That how it's gonna be, huh? After all we did for you?"

"I can't," she stammered, her fingers numb. "I-I'm not ready. I-I don't want this. I thought I did, but…"

Rip uncrossed his arms, the inked flesh of his bare torso sprouting thick grey fur. His snarled hands turned hairy as well, and curved black talons slowly emerged from his fingertips. The Old Dog's face transformed around those glowing eyes, popping and snapping into a wholly different shape. "Looks like we've come to an impasse, Red," he bellowed through an elongating snout filled with gleaming jagged teeth.

The crowds screamed and tripped over themselves to escape the wolf-man in their midst. Sara braced herself for an attack, readying her blade. She knew she couldn't kill Rip—that fate belonged to Michael—but Rip couldn't kill her either. Not if fate held.

Can he?

She determined that she didn't want to find out.

Rip snapped his massive jaws, flinging saliva into her face. He lunged for her, swiping at her with a tremendous paw. Sara channeled her anger, drawing from the tar-like pool of Rage that had settled in her gut, and kicked off with her feet into a perfect backwards somersault. She landed in a skid just in time to see Rip lashing out at her again, strike after strike, his claws cutting the air centimeters from her skin. She flinched away from each attack, nearly anticipating his moves. His arm swung for her, too close to slide away from it, and Sara dropped to a crouch, sparing her head. She came up with the blade, sticking it towards his side, but he twirled left of the thrust and caught her face in a backhand. The blow knocked her off balance and she crashed sideways over a table.

"Come on, Red!" he howled, leaping to land on the bar on all fours. "You should be so much stronger than this by now! Don't give up on me yet!"

He leaped for her, his hooked claws descending fast, giving her just a moment's notice to roll out of the way. Rip scurried about the dance floor, his talons scraping on the tile, as he righted himself and aimed for her. Sara bounced to her feet and kick-twirled, digging her heel into his face and spinning him off course. He landed in a tangle, overturning two nearby tables, laughing all the while.

"Much better!" the wolf-man exclaimed. He rose, pushing the tables aside, and eased his leather jacket off of him. Almost ceremoniously, he folded it neatly

148

and draped it over a table. He faced her again, snickering through fangs. "Let's see what *I* can do." Rip flexed his arms, and before Sara's astonished eyes, began to grow even more. Muscles bulged and rippled beneath his silver fur, his spine audibly popping into a higher arch. He growled throughout his new transformation, as his torso doubled in mass and potency. His wolf's mane sprouted fuller, forming a bushy cowl that framed his warped, snarling maw.

Once finished, the Old Dog chuckled as dark shadows spilled down his face. "Ready for Round Two?"

The gigantic beast dropped to all fours and galloped for her, snapping his jaws. Desperate, Sara hurled her curved chukrahas blade like an edged boomerang, but the wolf-creature brought up its paws and twirled over the knife. Sara watched her only means of defense spiraling to land somewhere in the recesses of the club, lost forever.

But Rip kept coming at her, growling and somehow laughing at the same time.

Unarmed and out of time, Sara spun on her feet, nearly slipping to the floor. She bolted for the exit, sliding over a table in her path an eye-blink before Rip swatted it out of his way. Sara crashed out the front doors and took the steps to the thoroughfare in a single bound. Rip exploded through the entrance, shattering glass and wood. Screams erupted from the street, but Sara pushed her way through the mob of spacers, frantic and trembling.

Throwing cautious peeks behind her, she watched in awestruck horror as the wolf-monster ripped through passersby as they tried to flee the carnage. Tentacles and appendages flew in bloody blue, red, and orange splatters, decorating Supernova's strip in gore.

"Move!" Sara shrieked, slamming into angry aliens right before Rip followed, cutting a gory path through the masses. Sara worked her legs furiously, ricocheting from building to building in a mad race for the rift. Escape was her only means of survival now.

"Come on, Red!" Rip shouted after her in some deep, demonic voice. "Come see what big teeth Gramma has!"

An oblivious long-snouted alien in a ratty coat and floppy stovetop hat pushed his small cart-on-wheels right into Sara's line of sight. She tried to stop herself, but tumbled over the cart, scattering gaudy jewelry everywhere. Out of breath and eyes brimming with moisture, she turned back and saw Rip, still tearing after her.

The alien vendor squibbled something in offense, but Sara ignored him, finally spotting the rift by Wurgyl's store. Still on the ground, she crab-walked backwards, then flopped to her stomach and dragged herself to the portal, even as the screams grew closer and the heat from Rip's hungry jaws warmed her chilled flesh. Her dirtied fingers stretched for the rift as it began to emit its rainbow-colored lights.

"Come on," she begged, almost there.

"*I'm coming for ya, sis!*" Rip shouted behind her.

She squeezed her eyes tight, ready to feel his claws cut into her back, when, at last, her fingers touched the rift and—

4

A flash of light dazzled her vision, and then Sara was lying flat on her face in silence, heaving painful breaths. When no sharp wolf claws shredded her flesh, she opened one eye, then two, and was met by the wonderful sight of her lavender walls. The large floor-to-ceiling windows were still open like she'd left them, the soothing beach breeze gently rustling her sheer white drapes. The sounds of seagulls and breaking waves instantly calmed her nerves, and she laughed to herself, beyond relieved.

She rolled onto her back, staring up at the wicker ceiling fan that circulated the cool air, and groaned out loud, chuckling through happy tears. Finally relaxed, she rose to stand on exhausted legs, taking in her spacious seaside abode with fresh appreciation, comforted by the familiar. On teak shelves rested—in perfectly arranged order—the alien idols, knick-knacks, books, and collectibles she'd accumulated on her journeys across the multiverse over the last couple years. No doubt a collection of this variety was invaluable to someone like Wurgyl, but Sara would never dream of parting with any of it. She'd tried once before to preserve mementos of her travels when she was married to Michael, but she'd only had a backpack then—and that had been destroyed by firestarters on Toby's world. Michael had never figured out the key to controlling their jumps, so they were never able to settle down anywhere and plant roots. They'd been transients, traveling to every world, but never a part of any of them. Once she learned the secret to traveling the worlds at will, and escaped Rip under cover of darkness, the first thing Sara thought to do was establish a home.

And what a home it was.

She crossed her clean living space, slipping off her boots and letting them clunk to the floor. Next she removed her socks, then walked barefoot to the balcony outside overlooking the Pacific Ocean. She found this little slice of California paradise in the year 1958. It was a good year. Good music, good style, and good neighbors. At first she thought seclusion would best suit her lifestyle, but moving into a seaside resort village proved to be the smarter move. Below, young people frolicked in the sand and surf, enjoying their afternoon, and completely oblivious that an inter-dimensional thief and professional adventurer lived just a few feet from them. Strangers were always coming and going on the beach, and no one paid her any mind or went snooping around her house. She, of course, made sure to play nice with the neighbors when she saw them, keeping up appearances as a busy office secretary so they wouldn't think her too strange.

"Welcome home, Mistress Sara," a synthesized voice greeted her from behind.

Sara casually glanced over her shoulder and watched as her six-foot-tall robot rotated at the waist to collect her boots and socks. The robot was from the far future of this world—the twenty-seventh century, to be exact—and adorned in all-white plastiron casing, its body built with proportions similar to that of a snowman's, each glossy globe spinning and churning to give the robot movement. Its face was flattened by a black monitor, and an 8-bit neon yellow smiley face gazed down at her in a poor mimic of kindness.

Nevertheless, Sara smiled. "Hey, Zeo."

The Z-O Series Autotron carried her dirty socks to the hamper in the corner and dumped them without another word. Servos whirring, its next destination was the welcome mat by her front door, where it deposited her boots. She'd acquired the bulky butler bot early in her solo adventures and had taken a liking to its dumpy, childlike quality.

"Hard day?" she asked, stifling a grin.

It rose up and swiveled to her, pausing while its processer hummed, searching for the proper response. Its digital smile shrank to a squat, single line, the squares that comprised its eyes expanding slightly.

Sara snorted and waved him off. "It was a joke, Zeo. Stand down."

The pre-programmed smile returned to the monitor as the 'tron shuffled off. "Shall I draw you a bath, Mistress Sara?"

She moaned in delight. "Oh, Zeo, after the day I've had, that would be lovely."

The motorized servant shuffled off and Sara smiled fondly after it, then returned outside and leaned against the wooden railing on her balcony, lifting her face to the clear blue heavens as the sun kissed her smudged skin, warming her. It felt good to be home. After her close call at Supernova, she fancied a soak in some coconut-scented bath oil, followed by sunbathing for the rest of the afternoon. Then maybe she'd have Zeo grill up some vegetables for supper, and afterwards she'd relax with a good book—perhaps the first edition of *The Adventures of Tom Sawyer* that nice Mr. Clemens gave her a few weeks ago on another world. Tomorrow she'd be off to Eox to spend the day at the Living Rocks and hear their endless ironic limericks that amused her so.

Eox was incredibly beautiful and interesting, just like the Crimson Palisades, the Well of Ponderous Gazing deep in the Lyric Jungles of Avor, the Five Rings of Junipereen, and an ever-growing list of other places she had visited in her jumps. Yet, as she stared out at the blissful beach people below, a somber mood overtook her. While watching families, young couples, and scampering children enjoying each other's company, she reflected that all the exotic places she visited, as well as her new home, were empty. They held no real purpose; there was nothing for her there, or here. Not really. There was never anything anywhere *for her*. For years she'd gallivanted around the 'verse, denying herself no experience. Every day was a vacation and a chance to see new things… But no matter where she went, she could never escape the void in her heart. Even her thrillseeking escapades for cash couldn't distract her long enough from the truth that never faded from her mind: She missed her boys. Of course she knew how to find them—no doubt they were right where she left them. Still looking up at her, terrified. Still clinging to each other in fear.

She frowned, ashamed. They were right to hate her. As Rip was so fond of pointing out, there was something dark and evil growing inside her. And if the future was, indeed, already written, eventually it would get out.

And destroy the worlds, she thought, grieved.

If…when that happened, she didn't want Toby anywhere near Ground Zero. She hated herself for abandoning him, but she had to believe it was for the best. *I'm no mother. I would only hurt him.* She needed to keep running, to stay ahead of her fate. It was better for all of them that way, though she did miss them. She'd hated Michael for lying to her. She'd been prepared to murder him that day years ago, but now the hate was softer. Now there was just sadness. And, while she did her best to push the thought away, not a day went by that she didn't consider returning for him. But then what? Could she just apologize? Go back to living in Michael's shadow, letting the Man in the Stetson dictate her life? No. She loved her freedom.

She just wished she had a friend to share it with.

Saddened, she re-entered her living room, drawing the French doors closed behind her, shutting herself inside. Zeo returned, a towel draped over its arm. "Your bath is prepared."

"Thanks," she sighed. Then, "Zeo, how would you like to get out of here?"

It blinked back at her. "I do not understand the question."

She frowned. "You know. Out. Outside."

"But you told me never to reveal myself to the primitives. My components are far too advanced for this era—"

"No, no, I mean you could come with me. On one of my secret trips. I could show you the galaxy. A thousand galaxies! Wouldn't that be nice?"

But the Autotron only watched her in detached silence. "I do not understand the question, Mistress Sara."

She slumped down on the edge of her sofa, glum. "Nevermind, Zeo. I just thought… I don't know what I thought."

"You seek companionship," it said. How pitiful that even a hunk of chips and wires could name the source of her misery so precisely.

She propped her chin on her palm. "Yeah. Guess so."

"I am sorry, but my model is not programmed for companionship. I am programmed for housekeeping, culinary applications, and security protocol."

"S'okay, Zeo. It was just a thought."

"And a fine one at that, Mistress Sara. But don't you have any friends in your own model?"

"I'm not *looking* for friends." she blurted, aggravated, recalling what she'd told Wurgyl.

Sara expected, hoped, that the 'tron would impart some words of wisdom, but instead her giant toy simply stood still, waiting for her to take her towel. As much personality as she imposed on the walking appliance, it was still only that.

"Your water is getting cold," the 'tron said, unable to soothe her heartache.

She stood, resigned to another lonely evening, desperate for a change. A funny thought struck her as she remembered feeling like this all too often back in high school, long before she ever met Charlie. Dateless and unpopular, confined to another night of reading until she drifted to sleep, unfulfilled and craving adventure. Of course, back in those days, whenever the restlessness grew so unbearable she thought she'd bust, she'd head to the store to see—

Suddenly, her breath caught in her chest and she grinned wide until grateful tears began to leak from the corners of her eyes. She released a "Yes!", struck now by the most wonderful thought. *Of course!* Instantly, her worries evaporated and she busied herself about the house, slipping on her jacket. She could hardly manage to dress, still giggling, thrilled, now, to have found a purpose.

All the while, Zeo watched her, its smile slowly shrinking again into a "minus" symbol. "Mistress Sara?"

"Change of plans, Zeo! I'm going out again!" Carried away by excitement, Sara beamed. *I just hope he's working.*

5

A small scrap fluttered down onto the darkened sands of the Desert of Choosing, and an explosion of light heralded the Old Dog's return. Rip sauntered out of the mystical sheet of paper from his gramma's ancient notebook once it touched down, newly restored to his human shape. He slid on his worn leather jacket, his muscles sore from his time as the wolf. While his transformation granted him incredible strength, it did not come without a price.

Power never did. His Gramma Moore had taught him that.

Adelaide Moore had taught him many things about the Void between the worlds. Rip missed his gramma. Missed her lessons, her wry humor, but mostly her singing, and the way she truly cared for him. The old witch had been dead for long years, but he still felt connected to her—and to her work. He treasured the notebook she'd given him and the magickal sheets within. Sheets that Rip still, to this day, handed out to the agents of the Dark, to bestow upon them the power to traverse the dimensions.

However, not all of his protégés were grateful for his gift.

Rip snickered to himself as he thought back to the petrified look on Red's face. While she had just managed to slip through his claws again, that look of pure panic was priceless and served as a sort of consolation to his loss. Rip never had any intention of killing Sara. His goal was to push her, to frighten her, but more than that—to make her angry. Only when she finally let go and allowed the Rage to fully take control would her destiny be complete. It was his job to make sure that happened, just as it had been his gramma's job to unlock the secret of the rifts. The Chaos had chosen his family to see to the destruction of the multiverse, and nothing would stop him from fulfilling his role. If that meant he needed to terrify his charges, to beat them, to destroy everyone they knew and loved, then that was his lot in life.

Exhausted by Red's cat-and-mouse game for another day, Rip trundled up the nearest sand dune and spotted his adobe hovel. Firelight from the hearth flickered through the cut-out windows, beckoning him to an evening's rest. He dragged his tired frame to the wooden door and pushed it open, releasing a sigh of relaxation as he crossed the threshold into his shack. His gramma's old rocker waited by the fireplace, a blanket of animal furs draped over the high back. On the mantle, his favorite pipe. He—

His hackles stood on end, prickly gooseflesh breaking out along his wiry arms. Rip stiffened, holding his breath. With his eyes, he searched the room.

"Who's there?" he said, his voice strange and hollow to his own ears. Heart quivering in his chest, he remained still, flexing his fingers, prepared to summon the wolf again, though he knew that to do so this soon after his last transformation would be difficult and would surely take its toll on his body.

A crack of thunder rattled his senses, sounding as though it were mere feet behind him. He let out a cry and turned, gaping through his open window across the sands. There, he saw a single streak of purple lightning punch the earth. Then another. Another. All striking the same spot, all accompanied by a bone-jarring rumble. After the fourth boom, Rip clapped his hands over his ears and flinched, then staggered out into the night.

Again and again the starless skies hurled one bolt after another at the earth, kicking up sand and grit. A shriek of fresh pain caught Rip by surprise and he thrashed about as though on fire, shrugging out of his jacket. He struggled to free himself from the leather covering, then hurled it to the ground.

"Aah!" he cried, looking down at his arms, turning them over. There, his tattoos squirmed like black snakes upon his flesh—up his arms and across his torso. The underside of his skin burned, and he clawed as though he could release the demonic ink and be free of its torment.

Still the lightning struck. Still the thunder shook the very foundations of the cosmos.

Rip dropped to the sand, clutching his arms across his chest, weeping under an intensity of pain he'd never thought possible. His breath left him, and he imagined it would be quickly followed by his sanity, then his soul. He shuddered and sobbed soundlessly as the abominable boom-boom-boom continued to fill his world.

"*Stop!*" he tried to scream, his voice a hoarse whisper.

Suddenly, the pain loosed him from its grip, and he dropped face-first to the ground. He sucked in oxygen without minding the sand he breathed in along with it, greedy for relief. As soon as his mind cleared, he realized the thunder and lightning had stopped as well.

Carefully, he rose to all fours, hacking and doing his best not to retch. Slowly the pain subsided, though his bones trembled. Fatigued, Rip managed to totter to a stand and lifted his sweaty head up to where the lightning had struck. And there, over the hill, he saw a figure headed his way.

Rip summoned his wolf's eyes and looked again. As the shape neared, it wobbled and dipped unevenly, like a colt on new legs. Peering deeper into the gloom, Rip could not tell if the shape was a man or a woman—indeed it had no defining details, but seemed to be a human-sized form, comprised entirely of charcoal smoke that whipped and flickered in the wind, as though on the verge of being snuffed out. But the smoke held together, growing denser and darker by the moment.

Mouth open in awe, Rip watched as the smoke turned to flesh. Now he saw the simulacrum of a man—though anatomically incomplete—lurching straight for him, nude with coal black skin, its flesh withered, puckered, and undulating as though it had a mind separate from the body itself. At first, the man had no face, just a blank mass of coiling blackness, but as he moved to Rip's doorstep, a face did form, with lidless eyes and a lipless mouth filled with eyes and teeth that were startling white against the black oil canvas of his flesh.

"Riiiiiiip," the thing moaned, and the ground beneath the Old Dog's boots quaked.

Rip's resolve faltered, and he took a step back as the weakened man-thing collapsed in front of him. This close to the creature, Rip's tattoos came alive, rattling in place in elation. In *worship*.

"No," Rip said in a hush. It wasn't possible, but… Somehow it was true.

He dropped to his knees and bowed low before the prostrate form.

Through trembling lips, he whispered, "Master."

6

Bright mid-morning sun shone in through the expansive glass skylight that encased the domed village. Just as Sara remembered, the thoroughfare was packed with busy customers, filling bags with items they really didn't need.

She stood still in the midst of the foot traffic, watching as girls her age rushed past, gabbing excitedly, pointing at boys, ogling dresses in the storefront windows. Their lives were empty…but they looked happy, which was more than she could say. Growing up, Sara had always thought that adventure and excitement would bring her life meaning. Instead, her wild capers seemed to have only brought her heartache. She was here to remedy that, though.

Leaving behind the rift, she traveled through her old stomping grounds, struck by how out of place she felt amongst the familiar. Once, the stacked apartments that flanked the streets had seemed to reach to the heavens, but now they looked so small. *Everything* looked smaller, and she wondered how she could ever have breathed in a place as confining as this.

Gazing at all the old buildings, memories pressed against her. She remembered her mom and dad, and laughed at anecdotes she'd thought long lost. Passing by a fork in the road, she paused a moment to glance to her left where, three blocks down, she knew she'd find the apartment where she'd made her home with Charlie. For the briefest of seconds, she considered going by the place, but feared the ghosts that still haunted those halls. Besides, that wasn't her anymore. That was some other girl's problem, some other girl's pain. That foolish little girl was long gone, now.

And good riddance, Sara thought.

Turning her back on her past, Sara picked up her pace, scanning the eyes of the people she passed. Surprisingly, she recognized many of the faces from her childhood. They weren't friends; she didn't know any of their names, and they certainly had no idea who *she* was. But she remembered them all the same, and they carried on as they always had—eating, shopping, *consuming*. She chuckled to herself, amused by their small town lives, but strangely comforted by it all, as well. In a way, it was nice that such a no-nothing world carried on, oblivious to the horrors she'd seen.

Stay ignorant, she thought as she gazed at the unsuspecting expressions of the passerby. *Enjoy every moment…before the Black Pillar comes for you.*

With new determination strengthening her legs, Sara marched faster, a smile broadening on her face as she spotted the old sign that read SUPERNATURAL SURPLUS. Tittering with giddiness, she raced ahead and stopped before the door, her heart dancing in anticipation. Through the storefront window, she glimpsed the large frame of a young man who stood behind the counter, happily ringing up a customer, and overjoyed tears stung her eyes. Unable to quell her excitement any longer, Sara opened the door of the occult bookstore. She stepped into the distinguished aromas of strange incense that instantly transported her back to a simpler time when she frequented this store. Or, rather, when she frequently sought the company of the boy who worked here.

Johnny Frawl looked the same as the day she'd left him. Still burly, but baby-faced, his blond bushy mop still uncombed. Adorned in simple dark jeans and a black button-up shirt, untucked and rolled up at the sleeves, he waited on a long line of occult enthusiasts, all stacking up at the counter with their various "hocus pocus" trinkets. In fact, as Sara's heartrate returned to normal, she marveled at just how packed the place was. Johnny's dad had opened the store years ago on a lark, driven by his own hobby to study the weird. Johnny had certainly inherited his father's penchant for the bizarre. Still, they had seemed to be two of a rare kind, as the store was regularly in debt and was little more than a mild curiosity to their village. To see it this crowded was a pleasant surprise, but also left Sara wondering what had changed.

Towards the rear of the store, she spotted Johnny's Nana, beckoning still more customers towards a back curtain—the old avaricious woman holding a liver-spotted hand out, accepting payment. Payment for what? Whatever she was charging, however, seemed perfectly acceptable to her marks. They happily paid and slipped inside even as other customers left the curtained area in a steady flow, their faces lit with enchantment and talking in thrilled hushes. Like a sideshow attraction.

What's back there?

"Sara?"

Unaccustomed to hearing her own name these days, Sara gave a start and turned to the counter where Johnny stood, open-mouthed, his expression widening in surprise.

Remembering why she was here, she shook aside her curiosity about the secret room and beamed. "Hey."

He looked to either side, as if trapped. "Uh…what are you doing here?"

She giggled. "I came to see you!"

"Me?"

Sara laughed and Johnny blushed. Slowly a silly grin touched the corners of his mouth and he waved down a dark-skinned full-figured girl in a silky shirt and jeans. "Maya, can you cover for me?"

The other employee nodded and unloaded an armful of scented candles on an empty spot on the shelf. After quickly arranging them, she moved into place behind the register as Johnny rounded the counter to join Sara. As soon as he was within reach, Sara wrapped her strong arms around his neck and squeezed. "I missed you so much!"

He stiffened in her embrace, and when they parted, his fuzzy cheeks were still crimson. Nodding towards her head, he remarked, "You cut your hair. I hardly recognized you."

Sara ruffled the back of her spiky do, having all but forgotten her new style. "Oh yeah, that. You like?"

"It suits you," he said. After surveying the busy store, he gestured to the door. "Maybe we should go outside."

Sara followed Johnny outside, resisting the urge to cling to his beefy arm as she used to. Rift jumping was not a precise science—she wasn't quite sure how much time had passed on this world since she'd last seen Johnny. However much time had passed, she knew that she'd ended their friendship in a pretty nasty way. She wasn't quite sure how he felt about her anymore, but she craved his forgiveness. His companionship.

"The store is crazy busy," she exclaimed. "I'm really happy for you."

He rubbed his neck, grinning sheepishly. "Yeah…business has really taken off. Mom and Dad made enough in a month to finally retire. I bought the store from Dad a year ago and hired Maya."

"I see Nana's still around."

"Yeah," he smirked. "Can't get rid of her. You know Nana."

"I know," she laughed, perhaps too eagerly. "I remember." *I remember everything*, she wanted to say. *And I'm sorry*.

Johnny nodded, the atmosphere of good humor lingering, and looked down at his thick-soled boots. "So…what are you doing here? I mean, back in town?" He faced her, his tiny eyes hungry for answers. "After all that mess happened across the street—" He jerked his chin to the clothing store across the street where Michael had rescued her from Charlie, killing her ex-husband in the process. "It was nuts! Charlie was dead and then you were just *gone*. I looked for you afterwards, but… What *happened* to you? Where did you go?"

Sara averted his questions, tucking her long bangs behind her ear. "It's…uh…complicated."

Johnny kept quiet for a moment, then ventured, "Did it have anything to do with Michael?"

She met his face, alert. How did he know about Michael? In a hushed, sharp voice, she asked, "What do you know about that?"

Now it was his turn to look away. "You'd better come with me."

7

It took a bit of convincing, but Nana finally cleared out the back room, to the groans and complaints of paying customers. Johnny thanked them for understanding and made his grandmother give them all a full refund. Then he pushed aside the curtain and allowed Sara inside, letting it fall closed behind the two of them. Sara scanned the room, remembering it as the Silent Reading section of the store. Johnny's dad had a bunch of musty old books back here that weren't for sale, but he made them available for any curious onlookers to read. Of course, before today, she'd only seen the place deserted. Everything looked more or less the same as the day she last saw it—

Except for the brick wall in the back.

Johnny kept his distance from it, but pointed at the wall and a crudely drawn circle in white chalk thereon. On the floor surrounding that patch of wall, rested rows of lit candles, flowers, trinkets, gifts—like an altar.

He seemed almost fearful of the spot.

Sara edged closer, the terrifying boom-boom-boom reverberating in the pit of her soul. She hesitated, too nervous to get any closer to the peculiar shrine.

Johnny narrated, "Michael came to me last year. He told me what he was: a rift jumper. He needed my help to crack a dimensional wall so that he could get to the In-Between. He said he needed to talk to God. To get out of his job." The young man quieted. "He said he was doing it all for a girl."

Sara turned to face him, aghast.

Johnny said, "I had no idea it was you. Then he left, and I heard gunshots across the street, and the next thing I know, Charlie's dead, and I saw you with Michael for just a second. But then you guys were gone—I mean, *gone*. No one saw you after that."

A bittersweet smile broke through as Sara recalled how her adventure with Michael had begun. "I went with him," she whispered.

Johnny frowned. "That's what I thought."

"I've only been gone a year?"

His brow furrowed. "Yeah. Why? How long did you think you were gone?"

She shrugged. "Time works differently out there. A year for you. For me, three. Maybe more. Hard to tell."

Johnny gasped, his face brightening. "How was it? Where did you go? What happened?"

"We..." She chuckled, warmed by memories of the good times. "We went

159

to different worlds. We helped people. Saw… We saw everything. The Living Rocks of Eox, and purple oceans on Ruggashosh, and the Forest of Pir with trees the size of skyscrapers—"

"Trees! You saw actual trees!"

Sara grinned. She'd forgotten that they didn't have trees on this world. When Michael had first shown them to her on a parallel Earth, she could've stared at a tree for hours. "Trees and more," she said. "So much more."

"Where's Michael?" Johnny glanced over his shoulder real quick, as though Michael might just spring out of hiding. "Did he come back with you? There was so much I wanted to ask him after everything that happened."

Sara looked down at the hardwood floor and shook her head. "It…uh…didn't work out. Michael and I…broke up." She twisted her wedding band, wondering why she still wore it. Wondering if Michael still wore his.

Johnny averted his eyes, looking suddenly ashamed to have been smiling. "Oh. I'm sorry. He… When he was here before, he…he seemed like he really loved you. He'd have to, right? To be willing to cross over into death for you?"

"Yeah," she replied under her breath, then turned back to the brick wall. "So what's up with this?"

Johnny stepped next to her, but maintained a respectable length from the altar. "It's our bread and butter these days. I don't know what it is, exactly. After Michael was done with his business in the In-Between, we sealed the rift. But it's like it's leaking or something. People just started showing up here—the sensitive ones, you know? Not just from here in town, either, but Bevenshire and some of the other settlements. Even as far as Centric. They say they dream about this place. About this *wall*. They say it speaks to them."

"It's like a pilgrimage," Sara commented, feeling the wall pulling on her, as well.

"I was fine with it at first. We were getting some recognition, and as long as they were here, they bought stuff. But… then they started bringing offerings to it. Praying to it. Worse…I think something's on the other side, answering them. Gives me the creeps."

"Do *you* dream about it?" she asked, worried.

"Nah. But I keep an eye out. The rift needs blood to open, and I wonder how many of *them* know that. Like if any of them would try something crazy." He shook his head, worry furrowing his brow. "I've looked through some of my dad's old books and cast a few binding spells on it. I'm pretty sure it's locked up tight. It's just creepy, is all."

Sara took a deep breath and neared the wall, going so far as to reach out with her hand—but stopping short of actually touching the brick. "Every dimension has places where the walls to the Other Side are thin."

In a discreet, reverent tone, Johnny probed, "What's…out there, anyway? In the black space between the worlds?"

Sara closed her eyes, the boom-boom-boom sounding in her stomach like a death knell. Blood pounded in her ears along that same steady rhythm, tribal drums beckoning her to the Black. Johnny's voice became dull and muted, like he was speaking from the end of a long narrow corridor. The warm lights of the reading room dimmed, finally surrounding her in dark. She swayed on her feet, light-headed. Free. In that all-encompassing black she suddenly heard the sweetest music, promising rest. And then, all of her fears subsided and—

She touched the brick.

The song ended, and a voice shrieked in her ears and stabbed at her mind. "*I ssseeeee yooooouuuu…Motherrrr.*"

A grinning obsidian face flashed in her mind's eye, slapping Sara awake. She jerked her hand from the wall and gripped the sides of her head. "Aaggh!"

The room returned, and Johnny was on her in an instant, catching her before she collapsed to the floor. "*Sara!* Sara, are you okay?"

She pitched to the side and stumbled about the room, getting her breath and putting as much distance between herself and the marked wall as possible. Johnny led her to a chair and helped her to sit. "What happened? You were like in a trance or something! I've never seen anything like that! Do-do you need anything? Water or—?"

"I'm fine," she croaked, coughing hard. "Just…let me…"

"Man, what did you *see*?"

She gasped heavy breaths, then glared at the wall. "You can't let anyone else go near that thing. There's something beyond it… I can't really explain, but trust me. You've got to board this room up. No one can get to it. Do you understand?"

Johnny appeared shaken, but nodded quickly. "Y-Yeah, sure. Sure, okay."

"If you need the money to make up for it, I'll get you the money. Just keep it off-limits."

"Okay, okay." He knelt before her, touching a hand to her knee. "What was it?"

Sara shook her head, a vague terror overpowering her. She still couldn't shake the afterimage of that grinning face—eyes and teeth glowing white inside an inky black face, its flesh churning. She felt the Rage in that face, but the Rage didn't have a shape, a face.

Did It?

It called me "Mother", she realized with revulsion and rising panic. *Oh, God, why did it call me "Mother"?*

"I…I don't know." She held her face in her hands and remained silent for a long time after that.

8

The thing in Rip's hut shuddered and pulled from his grip. The Old Dog did his best to steady his midnight visitor, but the naked shape drew away and collapsed to all fours.

"Master!" Rip bellowed, hurrying to his gramma's rocker and removing the animal skins resting over the back. He draped the furs over the shivering creature. "What is it? What—"

The beast lifted its black, rippling face, a sharp bright smile opening up like a gash. "I ssseeeee yoooouuuu…Motherrrr." Then the shape slumped forward, exhausted.

"What did you see?" Rip said.

The Master rose on his own, gathering the furs about him as a cloak. He gazed about the room, but seemed to look past the walls. Rip took a step back, feeling invisible to this thing's attention. The Old Dog had been trembling since the Master arrived at his doorstep, and he couldn't seem to stop. "Master," he whispered. "H-How is it that you're here? I-I didn't think you had a body."

The shape looked down at his own hands, turning them over and over again. Studying them with wonder. "Yessss…a body… Not miiinnneeee…but a hosssst."

As the Master regarded his hands, then his arms, Rip observed that his tar-like flesh never ceased to coil and twist, as if he were comprised of a mass of snakes. The sight caused his throat to sting with bile.

"I'm ssstiiillll weak," the creature said, its voice a hissing warble, like air being let out of a tire. "I have muchhh to doooo…"

"What do we need to do, Master? Say the word, and I'll get it done. Rip's your man."

"Fiiiirrsssst… We punissshhhh the non-believerssss… Then—" The creature turned its head in a 180 degree arc, a wet gargle emitting from its open mouth. "—Motherrrr…"

9

"Nana, be reasonable," Johnny began, but the old woman threw her hands up in the air, her wrinkled mouth screwing up into a snarl.

"Close the store?" she exclaimed, even as Maya worked to ring out the remaining customers and hurry them along.

Sara stood to her friend's side, watching him trying to wrangle his surly grandma, unable to quell an amused smirk.

"Never!" she cried. "Business is finally good!" Nana gestured wildly to the patrons still waiting in line at the checkout. "Look! Look, paying customers, and you want to get rid of them!"

Johnny sighed through his nose. "It's just for a little while, Nana. Until we get the back room sealed off."

"That's our biggest attraction! Fool boy, you never had good business sense! Just like your dead grandfather!" She spat on the ground at the mere mention of her late husband and stormed out the front door, still flailing her arms about as though she were swatting at invisible flies. "Ungrateful little…"

Finally she was gone, the bells above the door clanging violently in her wake. Johnny slumped and Sara sidled closer to him. "Will she be okay?"

He grinned, looking tired but relieved. "She'll get over it. Thanks, Maya."

Maya returned the smile, watching Sara closely. Perhaps even jealously. Sara turned to Johnny, a bit surprised. "Is there something going on between you and Maya?"

He blushed and Sara snickered, elbowing him in his abundant midsection. "Good for you."

"Anyway," he said too loudly, turning to his customers. "Thanks again for coming. Be sure to stop by once our renovations are done."

They all waved and offered their well wishes until, at last, only Maya remained.

"I'll call you," Johnny said to her. Maya smiled and gave him a peck on the cheek—shooting Sara a warning look—then made her way out of the shop, as well. Johnny trailed behind and locked the door, turning over the CLOSED sign.

Sara felt calmer now that the rift's admirers had vacated. Her threat level decreased dramatically, and she hopped up to sit on the counter, just as she used to back when they had the place all to themselves. "Look at you. Got your own business, a hottie girlfriend—I'm really happy for you."

He shrugged and tucked his hands in his pockets. "Yeah. I guess I have Michael to thank for that."

At Michael's name, Sara cringed and frowned. "How's that?"

"We opened a portal to the Other Side," he said with a laugh. "I stared into the abyss, you know? It changes you. I mean, *that* was terrifying. Compared to that, asking a pretty girl out on a date is nothing. Even for a guy like me. You start taking more chances, being a little braver."

"Yeah," she breathed. "I know the feeling."

Johnny leaned on the counter by her side, digging at the dirt under his nails. "So, you…uh…wanna talk about what happened? With Michael?"

"Not really." She kicked off the counter and stretched her arms over her head. "So! What do you want to do now?"

"The hardware store is closed by now, but I'll stop by first thing in the morning and get the stuff to brick up this wall. Nana is going to have a *fit*. It's for the best, though. I feel better already knowing we'll be getting rid of it."

She nodded, an amiable silence resting comfortably in the familiar room. Johnny winced, then said, "Look, I know the last time we talked, it was a weird time. There was Charlie and—"

"I'm sorry about that," she said, feeling a thousand pounds lighter to finally be getting it off her shoulders. "I was such an idiot. You were absolutely right about Charlie. You were always there for me, and I pushed you away when I needed you most."

"I'm really sorry about your parents. I don't know if I ever got to tell you."

"I'm sorry for everything." She extended a hand. "Friends?"

He grinned and opened his arms to her. She entered in and he embraced her, protectively and without condemnation. She felt on the verge of tears but denied them for now. When they parted, though, she saw tiny pools brimming in Johnny's eyes. She chuckled, and he did too. "You're not staying, though, are you?"

Sara shook her head. "I really can't. It's…"

"Complicated," he said with a nod. "I'm picking up on that. Besides, with all *you've* seen, I can't imagine a place like this holding your attention." He groaned, wistful. "Man, it's gotta be incredible."

"It is," she beamed. "Which is why I came here."

He looked at her, puzzled. "What do you mean?"

She took his large hand. "I want you to come with me."

He exploded in laughter. "Yeah! Yeah, okay. Sure, why not? What about the store? Maya?"

Sara waved him off. "I'll bring you back. We could be gone for months and I could bring you back in the morning. It'll be like no time had passed."

He eyed her, as though waiting for a punchline. "You're serious."

"Absolutely! Come with me." She tugged on his arm. "I'm…I'm lonely," she admitted. "I want my best bud with me. Anyway, didn't we always talk about traveling together?"

"Yeah, to *Centric*! Not to Venus!" He paused. "Could…could we actually go to Venus?"

She smiled, warming up inside. "My ride's outside."

Rip walked amidst the flaming settlement, dark crimson splattering his grey fur. He blew hot breath out his snout, still tasting coppery blood on his elongated teeth. All around his wolfen form, the last of the raiders scrambled, their half-white, half-black painted faces contorted in stark terror. When he and the Master first arrived to the Maestro's camp, the raiders had fought back, hurling their spears, firing their guns. Rip had transformed and went after their strongest first, shredding through them with his massive blackened claws and snapping with iron jaws. Then he'd put their homes to the torch and now basked in the chaotic beauty of their fear.

Ahead, he glimpsed his Master through a shimmering haze of heat. Rip headed in his direction, even as a hulking raider screamed a throaty roar and surged towards him with a baseball bat adorned in spikes. The raider swung and Rip dodged it easily, even as tired as he was from the massacre. Almost effortlessly, he came up with a swift swipe of his claws that rent the bulky man in bloody halves. The Old Dog carried on his way and stopped behind his Master. Standing out against the Master's blackened grip was the bright pink throat of a giant with an eye stalk on either side of its pointed head. The alien wheezed in the Master's clutches, struggling uselessly. Black oil detached from the Master's forearm and inched towards the alien's face, slowly circling it, slowly entering its mouth and nostrils, slowly suffocating the creature.

Eye-Stalk gagged and kicked at the air, until at last the alien writhed no longer. The Master simply dropped the carcass to the ground, then beheld his fiery surroundings with something like wonder. An open-mouthed grin stretched tight across his oily features as he pivoted about, spreading his arms wide and taking in the show.

Rip let the monster have his moment, casually glancing around. The screams had died off, and there were bodies everywhere in the dust. "I think we got all of 'em," he said in his gruff wolf's voice. "No sign of the Maestro, though."

The Master made no indication that he heard Rip, or even cared to. He simply watched the flames in childlike awe. His own rage cooling, Rip relaxed his muscles, and the fur shrank back into his leathery skin. He grimaced in discomfort as his bones and joints realigned themselves with loud snaps and pops until, at last, he stood before the Master in nothing but his jeans. Catching his breath, Rip dug around in his side pockets and procured his lighter and a joint. He popped the smoke in his mouth and lit up, wondering when the Master might speak. The black beast seemed in another world—maybe even *all* of them—and had a scary blank look in his eyes.

Rip released a long blissful stream of smoke and prodded, "Hey, uh, Master?

You all right?"

But the man-shape only stood motionless with his profile to the Old Dog, that giddy grin still on his face.

Rip frowned, found a large stone, and went over to sit on it. He smoked his joint for a while, watching his Master close. "So, this was fun and all. What's next?"

"Neexxxtttt…" The Master hissed immediately, startling Rip. Just when the Old Dog thought the monster might continue, instead the creature grew silent once more, his body stiff like a statue.

Rip groaned under his breath and flicked the butt of his smoke off to the side. "You said something about a Mother? What did you mean?"

The monster raised his head to the dark sky, his smile spreading wider, to grotesque proportions. "Motherrrr…"

Suddenly, the Master moved to something that caught his attention on the ground. He stooped over and picked up an item. Examined it. Wiped it off on the inside of his furs. Rip watched in confusion as the Master returned, handing him the object. It was one of the dead raiders' weapons—a simple knife, handmade, with a dark, misshapen blade, and a lion's head crudely carved into the wood handle. The Master extended it to him, handle first. Rip glanced up to the white, lidless eyes that studied him.

"What is it?" Rip asked.

But the Master did not reply. Just stared, smiling, unblinking. Rip squirmed a bit in apprehension, but quickly took the proffered blade and set it next to him. "Thanks, then. I guess."

"Thissss is where we paaarrrt," the beast said.

Rip stood now, jittery. "Wha? No, take me with you. I can help—"

The smiling demon-god hissed, "You are helpiiiiing. Fiiiiinnnnddd my sheeeep…"

Deflated, Rip nodded. "Yeah, I get it. Stay here, huh? Go back to handing out your fancy sheets of paper?" He kicked at a rock on the ground. "Will I see you again?"

The Master took the discarded blade from the rock and, once more, placed it in Rip's hand. As the Old Dog took it, the creature wrapped his slithering black fingers around Rip's, clamping down. "Yeesssss… In hell."

11

"Woooo!" Johnny's exuberant wail echoed through the ravine, and Sara laughed in the driver's seat beside him.

"Hold on!" She jerked the yoke to the side. The rudder on the glider-car pivoted, and the wings on either side of the lightweight aerodynamic vehicle angled to catch the tremendous gusts generated in the cavernous chasm. The glider-car bucked beneath them and Johnny clamped down on the side, his eyes enlarging behind the goggles he wore on his face.

Sara steered through the valley, sifting through the yellow clouds, pointing below. "Down there! Look at that one!"

Johnny leaned over and gaped at the volcanic surface of Venus and cheered. "Amazing!"

"We caught it just in time! It's gonna erupt!" she said, veering out of the way just as the volcano directly beneath them let loose a tremble and exploded in a magnificent display of lava, smoke and rock.

Johnny pumped his fists, craning his neck as they flew by, barely able to take his eyes off the active volcano's outburst. As the volcano faded into the distance behind them, he turned his head and blurted, "Whoa, what are *those*?"

Sara peeked over the windshield and spotted the eight-foot-tall crab-like creatures that piddled around at the base of another volcano. Their shells were dark like charcoal, lined with seams that glowed a bright yellow light. "Lavaspiders," she called over the roar of the wind. "Best we steer clear of them."

"Yeah, ha ha! It's crazy!"

She grinned at him, refreshed by his enthusiasm. Yes, this was exactly what she had needed.

"How is this possible?" he asked, finally tearing his eyes from the Venusian landscape to face her.

"Well, it's not. Not in *our* dimension. But in this dimension, Venus and Earth are in opposite position to the sun. It's still a little closer to the sun than Earth is in ours, and the environment's really not very healthy for us for too long, but it's great for a quick fly-by. Besides, the Egalia are super nice to outsiders. You can't always count on that."

He blinked at her. "Egalia?"

"Bird people."

He threw his hands into the air. "Of course!"

"So, you feeling like Alan Worth yet?"

Johnny laughed and reclined in his chair, taking in every alien sight. "Oh, it's better. This is… wow…" Jerking to attention, he faced her and took her hand. "Thank you for this. This… *wow*."

Sara released a carefree laugh, finally feeling like she'd found her place in the multiverse. Johnny whooped once more and half-stood in the glider-car to get a better look as another volcano exploded below. Sara watched him, fondly remembering her first jump with Michael. It'd been scary, with violence dogging them at every turn. But, oh, there had been such beauty. In the beginning, she'd always scolded herself for acting so childishly whenever Michael showed her some new alien thing, thinking she was making a fool of herself. After all, by the time Michael found her, he'd been jumping for five years. He'd seen everything—done everything. Surely, she had reasoned to herself, he wouldn't put up with her bewilderment for long.

But seeing Johnny so happy was like looking at the multiverse with fresh eyes. No doubt this was what Michael had seen in *her*. A chance to be born again. A chance to leave behind the cynicism and just embrace life again.

Yet, look how that turned out. Her smile downturned to a frown. She was meant to bring light back into Michael's life, but instead she'd only ushered in a new age of darkness. Would Johnny befall the same fate if he traveled with her long enough? Was that just the cost of rift jumping? It made sense, she reasoned. Rip said that, in their jumps, they were really only ping-ponging to all the cracks in the cosmos that the Rage had claimed for Its own. Their lives were spent jumping from one cursed patch of the multiverse to the next. No doubt being that close to Evil over an extended period of time, without respite, took its toll on someone's soul. It certainly had taken its toll on hers.

No wonder Michael had always wanted to quit.

Seeing Johnny come alive, she worried for him. In him, Sara felt she'd found her salvation…but if she kept him close, she could not deny the distinct possibility that she, in turn, would only ruin her friend. Just like she'd ruined Michael and Toby. *It's my Song*, she thought, soured by her fate.

A shrill whine cut through her senses, blurring her sight. "Ack," she said, wincing and touching her temple.

Johnny noticed. "You okay?"

"It's—" She stopped short of saying "nothing", knowing exactly what it was. It was her budding danger sense kicking in again. Which meant… "Trouble."

The roar of a turbine engine rattled behind their glider-car. She and Johnny both turned in their seats to see a floating galleon, its majestic sails catching the wind and its undercarriage outfitted with powerful burning thrusters, gaining speed on them. Sara narrowed her eyes and studied the figures crowding around the bow of the ship, clanging sabers on the hull. They looked hungry for action, for murder.

Sara's headache dulled and she thinned her lips in consternation. "Pirates."

Johnny gulped. "So…what do we do?"

With little effort, the warship pulled alongside them, the malicious faces of the villainous pirates coming clearer into view. They were pale white and mottled in complexion, though Sara couldn't tell if that was the actual color of their skin, or if they had dried mud caked on their exposed flesh. A row of ridges ran the length of their foreheads, tapering off into a broad snout, and their lips were black and pulled back to reveal mismatched needle-like teeth. Clunky armor that resembled volcanic rock covered most of their stout bodies, and each of their four hands were large and strong. Most wielded swords that looked cut from slabs of blackened stone.

"Underdwellers," Sara commented, confused. "What are *they* doing up here?"

"You know them?" Johnny balked.

"They live beneath the volcanos. They're birthed in rock, fire, and ash when the volcanos erupt. They ride those lavaspiders you saw." She grimaced. "We fought them once before on our anniversary. Me and…Michael…" She regained her focus. "But Underdwellers are terrified of flying," she said, disturbed by the sight of them in the air. "Something's changed."

Before she had time to reflect any longer, one of the craggy monsters screeched and leapt off the frigate, banging haphazardly into the backseat of the glider-car.

"Sara!" Johnny yelped, as the volcanic warrior got his bearings, grinned rows of fangs, then swung his sword.

Sara took her hands off the yoke and blocked the pirate's strong arm, then backhanded him, dislodging his weapon. It tumbled over the side of the car, rattling into the abyss. The pirate's wide, empty hands searched her out, but she slapped and parried each grab for her, as the glider-car slid further off course. "Grab the yoke!" she hollered at Johnny.

Johnny fumbled to obey, inadvertently bumping the controls. The car swerved hard to the left, banking straight for the humming undercarriage of the motorized ship.

"Down! Down!" Sara barked, her hands tied as she traded grapples with their brutal passenger.

Johnny hollered and pushed down on the yoke, and the glider-car dipped into a steep decline, missing the larger vessel. They swooped beneath the frigate and came out the other side. Sara blocked a hand chop and glanced up to see three more pirates dropping down for the car. One missed entirely and screamed as he plummeted to the volcanoes below. The other two, however, landed hard on the back end of the car and scrambled for purchase with their two sets of arms. They clambered up, sneering severely, onyx daggers clenched in their teeth.

Fear shook Sara, and she instinctively reached to the small of her back to retrieve her chukrahas—

Only to realize she'd lost it on Supernova. She cursed under her breath then stood out of the seat.

"What are you doing?" Johnny cried, frantically wrestling with the yoke.

Sara took both hands and wrapped them around the head of the pirate in the backseat. Shutting her eyes, she gave in to the Rage, opening a door for It to flood into her veins. Opening her eyes once more—feeling them flood with black ichor—she gave a sharp twist and snapped the pirate's neck in two. The Underdweller twitched and leaned to the side, clearing the way for her to reach the two stowaways on the car's stern.

One of the pirates came to his balance first and planted his feet on the trunk. He took the knife from his teeth and reached to his belt to pull another blade from its sheath. He let out a wild "Ha!" and lunged for Sara. She swayed back, but not fast enough, and the tip of the rock dagger cut a shallow groove in her shirt and shoulder. She yelped, but absorbed the pain. Fed off it. Her Rage grew.

The thug came for her again, but her heightened senses were better prepared. She easily slid beneath the pirate's outstretched blade, then sprang up, caught his arm, and yanked it clean out of the socket. He cried and staggered, and Sara wasted no time ripping the blade from his useless hand and shoving it into the side of his head, silencing his wailing immediately. She retrieved the blade, and its former owner merely slipped off the side of the car, tumbling end over end into the flaming top of the nearest volcano.

The last of the pirates had made it to a crawling position, but Sara didn't give him the chance to right himself. Instead, she dropped low and plunged the dagger through his hand, pinning him to the car. He squirmed in agony and she punched him hard across the mouth, twice. Then she yanked the blade free and pushed against the man's face with her boot. He, too, rolled off the car, disappearing in the yellow clouds.

Sara rose, her breathing slow and steady. Focused. The Rage shuddered in her mind, whispering of the pleasure It took in her gruesome actions, and she returned to the cockpit. "Move," she commanded.

Johnny did a double-take upon seeing her black eyes and immediately slid out of the way. She slouched into the seat and took the controls, righting the craft.

"Sara," he said, his voice a hoarse whisper. "What's…wrong with you?"

She did not reply, but concentrated all her energy on reining in her dark impulses. She shut her eyes and forced the black to recede, *willing* the Rage back into Its cage and locking the door on It once again. It struggled, though, clawing to remain free, to take her over like before.

"No," she growled, clenching the yoke tight, her jaw tense, teeth on edge. *Get back. Get. Back.*

"Are you okay?" Johnny asked again, sounding faraway, but worried.

At last she released her breath and opened her blue eyes once more. "Yeah. I'm…fine."

Out of nowhere a wide red beam grazed the hood of their car, shredding the lightweight metal and spraying them with sparks and ash.

"Whoa!" Johnny barked. He and Sara looked to their side where the frigate was bearing down on them, catching up and aiming cannons their way.

"This is really not good," Sara said.

Johnny whipped about to face her. "You *think*?"

The Underdwellers cheered on the deck of their warship, powering up their cannon for another shot. Sara bit the inside of her cheek, certain that the worry knot over her left brow was visible once again. She was about to tell Johnny to brace himself when a thunderclap caused her to jump. She feared it was the cannon, but instead, the rear of the frigate detonated in a glorious fireball. The pirates scrambled in fright and confusion.

"Look!" Sara pointed to the heavens as winged figures descended from the upper clouds. In the hands of these heavenly protectors, golden trident-like spears. "It's the Egalia!" The tips of the spears glowed and tremendous spouts of unleashed power blasted forth, shattering the frigate into fiery pieces. Pirates bailed over the edge or were jettisoned by the explosions.

Sara kept an eye on the path ahead to make sure she didn't steer into a mountain face, but she couldn't help but keep the majority of her attention on the spectacular sight of the Egalia warriors summarily defeating their foes. In a matter of seconds, the mighty ship was reduced to a flaming husk that veered down, down, down, until it collided into the valley with a burst of fire and released gases.

Johnny crowed at the top of his lungs and Sara joined him, laughing and raising her fists in triumph. Their moment of rest was soon interrupted, however, by a very stern Egalia warrior who glided down to their side and glared at them through the sloping brow of his metal helmet. With his spear, he pointed below to a landing pad coming into view. To her surprise, Sara saw three tall and lean figures waiting there.

Sara gave a sheepish salute to their new chaperone. "Yeah, okay. We're taking it down."

The warrior nodded, firm, then flew off to rejoin his kinsmen, vanishing into the stratosphere. Johnny watched him go and looked to Sara. "A-Are we in trouble?"

Sara chewed her lip, but did not reply. She brought the glider-car into a smooth landing despite its damage, and the three figures on the landing pad gracefully moved her way. They were each at least seven feet high and covered from head to clawed toe in beautiful white feathers. At the elbows, their arms extended into majestic wings that they kept folded across their lithe bodies like cloaks. Their heads were flat on the top, but a blue-tipped plumage sprouted in the back. Their dark round eyes were spaced much further apart than a human's, in order to make room for a rosy pink beak, and each downy brow was dotted by a crown of tiny horns. The most regal of the trio took the lead, and the two that flanked carried golden spears.

Sara kept her head down as she climbed out of the car. She muttered to Johnny, "Let me handle this."

Johnny looked as if he wanted to run, but instead stood still, trembling and speechless. Sara marched to the trio then bowed before the lead. "Lady Vasariana of the Egalia, it's my honor."

The Lady dipped her feathered head in a show of respect. "The honor is mine to bear, Lady Sara of the Morrisons. We are well met, indeed."

Sara curtseyed and rose. She gestured behind her. "This is my friend…uh…"

Johnny hurried forward. "Captain Alan Worth, m'lady! Noted scientist and explorer of my people!"

The Egalian Queen peered down at the young man, amused. Sara shot her friend such a hard look she went cross-eyed. He blushed and whispered to her, "Hey, don't spoil this for me. When am I going to get this chance again?"

She groaned under her breath and once more faced the regal bird woman. "Right." A bit nervous, she said, "I had spoken so much of my last visit to Venus that my friend, *Captain Worth*, here, just had to see your breathtaking home."

The Queen seemed pleased by the compliment and bowed once more. "As you say. It is only unfortunate that you were met with such a rude welcome. In any event, it is most fortuitous that you have arrived, Lady Sara. As you have just borne witness, the Underdwellers have ascended to the High Kingdom once more to wage war against the Egalia."

Sara gauged the woman, suspicious. Even as the Egalian Queen spoke, Sara's stomach slowly seized into a painful spasm, indicating she was coming to another moral flashpoint. She pressed a hand to her stomach, trying not to betray the attack she felt coming on. *No, no, no*, she begged. *Not now*. "But Michael and I toppled their leader when we were here. Took out their entire infrastructure."

Lady Vasariana cut in, excited, "But they are no longer content to simply occupy our land. It is now a holy war they wish to wage. We've interrogated one of their advance scouts. They speak of a Great Volcano at the heart of the galaxies that breathes a pillar of Black Fire. They believe that their god will be reborn in this Black Fire and is on his way to reward them for their service. They're desperate to purge us as a tribute to him upon his return. It's prompted them to take to the skies, even though they've always feared it in the past."

Johnny paled and looked to Sara expectantly. But Sara had no words, only a hot and squishy churning in her stomach. Could the Great Volcano be the Gateworld that Aztaroth had been looking for? As for the rest, *of course* she knew the god they spoke of… and the pillar of fire…

Vasariana reached out with a delicate hand and touched Sara's arm, breaking her from her dread. "Lady Sara, we owe you our way of life, and we wouldn't ask you for your assistance again if it wasn't vital to the preservation of our entire planet—"

Sara inched away, kindly slipping from the bird-woman's gentle caress. "I'm sorry, my lady. I…I can't."

The Queen regarded her guards, who met her expression with worry and anger. Even Johnny seemed taken aback by the decision. He leaned in while the Egalia conversed among themselves and whispered in Sara's ear, "We have to help them. Right? Michael told me that, on the worlds he went to, God brought him there to help."

Sara ignored Johnny as Lady Vasariana faced her once more. The Queen was stiff and displeased, but unable to hide the desperation in her words. "Lady Sara, we are a proud people, but I beg you—"

The Queen bowed low before them, and her guards hissed in shock and outrage. One stepped forward to pull his Queen back to her feet, but she *cawed* at him, and he retracted his hand in shame. Vasariana resumed her bow, her voice broken, "Lady Sara, we fear this Black Fire and know it to be the extinction of all life. I will…I will gladly hand you my throne if that's what it will take for you to save us."

The guards muttered to each other, furious but perhaps seeing there was no other choice. Sara's head throbbed and the sickening boom-boom-boom persisted in the pit of her stomach, prompting her to make her choice.

Help them, a voice cut through the noise in her mind, and she recognized it as the one that spoke to her at Supernova. The one who stayed her hand when she meant to slay the Dun.

But she shook her head, wringing her hands. "No, I'm sorry. No, I can't. I *can't*." With a sweaty, shaking hand, she gripped Johnny's burly arm. "Come on. Let's go."

He tugged against her, bewildered. "But Sara? We—"

"Let's go!" she snapped at him, and jerked all the harder. Concentrating as Rip had taught her, she summoned the rift to her location and watched in guilty relief as it drifted along the dirty yellow skies, coming for her. She did her best not to look back at the Queen, but her conscience demanded she face her one last time.

There, Lady Vasariana remained bowed low, but what had been intended as an act of humility was now only a display of disgrace. Tears streaked her feathered face, and the Egalian monarch's eyes were cold and hard and full of hate. Sara's lip quivered in remorse.

"I'm sorry," she said, but the Queen only glowered at her, defeated and devoid of hope.

Sara hung her head and, still holding Johnny's hand, stepped into the rift as it passed, abandoning Venus to its fate.

12

Rainbow-colored lights blasted from the rift, and Sara crashed into her California home, eyes clamped shut to refuse the tears that threatened to spill. Johnny was right behind her, caught in mid-shout. "Sara, stop! We have to—"

He froze, registering their new environs. Her friend grew quiet and slowly turned in place, eyeing her bright and spacious house and the unusual collection of artifacts from her travels. Outside, she could hear the call of seagulls and the calming *shush-shush* of the waves, just like always. Only now, what once had been her oasis from a chaotic multiverse seemed more like a barb in her side when she thought of herself living in luxury while Venus—and incalculable other worlds—suffered. Sara's hatred for herself only grew.

"What is this place?" Johnny asked in an awed hush.

"It's my home," she said, without any of the pride or excitement she had imagined she'd feel when she first brought her friend here.

"Welcome home, Mistress Sara," Zeo chimed its programmed greeting, emerging from its maintenance stall in the back room.

"Whoa!" Johnny backed up as the towering Autotron peered down at him, its digital face drawing up into an exaggerated *o*.

"Oh dear," Zeo intoned in a simulation of fret. "Mistress Sara, I fear one of the primitives has breached the perimeter." The kindly droid lifted a clawed hand that whirred as it re-composed itself into an extended blaster rifle barrel. "Shall I dispose of it?"

Sara raised her hand, huffing. "It's fine, Zeo. He's with me."

The 'tron considered, then retracted its weapon. A pleasant, though artificial, smile returned to its flat face. "Very well. In that case, shall I prepare a snack?"

"Maybe later. Just give us some space, okay?"

"As you wish," it chimed, then swiveled slowly and rolled away.

Johnny gulped and faced Sara. "Is he going to kill me?"

"Probably not," she sighed in a rush, then sat on the edge of her sofa. Her hands shook, and no matter how hard she tried to hold them still, something in her gut—in her heart—would not let her escape the fact that she'd just done something horrible. *No,* she fought against the guilt. *I saved them. If I don't give into the Rage, no Black Pillar. No danger.* However, her self-justification did little to ease her conscience.

Johnny watched her, frowning. "Okay, I admit I'm new to this whole rift jumping thing, but what happened back on Venus…that was bad, wasn't it?"

174

She stood and paced to the balcony, doing her best to focus on the beautiful evening outside. The sun was setting on another perfect day in '58. Surfers rode the waves, and the neighbors were firing up their barbecue grills in their backyards. Everyone was happy here, warm and relaxed.

"Sara?" Johnny braved.

She stared at the orange sun disappearing over the choppy waters. "It's complicated, all right?"

"Yeah, you said that already. Does it have anything to do with you and Michael breaking up?"

A weight settled on her chest, making her breathing labored and painful. At last, she stifled a cry and whispered, "I'm not the same person I was when I left home."

Johnny sat down, patiently watching her. "Okay. I'm listening."

She leaned the back of her head against the patio door frame and faced him. "I did some things that I'm not proud of…but I can't take them back."

"Why not?" he interjected. His tone wasn't judgmental, but sympathetic. Sara missed that the most about her friend.

"I…I just can't, okay?" she said, defeated. "I've got this ticking time bomb inside of me and…" She rubbed her face, willing herself not to cry. "You know that Black Fire that Lady Vasariana was so afraid of? Well…it's me. I'm the one who's going to cause it."

Johnny's eyes widened, then drooped. "Oh. Crap."

"There's this *thing* growing inside of me," she confessed. "It's this alien entity called the Rage. Every time I fight, It gets a little bit stronger. It's trying to get out, and if it does, then…terrible things are going to happen."

Sara realized that this was, perhaps, the first time she'd ever voiced her fate aloud. Hearing herself form the words—admitting the ugly truth—felt like an anvil slamming down and flattening her soul. Her throat tightened until at last she could hold back no longer. Overwhelmed, she finally wept, collapsing to the couch, burying her face in her hands, shamed by her disease.

"I'm so sorry," she sobbed, not even understanding to whom she was apologizing or which of her multitude of sins she was hoping to atone. She was just sorry. For *everything*. For absolutely everything.

Johnny was instantly at her side, embracing her shuddering frame. "It's okay," he whispered.

She shook her head fiercely then leaned into his chest. "No, it's not. It's *not*…"

"Isn't there anyone who can help?"

Sara laughed through burning tears, angry and sarcastic. "Oh, I'm sure *Michael* could come up with some crazy plan to bend heaven and the Earths to make a way…"

"Then go find him!" Johnny exclaimed. "What are you waiting for?"

She jumped to her feet, outraged. "*No!* You don't get it, Johnny! You *never* get it!"

Now Johnny rose, his broad shoulders expanding, provoked. His face grew uncharacteristically stern, and he growled, "Then why don't you enlighten me?"

She cooled, knowing she had offended him. But she couldn't let these words go unsaid. "My whole life, I've always been weak. I get scared, and I run to someone—anyone—to protect me. I did it with Charlie, I did it with Michael." She released a sigh and waved a dismissive hand at Johnny. "Now, I'm even doing it with *you*. I'm sick of it. I'm sick of being so *pathetic*."

Faced with her tirade, Johnny crossed his meaty arms and scrutinized her. "So you're just going to pound on your chest and handle this on your own, huh? Even if it means you fail and start spouting black fire or whatever?" He smirked. "I gotta say, you're kind of dumb."

She snarled at him and clenched a fist, then slumped. Chuckled, cried some more, then laughed. "Shut up."

He relaxed and stepped forward, pulling her into a hug. "What's 'pathetic' is facing something like this all by yourself and pushing away the people who care about you. If you ask me, *that's* always been your problem."

She pulled from him, studying his round face, taking in all the compassion and acceptance she found there.

Johnny continued, still cradling her, though now at a distance. "As long as I've known you, I've watched you wanting to be somewhere else. Wanting to be *someone* else. It always broke my heart that you never saw how wonderful you are. How beautiful and smart and strong you've always been—"

"Johnny…"

Suddenly blushing, he released her and ruffled his hair awkwardly. "Look, I know you're never going to see me as anything more than a friend. I'm kinda fat, and I smell sorta funny when I get nervous, and I collect shrunken heads, and read way too many comic books."

She laughed, caught off guard by his candor. The release was wonderful.

He grinned and finished, "But that's me. And I like me." Shrugging, he rambled, "*Maya* likes me. I think." Growing serious, he said, "What I'm saying is, you've got to stop trying to be something you're not and accept who you are. Mistakes and all. But accept the good things, too. So, yeah, you picked up some weird parasite out here in the multiverse. And, yeah, maybe that means you could turn into some sort of weird tentacle-y beast thingie."

She rolled her eyes. "Thaaanks."

"But I say 'screw that'. *Fight* it. Let people help you. Beat this thing and take back your life."

Sara considered his earnest charge, wondering when the silly boy she'd shared science fiction stories with had turned into a man. "Maya's really lucky," she said around a smirk.

"Meh."

She giggled and hugged him. "Thanks, stupid-head."

"You're welcome, ya big dummy."

When they parted, it was all smiles. "So what now?" Sara asked.

Johnny stretched and groaned, breaking the tension. "I need to be getting back home. I think I might have fooled around and actually gotten myself a life. Besides, you've got more important things to be doing, making sure this Rage thing doesn't get out."

She nodded, knowing he was right, but still a bit sad to see him go. "Okay. Is it all right if I come visit sometimes?"

"Sure. But try and keep your hands off me. Maya can be jealous."

She snickered and extended a hand, which he shook. "Deal."

13

Broken bodies lay scattered about the ashen landscape like so much refuse to be gathered for the fire. Demolished buildings—abandoned and crumbling—stared with open faces at a stranger wandering through their world. The Master moved about the destruction, admiring the husk of a city that once thrived with beauty and compassion. Even the sky, now, was dead and grey, emptied of wind, of sound, of life. A permanent chill clung to every wrecked car, to every hollowed-out structure, and slithered in and out of every crevice on this planet-wide graveyard.

Ahead, the last fortress of Chelkan stood like a silent sentinel over the spoiling corpses haplessly discarded to his right and his left. The structure was circular by design, double-leveled and open at the top. Barbed wire and mounted ebon spikes protruded from every square inch, creating a protective shell for the frightened men, women, and children who once hid within its walls. The Master's open-mouthed grin widened at the sight of the desolate outpost, his memory stirred. He remembered this place and the last great battle that had occurred here, but only as a dream. Indeed, he'd been there at that battle, but merely as a presence; he'd experienced it through the eyes of his faithful servant. Many had stood against his pale servant in that splendid hour of horrors, but his servant had felled them all, including the soldier known as Holstead. To finally be here in the flesh, so to speak, left the Master with a strange displaced sensation. Tapping into the mind of his current host, the Master attempted to conjure a proper analogy for his mood, at last settling on a picture: that of a viewer entering into a movie he knew by heart. Everything was immediately familiar—but only from a distance. Finally able to physically step into this world, the Master noted that Chelkan was magnified in vivid detail that he'd never been able to perceive while only living vicariously through those who had welcomed his dark taint into their souls. The experience was marvelous, but too easily stole his attention from his work.

And there *was* much work to be done.

The Master crossed the ruined threshold of the fortress, stepping across a floor of bodies. Human soldiers in armor attracted flies. He searched their faces, passing each one over until, at last, his white eyes rested on Sergeant Kleg Holstead, the magnanimous leader of this remnant of survivors. The valiant warrior was freshly dead, his body still cooling from the battle that had ended only an hour before, a peaceful countenance about his haggard face. Beside the soldier, the Master's own former vassal: the boy, one of many Michael Morrisons scattered about the multiverse. The fair youth—alabaster-skinned and clothed in black leather—was recently defeated as well, viscous obsidian blood oozing from the grievous stomach wound that released his soul to its final reward.

"Chiiiiillllld," the Master rattled, and knelt to the shattered concrete floor beside the body. He held out his hands, and the black sludge that bled from the boy changed direction, awakened to sentience, and raced for him. The Master shut his eyes in ecstasy as that part of him that had dwelt in the boy returned home and joined his own tar-like flesh, snaking up his arm to mingle with its kin. He moaned in delight and stood, feeling a new sense of completion.

With that business completed, the Master turned his attention to his other reasons for visiting Chelkan. Stretched over the theater of war, his marvelous creations loomed like grotesque statues over the victims they'd claimed. Impossibly balanced on the knuckles of curled toes and the deadly tips of their insect-like forearms, the grey, hairless figures hunkered on all fours. Their smooth faces—barren of eyes, nose, and ears—opened at too-wide mouths that matched their father's split grin. Cracked, blunt teeth filled those overlarge mouths, teeth that had chattered incessantly as they feasted on the denizens of many worlds. Now, however, the chattering was silenced; the teeth were still. Without the boy—or rather, without the Master's presence *within* the boy—the creatures languished like dying vines. Their mutated flesh was stony and fissured like the surface of ancient rocks, and the creatures slumped, motionless, their bodies bending towards the earth in surrender.

The sight of his children in such a state stirred great pity within the Master.

Known on a thousand worlds as the Grey Death, the Unspeakable Flood, and the Infernal Horde, the army of monsters had been the first of the Master's machinations to wreak destruction among the planes of the multiverse. He had hoped that their conquest would lead to the discovery of the source of the dimensional splits—the Gateworld—and unlock the door of his prison. Through the obedient angel Aztaroth, the first to hear his Song from his confinement, the Master had culled vassals from every reality, blessing them with his gifts, bestowing upon them new bodies and new minds, uplifting them to be the mighty hand of his reach. Over the centuries, Aztaroth's recruits were pitted against one another time and again to determine who would serve as the general of this army. Even angels sought to control the hellish soldiers, like the brutish Molok, who had warred for millennia over the right to command the Horde. Yet, none of them wielded the power to *truly* lead them—none but the Master who had created them—but to lead them himself had never been an option. At best, he had imagined he'd only be able to utilize his proxy, like Michael Morrison or one of his many equally lethal counterparts, to take charge of his servants.

But that was before Mother. Mother had changed everything.

Now the Master was here, a powerful host in his possession, able to physically walk through the rank and file. Able to admire the blasphemous beauty of his army up close. He prided himself in their profane construction and hoped that God shivered at the mere sight of them.

He stepped to the nearest twisted devil, this one still erect, with its mouth frozen in a silent howl to the darkening skies, and placed his hand against the beast's petrified cheek.

"Awaaake," the Master breathed.

Slowly, the grey creature trembled, then jerked its head to the side, shattering a portion of the hard exterior that had formed over its dying flesh. With tremendous effort, it raised its spear-like arm, loose rock breaking free. The Master smiled at his creation until, at last, the monster was freed of its prison. It galloped about, teeth clacking once more in hungry zeal. Lifting its head high, it screamed, bringing to life its brethren. The Master watched in delight as his children woke from their stony slumber and raised a ravenous cry to the heavens.

Yes. It was time, now. Time to begin.

Time to find Mother.

14

Sara and Johnny returned home, laughing and reminiscing about the woes of high school that had seemed so important back then, but so silly now. The sun had set in their village, and silver-blue moonlight shone through the sky dome above. Sara's arm interlocked with her friend's and she hugged him close.

"Thanks for everything," she said, beaming. "I really needed this."

"Happy to help. You know, if you ever get tired of running, you can always come back here. I might even give you a job."

She snorted in amusement and squeezed tighter. "I'm not so sure Maya would approve."

"Ha, ha, yeah, on second thought, she—"

Johnny halted, surprising Sara. She glanced at him, her smile becoming a frown as she watched his chubby face grow pale.

"What is it?" she asked, then followed his line of sight down the street to the store. "Oh no..."

While the rest of the village seemed cleared out for the night, the area around the entrance to SUPERNATURAL SURPLUS was crowded by throngs of men and women on their knees, bowing low in rhythmic repetition and lifting their hands to the darkened storefront windows. The worshippers chanted in unison, raising a haunting psalm in an unknown language to the vaulted glass ceiling.

"What *is* this?" Johnny snapped, in a whisper. His eyes widened in sudden understanding and he turned to Sara.

She frowned. "The rift."

The duo raced forward, wading deep into the bowing crowds. The worshippers ignored the interlopers and continued their pattern, moaning and weeping as they sang praises to their dark god.

"This is bad," Sara shouted over their loud invocations.

Johnny glanced up. "Look!"

Sara spotted Nana and Maya on the edge of the multitude, their faces ashen with terror. Maya saw Johnny and sidestepped the mob to reach him. She collided into his arms for a brief, but tight squeeze. When they separated, Sara could see that she was clearly frightened, but relieved to have Johnny near her. "Where were you? We looked everywhere—"

"It's okay," he soothed. "I'm here. When did *this* happen?"

She shook her head, smoothing her frizzy locks away from her face, staring at the chilling display. "I don't know. Maybe an hour? They just...they were just here!" Maya eyed Sara in accusation. "What did you do?"

Sara huffed, struggling to understand. "I didn't do anything. I don't know what this..." She touched Johnny's arm, a dreaded realization entering her mind. "We have to check on the rift."

"What, the *wall?*" Maya said.

Johnny held his girlfriend off. "Stay here, okay? We'll be right back."

Maya made to protest, but Johnny was already moving to the forefront of the congregation, with Sara close behind. They reached the locked door, and he fumbled to dig the store keys out of his pocket. Sara flexed her empty fists, missing the familiar weight of the chukrahas. "I really need a weapon."

Johnny nodded in a hurry, opening the door and slipping inside. "I've got a gun in a safe under the counter. Come on."

Once the door was opened, the worshippers outside immediately stood erect, crying and shouting in joy. "He is coming!" a woman announced at the top of her lungs. Soon, all of them stretched their fingers to the darkened heavens, exclaiming, "He is coming! He is coming! *He is coming!*"

Sara followed Johnny inside and slammed the door shut, locking it tight. "Crazies."

Her friend rounded the counter and disappeared from sight, working at the lock of the small safe he kept back there. After a moment, he popped back up, a tiny revolver in his hand. "Here!"

Sara took the piece and eyed it, disappointed by its size. "This is it? This is all you've got?"

He faltered, then shrugged. "Sorry. Wasn't really expecting to defend my dimension from some evil alien deity, you know?"

She checked the rounds in the cylinder, counting a full load, then crossed the room to the back curtain. Sara touched the edge of the fabric and prepared to pull it back, but paused to speak to Johnny over her shoulder. "Look, you'd…uh…better go. Take Maya and your Nana and—"

"And what? Catch a transport at *this* hour? Where we gonna go? No. I'm staying right here. I opened that door in the first place. It's my responsibility to make sure it stays closed."

Wham! Johnny and Sara both jumped and looked to the front glass. The crazed zealots banged their fists, their palms—even their foreheads—against the store windows, trying to get in.

"God…" Sara breathed, finding it ironic that she'd call on the Almighty now. Would he even help her, after all that she'd done to rebel against him?

Frustrated, she grabbed Johnny's arm and pulled him behind her. They backed away, watching in stunned silence as the worshippers continued to throw themselves at the storefront, finally cracking the glass into a fine spiderweb. The jagged glass cut into the skin of those seeking to get inside, drawing blood. Crimson flowed from nicks in hands, arms, and heads, but the mob only wailed and sang, pleading to be blessed, begging for ascendance.

"Go!" Sara barked and shoved Johnny beyond the curtain. She watched the glass breaking away, bit by bit, worried what would happen when the zealots finally got in. She didn't have enough bullets for them all, and they'd soon swarm her. In what she felt certain were her final moments, she thought of Michael and Toby. Wished they were with her.

Get over it, Sara. You're on your own.

But she wasn't. No, she had Johnny now. He certainly wasn't the warrior

Michael was—or even Toby, for that matter—but he had a big heart. He was her heart, and she would protect him, no matter what. She'd abandoned too many already. *Not again.*

Grimacing as the worshippers tore away chunks of shattered glass with their cut, bleeding hands, Sara finally turned her back on them and ducked inside the reading room—

Only to find that the portal had already opened. Brick and dust lay scattered about the floor, ruining the altar, and Sara gaped into the yawning chasm of the eternal night of the Void. Wind from the vacuum of the In-Between stirred the debris and pulled at her, awakening the familiar and sickening boom-boom-boom in her abdomen. It called to her, begged her to lose herself forever in infinity, and for the briefest moment, she considered it.

"Sara!" Johnny shouted for her, and she snapped to, looking for him, only to see him pinned to the wall, his face marred by tearful sorrow, as a grey insect-like claw lanced through the meat of his shoulder.

Indeed, something had already breached the portal.

"Johnny!" She aimed her pistol at the hairless apish devil that held her friend in place. The creature had no eyes or nose—just a mouth and fat, cracked teeth that chattered at a high speed. "Stop!" she begged, and the thing turned as if to regard her, its clacking growing louder.

Suddenly, another spear slapped her gun away and knocked her across the room. She shook the stars from her sight and saw a second mutation prancing around her, pulling itself out of the pit. And behind that one, still another shape crawled out of the Void… Her stomach churned heavily, and she cried out in startled misery. A blackened figure, his obsidian flesh made of something like eels or snakes that writhed into the form of a man, stepped into the room, the majority of his vague shape obscured in a cloak of animal furs like the one Rip kept at his desert hovel. And the thing's face was hideous, the darkness there broken only by two bright white eyes and equally sparkling teeth that widened into a smile twice the size of a normal human's.

The profane man-thing stepped closer to her, its ivory orbs probing her, as its mouth opened to hiss, "Motherrrr…"

She scrambled away at the sound of the voice, shrieking in shock. "No! No, stay away!" For she had seen that face before; she had heard that voice. It was the Shape beyond the rift, in the black spaces between the worlds. It was the Rage, given flesh. "Stay away!" she railed against the monster, crying. "Stop!"

"Sara," Johnny spat, grimacing painfully as he squirmed like a butterfly tacked to a board. "What…"

The grey beast twisted its claw and Johnny shouted, fresh tears of pain pouring from his eyes. Blood gushed from his wound. Trembling, Sara turned to the Shape, stuttering, "W-Who…H-How… I don't understand. How is this possible?"

The Shape crouched before her, tilting its head from side to side, exhaling a long, putrid breath that soured Sara's stomach. As It neared, the Rage's seed within her came alive, rattling against her insides, the way the cultists outside had beaten against the window. Trying to break the barrier. Trying to be reunited with the Shape.

"Motherrr…" the Shape croaked.

"Why do you call me 'Mother'?" she screamed, sobbing.

"Yooouuuu gaaave me liiiiffeee…"

"No!" She cried uncontrollably now. "That's not possible! I stopped you from getting out! I didn't create the Black Pillar! I—"

"There iiiisss anotherrrr…"

Her cries were silenced. "Wh-What?"

The Shape rose to Its feet, spreading Its chest proudly. Without any show of discomfort, It reached into Its wriggling flesh and pulled, ripping Itself apart with the sounds of snapping elastic. Sara clamped her hand over her mouth, screaming through her fingers, tears nearly blinding her. For there, in a deep slumber encased in a cocoon of black ooze…

Was Toby.

"*NOOO!*" she screeched herself hoarse.

The smiling devil released Its chest and the slimy flesh regrew over the sleeping child, imprisoning him once more. Sara doubled over, crying all the breath out of her lungs. She gasped and shook, and again the Shape spoke, Its voice like a chill wind blowing through a graveyard, "Yooouuuu maaaaddee meee, Motherr… Just as yooouu were alllwaaaayyys meant tooo. Now I haaaaveee returrrned to take yoou home to your rewaaaarrd."

But Sara no longer cared. She barely heard the monster. All her thoughts focused on Toby. *It's all my fault…*

She'd been running for so long, but now she knew that the damage had already been done. Rip had been right all along; she was never going to outrun her fate.

"Get away!" a voice broke Sara from her grief.

She saw Maya entering the back room, her clothes torn, her hair mangled, and her face bloodied. Behind her, the crowds pressed in like a legion of zombies, groping for her, for the rift, for their master. Maya stepped forward, her eyes lit with a righteous fire, and plucked the small revolver off the floor. She planted her feet and took aim at the Shape. Through gritted teeth, she demanded, "I. Said. Get. Away."

"Maya, no," Johnny coughed from his place on the wall.

Seeing him in so much pain threatened to shake Maya's resolve, but she narrowed her eyes, took aim, and fired off a round at the Shape. The bullet merely disappeared into the folds of black serpents that formed Its body, and Maya's face fell. Immediately, the zealots surpassed her, dragging her back, prying the useless gun from her hand.

Sara watched the young woman bravely struggling against them, unable to help her. The speed of the world seemed to lapse into slow motion. She turned her head to see Johnny trying to dislodge the claw buried deep in his shoulder, shouting Maya's name all the while. They were going to die—*all* of them—and she'd brought this damnation. Guilt, fear, and anger pressed against her from all directions until she thought she'd explode.

"Stop!" Sara roared and stood. "Get away from her!" she barked at the zealots, pushing the black into her eyes, letting the Rage within speak through her. Recognizing their god inside her, the zombies released Maya and she tumbled forward, breathing heavily, but okay. Now, the worshippers fell to the ground, cowering before Sara's majesty, shielding their faces from her wrath.

"Good," she snapped, recalling that day she left Michael and Toby. "You *should* be afraid."

Leveling her dark-eyed gaze at the Shape, she fought against the blatant fear in her heart and faced It without flinching. The Rage-Thing's expression, on the other hand, was lit up like a kid on Christmas morning as It beheld her. "Motherrr…"

"Leave them alone," she ordered It, realizing she had nothing to bargain with. Nothing to offer.

Nothing but herself.

Trembling, but determined, she declared, "It's me you want, right? I'm your Mother? Fine. Take me."

The pair of grey devils turned their attention to her, and the one holding Johnny released him at once. Sara's friend collapsed to the floor, clutching his wound and hissing through strained teeth. Maya yelped and raced for him, cradling him protectively. Sara smiled at them, bittersweet. "I'm sorry," she told Johnny. "I never should have come back. But I'll fix this."

He gawked at her. "What are you doing?"

She ignored him and faced the Shape once more. "Take *me*," she said again as the grey monsters scurried around her perimeter, their spear-arms clacking on the hardwood floor. "I've been running long enough. It's time this ended. But you have to do something for me."

"Anythiiiinng, Motherrr…" It cooed, like a child. "Anything for yooouuu…"

Her eyes flicked to Johnny and she felt the blackness in them melt away. "Leave this world alone. In your… in your terrible glory, you must spare these

184

people."

The Shape frowned. "Oh, Motherrr…"

"I'm your mother!" she commanded, pouring steel into her voice. "And I'm ordering you, as your mother, to leave them alone!"

The Shape considered, then nodded, its mouth opening in delight. "Yesss, Motherrrr… I will save them…for laaaassst."

She gulped, but knew that was the best she could do for now. Maybe if she could just get the Shape out of here, figure things out, she could save Johnny from the destruction to come. "All right," she said, doing her best to sound authoritative, though she felt like she might wet her pants at any moment. "That's that, then. I'm…ready. Let's go."

The Shape clapped Its hands together in giddy excitement, Its unblinking eyes looming nearer. "Yessss… There issss so much for youuu to seeee…"

It moved closer to her, tenderly and almost reverently, she noticed. This thing exuded pure power, but It was still only a baby.

Her baby, born from her arrogance and rage.

I'm so sorry, Toby. I'll get you out of there. I'll make everything okay. I promise.

The Shape approached her and put a black, slippery hand to her forehead. She clamped her eyes shut and screamed, dimly aware that Johnny was hollering her name. Then, to her horror, the floorboards beneath her bucked and upended, and her ears were filled with the howls of the damned. She heard the clanging of steel and smelled burning sulfur, and she knew. Oh, she knew…

Hell was below, opening its mouth to receive her.

Sara shivered and bawled in misery as she was pulled down, down into the ground, off to inherit her final reward.

PART NINE: END OF THE LINE

1

A rift tore open like a wound in reality, spilling rainbow-colored light. The Master stepped into the cramped alley alone, admiring his new environs. The sounds and smells of the filthy human ghetto assaulted his senses, and a torrential downpour pelted him from above. In just a moment, his new clothes were completely soaked. Gone, now, were the animal furs that he'd procured from Rip. Now the Master wore a long black leather trenchcoat to conceal the dark serpents that comprised his shape. A matching black stocking cap covered the top and sides of his head, leaving only his face exposed.

The Master exited the trash-laden alley and trod through the equally polluted streets of the human settlement, unnoticed by the grimy dwellers of this dilapidated encampment. The people milled about aimlessly, lost and without purpose, occupying themselves with idle chatter, drink, or narcotics. Roaming like ominous storm clouds overhead, large circular ships—alien to this planet— kept a cold and constant vigil over the humans. Chain link fences laced with electricity hemmed in the displaced refugees, sapping them of resolve. The people were dead-eyed and lazy, squabbling with each other over the simplest issues. They were a pitiful sight, like wounded animals begging to be put out of their misery.

But at last the Master had come to put an end to their suffering.

He was drawn here by a force other than his will. It was a new sensation that aroused curiosity in him. Curiosity—another emotion alien to his nature. The Master paused, considering that revelation, as well: "His". Funny, he considered that he'd never had a gender before, but had since adopted the sex of his young host. It was his young host who had brought him here, to this world.

He knew, now, that it was also his young host who had convinced him to grant Mother's request and spare her world, when he had every intention of destroying it upon his arrival. Mercy was a sign of weakness, and he regretted that decision now, but still couldn't bring himself to return to Mother's dimension and visit upon it his horrors. Closing his eyes, summoning his strength, the Master shoved down the boy's voice in his mind. He worried that his host had more influence over his behavior than had been expected. The boy—Toby—was still strong within him, and the Master feared to what extent the boy could control him. If only he could remove the boy! But the Master knew he was not yet strong enough to exist without being bound to his host. It was his host who anchored him to the worlds beyond his prison in the In-Between.

Soon, though, if he only could reach the Gateworld, he could shatter the lock of his cage and be free. No longer merely a ghost possessing the living, but a being in his own right, in his full power. In his full truth. And then Chaos would spread, blotting out all Light.

In the meantime, his powers were beginning to waken, giving him the strength, he believed, to destroy at least one bar in his cage. But he must test the extent of that might, and this dimension, the Master knew, would be the easiest to shatter. The boy deemed it so.

The Master moved between the raindrops, his naked feet settling on the threshold of an unkempt lawn. Motorcycles were parked arbitrarily on the overgrown grounds, and big-bellied men in chaps and denim staggered about the porch, shouting and laughing obscenities at the rain while chugging away on mind-numbing drink. Women in various modes of dress tipped and swayed between their brutish companions, squealing in delight. So lost were they in their revelry, it took some time for the Master's presence to be noticed. He stood before them, still as a statue, until at last a woman caught sight of him. Her giggling instantly ceased. She tapped on her beaus and the men gaped at him, then laughed.

"What do *you* want?" one hollered across the cluttered yard.

The Master's grin parted and he exhaled, "Tanyaaa…"

The bikers froze at the unearthly sound of his voice floating across the yard, then one brave fool hurled a beer can that bounced off the sleeve of the Master's coat. "Get lost!" the hairy man with expanded gut bellowed, immediately earning him a round of laughter from his drunken brethren.

The Master did not flinch, just continued to stand and smile, drawing more threats and hollers from the miscreants. Then, without warning, he extended his hand. Five jets of black sludge exploded from his fingertips, stretched the length of the yard, and grabbled the can-throwing scuzzo by the throat. The biker gurgled, bug-eyed, then gagged as the Master hefted him high into the air, crashing him through the porch overhang and showering those beneath it in wood and dust and rain. They screamed and ran for cover. With a twist of his wrist, the Master released the biker, tossing him into the air, his screams echoing until he finally landed with a bloody thud on the pavement some distance away.

More screams. Gunshots, as the bikers retaliated, firing shotguns or pistols. The Master spread his arms and accepted their offerings, grinning all the while. Another jet of black tore through his chest and slapped away the fleet of motorcycles, crushing a few fleeing partyers under hunks of metal. Screams wafted into the air like the sweet smell of burning incense, and the Master's mouth widened until a low, growling chuckle dribbled out.

A piercing tone split the scene, followed by a booming robotic command: "ATTENTION, HUMANS. VIOLENCE OF THIS SCALE WILL NOT BE TOLERATED. LEAVE OR SUFFER PENALTY."

The Master craned to look over his shoulder and saw three small rotating cylinders, with hundreds of blinking lights, spinning in the air, issuing the command once more, "ATTENTION, HUMANS. VIOLENCE OF THIS SCALE WILL NOT BE TOLERATED. LEAVE OR—"

He swatted at the alien drones with a large oily tentacle, obliterating them with ease in a cascade of sparks.

The crack of a shotgun brought his attention back to the house. He turned and beheld a lanky blonde woman emerging from the ruined porch. She wore a wrinkled slip, her exposed legs and bare feet covered in scabs and bruises. Her mouth, too, was blistered, and her dilated eyes circled by deep shadows. In her bone-thin arms, she held the fired shotgun.

In that moment, the Master knew her. "Tanyaaaa…."

The woman trembled as she took a step forward, aiming the barrel at the Master. "I-I'm Tanya Jeffries," she stammered, nearly weeping. "W-What do you want?"

The Master surveyed the carnage he had created in such a short time, then beheld the woman, tilting his head to the side. "Weeeee have returned hommmeee, Motherrrr…"

All color drained from her face, and Tanya lowered the gun. The Master reached into his chest and pulled apart his black flesh, exposing the boy to her. Tanya tripped backwards, gagging and sputtering, "T-Toby?"

"Youuuu should have beeennn nicerrrr to the child…"

"Toby? Toby!"

The Master sneered as a flood of black unfurled from within him, encircling the petrified mother. She jerked against his restraints, even as the goo submerged her, but he poured more hate into his flesh, tightening, tightening, *tightening*. Inside, he felt a flicker of fear from the boy. A child's plea—*Don't! You said you would just scare her! Don't hurt her!*

But the Master had already given in once to his host's sentimental nature. No more. He buried the boy's will deep inside and continue to strangle the woman until, at last, he felt the snap of bone. Heard the squishy pop of this frail creature. The Master retracted his blackness, and Tanya's ruined body collapsed in a heap. In the distance, an alarm was raised. More drones filled the skies, responding to his devastation. The streets were crammed with the fleeing and the frightened. He drank in their panic, soaked in their horror, and looked to the rainy skies. Yes, he was ready now. He was finally strong enough.

This dimension would be the first of many.

The Master beheld the swirling clouds. Forked purple lightning streaked across the sky, followed by a ground-rattling peal of thunder. Dozens of terrified humans raced past him, but the Master ignored them, focusing only on his task. He opened his hands to the stormy sky and loosed a primal howl. The heavens ripped open, and beyond the darkness the Master saw…it.

A pillar of swirling, crackling black energy plummeted from the starless void in the skies. The sinister twister punched one of the large motherships out of orbit, then slammed into the earth a block away, instantly vaporizing nearby buildings. Screams intensified as the whole city—this whole world—raised their cries in a single unified shriek. People stumbled over one another, bolting from the storm.

But it was useless.

The vortex ripped them off their feet, dragging men, women, and children through the air, churning them in the evil black-flaming pillar. Only the Master remained unaffected, watching, slipping his hands into his coat pockets. The whirling tower devoured everything and everyone in sight, until the very fabric of reality itself cracked. The alien drones and their master ships, buildings, pieces of the street—the sky itself—broke loose and hurtled for that pillar. This reality was coming to an end, just as the Gateworld—and after that, the multiverse—would soon follow.

The Master watched the murder of an entire dimension in delight, his smile widening, his hungry, lidless eyes enlarging. After a moment of exhilaration, he simply turned his back, opened another gash in reality, and left this world to die.

2

Sara choked for breath and opened her eyes, but saw nothing but the oppressive black that pushed against her. She was immediately bombarded by unsettling sounds—the hiss of steam, the clanging of metal, and petrified shrieks that could only loosely be considered "human". Her hands were cold and wet, and she realized she was lying prone on the ground. The metal floor beneath her was slick with a slimy ichor that seeped through the knees of her jeans. She shivered, a deep chill settling into her bones and joints. She rolled to a sitting position and clutched her knees to her chest, trembling, weeping, and frightened by the inhuman wails that echoed about her. Worse than the freezing cold, worse than the disorientation, there arose within her the awful truth:

This was hell. And she was in it.

She began to cry harder now as the pained howls of the tormented flooded her mind. "Please…" she begged, though to whom she was begging and what she expected to receive, she did not know. Her words were cut short, shut off by the tightness in her chest as she wept. Her mind bombarded her with memories of her life. She heard every laugh, saw every smile, felt the warmth that every good deed brought to her heart—and knew that was all gone. She'd never hold a loved one again, never feel the sun on her face, never race barefoot along the green fields of any of a thousand worlds. No more books, no more bad TV, no more music, no more life. No more love or hope or wonder or joy or—

"God!" she wept, her chest constricting painfully. No God. She'd turned him away, and now there was nothing. Nothing at all, but the cold, dank…

A sliver of light struck her face, catching her sight. Through puffy, stinging eyes, she looked up and saw a crack in the wall, bleeding a dancing orange glow. Still sniffling, Sara crawled to the thin crevice and pushed her face against it. There was light out there, emitting from some burning furnace that she could not see, whose heat did not reach her. Rusted catwalks crisscrossed in every direction, and pipes and ports wove through the framework like vines, spitting violent gouts of steam at regular intervals and dripping with moisture. Through her crack in the wall, she glimpsed a factory of nightmares lit only by fire. And in that wicked firelight, deformed shadows prowled about, snapping at each other, baying and moaning and yowling. Sara clamped a hand to her mouth to force back the bile, fresh tears dotting her eyelashes. Though she couldn't quite make out the definition of those forms, she recognized by their apish gait that they were the same grey, hairless, mantis-clawed creatures that the Shape had brought to her homeworld.

The creatures scurried along the catwalks and even climbed the rafters, their sharpened spears clanking on the metal. The ceaseless chattering of their teeth carried easily in the sonorous factory, rattling the pipes and even Sara's insides. Suddenly, a pair of clattering incisors, which belonged to a featureless head, appeared directly beyond the gash. Sara yelped and dropped backwards, as the creature—though devoid of eyes—seemed to have spotted her. Its chittering intensified in pitch as it stabbed at the small opening with its arm. A tremendous buzzing grew outside her enclosure, and Sara feared more of those bug monsters were forming up just beyond the wall. Their roar drowned out her own screams as talons scraped along the metal, digging at the hole, working to tear the steel.

"*No!*" Sara wailed, covering her ears, her heart on the verge of exploding.

At last, the misshapen monster peeled back a small portion of the wall, the metal giving way with an ear-splitting screech. The creature had just enough room to shove its head inside, jerking it from side to side, its teeth rattling, chipping its front flat teeth as a clear viscous drool oozed from its mouth. Just as Sara feared, beyond that one were more hideous abominations of flesh, calling for her, reaching for her, ready to devour her whole.

Sara braced her back against the wall and kicked with her boot, connecting with the thing's slick, pulpy head. With one foot she pushed on the animal, and with the other she shoved against the popping wall, as if she could keep these things out. Her hands roved wildly in panic. "Stop! No! *Stop!*"

Something square-shaped dropped beside her and landed hard on the floor with a sharp, reverberating crash. She screamed in fright and glanced to it. It was a grate covering. Fearful and confused, she jerked her head upwards and spotted a hole in the ceiling, leading to—*what? A duct?* There, half-concealed by the shadows of the air duct, a man. One she recognized, his face filling her with equal parts trepidation and relief. He was tall and lean, even thinner than the last time she'd seen him, with short, tight curly hair that was almost white. His gaunt face, still marred by a mouth-shaped scar on his cheek where she'd once bitten him, lit up with urgency. "Sara!"

Sara momentarily forgot the hordes grabbing for her. "Chris?"

Chris Thompson lay on his stomach and extended a hand for her to take. "Come on!"

Sara nervously regarded the beasts that had nearly torn their way inside, then abandoned her stance against them, scraping along the floor to stretch for the proffered hand. Chris' pale face reddened with exertion as he pulled up, giving Sara just enough room to grab onto the outer edge and crawl into the darkened duct.

"Hurry," Chris breathed quietly, scurrying down the shaft. "This way."

Sara lowered her voice, too, grateful to hear the devils' chattering growing faint behind her. "W-Where are we? What is this place? Is this… Is this hell?"

He huffed up ahead, still crawling. "Sure. Might as well be. It's where we go to get processed."

"We?"

He paused to look over his shoulder at her, his smudged face cloaked in great regret. "All of us who sold our souls to the Rage."

She frowned, her eyes lowering. "Oh."

Chris picked up the pace, leading Sara down the narrow corridor and rounding a bend. "We gotta keep moving. I'll fill you in later. Let's just try and get through in one piece."

Sara nodded dumbly. "O-Okay."

He came to a sudden stop and offered her a brief sincere smile over his shoulder. "It's good to see you, Sara."

"You, too," she chuckled through a sob, finding it ironic. The last time she'd seen Chris, he was with the Maestro's firestarter army, trying to kill her. Funny who one's friends turned out to be in hell.

"You cut your hair. I like it." Then he grunted, turning a corner and shimmying ahead. "Down here."

Firelight shone through more grates on the floor, casting bending beams of light across the walls of the duct. Sara passed by one opening and paused to look through the mesh to the factory below. The place seemed to stretch to infinity with no single design in mind. It was like an M.C. Escher maze, with no up or down, no pattern, no rhyme or reason. Just endless walkways, pipes, and large bulky chains that stretched in every direction—with every surface covered by roaming packs of those grey creatures. The sheer enormity and impossibility of the place threatened to undo Sara's already waning sanity, and she shut her eyes against the sprawling steelworks.

Swallowing hard, she muttered, "How big is this place?"

Chris snickered with contempt. "How big is forever, right?"

Metal groaned in their wake, and Sara halted, turning sharply behind her. There, in the dark recesses of the narrow duct—

"They're coming!" she shouted, watching in dumbstruck terror as the grey creatures scraped and clawed forward. For her.

"Move!" Chris roared and picked up the pace. Sara doubled her efforts as well, sliding along her belly, her fingers digging into every crevice, trying to pull herself along. The rattling of teeth rebounded off the walls of the cramped corridor, and Sara could not stifle a whimper. Tears clung to her eyes, but she blinked past them and crawled.

Soon, she felt something press against her boots and threw a haphazard look behind her to see she was practically standing on the head of the nearest monster, its sharpened talons too pinned by the confinement to stab at her. Instead, it just reached out with its wide mouth, biting at the thick soles of her boots.

Chkchkchkchk!

She screamed. "Chris!"

Up ahead, he said, "We have to—"

But that was as far as he made it before the flooring beneath them gave way and Sara crashed through a large grate, tumbling in freefall. She hollered all the way down, catching glimpses of Chris as he plummeted alongside her. With no time to orient herself, she merely fell end over end until finally catching her ribs on the side of a large, steel pipe. She coughed the air out of her lungs, toppling backwards, clipping the railing of a catwalk, then crashing two more floors down before laying out on the floor of some dungeon-like room.

She sucked in breath, her body singing with shock and pain. "Chris!" she croaked, still unable to breathe, to think. Clanging metal echoed above. She craned her head up and saw the monsters scurrying on the upper levels, communicating to each other in their soul-sick clicking, jerking their heads side to side—sizing her up. She inched back against the wall of her pit, watching the vultures circling. What would happen to her if they caught her? Would they kill her? She was already dead, right? Dead and in hell, and what was there now, after that?

She determined not to find out.

The beasts chomped their teeth in fervor and leaped for her. She screamed until a large metal door, like something on an old submarine, opened behind her. A hand reached out, grabbed hold, and pulled her inside. She tumbled off balance and dipped forward into another hallway. It was Chris, and he put his weight against the giant door, grunting. "Help me!"

Sara hurried to his side and pressed with him, finally pushing the door closed, just as the first wave of monsters landed on the other side. Chris worked the wheel and locked the door in place, stepping away from it and the pounding of the invading monsters.

He bent over and braced his hands on his knees, coughing a laugh. "Whew. That'll hold for a while, but we've gotta keep moving."

Sara watched him straighten, leaning back to pop his neck and back. He chuckled. "Crazy, right?" he laughed. "That was a close one." He waved her forward and turned down the dark hall. "Come on, let's go."

"Wait," she snapped, holding her ground. "Where are we going? What… Wait. I'm just…I'm having a hard time wrapping my head around this. We're in hell. *Hell*."

He groaned, impatient. "A *kind* of hell, I don't know. Really, Sara, what does it matter?"

Enraged, she stormed for him, in tears. "It matters because I have to get out! I have to—"

Chris leaned backwards and exploded in laughter. Sara narrowed her eyes at him, her teeth on edge. He met her angered expression, his own darkening. "Figure it out, will ya? You're not *getting* out. None of us are."

"I don't believe that!"

"Believe it!" Calming, he said, "Will you come on, already?"

Sara growled, clutched at his soot-covered shirt, and hurled him against the wall. Chris' eyes widened in alarm, as she pinned him there. "Whoa!"

"Why should I trust you?" she said. "You're a murderer! You killed your own dad, and Light Sphere, and you tried to kill *me*!"

Chris winced and faltered, his eyes saddening, shame dropping down over his face like a veil. "I didn't kill Light Sphere," he mumbled.

Sara snarled, unable to see the point in such an admission. "What?"

He steeled himself against her. "I said I didn't kill Light Sphere."

"But Michael told me that you said—"

His face turned crimson and he looked away. "Just tough guy talk, all right? I wanted to impress him." Chris faced her again, his eyes barely able to hold her glare. "Look…I'm not a good guy. Yeah, I…I killed my dad… And, yeah, I came after you, but…" He seemed lost in the past for a moment. When he returned to himself, there was a new boldness about him. "But if you'll recall, I died because I stuck up for you when the Maestro wanted you dead."

Sara's conviction faltered and her grip loosened slightly. "Why *did* you do that?" she demanded. "Why are you helping me now?"

Once more, he looked to the floor, his face red, his teeth clenched together in humiliation. "Because you talked to me. You weren't afraid of me or what I could do. Even after I hurt you… You still believed that I could change." He exhaled and relaxed in her grip, his shoulders slumping. "I wish I'd listened to you. If I had—" He eyed the steelworks. "Well…I wouldn't be down here, now would I?"

Her heart quieted, and her breathing slowed. She studied Chris closely, wanting desperately to trust him, but uncertain. Finally she released him, and he humbly smoothed out his shirt. "Where are we going?" she asked, softer this time.

He jerked his chin down the hall. "There's more of us. We've been hiding from those things."

"Then let's go meet the gang."

3

Chris led Sara throughout the steelworks, navigating a circuitous path through side chambers, hidden passageways, and ducts. They rarely spoke during their long trek, and more than once Sara worried that they might be lost. How could Chris possibly know where they were going in this nightmare labyrinth? Nevertheless, she trusted her unlikely guide. She supposed there was no other choice.

"How long have you been here?" she finally asked, after they'd gone a long time without hearing or sighting the grey devils.

He shrugged, ducking under a barrel-shaped pipe. "You're new here, huh? Still thinking in terms of space and time like in your old life. Nah, there is no 'how long' here? There's just 'here'. We're just 'here'. We always have been and we always will be. Welcome to eternity."

Sara frowned, her stomach souring with hunger. It churned inside, growling loud enough to give Chris pause. She blushed. "Sorry."

He smirked. "Better get used to it."

"What?"

"Feeling hungry. It's crazy. There's no food or water here and we don't seem to need it. It's not like we're going to die again, right? But, *man*, the hunger and thirst. It never goes away. Never. Just one of many itches that you'll never be able to scratch. It's like bugs under your skin." He snickered darkly. "Nice place, huh?"

She rolled her eyes, frustrated. "You seem really cavalier about all of this."

"Hey, things could be worse."

"*How?*"

He pushed aside low-hanging chains, holding them back so Sara could pass underneath. "We're not processed yet. 'Yet' being the operative word, but still."

"Yeah, you said that before. That this was where we get 'processed'. What do you mean? Processed into what?"

Chris stopped and faced her, looking tired and put upon. "What do you mean, 'what'? You saw them. They've been trying to catch you since you got here."

Sara's mouth slowly opened. "Those creatures?"

He tightened his jaw, looking away. "They catch us; they turn us. It's…well, I guess it's inevitable. Haven't you heard all the howling? Yeah, that's what it sounds like when they do—whatever it is they do—to you. All I know is, they catch you, take you some place awful, and when you come out… well you're one of them. If it's all the same to you, I'd like to put off finding out for myself, you know?"

Chris moved on, but Sara stood still, struggling with the revelation he'd presented. The army of monsters on Chelkan that the Maestro had always wanted Michael to lead… *They're us. They're all of us who sold out to the Rage…*

"We're here," Chris said from some distance ahead. Sara quickened her steps to catch up as he opened another heavy hatch. Inside, she saw a circular room that stretched possibly five levels to the roof. Stacked along the grimy and rusted metal walls were bunks with tattered bedding. Maybe two dozen dirtied faces lit up in fear at Sara's arrival, peering out of their darkened cubby holes. Startled, Sara halted in her tracks, facing them all down. Chris slipped past and addressed the frightened dwellers. "It's just me. I'm back. Picked up another one."

He gently pulled Sara inside, then closed and latched the door behind them. Sara's eyes adjusted to the gloom of the room. The only source of light was a dim radiance of hellfire coming from thin grates somewhere around the ceiling. It cast a dull, fluorescent glow over the bunks and their occupants.

Chris called to the others, nonchalant, "Come out, already." He glanced privately to Sara and shook his head, mumbling to her ear, "Brace yourself. They're losers."

One by one, the people emerged from hiding, dropping down to crowd around Sara. She retreated a step in fright, then held her ground. Examining the filthy faces of the damned, Sara didn't immediately recognize any of the others. There were men and women of most ages and an assortment of alien species, from young teens to elderly, but all had the same pallid tone to their sunken skin—no matter what color their skin had originally been—their eyes dark and hollow of life, their hair brittle and wild. Their bodies, some emaciated while others were bloated with gases, were bundled in mismatched and moth-eaten clothes, and they exuded the foulest stench Sara had ever encountered. She resisted a gag for propriety's sake and faced their dead dolls' eyes, then caught Chris wriggling his brow at her.

"What did I tell you?" he spoke aside with haughty disdain. "Losers."

"Who are *you*?" a young Asian woman snapped, the left side of her hair shaved and the other side long and dyed blue.

"Relax," Chris drawled. "She's with me, all right? She's new."

"I'm Sara," Sara said, and immediately a towering giant thundered forth, pushing others out of the way. His naked torso was a twisted mass of bulging muscles, and something like vines grew around his bald head. His color was a washed-out remnant of dark green. A vertical seam evenly split his stoic visage. The brute shadowed her, grunted once, then stamped his foot as though he were about to charge. Chris eyed Sara, anxiety clouding his face, before the green goliath's head split along the seam, unfurling like a deadly flower, fleshy petals adorned in tiny razor-sharp teeth.

The beast roared at her, saliva flying from his mouth. Sara grimaced, then kicked him in the gut.

"Whoa, watch it there," Chris chuckled.

The alien doubled over, his face pulling back together in shock, as Sara grabbed the sides of his head and brought it down into her knee. The creature snorted in pain and collapsed back onto the grated floor with a hard *thunk*. Startled gasps sounded from the crowd.

Chris groaned and rubbed his temple. "Aw, man. This is really embarrassing."

Three other beings circled the green alien and helped him to a stand. His sudden rage was now replaced by misery, and he moaned in discomfort, allowing the others to carry him to his bunk.

Sara faced the crowd, stern. "Anyone else?" Quickly, she spun on Chris and demanded, "What *is* this?"

Chris sighed. "Ah, that's just Jerry. He does that to all the newbies. Likes to scare them. Don't let him get to you." Shouting to the wobbly hulk of a man, Chris said, "Sleep it off, Jerry! There you go."

"I remember you," the Asian woman said, seething with contempt as she stepped to the forefront of the crowd.

Chris sucked in a sharp breath and winced. Leaning closer to Sara he said, "Sara, this is Mai. She was a firestarter like me."

Mai crossed her arms, snarling. "Yeah, and when your husband cried out that slime monster and turned it loose on us all, I got torn apart and ended up *here*."

"And she's still pretty sore about it," Chris said, scratching the back of his head.

Mai stepped closer, raising a fist. "Give me one reason why I shouldn't just turn you over to those monsters outside already, huh?"

Chris stepped in, holding out his hands. "Whoa, Mai, easy. There's not enough of us as there is. Sara's cool."

Mai pushed Chris away. "Get off me! I swear, if I still had my powers—"

"You'd what?" Sara barked, challenging the hothead.

"Enough," a bold, crisp voice cut through the standoff. Immediately, the crowd backed to the other side of the room, away from a new figure sitting up in his bunk. Even Mai lowered her hands and bowed her head in respect, real fear in her eyes. Chris snickered uneasily, "Hey—ah—guy. Look who I found."

Sara watched as a tall man in a raggedy hooded coat climbed down from his second-level bunk and dropped to the floor with a thud. As he approached, Sara marveled at his strong build and the way he carried himself. Only his beautiful lips and his hard cut chin were visible beneath the shadows of his hood—but she knew him. By his walk, by that mouth. A mouth she'd kissed a hundred times. A mouth she longed to kiss again.

Through tears she grinned, seeing her savior near. *Of course* he'd be here. He'd always be there for her, in her darkest of hours.

The man pulled back the hood to reveal his handsome face, and Michael Morrison said, "Hi, Sara."

4

The yellow skies of Venus were filled with the armies of Egalia. Lady Vasariana led the charge, the jagged wound on her forehead bleeding into her eyes and impairing her flight. Nevertheless, she kept her keen gaze forward, extended her trident, and squawked to the winged warriors behind her, "Give no quarter!"

Her army let out a deafening *caw* that trembled the heavens and shot forward, their glowing tridents poised and ready for battle. Facing down their charge, a fleet of galleons crewed by the volcanic Underdwellers. The subterranean savages had always been a thorn in the noble bird people's feathered side, scaling the walls of the High Kingdom on their giant lavaspiders from time to time. But now that the Underdwellers had finally overcome the acrophobia in their genetic memory, nowhere was safe from their brutality.

Below the Egalian Guard, lavaspiders spouted fiery streams of molten lava that pushed the warriors higher into the air and into the crosshairs of the mighty frigates. The Underdwellers shouted in victory and fired their cannons, bright crimson beams slicing through the cloud coverage. Vasariana swerved to the left and watched, helpless, as the men and women behind her were vaporized in the latest blast. She pushed through her anguish, flexing her wings to catch the powerful winds and swoop upward. More cannon fire sizzled past her, and she twirled expertly, just as her mother had taught her, pirouetting in between the deadly bolts. Finally escaping the torrent of fire, she halted mid-air, leveled her trident at the offending ship and let fly an energy blast of her own that tore the mast off the lead vessel, veering it off course. She hurled one shot after another, pelting the hull and deck, scattering the Underdweller vermin in all directions until, at last, the ship sped into its neighbor—both frigates fireballing in breathtaking glory.

Her soldiers cheered and pressed on in the attack, swarming the ships and trading shots, but their victory was not assured. The lavaspiders' reach claimed many lives, and the remaining galleons' cannons vaporized the very best of her soldiers without mercy. Through the haze of war, Vasariana glimpsed her soldiers landing on the decks of the vessels and taking the fight straight to the Underdwellers, but they were well-matched in combat—her valiant Egalian troops were unparalleled in their use of a spear, but the Underdwellers wielded their slab-swords with wanton zeal. And now, the Underdwellers had new and terrifying allies in the form of grey, faceless monstrosities with sharpened spears for arms. The alien creatures skittered about like beasts, decimating her frontline attacks.

In a moment of despair, the Egalian Queen imagined how this battle might have been different if only Lady Sara had come to their aid… But humans were fickle and weak. *No honor*, Lady Vasariana thought, bitter tears stinging her eyes. No matter. The Egalia had strength yet and would never surrender. Not while they still had breath.

Ships exploded all about her, but Vasariana's attention was stolen by a new vessel entering the fray. Another galleon—built just like the others—but a dark cloud occupied its stern. Something like living smoke billowed like a furnace, tendrils of black vapor plucking her brave fighters out of the skies and flinging them to the rocks below like broken dolls. This ship pushed ahead of the fleet, scraping against its brothers with abandon, aimed straight for her. Narrowing her gaze, Lady Vasariana peered past the death of her friends, past the battle, and beheld the wild figure on board this strange new ship. It was *similar* to a man, but unlike anything she'd ever seen, human, Egalia, Underdweller, or otherwise. *Hate* clothed him, and rot emitted from his touch. He did not move at all, merely stood still, a wide bright smile and enlarged white eyes fixed on her in a mad stare. Thick, slithering black tentacles detached from his shape and writhed about, slapping away her soldiers with lethal proficiency. All about this Beast, Underdwellers and their grey consorts lay prone, bending forward and sitting up and bending forward once again in rhythmic repetition. *Worshippers*, she knew.

So this was their god. This was the thing that had come to her world and emboldened the Underdwellers to seize the skies.

"Have at it then," she growled under her breath and clutched her spear the tighter. Loosing a battle cry, Lady Vasariana angled her beak and dove for the blasphemous creature. "For Venus! For the High Kingdom! For the Blessed Egalia!" Cannons tracked her position and fired, but she slipped through their grid, weaving through their destructive force, her eyes locked on that dark god. She neared it, drowning out the screams of her wonderful, brave Guard, vowing to avenge them all with the removal of the monster's black, grinning head.

"Ha!" she shouted, cresting the bow and landing on deck with a flourish of her wings. Crouched low, with trident burning bright—powered by her righteous cause—she charged the Black God. At once, his Underdweller worshippers rose from their adoration and took up their charred slab-swords, swinging wildly at her. The grey-skinned animals with them also surged, teeth rattling in their bulbous heads, setting her nerves on edge. Recalling wonderful memories of her childhood, sparring playfully with her mother, Vasariana forgot her crown and station, and returned to the spirited youth she'd once been, who craved excitement and courted danger. Sporting a savage grin, she engaged the ruffians, dancing around them as though they were stationary, dispossessing them of limbs and heads. Underdwellers and grey animals, alike, fell under the devastating might of her elegant weapon as she dodged and sidestepped their crude efforts.

All the while, the Black God watched, still smiling, his expression suggesting something like wonder. Like delight.

"Commeee tooo meeee…bird womannn…" he breathed, his voice a deep moan that caused the boards of the ship to bend and creak. At the sound of his soul-sick intonation, some weaker-minded Underdwellers shrieked and impaled themselves with their own swords, clearing a path for Vasariana. She leapt over an Underdweller's lunge, snapping the cretin's neck with a sharp kick, and flapped once with her wings to land before the monster. Sparing no time, she thrust out with her spear, stabbing the creature deep in his stomach—

But the end of her trident only vanished in his gooey darkness. She faltered in shock and looked to his face, expecting to see pain, but his wide, unblinking eyes and sparkling smile never faded. He simply stared at her and spread his arms to his sides, her spear still protruding from his stomach.

"N-No…" she said, her quivering hands slipping free of the spear's handle.

The Black God took hold of the trident, pulled it clean out, then tossed it effortlessly over the side of the ship. Strength left the Queen's legs, and she collapsed to her knees before the beast as he regarded her with a childlike smile. Slowly and deliberately, he took her chin in his icy, slick hand and carefully turned her around to face the distant skies, where storm clouds—surreal and nauseating—pulled together. Blacker than her darkest dreams, a pillar of ebon lowered from the heavens. Churning with a gravity of its own, it upended volcano, rock, and mountains, and pulled them into its greedy maw.

Tears froze in her eyes. "Eternal Spirit…"

Then she knew. It was the Black Fire. It was the end.

5

It wasn't her Michael, of course. Sara knew that the moment he removed his hood. He was an old man, deep frown lines creasing his once-handsome face, the evidence of a pained life. His hair was still long, but white, his dark eyes missing that devil-may-care spark that she'd always found so thrilling about her Michael. Nevertheless, Sara did know this Michael—he was the villainous Hooded Man that they had encountered on her first rift jump. Michael had killed him back then, but not before the Hooded Man had betrayed the Rage to help Sara to safety during an enemy attack.

Her first thought was to ask him what he was doing here, but she knew: Michael had condemned him to this place. *Stupid question.* Instead, she simply said, "It's you."

He grinned in a kicked-back, blasé way that somehow soothed her anxiety, even in a place as horrible as this. "It's me." Then his smile faded, his brow creasing in concern and something Sara thought might be heartache. He took a step toward her as though he were ready to embrace her, but held off. "What are you doing here? You're not…dead?"

She blushed at being this close to him, faced with the same questions that had flashed through her mind when she first saw Chris dangling from the hole in the ceiling. *Can I trust you? Are you friend or foe?* In her life, this Michael—like Chris—had been both. But hell, it seemed, was the great equalizer. Maybe old feuds no longer mattered.

"No. I was sent here," she said. "Some horrible monster—I think it used to be a friend of mine, but now…"

The Hooded Man traded guarded looks with Chris before facing her. "A demon? Like the Maestro?"

"Worse," she said without pause. "I've faced the Maestro, but this… This guy was in a whole other league. And he was covered in this black slime, like what came out of—" She hesitated, a strange vertigo washing over her as she spoke to this alternate version of her husband. "—out of Michael. It spoke in my mind, and… I think it might have been the Rage, itself."

Gasps and tormented moans followed from those crammed in the tight space. Worried conversations broke out, but through it all, Chris and the Hooded Man remained focused on one another, calm and calculating.

"But how is that possible?" Mai asked, aggravated.

Sara said, "It's my friend, Toby—"

"That little kid you were with?" Chris cut in, surprised. "The one the Maestro was so interested in?"

Sara nodded. "He was *inside* this thing. Like in a cocoon."

"He's an anchor," the Hooded Man said, rubbing at his whiskered chin. "The Rage is bound to Toby like a parasite. Using the boy to give Itself shape. Hold it in place."

Sara shifted her gaze between the two. "So what does that mean?"

Mai huffed and shook her head. "It means it's all over. The Rage is freed, just like It always wanted. Just like it used *us* to do. It's walking about and that's all she wrote." The girl sat down and looked away, dejected. "Can't tell if I feel good about that or not…"

"Not yet," the Hooded Man said. "If It's using Toby as an anchor, then It's not free from Its cage. An *aspect* of It might be, but It's only remotely controlling the boy as a means of working from the outside to pick the lock on Its cage."

"The Gateworld," Sara said.

The Hooded Man shook his head. "That's only a myth. Just something the Maestro fed Rip's gramma and she told him as a bedtime story."

Sara raised a brow. "You sure about that?"

Chris laughed, "So what if it *is* true? How's It gonna break the lock?"

But Sara already knew, all too well. "I've seen it," she muttered. "A pillar of black energy, capable of shattering a dimension."

Chris swore and Mai outright laughed in hopeless abandon. The strength in the Hooded Man's face faltered, and he glanced to the floor in quiet contemplation. Others in the room began to weep. Sara faced hell's inmates, overwhelmed by the desperation plaguing them all. She felt it creeping into her own heart, as well, seeking to convince her to join them. Find her bunk and get used to it. "No," she mumbled, then said louder, "*No*. I can fix this."

Mai glowered at her. Others continued to groan in misery as they made their way to their holes, crawling inside. But the sight of their surrender only served to stoke the fire in Sara's gut. "Listen! If I can just get out of here, I can—" A sharp pain like a knife's edge plunged in her mind, flinging her to the floor. She gave a startled shout and clutched at her pounding temples. Images psychically assaulted her—sensations of fear, of panic, of despondency—and she saw Venus. Lady Vasariana. Ships of Underdwellers and those same grey devils. The Pillar. And after that—

Nothing.

When she came to, Sara's face felt hot, and tears swelled her eyes. The Hooded Man was helping her up, while Chris stood frozen, frightened by her outburst. "What did you see?" the Hooded Man asked, out of breath, and Sara realized everyone was watching her expectantly.

Crying, she gasped, "I saw it happen. He just...he just destroyed a whole dimension... I..." She held her head, weeping. "Why am I seeing this? Why..." In her heart, though, she feared she knew why. *I'm his Mother*. They were linked now, and if she didn't get out of this place, she'd spend an eternity seeing that Black Pillar destroy everything beautiful in the multiverse, trying to find the Gateworld, tearing everything away piece by piece, until there was nothing left.

But maybe the link went both ways.

Drying her eyes, Sara said, "I can find him. I can *stop* him."

Mai stood now, enraged. "Forget it! Are you seriously that stupid? You're dead—"

"I'm not dead!" Sara cut in, but Mai pushed on, stepping into her face.

"—and there's nothing left now!" The angry girl circled to scowl at the others in the room and shouted, "There's nothing left for any of us but to be turned into those monsters for Its army! So what if we hide a millennium or more? We're going to get caught and they're going to turn us!"

Chris reached out with a careful hand, grabbing Mai's arm. "Mai, easy. That's not helping."

In tears, Mai hollered, "No, Chris! I'm not going to sit here and let her fill their heads with—"

"With what?" Sara interrupted. "With *hope*?" Now it was Sara's turn to face those frightened faces peering at her from every shadowed place. "The Rage used all of you! It used me, too. It made us all promises of power or freedom, but we were deceived."

The inmates listened attentively, hearing her out. Even Jerry rolled over in his bunk to face her, his hard countenance softening.

"But it's not too late," Sara said. "It *can't* be. You're all still here. You haven't changed into monsters yet. I can't give up. It can't end like this! Please. Please, help me. We can get out of here, I know it. My husband was sent here, too, and he got out, and he was able to renounce the Rage and get his life back. We can do the same. We can make up for all our mistakes."

No one spoke, so Sara turned to the Hooded Man. He watched her, carefully weighing her words, caught somewhere between faith and fear. She moved to him, impassioned. "Please," she begged him. "We have to try. The Michael I knew, he wouldn't give up. Not as long as he was able to fight."

Mai waved Sara off and sighed. "No way."

"No," the Hooded Man said. "She's right."

Mai propped her hands on her hips. "You can't be serious."

Chris moved closer to Sara, wide-eyed. "You really think we can escape?"

The Hooded Man studied Sara, then nodded slowly. "It won't be easy, but... There might be a way." He faced Chris. "The Rift Keeper."

Chris rolled his eyes into the back of his head and groaned. "Oooohh…"

"Who is that?" Sara asked, caught in a rush of excitement.

The Hooded Man explained, "This place—it isn't quite hell. It's more like a prison barge, floating in the In-Between. Those who have cut deals with the Rage come here when they die and get turned into his grey-skinned lapdogs. Then we wait until we're called into service. A rift opens, and those creatures are caught up in it and go, well, wherever they're summoned. But there's someone on *this* end of the rift who opens the gateway and lets them through. He's…kind of like a warden around here." The older man scratched the side of his face. "He's hidden somewhere deep, in the center of the prison. I made it there, once, when I first came here. We'd have to fight through hordes of things to get to him, but if we *could*…"

Sara grinned, flushed. "Then we could open the rift. Get out of here."

"Whoa, whoa, whoa." Chris waved his hands. "Yeah, okay, I've heard talk about this guy too, but the chances of us surviving to get *to* him, man—"

"I'm in," Mai blurted, arriving at Sara's side. The others looked to her in surprise and she shuffled awkwardly. "If you're all crazy enough to try this, then I'm in. It'd be better getting caught out there trying to get out of here, then to get caught in here sitting on our hands doing nothing."

"I'm in, too," a booming voice echoed. Sara twirled to the darkness and saw none other than Jerry climbing down out of his bunk. The giant seemed calmer, almost noble, rising to his impressive and powerful stature. "My blood boils for one last Great Battle."

Chris shrugged, huffing. "Sure, okay. Count me in. It's not like I had anything better to do for the rest of eternity."

Sara beamed at them all, proud of them and honored by their confidence. She turned to the Hooded Man, but he remained hesitant. "Will you help us?" she asked him, seeing her Michael in his eyes and missing him all the more.

The Hooded Man met the gazes of Sara's suicide squad, then firmed his mouth. "Yeah. Yeah, I'm in."

6

In the end, only Chris, Mai, Jerry, and Michael's *other* came with Sara. The rest stayed behind, content to weep and cling to each other in the dark, counting the seconds until their hiding place was finally discovered. Leaving them behind was difficult for Sara, but they had made their choice, and she knew she had to get out, find Toby, and fix this awful mess.

The enigmatic warrior Jerry kept to himself throughout the journey, while Chris and Mai brought up the rear and continued to bicker under their breaths. Sara pushed onward to walk beside the Hooded Man at the forefront. Despite his age, she saw her husband in the middle-aged man. His eyes were sharp, his face like flint as he marched through the labyrinthine steelworks. He'd pause periodically at the slightest sound, raising a hand to signal the group to hold up, and then, when the threat of danger passed, he'd lead the charge once more without a word.

"Thank you," she said to him after a while, out of earshot of their companions.

He nodded once, his dark eyes still alert.

She lowered her head, embarrassed and unsure how to begin. "I guess I never got a chance to thank you for saving my life the *last* time, either, back at that hotel when the Bug ship attacked."

"You don't have to," he said, somber. "I'm not a good man that you should ever thank, Sara."

"But why? You've shown me that you *can* be a good man. What…what happened that made you choose this?"

The Hooded Man turned a corner, and a dim firelight sputtered from somewhere up ahead. "On the world I'm from, humans served the machines. The machines controlled every aspect of our lives—what we ate, when we slept, where we worked, whether or not we could mate and produce children. Rip appeared one day and told me there was another way."

Sara balked, surprised. "Rip?"

"He talked about my power and how I had to discover it for myself. I was scared at first, but I saw the Rage as my chance to break free from the machines. In the end, though, I was really only trading one master for another. But there was this girl—" He faltered and shot her a quick glance out of the corner of his eye.

"Me," she said. "Another me."

He nodded. "Sara reminded me of the good man I wanted to be. She was everything I had been missing in life. Rip tried to convince me otherwise, but I wouldn't listen. I rebelled against him. Sara and I were married and we just ran. We found some nice, isolated cottage and lived there for years, away from the machines, away from the Rage. But…it was too late. I'd made my deal with the devil, and eventually, he came to collect." The shadow of his hood concealed his eyes, but Sara saw the man's lined mouth trembling with emotion. "The Maestro killed Sara to get to me. Then he told me he had this other Michael out there, running like I did. The Maestro tasked me with hunting your Michael down and bringing him back into the fold, and if he didn't come through, I was—" He quieted. "I was supposed to kill you. I agreed, Sara. But then…Then I saw you. You were the same as the day we first met, and I…"

"You saved me," she said, resisting some primal urge to hold him, just as she would her own Michael. *But it's not him.*

"I killed a lot of people to find you, though. I'm just as responsible for what's going on up there as you are. We *all* helped to bring this about. But I would've done anything to spare you from this place."

Sara grinned through a blush that quickly faded. A deep hurt ached in her heart. "Sad to say, I earned my place here, too. I wish I'd never listened to Rip. At the time, it made so much sense, but I don't know… It's nuts. I just wanted to be special for once. How pathetic is that?"

A smirk creased the Hooded Man's serious face. "Not pathetic at all. But you were always special, Sara. You didn't need the Rage for that."

The fire at the end of the hallway grew brighter, and Sara heard the clanking of chains. They were nearing something that she couldn't quite make out, but just the hint of it was enough to cause the hair on the back of her neck to rise.

"And your Michael?" the Hooded Man asked, startling Sara from her dread. "Where is he now?"

She bit her lip. "I don't know. Now that Toby's the Rage's anchor, I don't know what could have happened to Michael… I was pretty horrible to him. The things I said… I left him at his lowest and hurt him in ways…" Sara rubbed a tear with her palm.

"Sorry to hear that," he said, sincere. "He was kind of a punk when I met him, but then again," a chuckle broke his words, "I was like that when I was his age, too, as I recall. More importantly, he loved you."

"My marriage is another one of those things I hope to fix when I get out of here. If Michael will even *look* at me again."

"He will," the Hooded Man said immediately, strength in his voice.

"How can you be so sure?"

He smirked, humorless, and paused to look her way. "*I* would."

Chris called out from behind them, "What is that?"

Sara and the Hooded Man faced forward. The end of the corridor was fast approaching and seemed to open up into a great chamber. Here, the firelight was brightest, now accompanied by loud clanging, spitting steam, and ravenous growling. The Hooded Man held the others back and inched forward alone, one foot out of the darkness of the hallway and into the light. After a moment, he waved them forward. The squad kept quiet, but hustled to his side. Sara's boots edged to the end of a grated catwalk. Below, a canyon of fire and smoke. Narrowing her eyes, she glimpsed shapes in the smog—grey devils prowling on the walls and on more walkways beneath them. On the other side of a wide, monster-filled gap, another corridor that led into darkness.

The Hooded Man pointed to it. "That's where we're going."

"Awesome," Mai drawled, quiet but sharp.

"We can't cross this," Chris said. He cursed and paced, running his fingers through his tight curls. "This was your big plan, guy? What, that we'd just climb down, sneak through all those guys, then climb back up on the other side?"

"No," the Hooded Man said, patient. He gestured to the wall on their left. A network of thin pipes traced the wall around the chasm and to the other side. "We climb those all the way across."

Chris laughed. "No way."

The Hooded Man faced him. "I've done it before, kid. It'll be slow going, but we can make it, as long as we keep quiet."

Sara cut through the men and climbed out to the wall, settling a shaky boot on the first length of pipe. "Let's just go," she snapped.

Quiet Jerry obediently followed, and the Hooded Man offered Chris a proud grin before easing his way onto the pipes. Chris growled and fell in line, with Mai bringing up the rear. "I can't believe we're doing this," he grumbled.

"Just shut up, Chris," Mai whined.

Sara tuned them out, concentrating only on her next step. The pipe was a lot narrower than she'd anticipated, and the one above her hands that she gripped as she shimmied across was slick with perspiration. Ice cold, too. She couldn't understand why this pocket hell dimension looked like a boiler room, but every metal surface was freezing. In an effort to avoid focusing on the teeming monsters mere feet beneath her, Sara considered the Hooded Man's words.

Would Michael ever forgive her for leaving? Could they make things work? She hoped so—if for no other reason than that she needed him to help save Toby. If Sara was that creature's Mother, then Michael was the Father. Toby was their responsibility, their child. *We need to be a family again.* They would be. She had to find a way. She—

Visions struck her like a baseball bat across the face. Images of a world she'd never been to, but somehow she knew its name nonetheless: Myriad Prime. Towering obelisks, built with the sweat of human slaves, dotted frozen mountaintops and flat, weedy marshes. Presiding over their fearful servants, a race of powerful men with the heads and legs of horses, dark muscular bodies clad in bronze armor, and impressive and terrifying helmets. Surging forth from rock-hewn castles, the horse-men charged on hooves, brandishing broadswords made of glistening steel. Battalions of equine knights, led by their fierce lords, fell and died as they fought against legions of grey devils. Then the Shape. Smiling. Looking right at Sara. He knew she saw. He *wanted* her to see. The Black Pillar and—

Sara recoiled from the onslaught of destruction and let fly a startled warble. So disoriented was she that Sara let go of the pipe above and slipped backwards. She loosed a scream, feeling herself falling, then snapped to when a strong arm gripped hers. Jerry pulled her up, one-handed, his face turning a deep forest green as he strained under her weight.

"Got…you!" he made out through clenched teeth, his seam parting at the lip in exertion.

Sara's senses returned, the nightmare quickly dissipating, and she climbed up the large man's arm, grappling the pipe again. She braced her head against the wall, catching her breath. "Thanks."

Jerry dipped his chin, face stern. The Hooded Man leaned out to get a better look at her. "You okay?"

She nodded quickly, struggling through fresh grief. "It's happened again. He's destroyed another universe."

"Look!" Mai shouted, taking one hand off the pipe to point at their feet.

As one, the group glanced down and saw the devils climbing for them, their mantis-like spears clicking on the walls as they ascended, dull teeth making that gut-churning *chkchkchkchk* death rattle. Sara immediately knew it was her fumble that had brought them unwanted attention and scolded herself for being so careless. "Move!"

The group picked up their pace, shuffling along the ledge as the monsters' chattering grew louder and *closer*. The devils were now near enough to reach out with their talons, punching at the wall, missing the inmates by inches. One reared up to chomp at Sara's heel with its teeth, and she grunted and kicked at its head, knocking the beast off balance and sending it tumbling down the ladder of monsters. Beneath their weight, the pipes groaned and bent, and Sara quickened her efforts, her breathing labored and panicked. In her mind, she repeated *GoGoGo!*, doing her best not to fixate on the creatures that sought to drag her into the pit. From the smoking orange haze, a lance-like arm extended and cut deep into Jerry's back. His anguished squeal startled Sara, and she watched as he buckled at the knees, but did not let go.

"Jerry!" She reached out an arm to him to keep him steady, as the devil—its hook still in the meat of his shoulders—pulled itself up to perch on his back. "Get off!" She spared a foot to kick at the thing, but from this angle, it was useless. Jerry twisted under the creature's gangly frame, batting at it with his elbow, grim determination coloring his face.

Sara abandoned her climb and edged closer to him, pulling at the beast's spindly limbs, even as it lowered its crunching jaws on Jerry's neck. The thing bent forward to bite into him, but Sara managed to grab its leg and yank. The thing lost its foothold for only a moment, but it gave Jerry just enough opportunity to free a hand, grab the demon's head and smash it against the wall. It rebounded with a dull thud and relinquished its hold, dropping into the smoke.

Jerry inhaled raggedly, but his eyes were still clear and focused. Sara maintained eye contact with him, willing her strength to him. "You good?"

He nodded, snorting in pain, and picked up the trek once more. Sara led the way and, after a moment that seemed to stretch like taffy, her trembling boot finally found purchase on the catwalk across the chasm. She hopped on, nearly jumping up and down in released anxiety.

"Come on!" she urged her companions.

Jerry followed, and she helped the lumbering plant-man onto the platform. He sat, propped against the wall, his wound pumping bright green blood down his torso. The Hooded Man was next in line, quick enough, but Chris and Mai were still struggling on the pipes.

"Hurry!" Sara yelled, watching in horror as wave after wave of monsters inched their way up the wall, hissing and snarling. The devils reached for the pipes now, nicking them, tugging them. The beams gave a low groan as bolts snapped and popped, and the ledge dipped outward, away from the wall. Mai nearly lost her balance, but Chris gripped tight. "Hang on!"

"They're not going to make it," the Hooded Man observed, his tone cold and matter-of-fact. "We should go."

"*No*," Sara protested. "We're going to make it. All of us."

Sara sucked in a deep breath and moved for the pipe, ready to go back out into the fray. The Hooded Man clamped down on her arm, forcing her to face him. "I promised I would get you out of here," he said. "Not them."

"Then protect me," she snapped. "But I'm going after them."

She jerked her arm out of his hand and hurried out onto the pipes, shimmying along as fast as she could. Once more, her breathing turned shallow and fearful as the devils emerged from the fog. Chris and Mai teetered in place, kicking and stomping on the monsters that neared them.

"Hang on!" Sara hollered, digging the toe of her boot against the mouth of one of the chomping creatures. It gave a shriek and spun backwards, disappearing into the smoky abyss. Sweat dripped in Sara's eyes, stinging, but she pressed on, her hands slippery against the cold pipes.

A grey claw exploded from the mist and, in one lethal strike, cleanly cut the lower pipe in two. Steam whistled from the opening, and the rest of the supporting pipes wheezed and curled outward. Chris pinwheeled wildly, yelling as he fell backward. Sara shot an arm out for him and squeezed, sparing him.

But Mai was too far away to grab. She shouted, pitched backwards, and fell into the swirling hordes, her blue hair whipping around her anguished face.

"No!" Chris roared.

"Chris, come on!" Sara said, pulling him to her. His weight tugged against her center of gravity, threatening to pull her into the chasm as well. "We have to go!"

Chris stared into the abyss where Mai had fallen, the echoes of her petrified screams finally tapering off.

"*Chris*," Sara said, working to keep her voice calm and direct.

She caught his attention and he turned.

"We have to go," she said, and he nodded, getting his balance and sliding his feet along the piping.

The creatures' *chkchkchkchk* grew to an earsplitting volume, resonating throughout the steelworks. Sara tuned out the deafening sound, locking eyes with the Hooded Man on the platform. He waved her forward, his face earnest and deliberate. As soon as she was within reach, he extended his arms and took hold of her, safely clutching her to him.

"I've got you," he said.

She allowed herself the briefest of moments to close her eyes and return his embrace. Just a fraction of a second to pretend this was her Michael and all was forgiven. Chris' warble tore her from her fantasy, and together with the Hooded Man, she stretched and took Chris' hands, pulling him onto the platform.

The devils dragged their way out of the pit like a swarm of locusts, buzzing and snapping. Sara pushed Chris down the corridor. "Go, go, go!" Chris half-tottered, half-ran, and Sara hurried to Jerry's side.

"Can you walk?" she asked.

He nodded, but she marveled at how terrible he looked. His green skin was paling—he was nearly marble white—and it looked thin and clammy. *He's wrinkling.*

"Leave him," the Hooded Man said, halfway to Chris before he paused. "If those things bite or scratch you, the transformation starts."

"Wait, you mean he's turning into one of them?"

"And then he'll come after us, yes. He's already dead, Sara. Let's go."

As though that settled it, the Hooded Man disappeared with Chris around the bend, leaving Sara alone with Jerry. The man shivered, his vegetable skin papery and moist. His color turned ashen, and his face scrunched up, as though it were swallowing his features. Jerry's nose appeared pinched, and his eyes were nothing but swollen squints. Even his seam began to fade as his body conformed to that of the devils'.

"I-I'm sorry, Jerry," she stammered, her heart going out to him. He was a resident of hell, and she had no idea what poor decisions had landed him here, but he was still a person. A person who had saved her. "Thank you," she said, hating herself for the insufficiency of her words.

His eyes narrowed to slits before disappearing altogether, along with his nose and seam. His mouth cracked and widened as fat, dull teeth exposed themselves and began to vibrate in a death chatter:

Chkchkchkchkchk!

Sara scrambled to her feet and backed away. Jerry writhed on the ground, his transformation nearly complete, as he shuffled out of his flesh, his new body twisting into a lean, skeletal frame. Already, the thing reached for Sara, chattering. Sara grit her own teeth and kicked at the monstrosity. "I'm sorry, Jerry." The misshapen form slid over the edge of the catwalk, bouncing along the crawling armies.

Sara spared him one last pitiful look, then hurried along after the Hooded Man. It was time to get out of here.

7

Sara leaned against the wall of the corridor, shivering and attempting to rub warmth into her arms. She'd never accounted for how cold hell could be. Ice whistled through every joint, deep into every bone, and her muscles ached incessantly. Her teeth rattled so hard her jaw throbbed, and her stomach cramped.

They had managed to elude the roving packs of devils and were, for the moment, tucked safely away in a tight, dank corridor, its walls comprised of thick cables and wires that led who-knew-where. It was creepy, but it gave Sara a chance to breathe. To process what had happened to Jerry and Mai. The Hooded

Man was a bit further down the makeshift hall and had pulled back enough of the wires to get a peek at their constant pursuers. Chris, on the other hand, sat on the grated floor, arms draped over his knees, head hung low. His face was filthy, as Sara imagined hers was, and his eyes shone brightly against the darkness of his face. He was quiet—barely blinking—only staring at nothing.

Sara gave Chris his space and stepped nearer to the Hooded Man. "So…those things… They bite or scratch you and you turn into one of them? Is that what the Rage is doing? Turning all the multiverse into his weird zombie guys?"

"No," the man said, sparing her a brief look. "It only happens to us. In this place. That's what we have to look forward to."

"Not if we escape," she said with a small grin.

The Hooded Man turned to her sharply, as though surprised. His shock wavered to a sly, though sad, half-smile. "Right." He resumed his watch without another word on the matter, and Sara could see that he wasn't interested in any further conversation right now. She bit her lip and eased towards Chris. "Are you okay?"

From his place on the floor, Chris nodded slowly, but she doubted his certainty. "Who was Jerry?" she asked, unable to shake the guilt of knowing that a stranger had died to protect her. "I mean, what was he like?"

Chris shrugged, then said in a hollow tone, "On his world, he killed his family to prove himself worthy of the Rage."

Sara swallowed hard. "Oh."

Chris eyed her, his expression dead. Cold. "What did you expect, Sara? We're in hell. It's not exactly like we're saints down here." With that pronouncement, he resumed his watch of empty air, at last blinking.

Sara hesitated. "And Mai?"

At the mere mention of her name, a wall of tears built in Chris' eyes and his nose turned red. "Yeah… Mai."

Sara slid along the wall to sit next to him. "Were you and Mai…?"

"Doesn't really matter now, does it?"

Her heart broke for him, and without thinking, she rested a hand on his shoulder. "Chris, I'm sorry—"

He yanked from beneath her touch and jumped to his feet, infuriated. His stoicism broke as tears painted his dirtied cheeks. Gripping his curled hair, he raved, "I should've listened to her. This is all my fault. I brought you into the camp!"

Sara slowly rose, her heart pounding as his words grew louder. "Chris, shh. They'll hear you."

His shouting had drawn the attention of the Hooded Man now, who paused in his lookout duty to watch the scene play out.

"Who cares if they hear!" Chris hollered. "They're going to find us! We're already dead! And now we're gonna be turned into…" He suddenly quieted and paced. "We were safe… We should've stayed hidden." He wept, rubbing at his tears with his palms. "But, no. No, I screwed it up because I *listened* to you. Because it was *you*. Because you're Sara…"

Sara felt her own eyes water and involuntarily furrowed her brow.

"You always ruin everything for me," he said through clenched teeth. "Back at home, I *ran* that stupid town! I was a god! Then you came and convinced me to turn myself in. Then the Maestro found me and made me into somebody. I met Mai and… Then you show up again, and I stick my neck out for you and get my head chopped off. Now—now!—just when I start to get something for myself again, you're here, and I listen to you, and I put my trust in you, and Mai's gone!"

From down the hall, the Hooded Man called out in a stern voice, "Enough, kid."

"No!" Chris spun and pointed a finger. "No, old man. We're not getting out of here."

"Yes we will," Sara said, her voice cracking.

But Chris ignored her, locking a glare on the Hooded Man. "She's poison to us, guy. We can't tell her 'no', and it's just gonna get us killed. Let's leave her. Let's go back home. This isn't gonna end well for either one of us. You know it and I know it."

The Hooded Man's face hardened. He abandoned his post and marched forward. Sara trembled in his path, a cry caught in her throat. But the man stopped at Chris and clapped him hard against the ear, eliciting a yelp from the boy. Chris glowered at him for a brief moment before the Hooded Man struck him once more. Chris gripped the side of his head, bitter tears drying. Hate still radiated from him, but his outburst had been silenced, and the Hooded Man stared him down to make sure he was done.

At last, Chris broke off with a huff and sulked further away down the corridor. Sara watched him go, burdened by his words and wondering at their truth. When she looked to the Hooded Man, he was as impassive as stone and reported, "We can't stay here for long. We're almost to the rift, but the creatures will catch up to us soon enough. We need to hide and let them pass before we go any further."

Once more she looked to Chris, who kept his back to them, and hoped to talk their problems out. More than that, she wanted to know if the Hooded Man felt the same about her as Chris did. But her guide seemed in no mood to discuss feelings. "I know someone close by. If they haven't caught him yet, we should be safe there."

She nodded, composing herself, knowing now was not the time for the hard talks. Now they had to survive. "Okay, then, let's go."

He faltered, drawing her closer. "Sara, listen, this guy that we're about to see—you're not going to like it."

"It's not like we have much choice, though, right?"

"I know, but I don't want you to feel ambushed."

She crossed her arms, uncomfortable and impatient. "Okay, so what? What's the big deal?"

"Sara. It's Charlie."

Her arms dropped slowly to her sides.

8

The Hooded Man led them away from the chattering masses, and Sara's heart beat faster with each step. Chris remained distracted, trailing along behind them—almost aimlessly wandering—but Sara's focus stayed keenly fixed on the space before her.

For every step took her nearer to Charlie.

She didn't know what to expect, but more importantly, she didn't know what to feel. Her first instinct was terror. At the mere mention of her ex-husband's name, she was bombarded by memories of him standing tall over her, shouting, slapping, pointing that fat finger of his in her face and telling her she was a nothing. She'd always be a nothing. She felt the bruises, felt the strikes to her cheek, felt crushed beneath him as he forced himself on her.

And she'd felt that crippled by the thought of Charlie *before* Rip told her that her ex-husband had been the one to murder her parents. Knowing that extra piece of the puzzle made the idea of seeing him tantamount to stabbing herself through the chest with a jagged shard.

"Stop," she blurted, gripping her stomach and putting a hand to her mouth. "W-Wait, okay? Just wait."

Chris sighed in aggravation and trailed past her, but the Hooded Man paused and faced her with a look of concern. "What's wrong?"

"I can't do this," she said. "I-I can't face him again."

Chris snickered to himself and shook his head. "They're sooo gonna get us, man."

The Hooded Man cut him down with a withering glance, then approached Sara, carefully taking her arm. He pushed back his hood to reveal his wizened features and forced a reckless smirk that made him look twenty years younger. "You can. You will. And it's only for a while. Just long enough for the monsters to pass. Then we're out of there. But it's the only place I know where we can hide."

The sounds of spears clanging against metal carried down the hall, quickening Sara's breath. She jerked to look over her shoulder, but did not see the creatures. The Hooded Man called her back to the present. "Hey." She met his dark eyes and found a familiar strength there. It'd been Michael who saved her from Charlie in the first place, after all. "You're not the same girl you were," he told her, his face inches from hers. "Don't forget that."

She nodded quickly. "We need to hurry."

He gave her arm a gentle squeeze, then released it, rushing to the front. "This way. Hurry."

The devils' marching grew louder as the trio hurried down the corridor, scaling ladders, descending small flights of stairs, and turning a dozen or more corners. All the while, Sara heard the distant *chkchkchkchk* amidst the spewing steam and faraway wails of agony. She imagined Mai's voice intermingled with those terrified screams, and wondered if she'd know all too soon what these creatures did to their prey down in the dark.

At last, the Hooded Man stopped at a mass of leaky pipes and dropped to his belly. "Through here," he grunted, crawling beneath. Sara and Chris followed until they came out the other side into another dimly-lit passageway. At the end of the hall—a door. The Hooded Man brightened. "Here," he whispered, crossing to it in great strides. "Charlie," he hissed, inclining his ear to the door. "Charlie, it's me. Open up." He raised a fist to knock. "Charlie, it's—"

The man froze and shared an astonished look with Sara. "What?" she asked in a hush.

She leaned closer and saw that the door to Charlie's hiding spot was pried open just a crack. The Hooded Man held a finger to his lips, and she nodded. He waved Sara and Chris behind him and eased for the door, carefully laying it open with a tremendously long *creak*. Beyond the doorway, a pitch black room, only illuminated by the lone bulb flickering in the hall.

"Charlie?" the Hooded Man asked into the dark, peering in.

"They got him, too," Chris snickered. "This is awesome. Really, it's great."

A clang behind them. The devils' chatter intensified, and Sara tensed in terror.

"Inside!" the Hooded Man hissed, rushing into the pitch black room. "Hurry!"

Sara followed, even as Chris began to laugh. "Come and get us!" he shouted, guffawing madly.

"Shut up!" Sara barked, yanking him inside.

The Hooded Man pushed against the door and closed it, trapping them in eternal black. The inky shadows swallowed them whole, and Sara felt a scream of hopeless fright rising. Would they ever see light again? Had they descended into a new level of this hell? She opened her mouth to release her cry when, suddenly, gears noisily turned somewhere in the abyss. To her relief, slats opened up in portholes along the wall—something like vents—allowing thin cracks of hell-light inside. The light did little to warm her, but she relaxed nonetheless, as the room's features came into view. She saw her companions once more, with the Hooded Man still braced against the door and Chris lumbering off now that he could see in the gloom again.

Sara took quick stock of her surroundings, seeing a room similar to the one at Chris' camp. Moth-eaten blankets were piled high in a dryer corner of the wet room—like a nest. She turned back to the Hooded Man to see him in deep concentration, as though he were willing the devils not to find them, then turned her interest to the bundle of blankets. She knelt by them and was immediately taken by the scent. It was Charlie's scent. She'd never be able to describe it, but she knew it without a doubt. It had filled her home once, and its return brought down a deluge of terrible memories. In that moment she wondered if she'd ever left that old life. If she'd ever met Michael or gone on any of the amazing adventures since. In that moment, she was a teenage girl again, timid and afraid and foolish.

"They're moving on," the Hooded Man whispered, but he didn't look any less anxious. "I can hear them."

Chris flopped down on the floor, picking at a pebble and tossing it away, bored. Angry, Sara frowned at him, irritated by his childish pouting. Choosing to ignore Chris, she returned to Charlie's bed, reaching out a hand to feel the place where he slept, more than a little thankful that the man, himself, was gone.

Only—

"It's warm," she said, perplexed. Realization dawned on her, and she whipped about to the Hooded Man. "It's still warm."

He left the door and moved closer. "Then we've just missed him. Or maybe they already got him—"

"*Chris?*" a soft voice sounded from the other side of the door.

The young man perked up, his eyes wide with heartache. Sara and the Hooded Man, too, turned towards the sudden noise.

"Chris," the voice came again. Weak and hurt. A woman's voice.

Chris rose, his lip shuddering. "M-Mai?"

"Chris…let me in… They're almost here. Please, hurry."

He raced to the door. "Hold on, Mai!"

The Hooded Man intercepted him, slamming one hand on the door and holding Chris back with the other. Chris snarled at him and slapped his arm away. "*Move*, old man!"

218

"That's not Mai," he said, even and frigid.

Chris hesitated, then fought against him again, flailing. "The hell it isn't! Move!"

Sara stood and rushed to face Chris. "It's a trick, Chris. Don't let it in."

"It's not an 'it'! It's Mai, and she wouldn't even be out there if it wasn't for *you*!" Glowering through tears, Chris curled a fist and slugged Sara across the jaw. Unprepared for the strike, she fell to the floor, her face numb and throbbing.

The Hooded Man materialized at her side, hooking his arms under her, steadying her. They traded looks before both of them turned towards the door, but it was too late. Chris had already pried off the lock and was heaving the door open.

"Chris, no!" Sara shouted.

Standing in the doorway, Mai shuffled off-balance, her clothes torn, a small cut on her head bleeding. "Chris," she breathed in relief.

Chris barked a joyful laugh and crashed into her, hugging her close. "It's okay!" he exclaimed. "I've got you. I've got—"

Shurk!

A pale grey lance pierced through his stomach and out his back, spraying Sara and the Hooded Man in gore. Chris hacked and backed away, sliding off the spear-like claw. He looked to the fresh hole in his abdomen then into Mai's uncompassionate face. "M-Mai?"

"Chris!" Sara reached for him, but the Hooded Man held her back, wildly looking for an exit.

"Come on!" he roared.

Chris turned to offer Sara a pitiful, pleading look, then thumped over onto the floor, unmoving. Mai lifted her bloodied claw—pointing it right at Sara—and screamed like a siren at the top of her lungs. Sara clutched her hands to her ears, the splitting shriek as sharp as the claw that had claimed Chris. Even as the woman screamed, the skin of her face paled to white and stretched to the back of her head grotesquely, taking her eyes and nose with it, while pulling her mouth into a deathly rictus. And now her teeth began to chatter.

Chkchkchkchkchk!

A mob of grey devils spilled forward, flooding into the room. The newly transformed Mai joined their numbers as they clawed and bit the air around Sara. She spun into a roundhouse, jettisoning one monster across the room, only to face two more in its stead. She punched, kicked, and dodged, but they crowded her, *drowning* her. In the midst of their flapping, she only caught brief glimpses of the Hooded Man—long enough to see him knocked to the floor before vanishing from sight.

"Wait!" she cried, reaching for him, trying to clasp his coat. A pair of cracked teeth filled her vision, rattling loudly. The beast lashed out with its claw, smacking her against the wall.

And all she saw was black.

9

Soldiers in leather flight suits, skull caps, and goggles—like she'd seen on some Earths in the 1930s or 1940s—climbed atop their mounts. Brave men, all riding atop majestic and bizarre clockwork elephants. The bronze machines shot through the air on tiny bee-like wings, their impossible bulk strangely aerodynamic as they veered in between beautiful buildings with gold onions atop many towers. The pilots clutched their mechanical steeds, diving for the ground, firing translucent bubbles from elaborate ray guns. Below them: an endless flood of grey devils, roiling the land, toppling the population. The bubbles instantly imprisoned any creature they touched, but there were so many monsters... Too many. The elephant riders made many sweeping passes, doing their best to thin the herd, but the devils climbed each other's backs and leapt, digging claws into the mighty mechanical elephants and bringing them low. Pilots screamed as they were devoured. Then the wind picked up. Purple lightning stretched across the sky with jagged fingers.

The Black Pillar came into view and—

{*I sssseeee yooouuu, Motherrrrr...*}

Sara sat up, a scream frozen in her chest. She clutched at her breast, trying to massage the ache away, but her breathing was rapid and irregular. Nearly panting, she surveyed the room. She was in a cramped cage in a narrow room with high ceilings, filled to the brim with more cages—like an animal kennel. Hell-light and smoke filtered in through unseen passageways, and four-legged shadows prowled about in the half-lit recesses. In the other cages, lost souls wept and convulsed, screeching in pain and terror as their bodies endured the strains of their slow mutations. *This* had been the source of the wails she kept hearing.

Terrified, Sara cried as well, her sobs joining the broken chorus of suffering. Teary-eyed, she desperately sought the faces around her, but could not locate the Hooded Man. Grief, perhaps the darkest she'd ever experienced, weighed her down. Gripping the bars of her small box, she rested her head and shed what she thought must be the last of her tears.

"Sara?"

Startled, she turned and saw her neighbor in a cage to one side of hers. He lay on his side, his hands cupped against his stomach. He'd already lost most of his hair, and one eye was totally matted shut—vanishing. His skin was marbleizing by the second, and one of his arms was crooked like a baby bird's wing. Caught between man and beast, he was a piteous sight.

"Oh, Chris," Sara whimpered, crawling to be near him. She reached grimy fingers through the bars and managed to brush his arm. "Look what they've done to you."

With his one good eye, he beheld her. "You came back for me…"

She grinned through tears. "I'm here."

"You always…come back for me. About the things I said…I'm sorry—"

He shivered and his teeth clicked together once, raising the hairs on Sara's arm. "It's okay, Chris."

"I'm always hurting you," he said, voice breaking. "And you're always helping me. But I…I keep pushing you away. Why do I do that?"

She tried to snicker, but it became a sob. "I don't know. I do it, too."

He smiled, and she could see his teeth had grown fatter now. Dulled. "I guess we're just broken…huh?"

"I guess so."

"It's too late for me," he said. "But maybe you still have a chance."

She laughed and cried, her emotions a cluttered mess. "I don't know, Chris. It's not looking so good right about now."

He chuckled, his humanity fading. "But you're *Sara*. You're the girl who can do anything. The girl we would all die for."

His remaining hand shook as, with great effort, he reached out and gingerly stroked her low-hanging bangs. "I'm just glad that you were here with me…at the end…"

"I'm so sorry, Chris."

Suddenly his fingers tightened in her hair, bringing about a sharp pain. His last eye shrank to a slit before vanishing altogether, along with his nose. His mouth cracked and widened, and those fat, dull teeth exposed themselves and started a death chatter.

Chkchkchkchkchk!

"Chris, no!" Sara screamed, pulling against him but unable to break free. An insect-like appendage protruded from beneath his arm, shredding his flesh and leaving his hand ruined and useless. He caressed her face with his talon as she struggled. "No! NO!"

Sara planted her boots on the bars and pushed, finally slipping free as the Chris-thing reached for her, teeth clattering.

A pair of devils came to Chris' cage and opened it, releasing their new brother. He joined them as they circled Sara's cage, chomping at her and stamping their curled toes and spear-tips. More creatures flocked to her cage, their bony limbs clanging against the bars. She squinted her eyes and did her best to center herself—to prepare for whatever new hells they had in store. The things latched onto her pen and dragged, the metal grating against metal, causing her teeth to hurt and her eyes to water. She held on as the monsters lugged her across the slaughterhouse, beneath low-hanging chains and hooks.

"Where are you taking me?" she asked, though she knew it was useless trying to get an answer from these animals.

Instead she could only wait as they hauled her cage out of the room and through a gauntlet of thick, mildewed plastic curtains. When, at last, they breached, Sara took a great breath, stunned by the scope of the auditorium in which she now found herself. The monsters brought her pen into the center of an enclosed arena, amid rows of seats rising at least four stories high. On each level, Sara spotted droves of the grey devils, raising their lance-arms and clucking to the roof in excited frenzy. Her escorts popped the lock on her cage, but she resisted the urge to flee. Instead, she pressed against the back of the cage, watching them warily. Finally one—Chris, she imagined, though now he looked like the rest and she couldn't tell the difference—reached with his claw and prodded at her until she squirmed out. As soon as she touched down on the grated floor, the monsters began to clatter all the louder. Were they happy?

Her boots clanged on more grated and rusted steel, and she was lit from below by that same incandescent witch-glow that suffused this place. Steam rose through holes in the floor, obscuring her senses. Nevertheless, she stiffened her arms and prepared for an attack. None came right away, as her monstrous guards instead scurried to the stands, as if taking their seats to catch a bit of theater.

"What is this?" she called, her wavering voice echoing through the chamber.

"Well, hey there, Red."

She sighed at the sound of the voice behind her back. *Of course*, she thought. This was hell, after all, and every hell had to have a devil. Slowly, she turned about, releasing her tight fists, and faced the sand-worn drifter sauntering into the room. He appeared much the same as she had left him: grey hair braided, weathered jeans, boots with the dust of a thousand worlds, and a vest that exposed his wiry muscles. Only, she realized with great interest, his trademark tattoos were gone, as well as his leather jacket.

"Rip," she said. "That figures."

He hooked his thumbs in his pockets, moseying into view. As the firelight exposed him more clearly, Sara noticed he had company. To his left, one of the grey devils strode in, walking on its claws and toe knuckles. To Rip's right, another figure marched a few paces behind him. A young man, small in size, but carrying himself like a giant as he strode into the room, bearing a six-foot-long golden staff, intricately designed. He wore black leather pants and thick boots, but his torso was bare, displaying an immaculate, muscled frame. Her heart stuttered, for she knew this young man. His long blonde hair, his deep set black eyes, his familiar gait.

"Michael," she breathed. As with the Hooded Man, it wasn't her Michael. This one was nearly albino, blue veins wrapped like circuitry along his chest and face. And his naked core and arms displayed a tapestry of scars. A curious wound—it still looked fresh, though it didn't appear to be causing him pain—spread out on his stomach like a festering sore.

This new Michael sneered at her, and Rip offered the boy a glance. "One of 'em," the Old Dog commented. "The Rage has got a thing for the Michael Morrisons of the multiverse. Somethin' about them is just wired the right way. Of course, this one was always *my* personal favorite of all the ones I trained."

Sara kept her eyes fixed on Michael as he continued to leer at her, his eyes unblinking—his stare like a cunning animal sizing up its next meal. "He must not be all that great," she mused. "He's dead, after all."

Rip shrugged, nonchalant. "Got a point there, sis. We had a lot of hopes riding on his shoulders. He made it farther than any of the others. Who knew that Holstead cat would get lucky?"

"Holstead," Sara blurted, turning to Michael. "Then you're the one that died on Chelkan. The one who commanded Aztaroth's army."

And, she thought, *the one who might* still *command them*. Was this Michael the Rift Keeper?

"He did that," Rip answered for the silent brute. "You gotta understand—this army? It was originally designed so that only a demon could lead it. Or, you know," he paused and smiled proudly at the teenager to his side, almost like a father, "someone with a demon's capacity for hate. No, we burnt through a lot of folks—a lot of Michaels—trying to find one with the right stuff. Little brother, here, proved himself more than capable. The hate he's got inside of him… Hoo boy!" Rip laughed, but the Chelkan-Michael just sneered a Cheshire Cat grin. "When he fell in combat, we had to go find us a new general for the army—"

"My Michael," she said.

He pointed at her, still chuckling. "And you were a part of that plan, little darlin'. Break his heart and turn him dark, remember? You were meant to prepare him for his role, but, well, you both botched that all to hell." He glanced at their demonic surroundings, suddenly amused. "Ha, *hell*. Funny."

"So you're here," she announced. "I guess you didn't outrun your fate, either."

Rip groaned. "Yeah, it was a drag. You were right. That punk Michael shanked me. The thing of it is, he used *my* knife to do it. The knife that my Master gave me the last time I saw him. Makes me think the Master knew I was headed that direction. It's a trip."

"Can't say you didn't deserve it. Why aren't either one of you like those other creatures?"

"Well, that's a funny story." He turned to the young man beside him, the kid still coiled tight, like a spring about to explode. "See, Mike, here is still a handy guy to have around. The monsters, they still listen to him, even on this side of Creation. But the poor kid, he ain't never been much for schoolin'. He's a hammer, kinda like your boyfriend."

Sara watched the Chelkan-Michael, to see if Rip's sleight had gotten a rise out of him. But the killer remained emotionless. He only watched *her*, a sick grin never leaving his face. His eyes were totally savage, beyond comprehension.

But Rip's words confirmed one thing: this Michael was the Rift Keeper. Now she just had to figure out how he opened the rifts.

Rip clapped a hand on Michael's taut shoulder. "Mike still needs someone to do all the thinkin' for him. Keep him on the right track, you know how it is."

Sara crossed her arms, feigning indifference, but studied Michael out of the corner of her eye. "Let me guess. You."

"Nope," he grinned, revealing his extended canine. "You, Red."

She stiffened. "What?"

"I told you there was somethin' special about the Michael Morrison model. Turns out, the Sara Theresea model is just as special, too. You're a matching set, you might say."

Rip thumbed the tip of his nose and gave Michael a nod. The albino warrior returned the nod and hopped down off the raised dais before marching across the room. Sara tensed, unsure what came next, fearing an attack. But the Chelkan-Michael craned his neck to her—sneered—then jabbed his staff into a small hole in the floor that she couldn't detect very clearly.

The Rift Keeper gave a sharp jerk of his staff, and immediately, a bright hole of light opened up in the space before him, a rough breeze stirring his bangs. The portal's edges glimmered with bending rainbow colors, but within the rough square shape, Sara saw…well, *everything*.

The view whisked through the multiverse, cycling through images. Frozen moments in time. She saw majestic alien vistas and prehistoric landscapes. Robots, horse-drawn carriages, swords, mountains, underwater cities. Her eyes blinked rapidly, processing the snapshots of space and time, already beginning to see their common truth:

She and Michael were in every one of the images. Parallel Michaels and Saras.

They were all different, some subtly so, from the style or color of hair to the shape and build of the body. Some seemed more civilian than others—just an ordinary couple walking arm in arm in the park, or eating simple meals together in quiet homes with children between them. Others were soldiers. She saw one pair riding atop great dragons, soaring through a blazing sky, leading armies of helmeted soldiers into battle. Another Michael and Sara, their hair dyed black and wearing matching eyeliner, were dressed in black leather, riding together in the cockpit of a rickety space ship, snarling as they evaded capture. Explosions rocked the stars all around them, but the two seemed oblivious to the danger, having the time of their lives.

Other variations were far different: misshapen, discolored creatures, wholly alien and unrecognizable, yet she *did* recognize them. She saw their bond—the way they looked at each other—and knew.

Images flashed by and she saw herself, back home. Just sixteen, after her first date with Charlie. She barged into the auditorium where the Drama Class rehearsed the school play, nearly plowing down some tall, gangly, blond-headed boy in jeans and an overgrown olive denim jacket in the process. He stopped just short of getting smacked in the face by the door and slipped off one ear of his headset. "*Watch it*," he muttered, his voice echoing in the chamber as Sara watched.

"Watch it yourself, jerk," she mumbled to herself, in awe of the memory, realizing she'd already met a Michael on her world and never noticed. Was that meant to be *her* Michael? "Why are you showing me this?" she asked Rip, her heart fluttering.

"Told ya," he said. "You're a matching set. God made ya that way, I suppose. Think about it. Chaos entered Creation and fragmented it through a couple of star-crossed lovers. Seems kinda fitting, right, if It finished off the whole shebang through another pair. You're practically the new Adam and Eve, sis. There's some kinda power unlocked in you two lovebirds, and man, when that comes together, miracles happen."

Sara shook her head in a daze, unable to stop watching the images flashing by, losing herself in the eons of infinity. The snapshots of life turned darker and she saw *pain*. Michaels and Saras all across the multiverse, shouting at one another. Pointing angry fingers and bawling tears and throwing things against walls.

Rip narrated, "Why do you think the Rage is always after you? No matter what dimension it is, you two somehow find each other—and the Rage is always waiting, looking for a way to get in and put a stop to that nonsense before it begins. It turns you on each other. Sometimes Michael kills you, sometimes it's the other way around. So much drama! Always drama with you two! You're either madly in love or tearing each other apart!"

She watched as a version of her in Victorian dress pulled a flintlock and shot a version of Michael through the heart. Another scene depicted a teenage Michael in some Old West brothel. He sat on the corner of an unmade bed in a room upstairs, a Sara by his side. The décor struck Sara as familiar, and she watched as the other Sara—dressed only in a ratty slip, her hair a tangled mess, lipstick smeared on her face—gently stroked Michael's bare shoulder as he wept like a child. But Michael suddenly turned on her, embarrassed perhaps by his own weakness, and strangled her in the bed, his eyes feral—

Just like the Chelkan-Michael.

Sara faced the Rift Keeper and saw him watching the scene unfold as well, mad glee no longer shining in his eyes. Sara watched through the portal as Michael strangled the woman, murdering her. Then, just as soon as the deed was done, Michael's younger brother Seth barged into the bedroom, aghast at the sight. Sara held a hand to her mouth in shock as Seth leveled eyes on the dead version of herself, glared at Michael, then drew his pistol and killed him.

The Chelkan-Michael glowered at his own death replayed, and cycled on through the images.

"The Rage sends people like me," Rip was saying. "Like Charlie and Chris, and we come and poke and prod and get you two all riled up. Then, stand back and watch the fireworks happen. It's really melodramatic, ha ha. But, hey, teen love always is, right?" Rip absently bit at a nail, bored. "Of course, it doesn't always have to end that way. More than once the Rage has tried recruiting you. Think about it: get you cats both playing for his team and we make some sweet, sweet music."

Sara felt faint, her mind and heart racing, until she finally closed her eyes so that she didn't have to see anymore. After a moment, Rip called to his faithful soldier. "I think that's enough, Mike."

The Rift Keeper acknowledged, powering down the portal, removing his staff, then joining Rip once more on the stage.

"See, Red, this is your story." Rip gestured to the rows of monsters, watching her intently, their chattering finally silenced. "All this—all of us? We're just set dressing. You and Mike, you're the stars." He elbowed his sentinel in good humor. "Got a king, here, and now we've got his queen. And together, you'll rule this side of hell. Command the army, serve the Master, destroy pretty much everything."

"What about you?" she spat, overwhelmed.

"Retire!" He laughed and nodded to the devils. "I'm ready to be like *them*."

"They're mindless," she said.

"But happy. Above pain, above loneliness, above desire. They trample the worlds and devour everything in their path. Can't you see how simple that is? How peaceful?" Then, to her surprise, Rip beheld the grey devil that flanked him. Gently, he brushed a gnarled knuckle against the side of the creature's cheek, and the abomination seemed to purr under his touch in affection. He smiled at the faceless thing and said, "Besides, I get to rejoin my gramma. After all we've been through, we can finally be a family again."

Sara balked at the revelation, feeling a strange sort of pity for the Old Dog.

Rip shook his head. "I've played this game a long time, sis. A lot longer than you and Mike can realize. Now it's 'fun time'. We win! The Master is on his way to true freedom, and I'll have front row seats to the End of Creation. Now that you're here, I can step down—"

"*No.*"

Rip slumped, tired. "Aw, come on, Red. Are we still gonna play this game, even after we're dead? You can't run, get it? Just like I couldn't run from your boyfriend impaling me with my own pig sticker. I tried, but now I see. This is all about fate. All about design. We're locked in Life's little roller coaster, so when are you gonna get it? Belt down and enjoy the ride." He spread his arms wide and turned from side to side. "This is your *inheritance*, darlin'! Isn't that what you wanted? You and Michael, together forever—powerful? All your life you wanted power. This is why! You were destined to be a queen—to rule!—with Mike at your side. Okay, yeah, I'll grant you, this one's not quite as touchy-feely as yours was. But it's still him. Or…" Rip turned to another entryway and nodded. A pair of devils scurried through the plastic curtain and shortly returned with a prisoner draped between them.

The Hooded Man.

Sara took a step towards him, instinct commanding her to rescue him, but she stayed her hand and eyed Rip.

Rip shrugged. "But, hey, if my Mike's not good enough—and he's a specimen, believe me—then you can always trade up. Pick *this* Michael, I don't care. Michaels are kinda interchangeable around here. But the throne should have a Michael *and* a Sara. As it was in the beginning, and all that." He gestured to the Hooded Man, nonchalant. "Besides, why do you think he brought you all this way?"

Sara looked to the Hooded Man, but he kept his face down, eyes on the ground.

Rip whistled. "Oooooh, he didn't tell you. Man. Seems like no matter where you go, some Michael is always lying to you, little darlin'. Yeah, the old man, here, knows the score. Who do you think was king down here before my boy took over?"

Sara listened to Rip, all the while watching as the Hooded Man reddened in shame, still refusing to meet her gaze.

Rip carried on casually, "Yep, you're lookin' at a king in exile." The Old Dog stepped down off his perch and rounded the Hooded Man. "This one was always kind of a defect. He was never very handy in a fight. That's why my boy took him out so quick. But, man, what he lacks in brawn, he more than makes up for in that silver tongue and those pouty eyes. They sure did a number on *you*, sis. He's been trying to take back the throne ever since, but he hadn't found a way yet to take out Kung-Fu Michael, here. Once you came along, though—well, that evened the playing field."

"Is this true?" Sara asked, feeling a lead weight in her abdomen. "Were you just using me to be king?"

The Hooded Man did not look up or reply.

"Don't blame him, Red," Rip groaned. "He's been a mess ever since Aztaroth strung up his wife. I'm sure he could imagine worse ways to spend eternity than ruling down here with you sittin' beside him. You'd make a cute couple. I mean, he's all dried up and old enough to be your dad, but whatever floats your boat."

Sara bit her lip, using the pain to quell the tears that formed. At last the Hooded Man's eyes met hers, and she saw before her a broken man, a mere shadow of the noble protector she'd believed that he was. Once more she felt betrayed by a Michael and worried that she put too much faith in them. They were weak and she was, like the Hooded Man himself had once said, their kryptonite.

I make them weak. She regrettably understood her place in the cosmos. For aeons, the Rage had used her—or her doubles—to break those destined to challenge it.

But…maybe it didn't have to be that way. God had made them to be strong together; the Rage was only corrupting what was meant for good.

We have the power to stop this, she knew, her heart pounding in excitement. In hope. *We can stop this.*

Rip clapped his hands together, snapping her out of her thoughts. "Okay, then," he announced. "Let's get this going, yeah? I'm ready to have a little family reunion with Gramma Moore, so you pick one of these strapping gents to be your significant other, and I can transcend to my final reward."

"No," Sara said again, newfound determination breathing life into her body. She felt strong again, and clear-headed, and at last the damnable cold had retreated. Warmth stirred in her gut, lighting her blood on fire, and she smiled, her tears evaporating.

Rip rolled his eyes. "Oh, Red."

She ignored him, fixing her sight on the Hooded Man. "He said it himself," she told him. "There's a power inside of us. When we're together, miracles happen. Are we going to let these people tell us what to do? Are we going to let them keep using us, keep *breaking* us? We're more than just puppets," she shouted at him, willing him her strength. Her fight. "We do have a choice! We always have a choice. God gave us that. My Michael *showed* me that."

The Hooded Man's eyes cleared.

Sara continued, "You said that on your world the machines told you what to do, what to think. The Rage is doing the same thing! You told me so. But we can fight it. We *can* be free." Gritting her teeth, she declared, "And we can make them pay."

A quiet moment passed between them, and Sara sensed a deep kinship with the Hooded Man. His face softened into a warm grin—a strong grin—that communicated to her his love, devotion, and trust. It didn't matter anymore whether he had sold her out before. They could be a team, and they could claim the victory. Sara knew it.

The Hooded Man growled and ripped his arm out of his captor's hold, then punched the other devil in its flat face. Startled, the monster released him, and the man clumsily shoved against the first devil, breaking free. He looked to Sara, joyful, but surprised by his own daring, as well. Focusing, he snapped and pointed to Michael. "The staff! That's the key to opening the rift!"

Sara turned to the dais in time to see Chelkan-Michael leap off, pirouetting perfectly in the air. He landed before her in a fighting stance. A sinister sneer split his face like a slashed throat, and his dark, soulless eyes exuded malice and pure, all-encompassing *hate*. Sara's eyes widened as he swung with his staff, and she bent backwards, the metal narrowly brushing the tip of her chin. She landed on her back with an "Oof!", but came to quickly enough to roll aside as Michael slammed a thick boot to the floor where her head had been.

To her side, she saw the Hooded Man swinging wildly as more grey devils crowded about him. Rip hadn't lied—the old man wasn't much in a fight, throwing desperate haymakers to ward off the creatures. She worried she'd only pushed him to his own death, but she had to trust that whatever spark made the Michael Morrisons of the multiverse special was in him, as well, and would see him through. Sara instead concentrated on her own battle, jerking her head out of the way of the staff. Chelkan-Michael brought it down with a roar, and it clanged loudly on the metal floor, the sound ringing in her ears. She twisted and twirled, kicking out with her legs and landing in a crouch. Michael backed away, his sick smile broadening.

"I was hopin' you'd put up a fight," he said in a thick Southern drawl.

"I-I've met your brothers," she stammered, taking a step in retreat. "They're worried about you. Edward and—"

"Seth?" he chuckled as he advanced on her, twirling his staff, his body poised like a snake ready to strike. "Seth shot me in the back. Murdered by my own brother."

From behind Michael, Rip called out. "Ain't no use appealing to a sense of family with that one, Red. The boy was beaten by his father for bein' weak. He got it worse than his brothers did. When war broke out with them alien bugs, little brother, here, let all that rage out. Best weapon the South ever had. So what if he killed some women on the side? They were just painted ladies. Besides, there was so much death with the war and all, what were a few more, right?"

Sara eyed Michael in horror.

"I'm his only real family," Rip said, but Sara's glare remained on Michael, watching him twirl that staff, pacing back and forth with his teeth bared like a jungle cat. "When I found him in that desert after his own kin shot him for his crimes, I took him in. Raised him as my own. He's the best, sis. You can't beat him. Might as well marry the boy."

"No thanks," she said. "Besides, I've never been very good at the marrying thing, anyway."

She twirled and kicked, aiming for Michael's chin, but he was faster than she'd anticipated. He deftly blocked her attack with his staff, hooked her foot in it, and tossed her to the ground. She returned with a sweep to his feet, but he hopped over her leg and swung with his staff, clipping her cheek and coloring it with bright pain. Sara gasped and wavered as Michael brought the staff down in an axe chop. She sidestepped it clumsily, her balance thrown. He jabbed at her with its end once more, and she slipped around it, popping him in the side of the ear with her elbow.

Michael grunted and listed to the side, cupping a hand to his ear, and Sara saw her chance. She gripped the staff with both hands and yanked it away from him, but he recovered and shot his foot out, straight into her solar plexus. She cried and, in her surprise, lost the staff. It spun out of the fight, landing some distance away on the metal mesh floor. She made to reach for it, but Michael socked her in the mouth with a tight fist. He brought his knee to greet her face, but Sara slapped it down and snapped the back of her fist against his nose.

They parted, catching their breaths, until Chelkan-Michael lunged for her, pressing the offensive. Sara was ready for him this time and worked fast to block, to deflect, to dodge. Michael was like some creature bred for combat, but there was no rational thought behind his attacks. She could see it in that maniacal leer, that wild shine in his soulless eyes. He was a dervish of destruction, motivated purely by blind hate. He was too *emotional*, Sara realized.

And that, she understood, would be his downfall.

She ducked beneath another punch and came up, forcing a laugh she didn't quite feel. "I thought you were supposed to be good!"

He flinched in surprise, but pushed again. This time, however, Sara stepped out of the way of the attack, airy and relaxed. "Seriously? I was trained by the best," she told him. "A better Michael than you, anyway."

"*Rargh!*" He punched, kicked, twirled, but Sara dodged it all, anticipating his aimless attacks. His discipline was faltering, and she smiled.

"You're going to have to do a lot better than that to convince me to marry you! This is pathetic! No wonder you didn't last long on Chelkan! You're not a leader! You're no fighter!"

"Don't listen to her," Rip drawled, impatient. "She's just getting under your skin, Mike."

But Michael seemed unable to hear his mentor. His face was red with rage, his eyes nearly bulging and glistening with furious tears. He spun and kicked, striking Sara in the ribs. She gasped and tumbled to the floor, dazed by the power in him. Chelkan-Michael stood over her, his chest heaving, teeth on edge.

"Finish her, boy," Rip said with an air of resignation. "We'll just have to find you another bride. This one is defective."

Michael glared at her, and Sara looked through the stars in her vision to meet his baleful stare. "Better listen to him, Michael. Don't want to make your master mad. That's all you are, right? A dog on a leash? Just performing tricks, hoping for a treat?"

"Shut up," he spat.

"*Shut* me up, tough guy." Shaking her head in dismissal, though she feared a killing blow at any moment, she chuckled, "You're a joke, man. Did any of the other girls tell you that right before you killed them? What were they? Prostitutes, right? I mean, you paid them money to be nice to you, and they *still* didn't like you."

Michael fell on top of her, screaming, "*Shut up!*" He wrapped iron-like fingers around her throat and squeezed.

"You're…no warrior…" she wheezed, her sight fading to a bloody red blur. "You're not…strong… You're just a scared kid…whose daddy hit him…"

Michael's eyes narrowed and spewed forth tears. "I said 'shut up'!"

Softer now, she whispered, "I saw her…your Sara. She wanted to help you… She *loved* you." Glowering, she spat through clenched teeth, "And you killed her for it."

He gasped, as though she'd broken terrible news to him, and his fingers loosened, just marginally.

"Kill me," she croaked, teetering on the edge of consciousness. "But you'll never *beat* me… You're too weak for that—"

Michael roared himself hoarse, tightening his grip with furious strength, when the staff shot out of nowhere, slamming him in the side of the head. Instantly he released his hold and toppled to the floor, and Sara clutched her throat and hacked for life. Her senses slowly returned, and she glanced once to see Chelkan-Michael out cold on the ground, then looked up to see the Hooded Man standing over her, golden staff in hand. He panted laboriously, and his trademark coat was hanging from him in tatters. One of his eyes was swollen shut, and his body was adorned in a hundred tiny cuts, scrapes, and bites.

"You...okay?" he asked through heavy breaths.

Sara nodded, still trying to find her voice, and stood. Her throat was raw like she'd gargled with cement, and she barely managed, "You're bit."

His exuberant expression quickly turned to a grimace. He handed her the staff. "Go. You have to go."

She pushed aside the staff and clutched at his lapel, checking his numerous wounds. "Wh-What about you? You're coming with me."

"No," he sighed. "That was never going to happen."

"What do you mean?"

"I'm dead, Sara. We all are. But you're alive. You said so. You didn't die. You were *sent* here. This is a place for the dead. *You* can go back. But...I was never getting out of here."

She searched him, staring through tears, trying to rationalize. "Then why did you help me?"

"Isn't that obvious by now? You're Sara."

Once more he placed the staff before her. "Take it," he said, then nodded over his shoulder. "There's a lock in the floor. Put this in...turn it. You'll open the rift..."

All around them, the buzzing of grey devils grew louder, echoing in the chamber. Somewhere in the noise she heard Rip cursing at her as he climbed off his dais.

"Hurry," the Hooded Man said as the legions of monsters took to flight, scurrying down from the stands to join in the battle. "If they bite you in this place, dead or alive, you *will* turn."

"And you?"

A tear escaped his one good eye as his flesh slowly began to morph into an ashen grey. "Yeah, me too."

She knew she only had a moment, but had to ask. "Was Rip telling the truth? Could you have ruled this place? Could you have saved yourself from turning into one of them...if only I'd helped you?"

"Doesn't matter now."

The first of the devils reached them, gnashing its teeth and stretching for them with its claw.

"Sara, watch out!" the Hooded Man hollered, but Sara was already moving, taking the staff from him and twirling about to knock the mutated beast away. More were following, and she knew if she didn't leave now, she would never get a second chance.

"Come on!" The Hooded Man led the way, gripping his wounded side and staggering across the chamber.

Sara followed close behind, pausing to bat at the creatures nipping at their feet. Once she'd cleared the path, she joined the Hooded Man beside an intricately designed gold ring embedded in the floor. It resembled something like a Celtic knot that she'd seen on other words, and a perfectly circular hole waited at its center.

"You have to concentrate," he told her in a hurry. "Exploit the connection that you have to the Master. *Concentrate*, Sara."

The bays and growls of the devils approached, but Sara shut her eyes and tried to fall within herself, to touch that raw dark energy within her that served as some kind of despicable umbilical cord to her blasphemous child. Pushing aside her fear and doubt, she reached deep into her inner black and felt, and—

Images. A peaceful prairie. Nighttime celebration. The Glor is dead. The Krinvox are rejoicing. The Black Pillar arrives—

Something like an electric jolt touched her nerves and her eyes shot open. "I know where he is!"

But when she returned her attention to the Hooded Man, she saw the transformation had already begun. He was hunched over, his arms bent, ruined hands dangling like a pair of empty gloves. His face had already started to shrink, but there was still enough of the man there to stoke her pity.

"Go," he said, and his teeth clicked together once. "Find…your Michael…"

She wept and touched his face, unbothered by his deformities. Even now, at the end, all he cared about was her. She laughed through tears, although an ocean of grey was rushing towards her, readying to crash against her like a wave of decay. "Wh-What if he doesn't take me back?"

Through dry, cracked teeth, the Hooded Man said, "Sara…love is stronger…than what we put it through."

With a bittersweet smile, she leaned in and tenderly kissed Michael's lips. He returned her kiss, and she did not resist. When at last they parted, she brushed the side of his mouth with her thumb. "Thank you," she whispered.

"Thank *you*," he said, crying unashamedly, "For giving me…a chance to save you at last…"

She held his gaze as his remaining eye closed forever. In a moment, his nose disappeared in the fleshy folds of his face, and only that terrible mouth remained.

Chkchkchkchk!

Sara eased away from him, no longer afraid, then stabbed the staff into the lock. Still holding onto the image of the Krinvox homeworld, she gave the staff a sharp twist. A geyser of rainbow-colored light exploded from the lock, bathing her in warmth, in safety, but she hesitated a moment more, watching as the Hooded Man finished his transformation and joined his new brethren.

"Bye, Michael," she said, weeping.

The rift opened beneath her and—

10

A flash of white, and suddenly Sara's world turned muted and dark. In a split second, her mind processed her new surroundings. She'd landed on her hands and knees, the soft blades of tall grass of the planet Yur brushing against her bare palms. A clear, starry night sky stretched to infinity above her, and the gentle breeze caressed her dirtied face, carrying the calls of nighttime insects. A rush of gratitude overcame her as Sara pondered just how long she'd been in hell, in the world of metal and chains. There'd been no life there, nothing organic at all, and to be welcomed back to a world brimming with the sights, sounds, and smells of living organisms filled her with an unspeakable joy.

"I'm back," she gasped, her throat still bruised, her voice strained.

Shrieks startled her, and Sara raised her head to see a small, firelit camp nearby. Electric fencing ran along the perimeter, but beyond that she glimpsed simple huts and a simple people. The lanky, blue-skinned cyclopean aliens danced hand-in-hand around bonfires, and Sara understood they weren't screams they emitted, but laughter. Blissful peals of delight.

She rose to a stand, knowing this scene well. She'd been here once before, right after the battle with the Glor. The Krinvox celebrated, hugging and singing and dancing and laughing. The sight was like a beacon for a weary traveler, their happiness calling to her, promising home and friendship.

Their infectious mirth propelled her forward, and Sara raced across the plains, drawn by the warm fires and the smell of exotic foods. Drawn by the knowledge that *he* would be there.

"Michael…" she panted, picking up her pace, ignoring her sore body and shaking off the disorientation of her jump. Her muscles quivered with expectation, she was so desperate to see him again. She wanted to tell him how sorry she was, how she'd made so many mistakes, but was ready to set all that right. *Please take me back*, she begged, weeping now, but laughing too, ecstatic to be so near him, and ready to receive his forgiveness and love.

There! Her heart halted within her and she slid to a startled stop. He was right there, skulking alone around a fire pit, his hood drawn in quiet contemplation. Killing the Glor had weighed heavily on him, but Sara had dismissed his reservations at the time. How stupid she'd been, she now understood with tremendous weight.

I'm so sorry, she thought, watching him as he wrestled with his conscience all alone. *I won't leave you again. I promise I won't.*

Out of the corner of her eye, Sara spotted another familiar figure. This one, however, filled her with contempt and regret. There, striding across the camp towards Michael was a young, thoughtless girl. Her slender shoulders reared back and proud, the girl tossed her long ginger hair to the side, haughty and cold. Sara glowered at her younger self, hating her. Hating everything she would do to her family, to herself, to the multiverse.

But I can change it, she realized. She'd been given a second chance, and she wouldn't waste it. She would make this right.

The younger Michael and Sara talked by the fire, and she watched, remembering that conversation. At last, they stood, awkward in each other's presence, a thousand miles between them. She had to reach them, to *teach* them. She—

A rumble shook the earth, tossing her off balance, and Sara knew. *Oh, no… No, please, not yet.*

A roar like a freight train bore down on her, and a frigid gust of wind pressed the grassy plains nearly flat and slapped against her back. She closed her eyes, warm tears traveling her filthy cheeks, and slowly turned to behold the Black Pillar as it stirred in the sky, spinning straight for her. In helpless horror she watched as it broke apart the sky and earth, then sucked up the shattered pieces of reality into its vacuum mouth. In a flash of despair, Sara nearly slumped to her knees, ready to be embraced into oblivion, but she thought of all those in hell who had given up the last shred of their souls so that she could arrive here. Too many sacrifices had been made to allow her to fix her mistakes. She owed it to them—to the Hooded Man, in particular—to fight.

Straining her teeth, she turned towards the camp and sprinted. All the while, she begged the Man in the Stetson, or God, or *whoever*, to give her a few more precious seconds. Just long enough to warn Michael. He'd save the day somehow, just like he always did, if only she could get to him.

She raced along as the vortex uprooted the perimeter fence and drew it towards the sky. A post came spinning like a helicopter blade for Sara, barely giving her the chance to react. She flinched and dove for the earth, sliding along the field, as the post first impaled the soft dirt inches from her, then hurtled into the air, aimed for the pillar of black space. Sara clambered to her feet, locking eyes on Michael, watching him rush about the camp, trying to save the Krinvox.

"*Michael!*" she screeched hoarsely, but her voice was broken and snatched by the vicious gales.

The terrified tribespeople sailed past her, clawing at empty air, screaming to be saved, only to be devoured by the devilish tornado. She ignored them as best she could, mere feet now from the camp. Once more she opened her mouth to scream for her husband, when the gravitational pull of the world-eater tugged her feet out from under her. Sara fell forward, smacking her face on the ground, knocking herself dazed. Her feet rose in the air, being pulled, pulled, pulled, and she—like the Krinvox before her—groped at anything she could reach, digging ruts into the dirt, willing herself to fight.

"*No, no, no!*" she stammered, hysterical.

The cyclone effortlessly plucked her from the ground, and she twirled end over end, falling towards it. "*Nooo!*" More Krinvox screamed by, disappearing into the Void, erased from Creation, and Sara readied herself to join their fate, praying for annihilation as opposed to returning to those accursed steelworks. But as she slapped against the Black Pillar, her body froze, hovering in the air, a net of purple lightning fixing her in place. She struggled against the netting, but it held like a spider web of violet electricity, even as trees, rocks, and aliens splashed into the inky stuff all around her.

What was this? Why wasn't she taken? What—?

Below, she saw Michael, his back to her. The entire camp was gone, and he alone was left to survey the damage. There was still time! But he started away from her, looking for the rift. Looking to leave, before she could tell him everything she had to say.

"*Stop!*" she screamed, reaching for him, beckoning him back. "*WAAAIIIIT!*"

At last he spun to face her, stricken in horror at the sight of her. She tugged against the electricity, fastened as she was to the pillar, and stretched her arms for him. "*WAIT!*"

But then that girl appeared—her younger self—ruining everything yet again. The Young Sara gripped Michael's sleeve and pulled him away, practically hurling him into their rift. Sara watched in agony as her husband disappeared from sight, her last hope gone.

In fury, she pointed a lone, condemning finger at her younger self and wailed like a…

A banshee, she realized, a pit of despondency opening in her stomach. Here, at the end, she'd come full circle, becoming the very witch she'd feared and hoped to erase. The crone had been a warning…a warning she knew her younger self would never heed.

On the ground, Young Sara paled at the ghastly image of her older self, then hurried for the rift and vanished in a flash of beautiful rainbow-colored light. With its occupants accounted for, the simple piece of paper that another deluded young woman named Adelaide Moore had created with black magick, casually lifted from the ground and drifted away from the pillar before disappearing far over the horizon, off to the Desert of Choosing where Sara would ruin them all by listening to Rip…

There, still suspended on the pillar like a hanged criminal, Sara bowed her head and cried. Only a small patch of earth remained of Yur—an asteroid floating in empty black. She'd seen so much in her time as a rift jumper, but never the end of a world...

"Mooootheeerrrrr..." a soul-sick hiss greeted her.

With an audible pop, the purple lightning flickered off, releasing Sara and dropping her to what was left of this reality. She landed hard, spraining her wrist. "Ack!"

"Yoooouuu'vveee retuuuurrned, Moootheerrrr..."

Grimacing in pain, Sara clutched her wounded hand and rose to her knees. The Black Pillar churned in place, its devastating advance halted and its hunger sated for the moment. Standing before it, the Shape that had consumed Toby. He stood there, a living shadow adorned in oily snakes, his arms opened in a welcoming gesture, and his bright white eyes and teeth beaming in innocent elation.

"Stay back!" she shrieked even as she scooted away. Her heel, however, reached the end of Yur, the fathomless reaches of the In-Between surrounding her. She caught her breath and stood her ground as the Shape walked closer, as though planning to hug her.

"Haaaavveee you sssseeeen my wwooorrrkk...?"

"I've seen it," she spat.

The creature paused at her reaction, his open-mouthed grin faltering into a slight frown. "Aaaarreeen't you prrooouuuddd, Moootheeerrrr?"

"NO!" she barked a cry, when her foot brushed against something sticking out of the dirt. Impossibly, it was her other chukrahas blade, the one that she'd lost on the day when the Krinvox were destroyed. *This* day. Relieved to see something familiar, she plucked it from the earth and held it before her, angry. "And I'm not your mother!"

"Sara," a voice called her, stern but unbothered. She shivered at the sound, recognizing it as the one that had spoken to her in her mind, trying to lure her away from the Rage. She and the Shape both turned to see a wizened older man wearing a long duster, a red scarf wrapped warmly about his neck...with a Stetson cowboy hat perched on his head.

She gaped. "You..."

He held a hand to her, earnest. "Follow me, Sara. Right now."

Sara balked at his request, then, for reasons she couldn't process, she turned back to the Shape. Her "child" was watching her, and for the first time, his smile was gone.

"Mootheerrrr?"

She shook her head and took a step towards the Man in the Stetson. "No," she declared.

The Shape raised his arms and roared, a wave of black energy spreading from him and tossing Sara to the ground. She landed backwards, her head hovering over empty air at the end of the world. The creature continued to bellow, and the Black Pillar resumed its march. The winds picked up, tousling her bangs, as the ground beneath her broke up into chunks. She glanced to the Man in the Stetson. He waited for her, a hand outstretched. "Hurry!"

Sara gripped the chukrahas blade, tucked it in her belt, and raced for the Man. With every step she took, the ground was obliterated in her wake, but she did not dare look back. She shut out the despondent cries of the Shape, seeing the Man in the Stetson through a sort of tunnel vision. He bent forward, extending his hand to her, and she clenched her teeth and leapt for it. As soon as her hands met his she—

11

—stood once more in the Desert of Choosing. The high-pitched wail of the Black Pillar was instantly gone, along with the shouts of its master. The stark silence caused Sara's ears to ring, but she knew that she was safe at last.

She lurched off balance, allowing the flush of vertigo that always accompanied a rift jump to pass. Once it did, she looked up and around. The Man in the Stetson was gone, but she saw a high cliff in the distance, its dark jagged edge backed by a brilliant full moon. From there she heard voices, carried by the wind. Shouting.

"*Get out!*" a panicked man's voice echoed in her ears. She strained to listen, only picking up broken pieces of the man's words. "*...Hand...on you! The Rage...no part...! Leave! Go away!*"

Was that Rip?

Sara took a few steps forward, her eyes adjusting to the darkness. She glimpsed two shadowed figures fighting in silver moonlight. One was significantly taller than the other, but the smaller shape seemed to be winning—

She gasped as the smaller figure suddenly barreled into its opponent, and the two tumbled over the edge of the cliff as one tangled mass. They disappeared in the craggy rock formation at the mesa's base, and Sara jogged, then ran, to investigate. The cliff was farther away than she'd estimated, and it was rough country getting there. More than once she tripped over dips in the rocky terrain, but pushed on, hearing an anguished cry sound out like a gong on the night. With each step she grew more excited, nearly laughing in delight, for she already suspected what she'd just witnessed. And if she were right, that meant there was still a chance for her *and* the multiverse.

At last she descended into the shadow of the cliff and searched the ground at its feet. Into the dark, she whispered, "M-Michael? Michael, is that you? Are you there? Are—"

She paused, her gaze resting on a lifeless body. *Rip's* body. Then it was true…

Sara knelt beside the Old Dog's broken form. Congealing blood pooled from the man's nose and ears. He wore only a dusty pair of jeans, with his feet and torso bare. Rip's peculiar glyphic tattoos remained, writhing under his flesh like serpents, circulating around a fresh wound in the man's scrawny chest. Whatever weapon had caused that deep puncture was gone, as well as the Old Dog's trademark leather jacket, but she knew who possessed both artifacts now.

She smiled and quickly scanned the night, hoping to find him. Anxiety built inside her, and she felt the knot above her left brow tightening. "Come on, come on," she muttered, until she saw him. He was small, only a boy, with Rip's jacket draped too-large across his broad shoulders. The boy's back was to her as he wobbled along the desert floor, fading into the night. But it was him.

It was Michael. Not a double, not a mirror. It was *her* Michael. This was the day his life as a rift jumper began. There was so much horror, so much pain he was about to suffer, but she could spare him that. She could warn him about everything and stop this nightmare before it ever began.

She opened her mouth to shout his name, but another voice stopped her.

"Sara."

She reacted in fright and spun, face to face with the Man in the Stetson. His expression was one of understanding, but also somber. "No," he said.

She knew what he meant, but couldn't understand why he stopped her. Sara turned back to Michael's slight outline, watching him round a hill, about to disappear from her sight entirely. "Is that… That's him, isn't it?"

"Yes," the Man said.

"H-How old is he?"

"Twelve," he said. "And yet he's already caused incredible grief. It'll be a burden that he carries with him for the rest of his life, no matter how much good he does."

She walked a few steps towards the boy, her heart beating so furiously she feared it would burst. "But I could warn him. There's so much that he has to face."

"What would you tell him?" he asked patiently.

She wanted to answer, but found her mind blank and was no longer sure what words would be sufficient to change this young Michael. But he was right there! And he was leaving! "I-I don't know. Something! Just to…" Her heart quieted. "I don't know."

Finally, the boy climbed the hill and descended, gone now. Lost in the desert.

Sara slumped, feeling defeated.

"He's not ready to hear what you would have to say to him," the Man told her, his voice a soothing baritone that reminded her of home—but a home she'd never seen.

Sara faced the enigmatic man before her, her eyes contracting to slits. "Who are you?"

He studied her for a moment, his face calm and unreadable. "You know who I Am."

She shook her head and paced about. "No. No, I don't believe that."

"Yes, you do," he immediately replied, confident.

She halted, furious and unsettled. "So I'm just supposed to believe that you're God, then."

He held her gaze, unflinching, until Sara could no longer meet his intense stare. She glanced away for a moment, and without answering her question, the Man circled back around to Rip's body. As he drew nearer, step by step, the tribal tattoos on Rip's arms and chest squirmed all the wilder. As the Man knelt beside the cooling corpse, the living ink released a screech so high-pitched that Sara clenched her teeth and instinctively reached to cover her ears.

The Man in the Stetson gingerly waved his hand over the open wound in Rip's chest, and the churning shapes beneath the flesh oozed to the surface in a sticky, black sludge. The oil formed a single shape like a headless snake and screamed, fleeing Rip's body like a cockroach suddenly exposed to the light. The Man watched the grotesque creature slither to the ground as though he might let it go. Then he reached out, clutched the serpent in one hand, and stood.

The black thing twisted and rattled, squealing like a frightened hog, as the Man clenched a tight fist around it. Instantly, the serpent broke out in blazing blue fire, flash-cooking to a charcoal husk. The remains broke into ash, and the Man brushed his hands together, the last of the dying embers drifting away on the wind.

Meanwhile, Sara watched, open-mouthed and silent.

Without fanfare, the Man in the Stetson took a seat on a large boulder at the base of the cliff, his eyes kind and gentle. "I've been looking forward to this day."

"Why?"

"I've wanted to talk to you. But, like Michael, you weren't ready to hear what I had to say. Now you are."

The Man seemed prepared to stay put for some time, and Sara worried how this conversation was going to go. His calm nature was beginning to unnerve her. "Are you here to kill me?"

"No."

She relaxed, but only marginally. Careful to keep her distance, she watched his every move. "Michael prayed to you all the time. Why did you never answer

240

him?"

"Didn't I?"

"But he looked for you."

"And he found me. Not always in the ways he'd prefer—not always like this, like I am now with you. But he always found me when he searched. When he quieted his spirit, he heard my voice."

"You took away his powers. You stopped protecting him."

"I haven't stopped protecting him at all," the Man replied matter-of-factly. "He's no longer immune to pain, but I still hold his life in my hand, and no harm can befall him without my permission. As for his unusual strength, Michael is strong in other ways now. He's outlived his need for the invulnerability of youth. That was always intended to be a means to an end. Without those particular gifts, he's grown kinder, more thoughtful of his actions, less reckless. His faith, and his capacity for love, have grown, as well, making him stronger *now* than he ever thought possible." He considered for a moment and continued, "Michael has done everything I expected of him, and now he's moved on to a different period in his life. It was time for him to leave behind childish things. Because he has chosen the Light, he's broken the curse, and now, all across the multiverse, other Michaels are choosing a similar path. He has brought them hope." Thoughtfully he paused and said, "He's a good man. A good son. He trusts me, even when he disagrees with me, and he will not be forsaken." Then the Man's tone became firm. "But right now, this isn't about Michael. It's about *you*."

"About me," Sara said, knowing, "and what I've done, right?"

"Yes," he said without pause.

Angrily she snapped, "Is this the part where you tell me how bad I screwed up? Because I *get* that. What do you think I'm doing?"

"Running."

"No! I'm trying to fix this before it ever starts!"

"You can't change things by visiting the past. All you can do is move forward."

"I don't want to move forward!" she blurted before she'd even processed the words. "I don't want this to be my life! I want everything like it was!"

He shook his head. "It's not going to be. It can't."

"I know that! Stop being so calm about this! I...I..." her chest heaved and hurt, but she shouted, "You knew this was all going to happen! I mean, you're God, right?"

"I knew."

"Then why didn't you stop me!"

He frowned. "Why didn't you?" She halted, but he continued without condemnation or anger. "Sara, did you really think anything good was going to come out of listening to Rip?"

Gritting her teeth, she said, "I had no idea that—"

He stood, still unflustered, but not willing to buy her excuses. "You had some idea. Maybe you didn't know the extent of what would happen, but you knew people would be hurt by your actions. You knew it was wrong, but you chose to do it anyway."

Buried by guilt, she fumbled to remove the shame that pressed upon her. "And you let me."

"Yes I did," he said unapologetically. He studied her a moment more, then turned his face to the stars. He stared at them for the longest time, and at last Sara joined him. He sighed, his voice tender. "Beautiful, aren't they?"

She eyed him, unsure about this change in his focus, but unable to deny the truth. Breathing deep, she released, "Yeah, they are."

"It's all so beautiful," he whispered, almost to himself. "You create something and hold its life in your hands, and there's no greater joy…except what you feel when your creation embraces you in return. Part of being a parent is letting your children go their own way. Make their own mistakes. You can guide them, reassure them, punish them—but ultimately they must lead their own lives. Even if they choose to reject you. But when they come *back* to you, it makes all the pain worth it."

The Man's powerful eyes fell on hers, and she couldn't look away. She found she didn't want to anymore. "I was always there for you, Sara. I saw you sitting alone at night as a young girl, feeling isolated and unloved. I heard your prayers then."

She gasped. "I didn't tell anyone that."

"I watched as Aztaroth moved into your life and orchestrated the pieces into place to bring you pain—all in his futile effort to compete with me. He used you to hurt me, and it *did* work. I watched Charlie beat you." At this, the Man's stoic face broke and he frowned. "I heard you cry, long after he'd fallen asleep drunk. I was there with you in the dark, weeping with you. But I found ways to speak to you. A cool breeze, a book you'd thought you'd lost that you suddenly found, a smile from a stranger, or a funny memory that suddenly came to mind."

Sara listened, her face twisting and flushing as she began to cry.

The Man's voice cracked with tears. "I was there all the time, reminding you that there was still Light, even in the Dark. Reminding you to hang on, and that I would make all things right. I made promises to you, in your secret heart, that I would rescue you, and sometimes, in your dreams, you believed me, and you danced. Oh, how you danced."

She wiped at tears, but could not quell them. She stopped trying.

"I sent Michael to you when it was time, and I brought my retribution on

Charlie for all that he'd done." The Man's face hardened. "Just as my judgment is ready to fall on those who manipulated him."

The Man in the Stetson once more crossed over to Rip's body. He bent at his knees and reached beneath the Old Dog, into his back jeans pocket. Before Sara could ask what he was doing, the Man retrieved Rip's ratty old notebook, given to him by his gramma. It was folded in half and smudged and torn.

The Man regarded it, solemn. "There are doors that men were not meant to open."

"What are you going to do with it?"

The Man in the Stetson thumbed through the notebook, selecting a page. He tore it out, folded it, and offered it to the breeze, where it drifted into the dark, out of sight.

"Who was that for?" she asked.

"Michael," he said, nodding his chin towards the distance where the frightened boy had fled. "He's going to need it in a few weeks."

She nodded. "Then he's the last jumper."

"Not the last," the Man said with a smirk, then ripped out one more page. He held the book in an extended hand and, like the black serpent, it burst into flames and was instantly consumed. Then the Man stepped forward and held the final page to Sara.

She shirked away from it, wide-eyed. "You're giving it to *me*?"

"To everything there is a season. The time of rifts will soon be ending, Sara. But there are still battles to fight. One battle, in particular, for you."

Her mood darkened. "Toby."

He retracted the paper for a moment, thoughtful. "Sometimes the best way to defeat evil is to let it run its course. Like a pressure valve that needs to be released, it will hiss and roar and burn—but then it's spent and useless. Aztaroth, Rip—even the 'god' they worship—all the plans they've formed are collapsing. They've been undone by their own scheming and betrayal." His brow creased in heartache. "But Toby is caught in the middle. He needs you." With the hint of a grin, he finished, "His mother."

A blast of remorse tore through her heart, and she missed the little boy so much she thought she'd break. Still, she shuddered as she looked back at the page. "I still don't know why you're giving me the last one. After everything I've done? I've nearly destroyed the entire multiverse."

"Which is why I know that you can appreciate how serious this is."

Her stomach trembled. "Can I win? Can I save Toby?"

"Would knowing the outcome change what you have to do?"

She smiled and rolled her eyes. "Guess not."

Sara knew what needed to happen next. There was something festering inside her that she'd held onto for too long. It had been a part of her long before she'd fallen for Rip's temptations. Charlie had nurtured it, but even he hadn't put it there. Maybe no one did. Maybe she'd grown it herself, cultivating it, hiding pieces of hate in her heart to secretly feed it. But she'd reached the end of the line, and the time had come to let it go.

"Michael had a beast in him," she said, to the point. "It was the part of the Rage that he kept inside. It kept him connected to the source." Sara folded her hands and pressed them to her stomach, nervous. "I've got one in me, too…don't I?"

The Man answered with a wise smile.

"I need… Can you…?" She pursed her lips, frustrated. "Take it out."

"It will hurt."

"I know. But it can't hurt any worse than it already does."

"Do you trust me?" he asked, his voice playful.

She thought on it, then chuckled. "It's… a work in progress."

"That's okay," he said. "We have time."

"For me to come around?"

He paused, and his regal face softly glowed. "For me to prove myself to you."

She faltered at that, oddly touched by the sentiment, but before she could say anything else, the Man placed a hand on her forehead. He closed his eyes, peaceful, and Sara felt a stirring within her.

"What—?" she made to ask, then bucked as something tore loose inside. She screamed and crumpled to her knees, but the Man's hand did not leave her head. The evil inside her burned, and she squirmed but could not get away. Sara thrust her head back, her face staring into the night sky, and cried as a terrible shape rattled violently against her ribs, breaking free.

"Come out," the Man commanded, and something black and spindly crawled its way up Sara's throat, prying her mouth wider and poking its head into the world. Her screams were garbled as the thing climbed to freedom, its faceless head opening into a dripping mouth that produced a tinny, ear-splitting shrill. It chattered and shrieked until white light shone from Sara's eyes and mouth, vaporizing the fetus-like beast in a radiant display that turned the night to day.

Just as quickly, the light faded and the night returned. The Man removed his hand and Sara fell forward on the ground, gasping, choking. He bent by her side and stroked her short hair. She looked to him, breathing hard, but smiling now. He smiled, too. "Woman, where are your accusers?"

She laughed, exhausted but lighter, and he helped her to her feet. "Wow, you weren't kidding," she said. "That was pretty terrible."

"But?"

Grinning, she said, "But it was time."

He once more extended the paper to her. "Then this belongs to you. Use it wisely."

She faced down the paper, recognizing the implications it held, and carefully took it. A thought struck her. "But how am I going to control it now? Rip said you needed the Rage to control the rifts."

"There are other ways. There is a way stronger than rage."

"Love," she spoke slowly, remembering what the Hooded Man had said. "Love is stronger than what we put it through."

He gave her a wink. "Love will always be stronger than hate."

"Then I'm done running. It's time to finish it, once and for all."

Sara looked to the paper in her hand, closed her eyes, and concentrated.

12

In a shower of rainbow light, Sara stepped out of the rift, back in Los Angeles. Only everything was…wrong. Buildings looked like they'd been bombed, missing walls and ceilings. Blown-out brick littered the streets, along with loose trash. Broken down cars, their tires missing and windows shattered, lined the road, bumper to bumper, and a thick carpet of fresh snow blanketed the barren landscape. Not a soul could be spotted, and Sara detected no sound. No birds, no insects, not even wind. She couldn't tell if it was day or night, as the clouds overhead suffocated the city, and a strange dim glow suffused everything.

Had she miscalculated the jump? Had she landed in some sort of post-apocalyptic version of L.A.?

She looked over her shoulder, hoping the Man in the Stetson would be there, waiting to answer all her questions, but he was gone. She pressed her lips together, determination settling in.

"Right," she mumbled. "Faith. Great."

She next turned to face the direction where Michael's school stood. Over the treetops, she spied the second story balcony where her double had plummeted to her death so long ago, and over that balcony—

The Black Pillar.

Her breath caught in her throat and she froze, terrified, at the sight of the obsidian column connecting to the heavens. But oddly, the Pillar wasn't moving. It remained in place, churning, but without the vacuum pull she'd seen before. It seemed almost dormant. Above the school, purple lightning flickered within the coal black clouds that swirled round and round, but traveled nowhere. A spasmodic lightning storm turned inside the charcoal sky, rotating around the central beam of power, as if in worship.

Sara finally released her breath, not sure what the pillar's strange behavior might mean, but taking note of the fact that the school was in the eye of the storm. Circling the ebon column, Sara noticed moving shapes against the flash of lightning. They were ships, she realized, alien in design. It appeared that an entire fleet of mismatched alien vessels—which certainly did not belong on this world—patrolled the circumference of the storm's center.

But what are they doing? Why are they here?

A scream tore through the silence, surprising Sara. Without realizing it, she drew her chukrahas. Alert, preparing for an attack, Sara hurried across the devastated street, taking cover behind a burned-out sedan. Inside the car, amidst the snow that had drifted in through the broken glass, she spotted blood, but no bodies.

The scream sounded again, and Sara bounced on her haunches. Whimpering followed the screaming in the distance. She heard crying, pleas for help. Leaning forward, she raised her blade into position and advanced to investigate. The girl doing the screaming was pale with terror, dressed in rags. Her shoulder-length blonde hair hung over her pretty face in curly tresses. She couldn't have been much older than Sara herself. The young woman looked absolutely frigid, her panicked eyes darting everywhere—to the streets, the alleys, the rooftops.

"Help me!" the woman shrieked to no one in particular. "Please! Help me!"

Sara kept low and out of sight. Something didn't sit right about the situation. She'd walked into her fair share of traps in the past, and by now she recognized one when she spotted it. Instead of revealing herself, she waited.

Five long minutes passed, with the girl still pleading for aid, though she made no effort to keep moving. Maybe the girl was injured. Maybe she *couldn't* move. *No. This is a trap. She's baiting.* Sara grinned. She'd almost misjudged the girl as weak when she was, in fact, quite cunning. She had to respect that, but she wasn't going to fall for it. Sheathing her knife, thinking the girl would just have to find another mark, Sara slinked across the street, back the way she came when—

"AAHHH!"

The girl let loose her loudest scream yet, and it was soon followed by other, more hellish, sounds. Snapping and snarling. Sara dropped behind another car, peeking over the top, watching as a pack of grey devils dropped from the roofs and oozed out of the shadows.

Chkchkchkchk!

Sara grit her teeth and cursed under her breath. She'd hoped to go the rest of her life without seeing those things again.

The monsters crouched, their spears clacking on the concrete. The beasts hissed and chomped their cracked jaws, circling the blonde woman. One of the creatures growled and leapt through the air with blinding speed, tackling the screaming girl to the ground, slashing at her clothes like a feral beast.

Sara sighed. *Time to be the hero.* "Here we go."

She rose from her hiding place, and banged on the roof of the car. "Hey!"

Naturally, every monster paused and faced the newcomer.

She pounded again. "Come on!"

The pack disregarded their former prey, now fully focused on Sara. They galloped for her, bounding over cars, even scaling the buildings—running sideways along the brick walls—trying to take her from above. Sara sucked in a deep breath, flexing fingers around her chukrahas, suddenly not sure how she expected to survive this. With strong legs, a wall-running devil kicked off a building's face, its dark-stained talons outstretched as it sailed for her. Sara fell into a fighting stance, lashed out with her curved blade, and chopped the flying creature's featureless face. A black geyser sprayed from the wound, painting her face in blood. The thing went down without incident, and Sara wrenched her knife from its bulbous head, as four more monsters reached out for her.

She slashed and kicked, whirling out of reach of a clawed strike. The things advanced on her, more than she'd counted before, but she hacked at them, cutting at the creature on her right, while directing a boot to the face of the thing to her left. But no matter how many as she struck down, more took their place, swarming her like bees.

They cut into her, drawing blood, ruining her clothes. Somewhere in the melee Sara lost her blade. In the final moments of the struggle, she feared she'd end up infected by the devils and mutated into one of their own kind, but then remembered that the Hooded Man had told her that only happened in hell. No, here, she supposed she'd just be killed. After that…well, she hoped the Man in the Stetson would be waiting for her.

"Get down!" the blonde woman's voice broke through the din of snarling and growling.

Ker-krack!

A crashing blast echoed down the sonorous streets, and Sara barely had time to duck out of the way before a round zipped across the distance, catching an attacking creature in the back of its head, emptying its brains. Black bile splashed down on Sara as the headless thing lurched over. From her place on the ground, Sara saw the monsters turning away from her, one of them taking a rifle shot to the throat for the trouble. The thing pawed at its wound, but was dead before it hit the snow-covered concrete.

Ker-krack!

A rifle fired again and again, gunning down two more of the monsters, their obsidian muck-for-blood drenching Sara. She wiped at her face, finding her discarded knife on the asphalt in the process. She slid underneath a creature and grabbed the weapon, then flew up and stabbed the thing full on in the chest. It howled, vomiting black everywhere. She yanked the curved blade free, continuing to battle. Her strength returning, Sara danced around the rifle fire, adding her own numbers to the ever-increasing body count.

In no time, the monsters' numbers were halved. Then halved again. Soon only two remained, and one shot its predatory spears towards her, but flinched back, a bullet where its brain used to be.

One grey devil remained, and Sara smiled, black-blood covering her like a second skin. Gripping the blade tight, she raced for the monster, her chukrahas held high. She shrieked in a barbaric war cry, bringing the blade down with satisfaction.

"No, wait!" the blonde-headed girl shouted from somewhere behind her. "Don't!"

Sara ignored the waif, plunging her steel through the top of the devil's skull, cleaving it in half. The thing stood there, stock still, coughed up muck, then simply fell straight down. Sara pulled her knife free, breathing heavy and feeling better than she had in a long time. She wiped the curved blade on her jeans— realizing suddenly that her jeans were just as filthy as her weapon.

"Are you crazy?" the blonde girl again, shouting as she stood in front of Sara. The girl held a rifle by the barrel. It had been *her* gunning down Sara's attackers. The girl didn't look like she weighed ninety pounds soaking wet, but she sure could handle herself in a fight.

From behind them, the roar of an engine. Sara gripped her knife, ready for anything, and watched as an old red muscle car, decked out in spikes and caged windows, pulled up with a squalling halt. The driver's side door opened, and a man hurried out in military gear. He was lantern-jawed, with long sideburns and a smooth face. His brown hair was oily and slicked back, and a pair of glasses rested on the bridge of his pointed nose. At first glance, he was oddly familiar, but Sara couldn't place him.

"What just happened?" he demanded, out of breath as he approached, an M16-A1 assault rifle in his hand.

Sara kept her blade ready, feeling like an animal backed into a corner. The man joined the blonde girl, who still stood gaping before Sara like she expected an explanation for having her life saved.

"I *had* him," the blonde huffed, "then *she* shows up! I've been out here for an hour, and she blows the whole thing! Where were you guys?"

"We got jumped," the bespectacled man with the automatic rifle defended. "There were more than we thought."

Sara watched them bicker for a moment more, until Blondie leaned forward, nearly charging her. "Hope you're happy! What were you doing out here anyway?"

Sara stiffened, indignant. "You wanna try something? Bring it on."

The girl looked ready to hit her, but Glasses held her off. "Easy, Candice, easy," he calmed.

"Let me go, Edward!" she railed.

Sara froze, looking to the man. *Edward?* She remembered him now. She'd met his double once before, on her first jump. Edward was Michael's older brother, which meant—

"Sara?"

Her heart skipped a beat at his voice. *No…I'm not ready yet. I'm not ready to see him.*

A brown-haired man stepped out of the muscle car, his crisp blue eyes filled with shock. He looked different. Older, too. But still he wore his leather hooded jacket, T-shirt, jeans, and muddied sneakers. His face was dirty, his features hard—forged by battling those creatures, no doubt. He joined the group, standing behind Edward, watching her as long seconds passed.

It's not too late.

Forgetting the last two years, forgetting the betrayal and the hurtful words and the lies, she ran to him, his name like sweet chocolate on her lips. "Michael," she breathed, ready to hug him. To hold him and kiss him and pray he'd take her back. *Please love me… Please forgive me…*

But the blonde girl was immediately standing in the gap, barring her entrance into her husband's embrace. Sara skidded to a halt, confused and angry.

"Who do you think you are?" Blondie snapped.

Sara scowled. "I'm his wife, *chick*. Who are you?"

The girl leveled at Sara, her hands on her hips. "His *wife*."

PART TEN: TURN OUT THE LIGHTS

1

Sara Morrison struggled against her bonds and faced her three captors. The brothers huddled together, exchanging harsh whispers, while the third—Blondie—fretted, her thin, manicured eyebrows bunched together in worry. Sara watched her closest of all, as the blonde girl rubbed at her arms, her mouth hanging open as though a protest perched on her perfectly shaped lips, ready to hurry out.

As for the men, Edward Morrison—her brother-in-law, whom she'd never met properly, unless she counted his doppelgänger—grit his teeth in a snarl, gripping his rifle as he chewed noisily on curses. Tucked in his belt, her chukrahas that he'd confiscated from her. The shape of his face was different, squarer, but his thick brow and straight nose were identical to that of his younger brother, Michael.

She had the hardest time facing Michael, and only found the courage to look up at him when his back was turned to her. It was surreal seeing him again. Even stranger to be this close to him, but unable to talk. None of them had talked to her yet, content to keep her bound in zip ties and sitting cross legged in the corner of the room. As soon as their introductions had been made, they'd immediately taken her captive and thrown her into the trunk of Edward's customized cherry red 1969 Chevrolet Camaro SS. She rode in darkness over rough terrain, sensing many stops, many turns. Alien noises like massive engines grumbled by periodically, and she noticed the Chevy always slowed to allow the sources of such powerful sounds to pass before moving on again.

Ships, she reckoned. The same ships she saw circling the Black Pillar that rose from Michael's old school like a great onyx tree.

At last, Sara was taken out of the car trunk and brought inside the group's temporary camp—a hollowed-out three-story office building. The windows had long since been busted out, and the cold winter wind moved freely through the rooms, chilling her. Edward parked the Chevy in the adjoining parking garage, covering it in a camouflaged tarpaulin, saying something about it being too dangerous to move at night, so they'd have to wait it out inside the building before they could move on at first daylight.

Outside, Sara heard the prowling bands of devils—their distant snapping and snarling making it impossible for her to relax. Occasionally, an alien scouting vessel zoomed by, too. She had so many questions regarding this place, but right now none of those seemed important to her.

She was with Michael again…only everything was wrong.

Edward's voice rose, "No way," and Michael turned towards her, catching her glance. She blushed and looked to the side, and by the time she'd gathered the strength to meet his eyes again, he had looked back to his brother.

"Let me talk to her," Michael said.

Edward shuffled in place, flexing gloved fingers around the grip of his M16. "You're not thinking clear."

At his side, Blondie blurted at Michael in a desperate plea, her wavy curls bouncing, "Are you nuts? She's a *psycho!*"

Michael sighed and hung his head, rubbing at his brow tiredly. Blondie touched his sleeve with affection and Sara frowned at the contact. "Michael," the girl begged, softer now. "You can't trust her. She's dangerous. Please."

"Dude," Edward said, gruff. "We've already lost too much. We play this smart. We treat her just like any other monster the Rage throws at us." He grimaced. "We shoot her in the head."

"No," Michael cut through, not distressed, but sounding exhausted. "You're worried about me. I get that. But if the Rage has brought her into play, then that's gotta mean that we're nearing the End. She's got to know something."

"We'll get it some other way," Edward protested, real sympathy underpinning his contempt.

"It's not worth it," Blondie said, her grey eyes sad as she slipped her hand into his, their fingers interlacing.

Sara flinched, growing sick.

Michael smiled at the girl and gave her delicate hand a squeeze. "It is to me. I have to know. I have to… I need closure."

Edward blew out a breath, then hoisted his rifle. "Fine. But if she moves, I'm putting her down."

Michael nodded, then shared a caring look with Blondie before releasing her hand. The woman kept her distance as Michael approached Sara, hefting a rifle of his own. Unlike Edward's, the gun didn't appear Earth-formed, but alien, as its stock fit around Michael's trigger hand like a shield.

Sara's husband came to a stand before her, his long, chestnut-colored hair combed back behind his ears. His blue eyes were as true and bright as ever as he evenly held her gaze. Lips pursed into a tight line, he said, "Hello, Sara."

Sara relaxed and tried to stand, "Michael, I—", but he had his rifle aimed in an instant.

"Don't," he said, calm. "Don't get up."

She resumed her position, humiliated and angry. "You don't have to do this."

"Who are you?" he asked as though he hadn't heard her.

"You *know* who I am," she snapped.

"You're Sara. How do I know you're the Sara *I* knew?"

"This is stupid."

Behind Michael, Blondie aimed her rifle and commanded, "Answer the question."

Sara glared at her, then turned back to Michael. Frustrated, she rambled, "Your favorite band was Metallica. You love sprinkled donuts. You saved me from Charlie! On my first jump, we met Edward and Seth in some tech-poor dimension like the Civil War. We were *married* there." Seeing Blondie growing visibly uncomfortable, Sara grinned cruelly. "Want me to talk about our honeymoon? About the lavender silk nightie I bought and how you—"

"Enough," he said, harsh, his cheeks reddening.

She'd meant to hurt Blondie, but saw an ache in Michael's eyes that instantly grieved her. More apologetic, she continued, "It's me."

"The last thing I said to you," he said, his voice quiet and broken. "What was it?"

She didn't have to pause to think. She'd replayed that moment in her mind for two years. "You said 'I love you'."

Embittered, he asked, "And what did you say?"

"I…" She looked to the floor. "I said I didn't care."

Silence drifted in on the cold and Sara felt a sob in her heart that she would not release.

After a moment, Michael asked, "Why are you here?"

This time she met his eyes, praying he'd see the truth in her. "I need your help. I'm trying to fix this."

"She's lying," Edward called from the back of the room.

Michael watched her intently, his face totally unreadable. "Are you lying?"

"*No,*" she bit back, earnest.

"Rip said you would come back. We were fated to have a big throwdown. Is that what this is?"

She rolled her eyes. "No, of course not. Rip's… That's over, okay?"

He remained quiet for the longest time until Sara felt ready to burst. Nearing tears, she said, "Michael, please. You know me."

"No," he said, briskly. "I don't. Not anymore. It's been five years."

Sara balked. *Five years?* She'd only meant to be gone for days, not years.

Before she had a chance to reply, he demanded, "Who sent you?"

She considered then eyed him through her brow. "Your friend in the Stetson."

Michael's stony veneer finally cracked and recognition flashed across his eyes. His lips parted, just slightly, but he quickly closed them, tightening his jaw.

Michael lowered his gun and spoke to Edward over his shoulder. "I'm cutting her loose."

Sara beamed as Michael shouldered his alien rifle and knelt in front of her, slipping a knife from a sheath on his belt and beginning to cut her ties. Edward stomped forward, red in the face, and Blondie was right behind him.

"What are you doing?" Edward roared.

"Michael," Blondie hollered. "Stop! Don't do this—"

Michael raised up, and Sara stretched her arms, the tightness in her chest finally loosening. She stood, her legs tingly from being tucked under her for so long, but was careful to make no sudden movements. Edward had his rifle in her face again, nearly hopping from one foot to the other. "Don't move!" he ordered. "Don't you move!"

Sara lifted her hands in surrender, but Michael gently placed a gloved hand on the barrel of Edward's M16 and eased it down. "Stop," he said in a bit of an aggravated whine. "Let's hear what she has to say." He looked to the girl. "Okay?"

Blondie groaned, then lowered her gun. Edward's eyes bulged in outrage behind his glasses, but eventually he eased.

"Trust me," Michael said, and Edward shot him a hateful look.

"This better not—"

"It won't," Michael interrupted the half-thought, confident.

Edward shook his head and marched away. "I'm making a perimeter sweep." He banged out of the doorway, clanging noisily down the hall.

Michael watched his big brother go, his shoulders sagging now that the confrontation had abated. Putting on a half-hearted smile, he reached into a pocket of his jacket, which had acquired a few more tears since Sara had last seen it, and procured a protein bar. He tossed it to her. "Hungry?"

She greedily snatched the bar and immediately shred open the wrapper. She'd not eaten since before she was sent to the Maestro's weird hell prison, and she was absolutely famished. As she bit off the head of the bar, Michael stepped back, standing beside the blonde girl. They shared a quiet exchange—a question of certainty, an affirmation of security. Sara remembered those conversations.

Emotions spoken with only a glance or a nod. That's how it was to be married to someone. To know someone so intimately—to have them know you—so that words weren't even needed.

She slowed her chewing to frown, casting her eyes to the floor.

"You're here to help," Michael said to her. "How?"

Sara swallowed a bite and said miserably, "The Thing destroying the multiverse? The Thing behind the Black Pillar? It's Toby."

Michael didn't flinch at the revelation. Only blinked, solemn. "I know." His eyes dulled and he said, "I was there when it happened."

2

FIVE YEARS EARLIER

"I love you," Michael said, feeling something break inside him.

Sara turned to him, the winds of the building storm overhead rustling her long red hair. Her eyes were solid black as she effortlessly declared, "I don't care."

Then she and the Old Dog stepped into the rift in a burst of light and were gone…

Michael stood there, clutching his injured shoulder, panting laboriously, watching as the sheet of paper lifted off and vanished into the night, his every hope fleeing with it. Sara was… His chest hurt, as sobs broke loose.

Sara was *gone*.

But, no, it was worse than that. She was lost. Lost to him, to the Light. The Dark had claimed her, and Rip had left behind a prophecy of sorts: that they would have to fight.

I can't, Michael thought, a sharp pain piercing his heart. How could he fight her? *Please, God, don't make me do that.*

Sirens sounded in the distance, and Michael remembered where he was. He was at the school of his youth, on the darkest day of his life—now made darker by Sara's decision. The cops would soon arrive to discover the young girl Michael had pushed to her death when he was only a boy.

"W-We have to get out of here," he said, feeling numb and uncertain about his own future. He turned to the boy in his care, but Toby Jeffries stood stone still, trembling as he wept.

"She left," the small child whimpered, staring into the night, hysteria building in his frightened eyes.

Michael bent down and took hold of his arm. "We have to go!"

The two of them trundled across the street, hurrying a block away before ducking down an alley. A fog of pain enshrouded Michael's mind, and he struggled to stay on course, while Toby jerked in his grip. "Who's going to tuck me in?" the boy wailed. "Who's going to kiss me good-night and sing me songs?"

"Toby," Michael croaked, bleeding from the wounds Sara had delivered him, unable to collect himself enough to comfort the child. He was woozy, barely able to stand. He paused in the alleyway, bending over to catch his breath. "It's…it's going to be okay. But we need to—"

Toby screamed, wide-eyed, and terrified, "*She left!*"

Michael wrapped his good arm around the child and pulled him into a tight embrace. He wept freely, knowing how much Toby loved Sara. She was a mother to him, and now…

How could you, Sara, he cursed in his heart, hating her for what she'd done.

"Who will take care of me?" the boy cried pitifully in Michael's arms.

A crash sounded from the other end of the darkened alley. Michael pushed the boy behind him, bracing for another fight, although he wasn't sure he had the strength for it any longer. "Who's there?" he snapped. From the shadows, a black-cloaked hunched-over straw man shuffled forth, wagging a gnarled hooked finger.

Michael narrowed his eyes, recognizing the Maestro.

He left Toby behind and stomped for the hobbled creature, hefting him up by the lapel of his tattered garments. "You said I could stop her!"

But the Maestro only stared back at him, dumbfounded. "Past, present, future…all running together… I-I don't know what happens. What will happen…what *has* happened… Only that it begins here." He rasped, his dry voice the sound of a dusty tomb opening, spilling out death, "The end begins here."

The demon sobbed, as though lost and confused, and Michael dropped him to the ground, his own vision blurry, his thoughts disorientated. He'd lost too much blood—suffered too much tonight. He needed to hide, to regroup, to figure out how to stop Sara from… from doing what she'd already done.

God, where are you? What am I supposed to do?

"That's the Maestro!" the boy exclaimed, his ruddy cheeks bathed in tears. "Why are you letting him go?"

Michael faced the boy. "Toby, listen, you—"

"I thought you were a good guy," he cried.

"I am."

"Then why aren't you fighting him?" A cold wind suddenly took to flight, stirring the loose trash in the narrow alley. "Why was Sara scared of you?"

"It's not like that." Michael stepped closer, but Toby backed away, burning with anger.

"This is your fault!" he hollered, his tiny body quivering in rage. He clenched his fists as they slowly turned to ice. "You made her leave!"

Michael's heart beat faster as he waved down the boy. "No—"

"You're a liar!" Toby said. The ground trembled beneath their feet and the boy bowed his head, channeling his strength. A light snow swirled in the alley, and Michael feared what would come next. He thought of that frightening ice serpent Toby had used to eradicate the raiders in the Desert of Choosing.

"Toby, you have to calm down," Michael said, his voice shaky. "You're opening yourself up too wide, just like before. You're going to lose control."

When Toby rose, his eyes were black. "I *am* in control," he said, his voice deepening even as the words left him. It wasn't the boy's voice anymore.

Something was speaking through him now.

"No…" Michael gasped.

Impossibly, the shadows in the alley screamed and danced and slithered for the child, as though the boy were drawing them into himself.

"Toby, stop!"

The black lashed out like sticky tongues, wrapping around Toby's arms, his legs, his neck. The boy grinned all the while as living shadows coalesced around him, encasing him in a hideous cocoon. The blasphemous Shape pulsated and grew, taking on the loose form of a man, but could not maintain that outline for long. Shadows dripped and oozed and reformed, as if even they could not agree on what monstrous visage they would eventually retain.

Michael stepped away from the gelatinous blob, aghast. "Toby?"

But the Maestro stumbled forward, his skeletal hands held up in homage. "Master?" he moaned.

The vague Thing rose and swelled to fill the alley mouth with its sacrilege, its obsidian tentacles lashing out to lick the brick wall. Though it had no eyes—no face—it still seemed to watch the Maestro as the fractured demon bent his knee. "I've waited for you for so long, my Master," he blubbered. "I have written my song in the blood of the worlds…all for you. My music…it was always for you… *Please*, Master… Please tell me now…" The demon wept through a smile. "Did I please you? Did my concerto please you?"

The bodiless Thing clicked and gurgled deep within its formless bowels, and Michael held his breath. Then something like arms shot out of the muck and violently seized the Maestro, lifting him off the ground. The Maestro gasped in what sounded like delight at first, but quickly transformed to horror.

Frost crawled up the walls of the alley in a spider-web pattern, slinking along the floor and encircling Michael's feet. He shivered in the midst of this miniature blizzard and watched as a dark black *power* coursed like ebon lightning from the Shape and into the Maestro. The demon rattled in the air, bombarded by pure malevolent rage until—

A crack detonated and the Maestro was just…no more. A wave of ash pelted Michael and he looked with awestruck marvel at the Maestro's powdered remains mingling with the snow on the ground.

The demon had been totally vaporized.

"N-No…" Michael breathed in wonder.

The Shape merely regarded him emotionlessly as the storm clouds above parted. Then the slithering thing turned its amorphous body towards the heavens, beholding the awesome storm, its gullet lit from within by jagged purple lightning.

Against all reason, Michael reached for the monstrosity. "Toby?" he whispered.

The shadowed spawn spread its gelatinous bulk like wings, let out a howling squall, and shot up into the flickering clouds accompanied by a clap of thunder. Michael gaped into the sky, watching as the inky shape vanished into the starry expanse with a twinkle of fading starlight.

Michael glanced once more at the vanquished remains of the Maestro, then hurried out of the alley, shouting into the night. "Toby! *Toby!*"

Bright lights blinded him as he swayed into the street. A blaring honk quickly followed, and suddenly he was lifted off his feet, slamming face first into a windshield. The car's brakes locked and Michael was thrown, tumbling side over side to the pavement. His world continued to spiral, even as his body lay still, and he looked up through bleary eyes into the night, watching the storm that Sara had created as it slowly began to dissipate at last, its damage done.

His sight dimmed at the edges, and he felt himself slipping in and out of consciousness. Toby's wintry wind remained, chilling him to his core, and he wondered if this were the end for him. *I failed…*

From faraway, he heard a car door opening, then slamming shut. Heard the frantic clicking of heels on asphalt. Just as the black sought to claim him, Michael's vision was filled with a soft and pretty face. A young woman with wide and earnest grey eyes hovered over him, her kinky white-blonde locks caressing his scraped face and filling his head with the aroma of lilies. She searched him, hysterical, her thin nose crinkling at the end while her lovely mouth said, "Are you okay? Oh no, please don't be dead."

He wanted to laugh, even as she fretted over him.

"I'm so sorry," she rambled, flapping her hands wildly as though she'd just discovered an icky bug. "You were just…there!"

Michael watched her fuss over him. He tried to talk, but his mouth was dry. Encroaching darkness threatened to snuff her face from his view, when suddenly—

—he senses a sharp whoosh *as a switchblade knife cuts the air just below his ear and plunges hilt-deep into his shoulder. Snarling, he looks to see the knife still stuck in him, then turns further to see the blonde girl from the couch, backing away as her pouty lips part in mounting terror. The rubber string is still tied to her arm, and pink rings circle her wide grey eyes.*

He saw the girl, but *not* the girl. It was her. The same expressive grey eyes that instantly relaxed him. The same perfectly-shaped mouth, downturned in an adorable frown. But she was different. His vision flickered between one dimension and the next—here and another world, a future world, in the office of Salvatore "Sal" Frazetta that he visited a little over a year ago.

Michael wraps his hand around the knife and gives a jerk, wrenching it free, before tossing it aside. Growling, he surveys the fresh tear in his ratty jacket. "Don't. Touch. The Jacket."

The girl whimpers and staggers behind the table where she concocted her blue narcotic. Enraged, Michael takes an angry arm and smashes aside the equipment she used, splashing fluorescent blue liquid all over the floor. He reaches down and undoes the strap on her arm, throwing it to the side, then grabs her with both hands as he'd done to the late Tony Carlson. He slams the girl against the wall, suspending her bare feet off the floor so that she faces him at eye level.

In that moment, he feels the fear in her as her body shakes uncontrollably, but she is too numb from the drugs to fight back any more. She is helpless. He could kill her. Snap her in two without any effort and all of her pain would go away. He'd be doing her a favor, ending her miserable life.

It would be easy.

He studies her, curious. The girl before him is weak, and he pities her for it. There is something in her grey eyes, such surrender there. She's given up. Somewhere inside, he knows how that feels.

"What's your name?" he grumbles.

"C-Candice," she weeps.

"Where are you from?"

She scans his eyes, as though unsure of the reason behind his question. "Wy-Wyoming."

Michael cools and releases a heavy sigh, then glances to the table. He reaches over and picks up one of the needles to hold it before her, making sure she gets a good look at its glowing contents. "Go back there. And never do this again."

The girl nods to the best of her ability. Then he lets her go.

"You…" he breathed, his mind clearing from memories of another world.

The beautiful girl touched his face, full of compassion. "I am *so* sorry," she said, quieting. "I'll get you to a hospital, okay? You're going to be okay." She paused, combed her wavy hair over an ear and smiled, her cheeks dimpling as they blushed. "I'm Candice, by the way."

3

NOW

"Her name is Candice."

Edward had returned from his patrol relatively clear-headed, though he refused to speak to Sara or look too long in her direction. Reunited, the four of them collected assorted trash from the litter-strewn building and built two small fires in their temporary camp.

Michael and Sara sat at one of the fires near the window, while Edward sat next to the door, passing the time by reading a worn Tom Clancy paperback novel near another fire by the entrance. Next to him, Candice warmed her hands, rigid and hesitant, keeping a careful watch on Sara.

Michael didn't face Sara, just poked at the burning embers of trash with a stick. Sara, however, could hardly take her eyes off him as he spoke. "We've been married three years now."

Sara felt ill. Three years… She looked to the fire, tears frozen in her eyes.

No doubt Michael could sense her shock and hurt, but they were feelings he didn't share. Quietly, he explained, "She sort of hit me with her car." He chuckled. "I'd actually met her once before, on a jump. Another her. I saved her once when I had the chance to kill her." He grinned, reminiscing. "I actually met her on the world right before I met *you.*"

Sara brooded. "Funny how life doesn't turn out at all like you thought it would," she muttered into the flame, echoing words she had spoken to Michael on their wedding night.

Clearing his throat, he said, "Anyway, Candice had just come to the city, looking to be a singer. After she hit me with the car, she took me to the hospital and stayed with me. I was out of it for a couple days. When I came to, all of *this* started happening."

Sara eyed him, trying to put her emotions aside. "What *is* happening?"

His brow furrowed. "The storm came first. The blizzard. Days grew shorter, night stretched longer. Then the rift opened at the school, and the ships moved in. Ground troops soon followed. And monsters." His blue eyes glazed over, as though he were lost in the scary parts of a movie. "I recognized a lot of them—but there's no reason they should've all been together. They were all from different dimensions, but they were suddenly here with no explanation: Trigarian assassins, warships from the Filax Battalion of Igos 5, those Underdweller guys on the lavaspiders we ran into on our anniversary…there's even a Great Xanawhales Hortex floating around somewhere, though luckily we've stayed clear of *that* thing so far. Those are no fun."

A shiver clambered up Sara's back. "Underdwellers? From Venus?"

He nodded, meeting her eyes. She stifled a curse. "I ran into them a while back. They were preparing for something called 'The Black Fire'. They said their god was going to be reborn in it and reward them."

"Black Fire. The Black Pillar."

It was Sara's turn to nod. She gnashed her teeth, "I saw Venus destroyed. Lady Vasariana...all of them."

"*What?*"

She watched the flickering firelight. "I'm linked to Toby. I can... I get these visions. I see the worlds he visits. He makes me watch as he destroys them. But if the Underdwellers are *here* now—"

"Then that means Toby may be sparing those who have sworn allegiance to the Rage." He scratched at the dark stubble on his broad chin. "Makes sense. More have been showing up every day, like refugees from all the worlds Toby's destroying."

"And they're around the school," Sara finished the thought, "because of the rift there."

"They're preparing for something," Michael said. "But for what?"

Sara rubbed the chill out of her hands. "Have you ever heard of something called 'the Gateworld'?"

He shook his head, confused.

"Rip told me about it once," Sara said. "It's supposed to be the Origin Point for all the rifts—everything blooms out from it like stress cracks after an earthquake. The faultlines are always there, but when you put the right amount of pressure in the right place, it all opens up like a domino effect." She shrugged. "Apparently, that's what the Maestro and his army had been looking for all that time. Rip, too." Sara recalled the Hooded Man and his reaction to the tale, and said, "Not everyone believes it exists, but if it does, then it's the lock on the Rage's cage. If he can break *that* world, then it's all over."

Michael considered the information darkly. "How do you know *this* isn't the Gateworld?"

She leveled him a serious look. "Because, I'm thinking if it was, we wouldn't be having this conversation."

He nodded, his eyes roving over the fire. Sara could see the gears of his mind turning. "When I was in the White Place before, the Man in the Stetson said that the Rage wanted to shatter the mirrors of the multiverse to escape, but that didn't make sense to me. If the multiverse is near-infinite, how could It ever smash all the mirrors? But if there's just one, in particular, It has to smash to start a chain reaction—"

Michael turned and looked out the window across the frozen wasteland, at the Black Pillar rising into the heavens. Sara regarded it, too, and said, "The Rage is strong here, remember? It got to Rip's Gramma Moore, you...*me.*" Quieter, she finished, "Toby." Her heart aching for the child she once cuddled in her arms, she pressed on, "Toby released It. Not all of It, but enough that It's able to reach through the bars of Its cage, feeling around, trying to find the Gateworld and set Itself free."

"And destroying countless worlds in the process," Michael muttered.

"I could try and find the Gateworld," she offered. "But that could take forever—literally. No one else who has looked for it has been able to find it, and that's if it even exists at all."

Michael met her eyes. "It doesn't matter if it exists. The Rage believes it does, and It's going to wipe out every dimension in Its way until It finds it. Unless we stop It first." He nodded over his shoulder, "If that pillar *is* Its arm trying to reach around for the lock—"

Sara grinned, thrilled to be talking with him again. Not shouting, but talking. Planning. Coming up with a battle strategy to fight the bad guys. That was what they used to do, and they could have that again. *Please trust me.* Finishing his thought, she blurted, "Then we cut off the arm at the source. Close down the rift at the school, save the multiverse."

He stood, his anxiety building as the plan began to take shape, and paced around the fire. "It won't be that easy. Gateworld or no, Toby's been shattering the mirrors of the cage. With every dimension he destroys, the multiverse grows weaker, and the Rage gets a little bit stronger." He bashed his fist into his palm. "I knew it. We'd already seen their forces pulling back. They're circling the wagons. Creating interference so that nothing can get through. Toby must be *close* now. Or, at least, thinks he's close."

At the mention of Toby, they both grew sullen, and Sara found herself taking a deep breath and slowly releasing it. "This is all my fault." She looked to him, searching his steely blue eyes. "Isn't it?"

He wouldn't face her. Instead he crouched back down, stirring the burning trash with his stick. "It's both of ours." Michael glanced her way, as if testing himself, but quickly returned his attention to the fire.

"But we can fix it together... Right?"

His face firmed, and he nodded towards the entrance. "That's...up to the group. We're a team. We make decisions together. I don't trust myself to lead anymore."

His admission was colored with a great deal of remorse, and the corner of Sara's mouth twitched into a frown. Had she done that to him? Caused him to doubt himself?

"He's proud of you, you know," Sara offered feebly. "The Man in the Stetson.

He told me. He said you're stronger now than you ever were with your powers."

Hope and relief flickered on Michael's handsome face, but he quickly diffused it.

"He said you won't be forgotten," she told him.

He nodded, accepting the praise, but was careful not to reveal any emotion. "Thanks."

She rested in the quiet moment that followed, needing a small breather from the great stakes they'd been discussing. "You found your brother."

A ghost of a smile played at his chapped lips. "Yeah. When I woke up in the hospital after Candice ran me over, Edward and Seth were there, too—bringing *me* in. The *other* me. The twelve-year-old version of me that had just been shot by Big Joe's men. Little Me was taken out of this world and thrown into the Desert of Choosing to face Rip and all of that. At the same time, *I* woke up. I found them. Told them everything."

Sara gauged him closely.

Michael seemed to sense her unspoken accusation and said, "*Everything*, Sara. What I did to the other you when I was twelve. I told them about Rip and rift jumping and…meeting you again. How you left. Everything."

Sara considered this and glanced at Candice out of the corner of her eye.

"Candice knows, too," Michael said, as if reading her mind. "They all do. No more lies. They cost me too much last time."

Sara frowned and resumed her fire-watching. Now she envied Candice all the more. "How'd they take it?"

He flashed a cavalier grin. "Not great at first, but the aliens showed up, so they couldn't really afford to doubt me then. We've been together ever since, trying to fight back."

Joy bloomed in her heart, and Sara wanted to throw her arms around Michael. He'd wanted for so long to be reunited with his family. And now he finally was. She was so happy for him.

"That's really great," she said at last, feeling her words were inadequate. "Where's Seth?"

Michael stiffened, his eyes dulling. "Seth—ah—died. Two years ago. Sniper round. He was thirteen."

"I'm so sorry."

Every instinct in her told Sara to move for him. To hold him.

But Candice was still watching her, anxious and unsure.

So instead, perhaps it was time to address the blonde-headed elephant in the room. Growing dour, Sara muttered, "So. Candice."

The tips of Michael's ears turned bright red, his high cheek bones flushing. "Believe me, it's not something I was looking for." He regarded the darkened landscape beyond, watching the patrols that dotted the night like fireflies. "For the first year after you left, I thought you would come back. I prayed every night that you would, and… I don't know. I guess I hoped that you would change your mind. Then all this started. I didn't have a rift out of here, and the invasion came in full force, and every day looked like it was going to be our last. It just…it changed things." He shook his head and tossed his stick onto the fire. "Candice was so patient with me. I put her through hell… It was like I was broken, and I didn't know if I'd ever get fixed. But she was there with me. She loved me—"

"I get it," Sara mumbled, wiping at her eyes with the back of her hand.

Michael looked up to her, his face taut, but his tone gentle. "Sara, you *left*."

Sara caught Candice trying unsuccessfully to look discreet while eavesdropping, and she hated her. Wanted to kill her. She hated her even more for looking so gorgeous, like even in the midst of this warzone, she still had time to fix her hair, to put on makeup.

I never wore makeup.

In all fairness, Sara wasn't even sure Candice had on makeup, but she was so beautiful that it was hard to tell. It was infuriating.

"She's kind of ditzy, isn't she?" Sara smirked, needing badly to point out a flaw in Michael's new flame.

"That's not fair. You don't know her. What she's been through."

"We've all been through a lot," she snapped, a fresh wound prodded.

This time, he narrowed his eyes against her in scrutiny. "What happened to you? Where did you go?"

Sara reflected on the last two years and shrugged a shoulder. "Everywhere. Nowhere. Rip and I had a falling out, so I left. Slummed around the multiverse for a couple years. Then…I went to hell."

Michael nodded as though she'd described a trip to the corner grocery store. "How'd that work out?"

She returned his nonchalance. "Learned a lot. Got my head straight. The Man in the Stetson picked me up and dusted me off—"

Michael chuckled, the sound like water in the desert, and Sara felt alive again. "Yeah. He's good at that."

"And he sent me here," she said, all business. "To help you. To stop this, once and for all."

Michael considered her very closely, a warm smile spreading. Then, just as quickly as the smile had appeared, it evaporated. Michael stood, his brow creasing. As soon as he did, Candice jumped to her feet, too, looking as though she were working hard to restrain herself from butting in where she didn't belong. *Stay back, chick, if you know what's good for you.*

"We'll talk more in the morning," Michael said, without any air of familiarity.

Like he was talking to a stranger once more. "It's late. We should try and get some rest. I'll introduce you to the rest of the Resistance tomorrow."

He took a step back, and Candice was there in a heartbeat, taking his hand. Her eyes roved up and down him, pleading for reassurance that she was still his beloved.

"Make yourself comfortable," Michael told Sara, ready to walk away. "We've got some food. I've told Edward to play nice, but don't push him. You're welcome here, so long as you abide by the rules."

Sara huffed. "Well, don't I get my chukrahas back?"

"We'll talk in the morning," he repeated, his walls quickly raising. He grinned awkwardly. Even offered a little wave. "Good night."

Sara watched him walk away, Candice leaning her head against his shoulder. *That should be me. That's* my *shoulder.*

"Good night," she whispered after him, but he wasn't listening to her anymore. Michael and Candice disappeared down the hall, and Edward stood, tucked the battered paperback in his vest, and blocked the doorway. He faced down Sara, his jaw clenched.

"Better get to sleep," he said, and it sounded more like an order than a request.

Sara sighed and stood alone in the drafty room, then turned to watch the pillar of black fire working outside.

4

Sara sat against the wall, her head leaned back, feeling the wintry wind stirring her long bangs. The fire Michael had built still glowed beside her, warming the side of her face. In the distance, against the purple light of the humming beam that protruded from the school, she saw black shapes buzzing about in regular routines. Surely Michael had a plan for fixing this; she just wished he'd trust her with it. Of course, she couldn't blame him for keeping her at arm's length.

"I love you." That had been his last words to her before she joined Rip in the rift.

And she had said, *"I don't care."*

That's how it had ended for them. Her heart ached with "what ifs". If only she'd listened to Michael when he tried to warn her about Rip. If only she'd told the Old Dog to go to hell. If only she'd held her family close instead of forsaking them in her own misguided pursuit of...

Of what? Freedom? Independence?

Even she didn't know anymore.

She wondered—hoped—that in some alternate reality, she'd made the right choice. Running her fingers through her messy hair, listening to the wind howl through the toothless opening of the window, she wondered what *that* Michael and Sara might be doing now. Maybe they were engaged in deep conversation, maybe they were making love. Maybe they were staying up late with Toby, eating pizza and playing video games. Laughing and rejoicing that what was once ruined had been restored.

She couldn't imagine any real, genuine laughter in this dimension. This place was a cold, dead world, with the Rage towering over it like the king of hell.

But I'll take that king down. This is Its fault. It's all Its fault.

Blaming the Rage was the easy way out, though. In her heart, even as wounded as she was, Sara understood that she had brought her miserable situation upon herself. All of it. She had even pushed Michael away and into the arms of that beauty queen bimbo, Candice.

She shuddered to think what the two of *them* were doing now.

Sara tried to close her eyes, but sleep was denied her. She slid to her side and lay on the hard tile floor, feeling grit underneath her clothes. Thankfully she'd managed to get the grey devils' blood off her skin, but her clothes still reeked of death. Maybe tomorrow Michael would hook her up with some new clothes and she could burn these. A clean start.

She'd kill for one of those right now.

Minutes seemed like hours, hours seemed like days. The sun had yet to rise, but she wasn't so sure it would rise here, not with the Pillar blotting out the skies with its evil. She cocked an eye towards the door. Edward remained on watch, but he had dozed off, slumped against the wall with his rifle across his lap, her chukrahas still tucked in his belt.

Sara crept to a stand and silently moved across the room. She considered taking the blade from him, but she'd never earn Michael's trust that way. Instead she watched Edward sleeping fitfully, mumbling in his sleep and giving a startled jerk. Once he settled back down, Sara stepped over Edward without a sound. He slept on, and Sara made her move. With speed, she snuck down the hall, heading off in the direction Michael and Candice had gone earlier, already wondering why she was torturing herself this way.

Voices drifted down the darkened hallway, and Sara slowed, hugging the wall and creeping towards the sound. As she neared a new room, one with a flicker of candlelight warding off the night, she recognized Michael's voice. She wasn't able to decipher his words yet, but knowing he was so close set her skin on fire. He sounded upset—not angry, but heated—and Sara knew he and the missus were having problems.

She grinned, easing closer to the doorway.

Edging one eye around the corner, she spied Michael standing, pacing.

Candice sat on a small mattress on the floor, perhaps left over by squatters. Her face was red. She'd been crying. The girl looked pitiful. Neurotic and suspicious. Any respect Sara had awarded this girl for being able to handle a gun in a fight was revoked.

This girl is a wreck.

"You still love her…" Candice half-said, half-asked. She looked hurt and scared, as though she were about to be thrown out in the cold with the garbage.

Sara's smile widened, her heart beating wildly with hope.

Michael knelt down to his wife—his new one—and wiped the tears off her face, before tipping her chin so that her grey eyes met his. "The part of Sara that I loved is gone. What she is now…she's just a creature. Just a tool of the Rage."

Outside the room, Sara's heart sank. She leaned against the wall and slid to sit.

"I love you," Candice whimpered inside the room. "I don't want to lose you."

"You won't," Michael promised, and he sounded so sure. Sara missed his surety the most… "When Sara and I met, we were just kids. I didn't know the first thing about love or what it was supposed to look like. It seemed all we ever did was hurt each other."

Sara bit her lip, feeling a knot form in her throat.

"But you— You showed me what love *could* be if I didn't worry so much about getting it right. Loving you is the easiest thing I've ever done. Remember when I told you that we'd met before? When I found you in that other world, I was the darkest I'd ever been, but I saw something in you that started to bring me back. I don't think I would've even been capable of loving Sara in the first place if I hadn't found you first. But seeing her again…" He sighed. "No matter how long we were together, whenever I looked at Sara, all I saw was the girl I'd hurt once."

"What about when you look at me?" Candice asked, growing bolder in his love. Confident in her place at his side.

Somehow, Sara could hear a smile spreading across his face. "When I look at you, I see a girl that I could've hurt, but I didn't. You got through to me, babe. You still get through to me."

She heard them kissing. Heard Michael shuffling into bed with her, as Candice slipped into his arms, their soft declarations of love fading into the hall.

Sara quickly rose to a stand and left the way she had come, her chest heaving with silent sobs. What was she doing here? She obviously wasn't wanted—wasn't needed. It was all wrong. Everything was wrong and broken…

"Hello, Sara."

Sara gave a start and swallowed her tears, turning about to see the Man in the Stetson a step behind her. He offered her a sympathetic smile, his hands in his long coat's pockets.

She smiled through tears. "He's married." Weeping now, she said, "But you knew that already."

His blue eyes twinkled, moist with tears of his own. He simply removed his hands from their pockets and offered his arms to her. Sara gently entered his embrace and buried her head in his chest. With tender care he encircled her in his strong arms and let her cry for as long as she needed.

5

A crack tore open just above the tall, windswept grass like a mortal wound in reality. Black energy flickered from the rip, and a viscous, obsidian goo dripped and stained the weeds and wildflowers. One blackened foot emerged from the portal and lowered to touch down on the rough gravel, the rest of the figure following behind.

The Master stood erect, casually observing his new surroundings.

He'd seen many worlds in his long quest to discover the Gateworld—the weak spot in the multiverse that, if shattered, would finally set him free. Compared to the bizarre and alien landscapes he'd previously glimpsed, and subsequently destroyed, this world was simple and unremarkable. Mighty leafy trees moved in rhythm to a warm mid-summer breeze, the sky cloudless and bright. Ahead he spotted a cliff rising to stand guard over a pedestrian and rural town. Hovering to the sky, he briefly considered the quaint village below, snarling in disdain. Settling back to the earth, he regarded an old structure alongside the beaten path—a church. The ramshackle house of worship was crumbling and nearly consumed by the woods that flanked its sides. A weather-beaten sign out front proclaimed it to be the "Good Church of the Faithful", and the Master's lip curled in disgust.

Still, there was something about this place, as *righteous* as it was. Something sinister that tainted these picturesque woods. There was a stain here, a stench lingering over the whole town—no, even beyond the populated area. He could feel it lurking in the dark recesses of the woods around him, and knew it for what it was: Rot. Decay. Squalor.

These bled outward from the Source, like an unmistakable thumbprint on this world.

His already wide smile stretched grotesquely across his swirling black face. Could it be? Had he finally found it?

There was something, yes, but perhaps the pulse of evil was not quite strong enough. It wasn't here. Not in this town. But close.

A deep chuckle rumbled behind his clenched teeth, and he spread his arms and rose high into the air, above the treetops. Angling forward, he shot ahead at a dizzying speed, his long coat buffeted by the force of the pummeling winds. Below his naked toes, the countryside blurred past as he traced the river of wickedness. He laughed, now, as he left behind that sickeningly *happy* place and the landscape began to change. The light seemed dimmer as storm clouds drew together overhead. The wind chilled, and cold rain slashed and stabbed at the earth. Yes, he felt it now. He was drawing near to the place where the evil began in this world. He was coming to the Source.

To the very gate of Chaos, itself.

In mere moments, he was miles away from that peaceful hill and slowed to float above a darkened dreary City, frigid rain drenching him as he descended to the slick streets. The pelting rain ran down his shifting features, dripping off his chin. In stark contrast to that deceptively peaceful town nearby, this was a place that wallowed in degradation. Here, he breathed in nothing but hopelessness and depression, and he shut his eyes in ecstasy, swaying in the stormy night as though the misery he felt in the wind were a gentle caress. He had felt sadness, pain, bitter agony in other places, but never so pronounced. And he understood why...the Source *was* here.

The Master opened his eyes, his gaze settling on a ritzy club, lively big band music drifting from the front doors and into the night. The sign above told him this was the Silver Pearl, but behind the glamor and colorful lights, the Master sensed his own within. Locked beneath this night club was a well of Evil, the very door to the prison keeping Chaos at bay.

Yes, this was it. The cause of the rifts—the fractures in the multiverse. This was where blasphemies had been committed and terrible profane rites performed. This was where true hell had been opened up, if only for a moment, and where the Source—in all of its fullness and majesty—waited, trapped beneath.

But I have come to bring freedom.

"Aaaatt lllaaaasssst..." he breathed, hovering closer for the door.

He would rend the gate open. He would free himself and re-enter the Source and be made whole once more. Then Chaos would reign forever and ever.

Leering, he reached one hand for the door, ready to greet the worshippers who had been waiting for this day, but something stirred within him. He paused, his writhing fingers inches from the handle.

But what about Mother? he thought.

The Master tensed, rigid at the mention of her name. Yes... Mother. What would it profit him to regain his full power and lay hold of his destiny, if she were not here to witness it and weep in anguish?

No, that wouldn't do at all.

The Gateworld could wait for one more moment. First, he needed to find Mother. Her suffering would complete his joy.

"Motherrr…"

6

"Wake up," Edward barked, kicking loose gravel against Sara's chest with his boot.

She opened her eyes to find him standing over her, poking at her ribs with the barrel of his gun.

"Come on," he said, gruff, but cooling. "Losing light."

She sat up, wincing with stiffness, and surveyed the cityscape through the window. The skies were gunmetal grey, accented by the supernatural lightning storm above the school. She rubbed sleep out of her sight. "What time is it?"

"Ten in the morning," Edward said, taking a step back to give Sara room to crawl to a stand.

"Looks more like it's nearing dusk already."

"Time moves differently these days," he said. "Come on. We gotta get moving."

Sara stood the rest of the way, her body scolding her for sleeping on the hard floor. She wasn't sure how or when she'd returned to the room after her crying fit with the Man in the Stetson, but she was ready to push on.

She eyed her chukrahas in Edward's belt, and he sensed her eyes on him. He tightened his fingers around the grip of his gun. "Forget it," he said. "You're still our prisoner until the group figures out what to do with you."

Sara grimaced, but did not press an attack. Hearing voices coming from the door, she glanced over Edward's shoulder and spotted Michael and Candice, both with guns in hands, looking ready to move out. Michael seemed to make a point not to look at her this morning, or even acknowledge her, instead taking a peek outside.

He popped back in and whispered across the room to his brother. "Clear."

Edward nodded. "Let's get to the Chevy." Using his barrel as a prod, Edward shoved Sara forward, following close behind. Michael took point, easing into the hallway, his alien rifle raised. Candice followed after, her rifle raised, too, covering every angle Michael wasn't. They moved efficiently as a unit, communicating with only looks and nods.

Sara kept her hands slightly upraised as they moved down the hall and mumbled over her shoulder to her armed escort. "Aren't you going to give me a weapon? What if we run into trouble? You've got to let me defend myself."

"No, I don't," Edward remarked, matter-of-fact. "No skin off *my* nose if you take a stray round to the head. It'd save me the bullet."

Sara grumbled and kept shuffling along, forcing herself to comply. Edward might talk a tough game, but he was small potatoes after the foes she'd faced. Just a guy with a gun and a chip on his shoulder. Still, she missed the Edward she'd met first, the one who had stood as Michael's best man at their wedding.

Up ahead, Michael and Candice stacked up against the outer wall to the stairwell, trading non-verbal signals. Candice removed one hand from her rifle to push the door open, then stepped back as Michael hurried in, barrel out. After a tense second, he returned, locking gazes with Edward.

"Clear."

Sara felt the M16 shove into her back and rolled her eyes, following after the couple. The foursome descended the staircase in silence, and Sara noticed the walls marked by gunfire, with blood dried dark in grotesque splatters.

Once they reached the bottom, Michael pressed his back to the wall, ready to breach it, but Candice stayed his hand, making a cutting motion at her throat and shaking her head. He grimaced, but opened the door for her. Blondie slipped inside and almost immediately waved them forward. At last they entered the parking garage where they'd left the car the day before. Only a handful of broken-down cars dotted the littered lot, but Sara spotted the Chevy under its tarp on the other end.

It was a straight shot, but Michael turned to Edward, waiting.

Softly Edward said, "Go."

Michael led the way, scurrying across the garage with his head down. Candice was right behind him, and Sara after that. Halfway to their prize, however, they heard the grinding of tank treads.

"*Down*," Edward hissed and the four slid to the ground, scampering to take refuge behind the wall of the parking garage.

As one, the four peered over the top of the wall, and Sara saw the bogey in question—its metal was stained black and it had treads like a tank, but at the top it extended into some crude machine-man. Its three-fingered arms were poised at its side, and its head, a metallic humanoid skull with glowing red eyes that scanned either side of the street. The scanner turned in their direction, and the four humans tucked back into hiding. The red sensor shot over their heads and raked against the garage's support beams and parked cars, but could not pierce the concrete wall.

Once the laser dissipated, Michael was the first to spy once more. Sara rose, too, and saw the tank-man rolling on, leading a parade of captives. Humans, smudged with soot and whimpering loudly, were manacled together and followed along. At either side, herding the humans, were the charred Underdwellers, poised haughtily on their gigantic lavaspiders. The barbarians barked orders and poked with their slab-swords, hurrying along the spoil.

"Where are they taking them?" Sara said, looking to Michael. His eyes remained locked on the helpless captives below, his jaw clenched in anger.

It was Candice who answered. "To the school. They give them a choice, swear allegiance to the Rage, or die. And if they choose the Rage, they get stuffed through some portal, and when they come out…they're those grey *things*."

Sara looked out once more at the pitiful victims below and firmed her mouth. "We have to get them out of there." Again she turned to Michael, but he said nothing. "Hey," she snapped at him. "We have to get them out of there."

He would not face her, and the march carried on, now a safe distance away.

Edward stood, calmer now that the danger had passed. "Too risky. Keep moving."

Candice obeyed, and Michael stood as well, but continued to watch the scene on the street, a terrible sadness swallowing his features. At last, he turned and followed his brother.

But Sara remained still. "Wait. Michael. You're just going to leave them?"

He showed her his profile, his eyes hooded and defeated. "What do you want me to do? I'm not invincible anymore, remember?"

"But we can *fight* them. That's…that's what you do."

Michael hung his head, and Edward stepped in, blocking his brother from Sara's view. "We don't have the numbers to go picking fights," he said in a clipped tone. "We fight when we have to. Otherwise, we keep moving."

"*Michael?*" she half-laughed, half-whined. "You're really going to stand there and let him decide something like that?"

He ignored her question and turned to Candice, offering his hand. She took it with a sympathetic frown, and they started walking away, headed for the car. Sara stalked after them, furious. "Michael—"

Edward let his M16 hang on the sling off his shoulder and brusquely gripped her arms. "Hey!" he protested, but Sara reacted, twisting free, popping him with a fisted backhand to his cheek, then curling his neck and slamming him against the nearest car. He rebounded and slid to the hood and Sara charged him amidst Michael's shouts of "Sara! Stop!"

But she didn't. She tore the M16 away and tossed it to the ground, then retrieved her chukrahas blade and tucked it under Edward's chin. His eyes widened behind his glasses. "Shoot her, Mike!" he shouted.

"Sara!" Michael roared, charging up his rifle. She glanced out of her peripheral and saw that he and Candice both had her in their sights. "Don't," Blondie hissed at her.

"Take the s-shot," Edward stammered.

Michael got a tighter grip on the rifle, faltering. Candice shuffled at his side, anxious. "Michael."

He held one hand out, signaling Candice to back down, and she lowered her gun, if only marginally.

Edward swallowed hard against the edge at his throat. "Shoot her, man. I told you. She's *one* of them. She's playing you, Michael. Shoot her!"

Sara held her breath, watching Michael. Sweat rolled into his eyes and he blinked it away, his hands jittery. "Don't make me do this," he said.

Through gritted teeth, Sara growled at Edward, "I'm *not* your enemy."

She stepped back, taking the blade off him. Immediately, he massaged his Adam's apple, then took up his gun. Once he had it, he aimed it at her, but she put her back to him and faced Michael. Calm, now, she flipped the chukrahas blade in her hand and offered it to him, handle out.

He considered, then lowered his rifle and took the weapon from her. She sought his eyes, worry furrowing her brow. "And I'm not a 'tool of the Rage'," she said, mimicking his condemnation from the night before. He blushed, realizing she'd heard his intimate conversation with Candice, and Sara finished quietly, "Not anymore."

7

The group arrived at the entrance to the Resistance Headquarters. A chain link fence stretched around a perimeter, though Sara couldn't see what secrets they were protecting within. Boards and rusted sheets of metal were attached to the fencing and strips of barbed wire coiled about the tops in bushy tangles.

Edward drove the armored Chevy up to the front gates and slowed as three guards—slim youths in thick coats, baggy cargo pants, oversized sunglasses, caps that sat high on their heads, and checkered handkerchiefs pulled up to conceal their noses and mouths—approached with AK-47s, commanding the vehicle to stop. Edward had both hands on the wheel and his shoulders rose higher, tensing. In the passenger seat beside him, Candice let her own M16 lean against her leg and raised her hands to the ceiling.

Sara rode in the backseat, Michael sitting stiffly beside her. He, too, lifted his hands, and nudged her with an elbow. She followed suit as the three guards circled the car, peering into the windows curiously. One even went so far as to stick his head inside Candice's window, and Michael sat up even straighter, on the alert. The kid gave the car a once-over and jerked to Edward.

"What do you want?"

Edward kept his hands on the wheel, but nodded to the back. "We caught one of them. Need to show her to the Boss Man."

The guard considered Sara, but with his face covered by the kerchief and sunglasses, his reaction was unreadable. Nevertheless, he stared for a long time, and Sara felt the air leaving the car as everyone remained achingly still.

Finally, the guard withdrew his head—Candice released a long breath, her shoulders slumping as though deflated—and whistled shrilly to his cohorts. They hurried to the gate, which consisted of four sawhorses bolstered by corrugated metal siding. Still anxious, Edward eased the Chevy inside, revealing a gravel parking lot marked with potholes frozen over by the winter wind. Ratty tents dotted the expanse, and rattier refugees congregated around a number of oil drum fires, their despondent and dirtied faces highlighted by the orange glow of flames.

Only a few vehicles were visible: jeeps or trucks and one dented convertible—all outfitted with armor and weapons similar to Edward's Chevy. Sitting atop the parked cars in nearly triumphant poses, with their AKs on full display, more youths in sunglasses and facemasks oversaw the refugees like mini-dictators.

At the direction of an agitated gunman, Edward steered the Chevy into a spot and parked it. Without a word, Sara's company exited the vehicle, stone-faced and on edge. Michael gave a small signal for Sara to follow him, and she did, wading into the tension of the encampment. Outside the confines of the car, she could hear the raucous laughter and catcalling as groups of soldiers formed and strutted before one another, showing off with their guns or puffing out their chests in displays of Alpha male aggression.

"They're just kids," she whispered, watching the boys push each other around and whoop at one another in a tribal ritual of dominance.

The closer Sara looked, the more she noticed how fearful the refugees were as they watched the rowdy soldiers. One woman was pressed against a wall—petrified stiff—as a guard nuzzled her neck. The woman's tear-filled eyes met Sara's and silently pleaded for rescue. Shouts stole Sara's attention to a soup line, where two soldiers were shoving their way ahead of families, yukking it up as they cut to the head of the line and got a larger helping than the others. One old man protested and they pushed him aside, knocking him to the mud, which only drew louder laughter out of the goons.

Sara scowled and muttered to Michael, "*This* is your 'Resistance'?"

She glanced to Candice, who was biting her lip nervously, her rifle clutched like a security blanket. Beside her, Edward spoke to Sara over his shoulder, his voice betraying his own disgust. "Let's just do what we came here to do and get out of here."

Next Sara faced Michael, hoping he'd answer, but he remained taciturn. His eyes were locked ahead, jaw clenched so hard his teeth squeaked. He was purposefully ignoring these petty thugs playing protectors, and it looked to be killing him. She wanted to demand that he explain why he hadn't done something, but supposed that, like their episode with the tank, it came down to his vulnerability. Everything in his body language screamed to her that he wanted to help, but he felt powerless.

Seeing him struggling with helplessness broke her heart. She remembered all the places they'd been, all the people they'd helped. This was *Michael Morrison*, the man who toppled evil empires. He had fought giants and rescued whole planets. He'd been to hell and back and couldn't be broken by something as all-encompassing as the Rage…and yet, now, he was subjected to following orders from teenagers with guns and attitude.

I'm sorry, she wanted to say to him, and fought the urge to take his hand.

Michael halted, startling Sara, and she realized her troop had stopped before a building. Two guards flanked a black-tinted glass door, the luminosity of pink neon shading the tops of their heads. Sara glanced up and read, "The Pony Palace?"

Snarling in contempt, she looked to Michael, but he wouldn't face her. The guard at the door huffed, "What do you want? He didn't send for you."

Edward spoke in a controlled, but firm tone. "We need to talk to the Boss Man. We caught one of them—"

The guard pushed Edward out of the way so that he could get a better look at Sara. The boy raised his sunglasses, revealing that one of his eyes had been gouged out, a jagged scar slashed across the lid. "She don't look like no alien, man."

"Just let us in," Edward said patiently. "Big Joe will want to see her. Trust me."

The guard pressed his one eye in Edward's face, tugging down his kerchief to scowl, "I *don't* trust you, man. And I don't gotta, you got that?"

"P-Please," Candice stammered, uneasy, then flashed her flawless cover girl smile. "We wouldn't come if it wasn't important."

One-Eye jerked towards Candice now, looking her up and down as he slithered closer. "Well, hey, now. Important, huh? Maybe you'd—ah—like to convince me. *Educate* me on how important this really is."

Sara heard the high-pitched whine of Michael's alien rifle powering on. He brought the gun up in half a blink and had it pressed to the side of One-Eye's face.

Sara grinned. Now there was the Michael she remembered.

One-Eye didn't back down. Only jutted out his chin as four more soldiers materialized, seemingly out of nowhere, their AKs aimed at the group. One-Eye chuckled. "Come on, now. Whatcha gonna do? Huh?"

Grey eyes downcast, Candice turned to her husband and eased a delicate hand over his. "Michael."

Edward watched his brother carefully, as though he half-expected Michael to pull the trigger. Then, after a moment, he turned back to One-Eye, annoyed. "Can we see Big Joe now?"

One-Eye continued to grin, but finally stepped aside without offering an invitation. Michael powered down the rifle and let it rest, glaring at One-Eye even as he passed. Edward led the way inside, and Sara entered into a sickly-sweet fog of smoke. A steady bass line drummed against her chest, and the dazzling, dizzying lights rivaled the glitz and excess of Supernova. On small pedestals spaced throughout the club, limber girls danced suggestively on poles—though the bruises on their arms and legs and the hollow looks in their deadened eyes gave Sara the impression they weren't entertainers, but prisoners.

Her stomach soured.

Seated around the writhing women, more soldiers gathered, smoking cigars or joints, taunting and whistling, and chugging large bottles of liquor. Still more soldiers, their guns carelessly discarded to the side, played arcade games positioned along the edges of the club, reminding Sara once more that these were only boys playing at being "men".

Marching beside her, Michael muttered, "Big Joe's the only game in town."

Sara started at the sound of his voice, wondering if this was Michael's way of apologizing. But the moniker struck her. "Big Joe. Why do I know that name?"

Michael's eyes faced forward, his lip a tight line. "Because he's the one who had me killed when I was little."

"Oh."

"After the aliens came, the police were totally useless. Military came in—didn't make a scratch. Eventually, Los Angeles was quarantined. They bricked us up with a forty-foot-high steel and concrete wall all around the city. No one gets in or out, which seemed fine by the aliens—"

"Because they just need the rift."

He nodded. "After that, the city fell into anarchy. We didn't even need the aliens to finish us off—we were killing ourselves. Big Joe, though, had the men and the guns. Didn't take too long for him to seize control. He's the Boss Man," Michael said, with a healthy dose of ironic disgust. "Look, I don't like it, but we don't have a shot at fighting the aliens without him."

Sara raised her eyebrows. "Doesn't look like much of a resistance. Looks more like a bachelor party."

"Joe sends his men out on raids for food, supplies, weapons, ammo. We've made a tiny dent in the Rage's forces, but Edward and I felt we needed more intel. We've been trying for months to *catch* one of those grey bug-things."

Sara turned to him, recognition lighting up her mind. "That's what Blondie—

uh, Candice—was doing yesterday, when I came by. That's why she didn't want me to kill all of them."

Michael grimaced. "Yeah. It was the closest we'd ever come to grabbing one."

"Sorry," Sara said.

He shrugged, a dark grin spreading. "S'okay. Now we've got you."

She slowed, drawing closer to him. "What do I have to do to convince you that I'm not working for the Rage?"

When he didn't reply, she gripped the sleeve of his jacket and tugged slightly. "Look in my eyes. They're not black anymore, all right? I told you—the Man in the Stetson saved me. He gave me a chance to make this right."

Michael kept moving, his face slackening.

"Michael," she hissed. "Please."

"We're here," he grumbled.

Sara fumed but looked ahead as Edward climbed a spiral staircase that led to the Pony Palace's second story. Sara followed Candice while Michael brought up the rear. At the sight of the VIP area, Sara paused, struck sick by the sight. More soldiers—older and dressed in gaudy pinstripe suits that were only mildly moth-eaten—lounged on cushions, sipping tall glasses of bubbly champagne while more women sashayed around them, again wearing little more than vacant expressions. The men—Big Joe's lieutenants, Sara surmised—sat impassive, almost bored, as their slaves paraded in front of them.

At the center of this harem, the esteemed "Boss Man" himself, a hulking dark figure in a bright white suit that pinched the fat folds of his neck. The man was massive in bulk, a victim of his own appetites. He reclined with his knees spread to balance his oversized frame, an ornate cane—complete with a silver skull handle—serving as a perch for his arms. An impressive crown of dreadlocks framed his sweaty face, and a beard all but hid his lips and dangled down the middle of his chest. Only the prettiest of the slave girls twirled about him seductively, but he stared through them as though they were meaningless gnats in the presence of his greatness.

Upon spying Edward, the King of Los Angeles swatted his half-naked toys away and slightly leaned his incredible girth over his cane. A silky deep voice trickled from the onyx mountain like a cool stream, "What do you want, Eddie?"

Edward bristled at the abbreviation, but said, "It's important. We—"

Big Joe eyed the group, suspicious. "Thought you said you were gonna find me one of those chitterer things."

"We did," Edward said, flashing angry eyes at Sara. "Then she came along."

The fat man scratched at the corner of his mouth and nodded in appraisal. "Am I supposed to know who this is? Am I supposed to care? Or did you just bring her to me as a present? Could always use more girls."

"This is Sara," Michael spoke up, drawing a disapproving look from his brother.

Big Joe paused in thoughtful consideration, then barked a deep belly laugh. "*The* Sara? The one that used to be your old lady?"

Michael answered with a nod. Big Joe tapped the handle of his cane in quiet thought. "Well, well."

"She's got information," Michael said.

The gangster exhaled a low, gravelly chuckle. "Let's hear it then, girl."

Edward jerked his chin, indicating for Sara to move forward. She did, presenting herself before the Boss Man. "The Rage is looking for something called 'The Gateworld'. It's a parallel dimension from this one, but I think it's the source of everything. It's the one world keeping him trapped. If he can reach it—destroy it—then it's game over."

Joe listened carefully, his eyes narrowing. When he didn't speak, Michael said from the back, "We need to press our attack while there's still time. We might not get another chance."

The gangster shrugged. "Why should I believe you?" The man took hold of his cane and made a sweeping gesture over the expanse of the Palace. "Way I see it, we've got the aliens on the run. They haven't made a move on our turf in months."

"That's because it's not about you," Sara snapped. "It's never been about you. This invasion isn't just some bid to take over your planet. This dimension is only a staging point for the *real* invasion. That beam is out there looking for the Gateworld, and it's destroying realities left and right trying to find it, but we have the opportunity to stop it."

The man quieted and sneered. "And how do you propose that?"

She stepped closer, feeling herself grow bolder. "By shutting down the rift at the school. We'll cut it off at the source."

"Silly girl, the school's a fortress. We'd never make it within three blocks of that place."

"But you've got the soldiers and—"

"That's right. *I've* got the soldiers. These are my men. Y'see all those people out there? They're under *my* protection. I run these streets, and I'll do what's best for me and mine."

Sara glowered at the fat man. "Like sitting in here in your little love nest? Hiding? Lording over these people like some kind of dictator?"

"Woman, you listen here," he roared, but Michael stepped up to Sara's side.

"Joe," he began, calm, "we need to seriously consider this. We're looking at the extinction of all life everywhere. Not just on this world, but all the worlds. It's too big to blow her off." He sighed, but recovered quickly. "I don't trust her any more than you do." Sara flinched, her heart sinking, as Michael continued, "But if there's a shot that she's telling the truth and we can end this thing, then we've got to try."

Big Joe remained still, save for the slight flexing of his large hand over the skull on his cane. When at last he spoke, his voice was a menacing rumble, "And if she's wrong, then I stick my neck out and lose everything. I'm not willing to take that risk. Especially not on *your* word...'little man'."

Michael clenched his teeth, visibly frustrated, as Big Joe rose with great effort from his sunken couch. "Maybe you forget your place. The only reason I let you and your brothers live in the first place was out of the kindness of my gracious heart, and on account of Eddie being a good wheel-man. Don't think I've forgotten that you rolled with *Rip* before all this started." He chuckled sardonically. "Rip's Mongrels. So if all this nonsense you've been telling me about 'parallel dimensions' and 'dark anti-gods' is true, then Rip's responsible for all of it, and the way I see it, that makes you accomplices."

Now it was Edward's turn to protest. "Come on, Joe, we had no idea this was what Rip was about."

"Eddie, I ain't talking to you yet," the man barked, then craned his meaty head back to Michael. "I'm talking to the little brother, here. Rip's big hitman, that it? Come on, kid, we all know Rip was just grooming you to be his successor. Maybe this is all part of the Big Plan, that it? Maybe you and Rip are playin' me. Maybe I should just finish what I started back in that cemetery when you was just a snot-nosed kid."

Joe gave a slow nod, and his lieutenants rose, shuffling under their coats for pistols. Edward braced for a fight, leveling his M16 but unable to settle on one target in the half-dozen that flanked them. "Joe, don't," he implored.

Candice raised her gun, too, but looked too frightened to fire, her distracted grey eyes darting from Michael to Joe.

Michael, meanwhile, stood in place, fearless, as Joe sneered.

"Are you kidding me?" Sara growled and faced all the hard-eyed predators. "Do you know who Michael is? Do you know what he's *done*? He's been to more worlds than you can count! He's killed thousands! He's led armies! He's fought every terrible monster that hell's ever made and he's killed everything— *everything!*—that's come against him!" Red-faced, she shouted, tears building. "You should all be *shaking* when he walks into the room. *He* should be in charge of this whole thing! If you want to live past tomorrow, you have to listen to him!"

Big Joe's snicker caught Sara off guard, silencing her rant. "*You* didn't. Not if the stories are true."

She faltered, breathing heavy, and faced Michael. He'd been watching her with a strange sort of gratitude, but now his blue eyes held within them a question.

Sara frowned. Quietly she told him, an apology in her heart, "I should've."

Edward cut through the awkward pause, "Okay, Joe, you've made your point. We're grateful that you've kept us around—given us a place. You're the Boss Man."

"That's right, I am," Big Joe immediately echoed. He flicked a dismissive look to his gunmen, and they lowered their barrels. "Eddie, take your attack dog, here, out of my sight. Leave the red-head with me. We'll figure out if she's lying or not," he said, finishing with a dissolute grin.

Edward took a tentative step forward, nearly shielding Sara from the gangster. "But she's *our* prisoner."

"Did I stutter?" the big man roared.

"No," Michael declared through his teeth. "She stays with us. And for the last time, my brother's name is *Edward*."

Big Joe's nostrils flared, and the men in suits eased forward once more, guns out. "You wanna take a shot at me, little man?"

"Michael, don't," Candice pleaded, her voice quavering.

The fat man stomped closer, rattling the floor beneath him as he stood to shadow Michael. Pressing his dark, sweaty face near, he growled, "You might've been some bad dude out there on your little space adventures, but down here, you're just a punk. I can kill you anytime I want. I—"

The low whirring grind of an air raid alarm interrupted Big Joe's threat as the distant chatter of gunfire erupted outside. Inside the Pony Palace, time slowed to a single instant that stretched infinitely as the jarring music was abruptly cut off, filling the club with the sounds of commotion coming from outside the entrance. A cloying quiet hung in the air as the dancers below whimpered and quickly collected themselves, inching for the rear of the club. As one, Joe's men turned to him and he nodded a silent order.

The muted sounds of battle echoed indoors and Sara watched as the soldiers shuffled about, preparing for anything.

"Who's with you?" Joe whispered to Michael.

He grimaced. "Nobody."

From the front door, the sound of a shattering window, and One-Eye crashed into the club through a shower of glass. His body tumbled over a table, accompanied by the screams of the dancing girls. Big Joe shoved Michael aside and gripped the second story railing, leaning his girth over the bar. "On the door!"

His men cursed and hollered and hoisted their guns as they charged the ruined front door. Sara gaped in dread as lumbering dark shapes stomped inside the jagged opening, their massive bodies adorned in craggy armor made of volcanic rock. Each of the figures' four powerful hands carried slab-swords.

Underdwellers, Sara knew. The invasion was here.

8

Big Joe's adolescent army opened fire on the aliens, tinny pops instantly deafening Sara. The first line of bestial marauders shrugged off the rounds, then spun, bifurcating the nearest gunmen with a single tremendous swipe. Sara turned to Joe, but the fat man only stood dumbstruck as more Underdwellers hurried inside, mowing down his feeble opposition.

"Aim for the seams in their armor!" Michael was suddenly shouting, rallying the gunmen in the second-story VIP lounge. He clamped a hand on Edward's shoulder, drawing his attention. "They're vulnerable in the seams of their armor."

Edward nodded in a daze. "Right." Composed again, the elder Morrison brother lay his M16 over the railing and popped off calculated shots. Michael next turned to Candice, and Sara watched real fear cloak her husband's face. Candice's large grey eyes betrayed no tears, but the terror there was palpable.

"Conserve your ammo," Michael said, his voice almost a whisper drowned out by the chaos below. "Stick with Edward. Pick your shots. You'll be fine."

"What about you?"

"Michael," Sara interrupted, the club beneath them echoing with the screams of dying youths. "I can help."

He considered her briefly, and her eyes fell on the chukrahas still tucked in his belt. Michael's mouth tightened to a line, and, with great trepidation, he withdrew the curved blade, eyed it carefully, then tossed it to Sara. He said not a word, but his expression carried a silent plea that she prove herself trustworthy. Sara caught the handle, her slender fingers flexing around the familiar grip, and relished its pleasant weight. She mouthed "thank you" before diving over the edge of the railing, pirouetting in a downward spiral before righting herself into a deadly crouch in the center of the bloody melee. Forgoing everything but her instinct to survive, Sara rushed forward, keeping low.

To her left, a ganger sprayed with his AK, screaming a throaty wail that was cut short by an Underdweller's blade. The dying man kept a tight grip on the trigger, but his aim went wild, spitting bullets in Sara's path. She slid to her knees and bent backwards, deadly rounds passing over her like a limbo bar, then rose to a stand, twirled, and hacked with her chukrahas blade, catching the killer Underdweller in the throat. The monster gurgled, its warm blood jettisoning against Sara's face. She spat it out of her mouth and dislodged the blade just as the next combatant advanced. Whirling, she hacked and stabbed, each blow glancing off the rock armor. Ducking beneath a strike, she bounced up and shoved the blade into the Underdweller's armpit, plunging the chukrahas deep to puncture his heart. Two more creatures flanked her, and she roundhouse-kicked one before dropping to her knee and lashing out with a foot that knocked the second four-armed monster off-balance. Bloodied blade still in hand, she leapt onto the downed Underdweller and stabbed it in the throat, riding the creature's body as it writhed and gasped for a last taste of life.

Strong arms gripped her from behind, shaking free the dagger in her hand before hefting Sara off the ground. Two large hands painfully clutched her arms while another lower pair squeezed her legs. She twisted uselessly in captivity, at last baring her teeth and throwing her head back, smashing against the broad bony ridge of the Underdweller's face. He yelped, and she saw red flash across her vision, but her desperate move earned her freedom. Deposited on the floor, Sara found her chukrahas and brought it up with both hands before laying the sharp edge of it against the Underdweller's face, splitting it in twain.

The dead weight dropped backwards and Sara heaved giant, ragged breaths, her body shuddering with exertion. A roar from behind startled her, and she spun to see another Underdweller charging, its two slab-swords forming a blurring X, before a splash of glittering-silver caught the attacking alien and jettisoned him across the club.

Sara turned in place and saw Michael at her side, his alien rifle discharged.

"Thanks," she huffed.

"You still lose yourself in the fight," he shouted evenly over the clamor of war. "Gotta stay focused."

She grinned. He might have admonished her, but still, he had acknowledged their shared past, their bond.

He glanced her way, swinging his rifle around. "Down."

She bobbed without hesitation, and he fired off another jet of something like sparkling silver paint that detonated two Underdwellers. Sara glanced up and saw Michael's flank unguarded, then hurled her chukrahas end over end, burying it hilt deep in her enemy's face. Michael casually noticed the save and smirked. "Thanks."

A warm moment settled between them, and Sara felt her heart pounding in exhilaration. Gone were the arguments, the petty competition, the hurt feelings. Two years evaporated in seconds, and at last, she was reunited with her husband. He grinned, too, his perfect smile shattering the gloom, and she felt their spirits connect. Prayed that he felt it, too.

Suddenly, Michael's eyes flicked to the left, and his gun was up. In turn, Sara's eyes turned to his right, detecting another foe, and without a word, the couple fell into perfect step, sliding along the floor to press back to back. Michael fired twice and turned, while Sara kicked and punched to defend his rear guard. She somersaulted to the ground, scooping up her knife, as Michael covered her, picking off targets with ease. She rose and stabbed to his left, while he half-turned and bashed the rifle butt against an Underdweller's nose. One-two, one-two they fought, trading punches, slipping in and out of each other's movements, breathing, moving, killing as one. Sweat covered and cooled her bare flesh as her body slid against his, brushing against his hands, feeling his breath on her shoulders. Gooseflesh rose and she gasped in excitement, entangled with him as their breaths swelled and broke in unison. Sara beamed through it all, laughing in delight now as they moved about the carnage, dodging, ducking, weaving. It was a dance that she relished.

When at last the music of battle ended, the Underdweller forces lay dead at their feet, and Michael and Sara were facing each other, each smiling wide and breathing heavy. His cheeks were flushed, and she imagined hers were the same.

"That was…" Michael gulped and chuckled. "A lot of fun."

She snickered. "Yeah. Been a while."

He almost managed an easy laugh, but he broke off, paling suddenly. "Candice," he said quickly. Sara turned and saw Michael's wife and brother descending the staircase.

Edward raced forward, excited. "I-I can't believe you just did that, dude! That was amazing! I didn't know you had that in you!"

Michael emitted an embarrassed chuckle between greedy gulps of air, turning his focus to Candice. The woman appeared heartsick, hurt eyes passing accusingly between Michael and Sara.

"Are you okay?" Michael clumsily asked, but Candice took a step back, her expression downcast. He frowned. "Candice—"

The roof gave a crack like a thunderclap, and huge chunks of ceiling broke away, smashing into the dance floor. Everyone scattered in the raining debris, dashing for cover. Sara hurried out of the way and looked back to see a hive of grey devils spilling inside like cockroaches. The few of Big Joe's guerrilla fighters who remained aimed at the descending hordes and fired. Devils toppled soldiers, biting into their heads or prying off limbs. Still more beasts burrowed those long spears into fresh prey, sending blood cascading over the tile.

Sara jerked to Michael and saw him gripping Candice by an arm, ushering her away from the immediate carnage. Edward held his ground, blasting M16 fire and perforating only a few of his targets.

A devil neared Sara, raising up on its spindly haunches to launch a clawed attack. She backrolled out of its path and torqued forward out of the roll, spinning at the hip and decapitating the beast with a chukrahas chop.

More and more monsters fell from the blackened sky, and Sara knew they'd never survive if they couldn't get out of the club. Underdwellers were formidable, but they were still men. They still thought, still feared. These things were pure instinct, operating only on the mindless urge to kill, kill, kill.

But the devils' sudden arrival was not to be the end of their trouble. A single bolt of purple lightning punched through the masses, shattering the floor to instant ash. At once, the devils quieted and formed a sort of living wall around the fresh crater. Sara caught her breath and watched in mounting horror as the Shape descended, riding the lightning. The Shape with the long dark coat and the sentient flesh that writhed and coiled about like snakes.

"Toby," Sara breathed, and searched for Michael in the panicked crowd.

The god spread his arms and lifted his bright, unblinking eyes and profane smile to his audience. He called in a whisper that still managed to rattle the glass that remained in the windows, "Mmmoootthheeerrrr... Whhheeerreee are yoouuuu? I can ffffeeeel yyooouuu here..."

Michael met her glance from the shadows, Edward and Candice huddled close. He shook his head vehemently, but Sara bit the inside of her lip and walked out into the light that poured in through the roof's opening. "I'm here, Toby."

The Shape snapped to attention and hissed, "Yeeeessssss... I ffffeeelt your presencccee here on thisss wooorrrldd..."

"What do you want?" she bellowed. "You've already sent me to your hell. I got out." She shrugged, feigning bravery, though her stomach lurched inside. "If you're going to kill me, just do it. I'm tired of having you inside my head. I'm tired of seeing all the people you're hurting."

The Shape regarded her, craning his smiling head from side to side in curiosity.

"Kill me!" she snapped, even going so far as to tuck the chukrahas in its sheath. "I'm tired of running from you. Just do it!"

But the Shape only watched her, passive.

Sara nodded, narrowing her eyes. "But that's the thing, isn't it? Toby, you're still in there. The Rage wants to kill me, but *you* don't. You're fighting it. You *can* control it. You want me to help you. Let me help you." She threw a quick glance to Michael, still hiding in the shadows, before turning back to Toby. "Let *us* help you."

The Shape craned its neck at a horrible angle and watched in leering bewilderment as Michael walked forward. "Toby," he said.

"Miiichaeel..."

Michael joined Sara's side, stoic and strong. "This has gone on long enough, Toby. Please. Please stop."

The slap of a shotgun blast split the anxious quiet, and Sara flinched. The

Shape took a direct round to the chest, but did not falter. Did not even regard the impact. Instead, the creature slowly looked up to the VIP lounge, and Sara's gaze followed, landing squarely on Big Joe. The fat gangster stood there with a smoking shotgun in his hand, sweat pooling down his face.

"You think you can come in here?" he screamed at the Shape, and pumped the gun again. "Into my house?! Into my city?! This is *my*—urk!"

The Shape gave a flick of his fingers, and vines of surging black exploded forward from his hand, wrapping Joe's fatty head in their grip. Sara turned to the thing. "Toby, don't—"

"The boooyyyy is not in controooollll…"

The Shape flexed its tendrils, and Joe's head gave a wet *pop* before the headless bag of meat tumbled over the railing and pulverized a table. In retaliation, the last of Joe's gunmen pushed their attack, firing into the grey horde. Without any spoken command, the Shape unleashed them on Joe's army. The chattering devils sprang forward, feasting on their kill.

Michael left Sara, blasting huge swaths of the creatures, clearing a path for Candice. She ran for her husband, pelting the galloping abnormalities with three-round bursts. Before Sara had a chance to process the sudden violence, Edward was there, tugging on her elbow. "Out! Go! Go!"

Sara kept low and headed for a side door marked EXIT. Edward trailed behind, laying down suppressive fire in their wake. "Michael!" he roared. "Move!"

Michael and Candice joined Sara at the door, swatting at the buzzing creatures that swarmed and swooped through the air, tackling gunmen and rending flesh and bone with their sharp spears. Through the locust-like haze, Sara glimpsed the Shape watching the massacre with an almost innocent delight.

"Wheeerrreee aaare yooouu, Mooothheerrr…?"

Sara frowned, grieving for Toby in her heart, then disappeared out the door with her crew.

9

They left the Resistance in flames. Edward drove the armored Chevy down the deserted, littered streets, weaving down side roads amidst tall, gutted skyscrapers that stood dark against the early moon's light like gigantic mausoleums. The car ride was silent as the four survivors sat speechless, soot covering their faces, nerves still rattled as they cradled their warm weapons. Michael rode shotgun next to his brother, while Sara and Candice occupied the backseat, a strange gulf between them. Both women kept their eyes fixed ahead in an almost painful attempt not to look at each other. As Edward sped on he finally shattered the quiet, banging on the steering wheel and cursing a tirade in pent-up frustration.

"What are we doing to do now?" he shouted. The sound of his angry voice reverberated in the cramped car, causing Sara's ears to ring. "Where are we going to go?"

Michael remained eerily still, watching the dead streets blur by them. "Let's go home," he offered.

Edward nearly did a double take, then blew a hot breath out his nostrils. "No. We need to keep moving."

At last Michael faced the driver, his mouth firm. "No."

"Just let me think, all right?" Edward snapped, removing one hand from the wheel to rake through his sweaty hair. "I just gotta think. Gotta—"

"*No*," Michael said, louder. A command. Sara perked up. Edward did, too, snarling. "You're not in charge anymore," Michael told him. "I am."

Edward chortled. "That so, little brother?"

"I'm not so little anymore."

"He's right," Sara chimed in, and Edward veered to the curb in response.

"That's it," he barked. Throwing the car into park, Edward nearly kicked open his door and reached inside, dragging Sara out. "Move!"

Hurling her off balance, Edward leveled his M16 at her. Michael and Candice were already hustling out of the vehicle when he shouted, "Start walking! Go!"

"Edward—" Michael bellowed.

"No! We were doing fine until she got here! That creep in the black slime wants her! Calls her his mother, right? She's got a frickin' target on her back, and I don't want her anywhere near us!"

"He's right," Candice said with a solemn nod.

Michael cut hard eyes at both of them and moved closer to Sara. "No, she's one of us. She could've turned on us back there, but she's on our side. We need her if we're going to stop Toby. There's no one left."

"I don't trust her," Edward said. "And *I'm* in charge."

"No, you're not," Michael rose taller, his tone edgy. "You had your shot, but we haven't made a dent in this thing! We *never* should've been playing by Joe's rules. You trusted him after all that he did to our family?"

Edward glared at him, red-faced. "Shut up."

"Seth's dead and—"

Edward swung his rifle around, connecting with Michael's jaw and scattering the younger Morrison to the frosty street. "*Shut up!*"

Michael growled and tackled Edward, splaying him out on the Chevy's hood, knocking the gun free. Sara eyed the rifle, but Candice had hers up in an instant, daring her to move. Sara decided it was best to stay her hand and watched as the brothers struggled on the hood, swapping punches and tangling each other in holds.

"I'm gonna beat you down, dude!" Edward hollered.

"I'm not your enemy!" Michael roared back, then punched Edward across the cheek. "I miss him, too!"

"Shut up!"

"It wasn't your fault that he died!" Michael blurted, and Edward replied with a solid right hook. Michael took it, spitting blood to the ground, and said, "But we're still a family!"

"I know that!" Edward shouted, his anger breaking off into a sob. "I'm trying to protect our family! Just like I always do!"

Out of breath, Michael backed away. "Then let me play this. Trust me—for once."

"I…" Edward swiped at the blood on his nose with the back of his hand.

"This is what I do, man," Michael said, earnest and calm. "I can *do* this."

Edward hocked a wad of blood onto the street, then glowered at Sara. "And she's part of it?"

Michael nodded. "Sara said the Man in the Stetson sent her to help us. I believe her."

He shook his head, yanking the discarded rifle off the pavement. "You're playing a dangerous game, bro. But we'll do it your way. For now."

"Thank you."

Edward groaned and climbed back in the car. "So, what, we're headed home?"

"We'll lay low there until we figure out our next move."

"Whatever." Edward cranked the engine and revved it once, then craned his head out the window. "You coming?"

Michael turned to Candice. "Are you okay?"

She shrugged, indifferent. "Does it really matter what I think? I trust you." Shooting Sara a dirty look, she continued, "I don't trust her, but I trust you."

"Thank you," he repeated, and Candice climbed back into the Chevy, her back to him.

Alone now on the street, Michael and Sara stood under the silver moonlight, their breath leaving them in frigid plumes. In the distance, Sara could hear the murderous howls of the grey devils, and the screams seized her heart. Michael weakly nodded for the car. "Come on," he muttered. "Let's go."

10

Edward pulled the Chevy up to the old apartment, and Michael stepped out, giving the rundown heap a once-over. It'd been two years since they called this place home, and since then, the upper floors had taken a direct hit from a Filax warship. The fires had since been put out, leaving the brick facing of the old apartment nothing more than a blackened hull. The place looked like hell, and seeing his childhood home in such a state bruised Michael's spirit.

But it was all they had left.

He and his brother shared a cautious look and hoisted their rifles, taking point. They descended the steps on the sidewalk down to the lower basement level of the building where their apartment rested. The door stood open, but no movement from inside stirred.

Michael glanced to Candice and Sara, and both girls drew their weapons, their eyes on the street to cover their backs. Edward held up a hand with three fingers and counted down. At zero, he pumped his fist, and Michael shoved the door open with his foot. The Morrison brothers piled in, swinging rifle barrels all along the darkened living room.

"Clear," Michael muttered.

"Rooms," Edward said, and the brothers split up, rushing into the cramped apartment, checking both bedrooms and the bathroom in a matter of seconds. They reconvened in the disheveled living quarters, and Edward eased down his M16 with a sigh.

"All clear," he called out, and Candice and Sara hurried inside. "I'll go out in a sec and put the tarp on the Chevy. That should keep it camouflaged from the air." Edward noted. "I can take first watch."

Michael slung his alien rifle over his shoulder and went to work dragging the moth-eaten couch towards the door. "We can barricade the entrance."

"Not that it'll do much," Edward sang glumly.

"It's something."

With their immediate security determined, Michael relaxed for a moment, taking a small measure of comfort from being home. The place was in shambles, destroyed during the last attack that took place here when Seth fell two years ago. They'd all been asleep, thinking they were off the enemy's radar, when the shooting started. They'd fought off the intruders—a mixture of assassin 'bots, and dog-like verryl mercenaries—in their home and made a run for it, but more soldiers had been in wait on the rooftops outside. Seth was dead the moment he opened the door. The remaining three of them barely made it out alive, but somehow they did, and they piled into the Chevy and tore away, never looking back. After that, Edward decided they'd throw in with Big Joe and his goons and take their chances.

But we see now how that worked out, Michael thought. He watched his brother trail about the living room, a morose silence consuming him. Lying haphazard on one of the shelves, a framed photo of seven-year-old Edward at the hospital, holding his newborn brother Seth in his arms, bundled in a fuzzy cap and blankets. Squeezed in the chair next to Edward, Michael, himself, when he was only fifteen months old—still mostly bald, still a little ball of fat with a chubby face looking bewildered at the flash of the camera.

It was the one and only picture ever taken of the three of them before Mom and Dad died.

Michael frowned, watching his brother carefully right the frame on the shelf before gripping his rifle and marching on. But Edward wasn't the only one affected by the past. Michael noticed Candice stirring through the ruined junk, too. This had been her home, too, for a while. When Michael first met her, she'd just moved to L.A. from Wyoming, looking to make her way as a singer/actress.

Of course, the aliens had destroyed those dreams, as well.

Her parents were still in Wyoming; at least, she hoped they were. Los Angeles was quickly cut off from the rest of the world when the pillar took root, and they'd not been able to get word out in years. The Morrisons had taken Candice in, first in thanks for saving Michael's life, but then an unlikely romance developed between her and Michael, and she had become a part of the family. Michael smiled suddenly, recalling those early days of their relationship, when the world outside was falling apart, but his world had still managed to seem brighter day by day.

Candice sifted through papers, her grey eyes sparkling as she retrieved her guitar from the wreckage. She shouldered her rifle and turned the guitar about, marveling at it. Tears welled despite her smile, and she focused on Michael. Holding the guitar for him to see, she grinned. "It's still here."

Five years of fighting for survival was instantly stripped away, and he saw his wife as the exuberant girl she'd been when she saved him. She'd laughed so much back then, never losing hope that they'd make the universe right again. She'd pass the time in the evenings singing for them until Edward and Seth went to bed, and then she'd sing softer songs for Michael. Songs she'd written, full of her dreams and innermost thoughts. They'd hold each other and kiss and make love. She'd brought beauty and joy back into his life. His Candice.

His love for her overflowed suddenly, and he crossed the room, desperate to be near her again, but Sara called him back. "We need to figure out the plan."

Candice's smile faded, her good mood interrupted. She set aside the guitar, and Michael saddened as her face became hard, donning once more the expression of a soldier.

Michael caught Sara watching him intently, the knot above her left brow prominent. Jealousy and hurt were in her eyes, and Michael still didn't know how to deal with that. Since she'd returned, he'd been in nearly constant prayer to

God, begging for clarity. For answers. *Why now?* he asked. After all this time, after meeting Candice and being reunited with his brothers… Things were hard, but there was a certain sense of normalcy they'd established. He finally had a home, a family. Just like he'd wanted since he was a kid.

And now Sara had come back and changed everything.

She stood before him, more beautiful than he'd ever seen her. Sure, she was filthy and bloodied, but his heart looked past all that. Her body was toned and tough, and she was in perfect command of every movement. Her short, choppy locks only accentuated an air of playfulness and disregard for danger that excited him. But more than that, her eyes were soft again. Pure. He didn't know what she'd seen—what had happened to her—since they parted, but she had grown and matured, and he was captivated by her mystery, wondering about the stories she had to tell. After all this time, she seemed finally at peace with herself, willing to accept her choices, and he gravitated towards her confidence and strength.

She'd become perfect. At least, perfect for him. They were perfect together. If there'd been any doubt, their display on the dance floor had cemented it.

Why now, God? he begged, guilt-ridden and confused.

He forced himself to look away from her, tempted by her body and his vivid memories of touching her, kissing her. Michael moved into the kitchenette and swiped away the dust that had accumulated on the counter over the last couple years. Quickly digging through debris, he found small chunks of plaster and rock and laid them out on the counter for a makeshift diagram. The others crowded around, watching, as he narrated, "Plan's simple. We get inside the school and close the rift."

Edward shook his head immediately. "No way. Joe was right. That school is the most heavily guarded place in L.A. *Especially* with their leader here. We couldn't take that place even if we had an army. Which we don't."

Michael countered, "Which is why we're sneaking in. We exploit Toby's weakness. Because he has so many loyal followers crowding around the school, he won't notice a small team of four people."

Sara scratched her temple in thought. "And the rift? You can close it?"

Michael thought of a kid named Johnny Frawl on Sara's world and blushed. "Well… I knew a guy who did it once. I think I can manage it."

"Think?" Edward blurted. "We're gonna need a lot more than that if we're doing this."

"It takes blood to close a rift," Michael defended. "I'll do it."

"How much blood?" Candice asked, paling.

"I don't know that yet. Last time it just took a few drops, but that was a smaller rift than this. It…might take more."

Candice bit her lip, angry and scared. Michael pointed at Edward. "Look, we've got their patrols memorized. We catch them moving a fresh batch of prisoners, take out the guards, and commandeer one of those skull-tanks."

"Then we ride on in," Sara finished, her mouth hinting at a smile.

"That's suicide, dude," Edward drawled.

"That's why they'd never expect it," Michael said, his adrenaline pumping.

"What if we run into Toby?" Candice argued. "We can't kill that thing. Michael, you said so yourself. You watched it *unmake* an angel."

Michael considered, replaying horrible memories of the Maestro's demise. "Leave Toby to us," he said with great regret. Then, even though he knew it would wound Candice, he faced Sara, acknowledging her importance. "You saw him back at the club. Having Sara here has him confused."

"Toby's still in there," Sara agreed. "I can get through to him. I just need more time."

"Sara and I started this," Michael said through a frown. "We really messed up…with Toby. We've got to try and save him."

Edward pushed away from the pow-wow, fuming. "He's gone, man! Hey, I get it. I'm sorry about the kid, too, but I've got to look out for this family."

"Toby is my family," Michael snapped. Faltering, he stammered, "S-Sara too."

"Are you frickin' kidding me?" Edward blasted. "*Sara's* your family? The chick who fried you with purple lightning and left you and that little boy here to die? So, what, she's back and says she's on God's team now, and all's forgiven?" Edward wildly pointed at Candice, railing now. "Do you have any idea what you're doing to your wife? Your *actual* wife who didn't try to kill you?"

"Edward," Candice quietly protested.

"No!" Edward cried. "He needs to hear this. *This* is your wife, Michael. *She's* the one carrying your baby."

"Stop it!" Michael punched the counter, cracking the rickety top. His ears rang from the volume of his own command, and his cheeks flushed with embarrassment. Three pairs of expectant eyes locked on him, burning down into his soul, but he couldn't face any of them.

After taking a breath, he growled in a steady rant, "This is the plan. This is what we're doing. We spend tonight checking our ammo. We left in a hurry last time, so there should still be some more hideout weapons and rounds in the apartment. First light, we set up and ambush a prisoner transport. Take the skull-tank and drive right through the city to the school. Get inside, kill only when we need to, and close the rift. Got it?"

Edward stormed for the door. "I'm taking watch."

"Edward—" Michael began, but his brother disappeared through the front door, slamming it behind him.

At last, Michael faced Candice, but she wouldn't return his gaze. His spirit wilted. "I'd better get some sleep," she said. "I'll take second watch."

She gently broke away from the group, grabbing her guitar as she passed, and slipped inside their old bedroom, softly shutting the door.

Alone again with Sara, Michael rested his head on the counter and released a long, tired breath.

"Wow," Sara breathed into the quiet, stale air. "You're...going to be a dad."

He nodded.

"How far along is she?"

"Not sure. No doctors, right? About three months, we think."

"That's... wow..."

"I'm terrified," he blurted, never able to confess that before. Not even to himself. "We... we talked about kids—we *wanted* kids—but now isn't a great time..."

"H-How does Candice feel?"

"We haven't really talked about it," he said, his head still on the counter, his emotions rising in a dangerous, but unstoppable, crescendo. "I think we're both too scared to get excited. Out here...everything changes in a moment. We just need to get through tomorrow. After that...well, we'll see where we're at." He sighed, his sinuses stinging. "If she'll even want me now."

"I really screwed things up," Sara offered.

Michael felt a sob in his chest, but refused it. "Why did you have to come back?"

Her voice broke into a small cry. "I missed you."

He rose and faced her, the moisture in her swollen eyes matching his own.

She blinked tears out of her long lashes, her lip curling as she wept. "D-Did you miss me?"

"Don't ask me that," he snarled, his chest shuddering. "You can't ever ask me that."

"Michael," she begged, and brushed his arm, but he flinched away from her, gasping a startled cry.

"Don't touch me," he snapped. "Just...leave me alone, okay?"

Wiping at his eyes, he hurried away, locking himself in the bathroom.

Sara sat in the dark living room, her body numb and shaking with Edward's revelation.

Michael was going to be a dad... of another woman's child.

She sniffled and scratched an errant tear on her cheek. He was still in the bathroom, hiding from her. From all of them, she supposed. Once, she pressed her ear against the door and heard him weeping.

Not for the first time, she wondered why she was still here. She was only making everyone miserable. *As always*, she mused fretfully. But they needed her. Stopping Toby before he reached the Gateworld was all that mattered. If they could do that, then... then she'd leave. Where she'd go after that, well, she had no idea. She supposed she could go back to her house on the beach. That large empty house, with no one to share it.

But she couldn't worry about that now.

Standing, she straightened the creases in her lap and dried her face, tossing her bangs to the side to affect a return to confidence. Her heart pounded inside, but she pushed to the other side of the room, easing towards the bedroom door where Candice had disappeared. From her side of the closed door, Sara could hear the faint plucking of guitar strings. It was a beautiful melody that nonetheless stirred in her a great sadness. Curious now, she carefully pushed open the door and saw a number of lit candles set around the room. Candice's back was to her as the girl sat on the edge of the messy bed, one leg draped over the other as she propped up the guitar and played. Sara listened, taken aback by how talented she was.

Still thinking she was alone, Candice hummed softly along with the guitar, then sang. Sara didn't know the song, but it moved her. Candice's voice was bright and powerful, and Sara imagined her singing to her and Michael's baby one day. Fresh hurt struck Sara, and she bowed her head, solemn.

Abruptly, Candice stopped playing, and Sara realized she'd been discovered.

"What are you doing here?" the girl demanded.

"I'm sorry," Sara said, realizing that, without thinking, she'd entered the room. She looked around the candlelit space that Candice and Michael had shared and saw snapshots of the couple everywhere. They weren't professional photos by any means—just quick Polaroids taken in calm moments between battles over the last five years. No vacations or faraway places. Just pictures of the two of them snuggled on the couch that now lay in tatters in the other room. Self-taken photos of the couple sharing a laugh, their faces smudged with ash, rifles on their backs.

They looked so in love. Michael had never seemed so happy since Sara had known him. Never so free. He'd wanted out of rift jumping for so long. Wanted to settle down and have a family. Now he had that, and she'd missed her chance to be a part of that life. She was an intruder here, in this holy place where Michael and Candice had built for themselves a life. Sara resisted the urge to flee from this temple, and gulped hard. "That's—uh—a really beautiful song. Did you write it?"

"No," Candice said, unimpressed. She stood and rested the guitar in the corner. "It's Garth Brooks. 'The Dance'."

"Who's Garth Brooks?"

"Right. You wouldn't know. You're not from around here."

Candice busied herself about the room, not looking at Sara as she brought some order to the chaos of her belongings. "Anyway," the girl blurted, her tone clipped, "what do you want?"

Sara stuck her hands in her pockets, shifting her weight awkwardly. "Tomorrow is a big day, and Michael's plan kinda revolves around the four of us working together. Trusting each other. I wanted to—"

Candice paused and put a hand on her hip, cocking her head to the side. "What? Be best girlfriends?"

"No. I... I don't know. I wasn't really expecting you."

Candice snatched a discarded shirt and gave it a pop, loosening the dust that had settled in the folds of its fabric. "Yeah. Ditto."

Sara smirked despite herself. Blondie had some bite. Under any other circumstances, she imagined the two of them could've been friends. "I can see why he loves you," Sara said, surprised to hear herself utter the words.

Her comment surprised Candice, as well, whose grey eyes widened and cleared. Then the beauty queen relaxed and sat back on the bed. "He's an idiot," Candice said, her full lips in a pout.

Sara laughed. "Yeah. He is that sometimes."

Now Candice leveled those dreamy eyes on her, with a hard, sincere gaze. "But I love him."

Sara nodded, growing serious. "I know. I do, too."

"I know."

Sara groaned and dared to sit next to Candice, her shoulders slumping. "So what do we do?"

Candice was silent for a moment, then posed thoughtfully. "I get him Monday through Thursday. And every other weekend."

Sara exploded in unexpected laughter, and Candice joined in after a moment, until Sara's vision turned blurry with happy tears. How strange to be sharing this moment with Michael's new wife. "Sounds fair," she said. At last, the mirth faded into a nice, warm quiet. "No," Sara murmured, "I'm not hanging around. We get through tomorrow and... I'll leave."

Candice seemed to breathe easier, but didn't press it. "So what are our chances tomorrow? Really?"

Sara shrugged. "Well, it's not much of a plan. I mean, seriously, hide in a tank and drive through the front doors?" She chuckled wistfully, "But that's Michael. He's never been one for strategies. He's too to-the-point for that."

296

"He is," Candice agreed.

"But I don't know," Sara added. "He's kind of this unstoppable train, and you just *want* to believe in him. He—"

"He makes you think that nothing is impossible." Candice considered then said, "I do wish we had an army, though."

Sara grinned, struck by a funny memory. "Did he ever tell you about the time that we were on Ruggashosh? We were there for three weeks, and it was just us and this small crew of fish people, and we were up against this *giant* sea monster that had chased them out of their homes. And Michael, he was incredible, *wrestling* this Leviathan!" She chuckled. "That was a wild jump."

Candice laughed, but shook her head, a cloud falling over her face. "No, he doesn't ever talk about that stuff."

"You kidding me?"

"He doesn't like to talk about his life before all of this."

"What's going on?" Michael brusquely cut in, startling the women. As one they turned to the doorway and saw him standing there, tense and red-faced from crying.

Sara smiled. "How come you haven't told Blondie about Ruggashosh and the Leviathan? That's a solid story, there."

He cut his eyes at her, his face a hard scowl. "That was a long time ago. It doesn't matter now."

A frown flickered on Sara's face as she reflected on her dad saying the same thing about his own wars and the hurt he'd caused her by remaining silent.

Gruff, Michael switched topics, "Candice, what's our gun situation?"

She stood, biting her lip, keeping her anger in check. "Haven't looked."

He hesitated, then broke eye contact. "You probably should."

Sara watched Candice close a fist, but march away, nonetheless, passing Michael without a look. Sara rolled her eyes and stood, as well, while Michael watched her with a grimace.

"Leave her alone," he said under his breath.

"Just having some girl talk, Michael. Your wife is kinda cool. And pretty hot, too, I have to admit."

"Stop it. I don't know what you're trying to do—"

She approached him, tender but firm. "I'm not trying to do anything, but keep us all alive past tomorrow. You and the new missus included."

"She's not your concern."

Sara growled. "You never change, I swear. Even after everything, you still push away the people who love you most."

He turned to leave, but she grabbed his arm and spun him back around. "No," she commanded. "You listen to me. We totally messed up everything about our relationship. I get that. I hate it, but I accept it. But you've got a real shot at making something great with that chick in there and you're going to blow it. Again."

"You are *not* giving me relationship advice."

"If not me, who?"

His anger diffused and she saw him beginning to listen to her. "She *loves* you, stupid. And I know you love her, too. But you've got to learn to let her in before it's too late. As long as we were together, you walked around terrified that people were going to figure out who you 'really' were and not want you anymore. Hello? We all know your secrets, and we're still here. Still following you. Still trusting you. You're not invincible anymore. You can't do all this by yourself. You need her. She needs you. Your baby needs you." Shaking her head, she looked to the floor. "But what do I know?"

"Thanks," he grumbled after a moment.

She eyed him and caught him fighting a smirk. "You're welcome."

"Why are you doing this?" he pleaded.

Sara frowned, but did her best to turn it into a grin. "We may not be together anymore, but we still make a good team."

Michael's eyes creased into a smile. "Yeah. The best."

12

Sara took her leave out the front door to check up on Edward, and Michael stayed behind in the quiet apartment. Candice shuffled through scattered junk, and Michael watched her, hands in his pockets, defenseless before her. He stepped closer, but hesitated to disturb her. Instead he watched her a moment more, combing her white-blonde curls behind her ears, focused on her task. She'd already accumulated a small pile consisting of a handgun and some spare clips. Michael knew it wouldn't be near enough to wage their crazy war tomorrow, but he'd hoped they'd be able to scavenge additional weapons as they took out more patrols on their last push to the school.

"Hey," he finally said, but she did not start, indicating she'd known he was watching her.

"We cleared it out pretty good last time," she said, still working.

He brushed his hand against her waist. "Hey. Stop for a sec."

She rose quickly, aggravated, rolling her eyes to land on the ceiling. "What?"

He pulled her closer, waiting for her eyes to meet his. When at last they did, he saw them watering with emotion, and he touched his forehead to hers. Breathing deep, he said, "I'm sorry."

She shut her eyes, her lip trembling. "Sara said she's leaving after tomorrow.

Are you… If you go, too, just… don't tell me 'good-bye', okay?"

He parted from her, shocked. "What?"

"Michael, you only stayed here because you didn't have a rift to get you off-world. Now that Sara's… You two have done all these things together. Seen so much and… Why would you ever stay here? I can't compete with the multiverse."

"You're insane," he said, feeling his face flush. "Are you kidding me?"

"This isn't who you are," she wept. "You're that guy *out there*, in Sara's stories. Fighting sea monsters and saving galaxies. You said it yourself. I was just an accident, and the baby—"

"No," he cut her off. "Yeah, maybe I didn't plan any of this. Maybe it's all an accident, but if it is, it's the best accident that's ever happened to me." He cupped her face, stroking her chin with his thumb. Her lips parted, quivering with fear. "I love you, Candice. I was lost out there. And Sara's stories are just… they're just stories. That's stuff I did, yeah, but that was never really me. I never knew who I was until you found me. I owe you everything and all I've ever brought you is trouble."

She touched her head to his and ran her fingers through his chestnut-colored hair. "No. No, you've brought me beauty and love and passion." She broke down, sobbing into him. "I love you so much."

He took her in his arms, squeezing tight, like he might drown without her. "I love you, I love you, I love you."

"Please don't leave me."

"No, never." He parted from her and again gently took her face in his rough hands and kissed her softly. She returned the kiss, pulling him in harder, deeper. They came up for air as she decorated his dirtied face with tears and kisses. "Sara is my past, but you are my future. We'll write our own stories," he whispered to her, clutching at the small of her back. "Okay? And we'll tell them to our baby."

She nodded quickly, refusing to let go. Michael bent down and scooped Candice into his arms. She stared at him, tears drying, her grey eyes alight with love and a bit of mischief. She traced his cheek to settle on his chin.

"Do you really want to talk about the Leviathan on Ruggashosh?" he asked.

Grinning seductively, she shook her head "no."

He smiled. "Good. Me, neither."

They kissed as he carried her to the bedroom.

13

Sara left the basement apartment behind and climbed the steps to street level. Edward sat there, hunched over in a corner, his rifle draped across his lap as he smoked a cigarette. At the sight of Sara, he took hold of the gun and aimed it at her.

"Stop. Right there."

She held up her hands in tired surrender. "Easy. Truce."

He narrowed his eyes at her. "Where's Michael?"

She blushed. "He and Candice need a little privacy."

Edward read the meaning behind her words and smirked. Laying his rifle at rest once more, he went back to sulking, watching the quiet streets.

"Mind if I join you for a while?" she asked.

He shrugged. Sara took that as a "yes" and found a spot next to him on the sidewalk. They sat in silence for a moment, and Sara spotted that he'd draped their filthy tarp over the Chevy, making it look like just another piece of devastated junk in this accursed city.

"How's it look out here?" she asked.

"Quiet for now." He leveled her with a withering glare. "But looks can be deceiving."

She huffed, overwhelmed by his suspicions. "I'm not going to hurt your family, Edward."

"Oh, I know you won't. I'll drop you long before you get the chance."

She watched him, bemused by his unrelenting disapproval of her. "You know, we've met before. I mean, another you. On another world."

"Yeah, Michael said something about that."

Sara giggled. "You paid for my honeymoon."

He darkened, frowning. "Oh."

"Believe it or not, you even liked me." When he didn't reply, she dared to give him a playful elbow to the ribs. He didn't shoot her for that, so she hoped he was slowly warming up to her. Draping her hands between her knees, she spoke into the night, "I get it, you know. You're looking out for your brother. The other you was the same way. He would do *anything* for his brothers."

"They're all I have," he said immediately, without any warmth in the declaration.

"Yeah, that's what Michael used to tell me. He said you watched out for them. You took care of each other. Must've been tough."

"'Tough' doesn't come close."

Edward didn't elaborate, his bespectacled eyes keen and alert as he searched the shadows. Sara searched, as well, but didn't sense any trouble, though she reasoned she'd lost her danger sense now that she'd made her "once and for all" decision, as Rip put it. Nevertheless, she remained mindful of the chukrahas in her belt, just in case. She was grateful she'd found the blade back on Yur. It was nice having something that was her own when everything else in life seemed to be denied her. No Michael, no family, no friends.

Just her dagger. Well, that and the Man in the Stetson. She sensed he was nearby, a quiet comfort to her emotional upheaval. *I'm doing it*, she thought out to him. *It hurts, but I'm doing okay. I'm trying to do good while I'm here.*

A Voice filled her inside, speaking a wordless message of peace and approval, and she smiled.

"I was seven when our parents died," Edward said, catching Sara off guard. She had not expected the conversation, but was grateful to be having it.

"How did it…" She paused. "I mean, Michael never talked about his parents."

"He didn't know them. He was just a baby when Seth was born. It'd been a hard pregnancy. I remember mom being sick a lot. When she finally had Seth, everybody was relieved. She was on bed rest for a while after that, and she finally got better. Mom was a nurse, and Dad was a supervisor at a factory or something. Work was never very important to him. He loved my Mom. Mom made breakfast in the morning before school, and he'd come and take her, and they'd dance around the kitchen." Edward frowned and picked at the concrete with a dirtied nail. "I still remember that." He sniffed hard and continued, cold, "When Mom got better after Seth, Dad convinced her to go out for dinner. Grandma was watching us. Mom didn't want to go. She was afraid to leave Seth so soon, but Dad… He got her to go." Edward's jaw tensed. "They never made it to dinner. A truck driver got distracted at the wheel. Crossed the median and…"

Sara hung her head. "Sorry."

"We stayed with Grandma for a while, but she had her own health problems and wasn't really equipped to raise two babies and a traumatized kid, right? We got passed around a lot. Got lost in the system."

"But you took care of Michael and Seth."

"You bet I did. That was the last thing my mother said to me. 'Take care of them, Eddie'."

Sara flinched at Edward's use of his hated nickname. Was that why he hated it so much?

"I always wondered why all that happened to us," he said, his brow creased. "Made no sense to me. I thought God was supposed to take care of good people. Things got worse after that, as Mike and Seth got older. No one would've believed it, but I could've sworn there was, like, a shadow following our family. Following *Michael*."

"The Rage," she said, dawning.

"Yeah, I know that now. That truck driver that killed my folks? Police said he fell asleep, but the guy swore that wasn't it. He said he was being chased by demons. I thought he was nuts at the time, but… Now I know he was probably right. Michael grew up *dark*. His eyes turned black pretty early on, and sometimes I'd catch him up at night, wandering around, talking to himself. Scared me. *He* scared me. Seth was afraid of him, too. Used to stay out of the house as much as he could."

"I didn't know."

"When I turned eighteen, I took legal custody of them. I thought I could be as great as Dad and figure out what was so broken inside of Michael. But then we fell in with Rip, and it just got even worse. Man, I was stupid. Police came around one morning. They had witnesses who thought they saw someone who looked like Michael at the school. They wanted to question him about a murder. A little girl—"

"Me," she said, remembering how she'd watched Michael push her other, younger self.

"I lied for Michael. I didn't want to believe it, but… I knew." Nodding, he muttered, "I knew." Sighing, he finished, "Then Big Joe shot him, and he disappeared from the hospital, and about ten seconds later this *new* Michael shows up in Candice's backseat. He's, like, my age now, and he's totally different, but he knows everything about us. It's him, but it's not my brother. Not quite."

"You're still scared of him," she said, gauging him carefully.

He nodded. "Yeah. Maybe not for the same reasons I used to be. The darkness is gone in him, thankfully, but… It's just a lot to take in. The multiverse and anti-gods and aliens. A lot to take on faith." Pointedly, he turned to her. "So you'll forgive me if you're one variable too many." He stood and brushed off his pants. "I gotta take a leak. Keep watch for a second."

"Sure," she said, and watched him leave, a scheme coming to mind.

14

"Mike! Wake up!"

Michael jerked awake, shaken to discover warm sunlight filtering in through the threadbare sheets hanging on the small basement window, casting their bedroom in dull, orange light. He rose up in bed, quickly spotting Candice beside him, both of them still undressed. With wild hair and puffy, frightened eyes, his wife gathered the sheets about her nakedness. Michael saw Edward standing in the doorway, holding his gun.

"Edward!" Candice snapped. "Knock!"

But Edward looked just as beside himself with panic, as though he'd only recently woken as well. "Dude, she's gone!"

Michael hurried out of bed, slipping into his pants and yanking his alien rifle from its perch against the wall. "What are you talking about?"

"Sara! She volunteered for second watch. I came inside. Fell asleep. I went out to check this morning, and she's *gone*, man!"

Michael's heart raced as he followed Edward into the living room, giving Candice a chance to rustle into her clothes and grab her gun in privacy. The brothers stormed outside, taking the steps up to the street two at a time.

"No," Michael said, adrenaline trembling through his veins. "No, she wouldn't do that."

"She turned on us, man! I told you! She waited until we were asleep, and now she's gone to the other side to tell them what we're planning for today!"

"No!" Michael shrieked. "No. That's not—"

Candice raced to catch up to them, hastily dressed, huddled beneath the hood of her coat, rifle in hand. The three of them scanned the streets as Edward railed, "That witch! We have to move before she brings the whole invasion here! We have to—"

"Would everybody relax?" Sara's voice called from a distance.

As one, the three spun. Michael saw Sara headed down the road, a motley crew at her back. His eyes struggled to register the band of strangers, most prominent among them a tall, white robot on treads—its snowman-like orbs pivoting as it advanced, regarding the ruined streets.

"What is this?" he demanded, flexing his grip around the rifle.

"Well, Blondie said it herself: We need an army. I got us one."

Michael opened his mouth to respond but closed it, struck speechless.

Sara shrugged, grinning knowingly. "Besides, what's the good in saving the multiverse a few dozen times if you can't call in favors from some old friends?"

She patted the robot at her side. "I went back to my rift this morning and swung by the house to pick up Zeo, here."

The robot scanned the new faces, its digital expression a poor mimic of human surprise. "Mistress Sara, many primitives are detecting my presence. Shall I self-destruct to terminate the violators?"

Michael gulped, but Sara laughed. "Nah, Zeo. It's cool. Relax."

Ignoring the suicidal 'bot, Sara turned to her side, where Michael recognized a husky young man wearing a long black coat, his dishwater blond mop top uncombed, his shoulder in a bandage. "This," she said, gesturing to the gentle giant, "is my oldest friend from back home."

"Johnny," Michael breathed in excitement, stepping in to shake his hand.

"Hey, Michael," Johnny Frawl greeted him and smiled.

"Man, it's been forever." Michael turned to Sara, "But I don't—"

"We need an expert to close the rift, right? I thought we could either bank on you fumbling your way through it, or I could just go get the *last* guy who closed one."

"Though," Johnny pointed out, raising a finger, "I'm not really an expert. Just a dabbler. Let that be known on the front end of this crazy plan."

Michael chuckled, and Sara turned to her other side, hooking a thumb in the direction of a misshapen alien that closely resembled a hairless rabbit, complete with buckteeth and drooping ears. He was a miserable, repulsive thing, and in each warty hand he drug twin black crates filled with what, Michael could only guess.

"That's my fence, Wurgyl," Sara introduced the creature. "He's got enough toys and noisemakers in those trunks to even the odds, I think."

The nervous alien glanced about, his eyes wide. "I'm here under protest, Red," he gargled. "I'm not combat-ready."

"Relax, Wurgyl. I'll owe you one after this."

"You'll owe me two!"

Behind Sara, a colorful quartet in garish costumes—complete with masks and capes—stepped forward. One man—blond, blue-eyed, and all-American—broke apart from the rest and approached, extending a hand encased in an ornately designed iron mechanical gauntlet. "Hello, again, Michael."

"Light Sphere!" Michael shouted in delight.

"Sara said you needed a hand. Hope you don't mind that we crashed your little party. This is my team, The Illumiknights."

"*Your* team?" Michael asked, surprised.

He winked. "I'm a free agent these days. Working for the military didn't agree with me." Light Sphere nodded to each member in turn: a grumpy-looking beast of a man, giant and hairy and dressed in a bear skin complete with head that served as a cowl; a regal Arab woman in mask, cape, and costume of whites and purples; and another smaller, spunky dark-headed girl in a skintight black catsuit with electric blue piping, wearing goggles on her face and something like rollerblades constructed of pure light on her feet. "This is Grizzly, Eon, and Slyder. Guys, this is Michael Morrison. We nearly killed each other one time."

"Isn't that how you make all your friends, Rick?" Grizzly remarked with a low chuckle.

The others nodded to Michael, all-smiles, but distant, as strangers.

"Thank you," Michael said. "Thank you for coming."

Light Sphere gave a firm nod—almost a salute—and stepped back in rank. Michael turned to Sara, dumbly shaking his head, even as he laughed. "I can't believe you pulled this off."

She smiled demurely, twisting her fingers awkwardly. "I'm not quite done yet. We've got one more."

Sara turned to her crew, and the others parted, making way for a figure that took Michael's breath away. From behind him, he heard Edward let out a startled cry. Walking towards them was a young man with a stern, mean face and longish dark hair. His chin was razor sharp, and his gaze was just as piercing. He was older than Michael had last seen him, but it was him.

"Seth…"

The gangly figure shrugged, hands in his back pockets, looking about uncertainly. "Hey," he said in a thick Southern drawl, and Michael suddenly realized with a bit of disappointment that this wasn't his actual brother, but his *double*, whom he'd met and befriended on Sara's first jump.

Sara quickly explained, "I picked him up from his world. After the Hooded Man killed Edward and we left, he didn't have any brothers to look out for him. I…dunno. I just thought the Morrison brothers should always have each other."

"Besides," Seth added coolly, careful not to look up at them, as though embarrassed, "Yanks won the war, so there wasn't much point in sticking around and letting the tide of progress wash us out."

Michael listened but didn't hear anything. He staggered forward, reminding himself that his real brother was dead—still, the young man before him was the next best thing. He clapped a hearty hand on his shoulder, overcome with emotion. "Good to see you again, man."

Seth seemed unfazed, shy almost, then glanced over Michael's shoulder and paled. At last his cool exterior was broken, his mouth slightly agape. "Edward?"

Michael stepped aside and saw his older brother scuffling forward, trembling. Seth, too, moved closer, drawn as if by gravity. The estranged brothers, separated by worlds—by death—stared captivated by one another. At last, Edward nearly fell on his brother, wrapping him in his arms. Seth hesitated, but returned the hug as Edward wept. "Aw, man. We lost you there for a while, little brother."

"Lost you, too," Seth said, his voice breaking beneath the weight of his sorrow.

Edward buried his face in Seth's shoulder, crying unashamedly. Then, suddenly he parted long enough to pull Michael into their hug as the brothers held tight.

Pulling away, removing his glasses to wipe at the wetness on his face, Edward glanced at Sara, who seemed to be crying, as well, through her pleased smile.

"Like me yet?" she asked.

He nodded, appreciative of her efforts.

Candice slipped in beside Michael, hugging him at his side. He looked down to her, drawing strength from the serenity in her big grey eyes. "We can do this," she whispered.

"Yeah," he breathed, kissing her gently. "We can do this."

15

Back inside the Morrison apartment, the final strategies were drawn up. Michael, Sara, Candice, Edward, Johnny, and Light Sphere crowded around the counter in the kitchenette, going over the makeshift diagram that Michael had made with loose trash. Meanwhile, Sara's robot butler Zeo fussed over the apartment's disrepair, muttering an exasperated "Oh dear" at regular intervals, taking it upon itself to arrange the toppled furniture and dust the filthy surfaces.

Michael watched the 'bot for a moment, smirking, then turned back to the counter. He drew a line down the center, narrating, "The prison transport will head down here. Light Sphere and Edward—you guys will flank them on either side. Draw their attention. Then Sara and I will hit them from the rear, get the captives free, and move for the tank."

Light Sphere crossed his arms. "Sounds easy enough."

Michael said, "After the tank's secured, Sara, Johnny and I will head for the school. It'll be a straight shot."

"What do we do?" Candice asked.

"There's nothing to do," Michael said. "Hopefully, anyway. After we get inside, it's pretty much up to us to close the rift and…deal with Toby."

"We'll make sure they stay off you," Edward said. "I get that stealth is key, here, but eventually they're going to catch on that there's a fox in the henhouse." He turned to Candice. "When that happens, we'll make some noise outside. Draw them off as best we can."

Sara said, "And that's where Wurgyl comes in."

At once, everyone looked over their shoulders to the pink, wrinkly creature in the living room. Presently he sat on the couch, surrounded by his cases, his long ears twitching at every outside sound. "What?" he asked, seeing all eyes on him.

"Open 'em up," Sara said.

Wurgyl hurried to a stand and depressed buttons on the trunks. The cases gave a hydraulic hiss, then opened to reveal an armory inside. Edward whistled, moving closer.

Sara reached into the collapsible drawers, grabbing firearms of various alien makes and models while Wurgyl described with growing pride. "That's a Y-85 Plasma Assault rifle. Very hush-hush. No one outside the Oran Hierarchy is supposed to even know those things exist, let alone get their hands on one."

Sara tossed the rifle to Edward, who caught it and observed it like a work of art. "Whoa…"

Even hard-faced Seth grew curious enough to poke his head closer. Wurgyl retrieved a long scope rifle, presenting it thoughtfully. "Numian Longshot.

Punches through Vidor steel—and that ain't easy. Trust me."

Seth took the rifle and practiced looking down the scope. Then he looked to the grip and frowned. "Where's the trigger?"

"Thought-activated," Wurgyl said. "Fit your fingers in the grooves there. Creates a neural link with the gun. Line up your shot through the scope, concentrate on your target, and imagine your target dead. They soon will be."

Seth chuckled darkly.

Wurgyl glanced to Light Sphere, but the Super Power held up his gauntlets. "That's okay," the hero said. "We brought our own."

The alien shrugged. "Suit yourself, human."

Sara helped herself to a blaster pistol, giving it a cursory examination before shoving it in a holster and strapping it to her thigh. "MagTech5 is mine. I'll need a backup for the chukrahas."

Wurgyl's ears drooped. "But that's my only one."

Sara laughed and patted him on the back, but did not return the weapon. "I also need the two flash-pops, and an Ifod Paradox Generator, just in case."

The alien groaned, but grabbed a handful of clutter that Michael did not even recognize. He handed them over, and Sara stuffed them into the various pouches on the belt she now wore.

"You're killing me, Red," Wurgyl said.

Candice was next in line. "Give me one of those Numian things."

Wurgyl obliged, and Michael saw her getting a feel for the gun, stone-faced and natural. He turned to the creature. "What about me?"

The hairless alien opened his mouth to reply, but Sara cut in, snapping her fingers. "I've got something special. Just for you," she said. Nearly pushing Wurgyl out of the way, she dug deep into the case and brought out a pair of metal-looking bands, like brass knuckles, only smooth.

With great care, she placed them in Michael's hands. "Arkonian Power Bands. Grants the wearer the strength of ten Xylocks. The might to knock a small moon out of orbit, right, Wurgyl?"

Rubbing his knotty hands together, the anxious alien corrected, "Ah, according to the brochure. If it doesn't quite live up to that... Well, no refunds." Grumbling to himself, he added, "Not that you're paying me for any of this anyway..."

She faced Michael again, softly smiling. "It's not quite the same as having super Rage-strength, but I thought you might like to smash something. You know, for old times' sake."

Michael took the power bands and slipped his hands inside. Instantly, he felt more solid, like he was made of pure iron. A charge raced through his veins, better than adrenaline. "Thanks, Sara. These are perfect. All of this, really."

"Um…" Johnny cut in. "You guys seem to have this all figured out, but I'm still not sure how you expect me to survive all the way to the rift. I'm not a fighter or a superhero or a weird alien guy with lots of guns."

Wurgyl bowed in acknowledgement.

"I'm just…" the doughy boy looked around the room, "Well, I'm just me."

"Don't worry," Sara said. "I've got you covered." She flicked her chin to the 'bot in the corner, its large frame comically sweeping a small pile of broken ceramic knick-knacks into an internal dustpan in its bottommost globe. "Zeo."

As if startled, the 'bot rose. "Yes, Mistress Sara?"

"Activate Protocol 7."

"At once, Mistress Sara."

Suddenly, Zeo went perfectly stiff, its orbs locking, then grinding with turning gears. Before Michael's astonished eyes, the robot simply transformed into something more man-like, large and imposing. Then a seam split down its middle, and the mechanical man opened up like a clam and remained immobile.

Sara nudged Johnny with an elbow. "There you go. Step inside."

Johnny's eyes widened. "You mean, it's like a mech suit?"

"More of a partner than a suit. Zeo's consciousness will be in there with you. But he'll let you take lead. Won't you, Zeo?"

A series of beeps emitted from the opened shell and Zeo's pleasant voice replied through hidden speakers, "Of course, Mistress Sara. I look forward to the destruction of many primitives. Present company excluded, of course."

"Uh…" Johnny began.

"You'll do fine," Sara laughed.

Edward turned to Michael, looking quite confident. "All right, bro. One last round. You're the leader. Lead on."

Michael felt a swell of gratitude as he beheld all those who'd come to his aid. "Thank you all," he said as everyone quieted. "This is it. The multiverse rises or falls on what we do here today."

"Can I leave now?" Wurgyl interjected, and Sara punched him in the arm.

"Shut up, Wurgyl," she hissed and he slumped on the couch, clutching his now closed trunks like shields.

Michael carried on, "I did this alone for so long, I… I never imagined I'd make such good friends." Gently taking Candice's hand, he finished, "We're family. And it's going to be that bond that will be our greatest weapon out there today." Looking across the faces before him, seeing Edward and Seth together again, Michael felt his eyes stinging and smiled. "Lock and load. You know your positions. Let's end this war."

Edward raised his rifle and whooped in triumph. The crowd broke off into smaller conversations, their armor and guns clattering as they prepared to leave.

Sara and Johnny moved for Zeo, and Michael could hear Sara trying to coax Johnny inside the suit with humorous difficulty.

In the midst of the busyness, Michael pulled Candice closer. "Once me and Sara get in the school, stay close to Edward and Seth. After it's over, I'll find you."

She nodded quickly, her eyes never leaving his. "Don't keep me waiting."

He leaned in and kissed her, breathing her in, drawing strength from her unwavering love. "I won't."

Without warning, the ground beneath them let out a bellow, and the building shifted and shook, grit from the rafters raining down. Candice stumbled into Michael and held onto him as everyone looked about.

"What was *that?*" Edward hollered.

But Michael knew. "Outside!"

16

Sara and Michael led the way outside and up the stairs to street level. When they beheld the sight before them, Sara's stomach plummeted. "Oh no."

A giant mechanized mastodon lumbered down the street, swinging twin lethal trunks to devastate all in its path. It twisted its massive head, obliterating the three-story building across the street, reducing it to refuse in an eye blink. But the destructor was not alone. An army of Underdwellers roared at the sight of Sara and the others and charged, slab-swords upraised. Mixed in the sea of violence were still more soldiers—humans and aliens of various stripes and armament. Orcs were there, too, riding astride feral hogs, and cybernetic assassins leveled laser rifles similar to those in Wurgyl's selection and fired.

"Down!" Michael roared, and everyone took cover, pelted on all sides by spears, bullets, and laserblasts.

Seth, hailing from a dimension where he'd spent the majority of his adolescence fighting off alien invaders, remained calm in the face of the advancing hordes, wasting no time in forming a one-man firing line. He picked his shots efficiently, methodically working his way through the front lines. He took off the side of one orc's face and put another round through one of the charging hogs, creating a domino effect that tripped up the infantrymen.

He looked up from his initial slaughter to see Edward watching him in awe. "Not bad."

The hatchet-faced youth shrugged, nonchalant, and resumed his deadly work. Edward stacked up beside him and began firing his Y-85, sending a series of three-round bursts down range, picking off targets.

An Underdweller roared and leapt at them from the side, but Sara was there, catching him in the neck with her chukrahas, then filling his face with a volley of rounds from her extended MagTech5.

Candice visibly struggled to keep her presence of mind in the face of the impossible odds, but Sara was proud to see Blondie take her place in Seth's firing line, returning the cyborgs' fire.

The mastodon made another pass, its huge steps pulverizing the street beside them. Vibrations knocked everyone off their feet, and Michael focused his attention on the towering beast. "We need to take that down!"

"Leave it to us," Light Sphere announced as his Illumiknights rushed out into the middle of the road. The Super Power leveled his iron gauntlets at the beast and Sara watched in nostalgic excitement as his gloves turned red hot as Light Sphere charged their energy, generating a pulsating orb of pure white light. He hurled the projectile like a bomb that stuck to the mastodon's undercarriage for a split second before a tremendous explosion detonated from the belly of the beast. The mechanized creature let out an ear-splitting mechanical roar before listing to the side, swinging its trunks. Light Sphere ducked in time to spare his head and nodded to his compatriots.

Grizzly returned the gesture, and then the grungy barbarian ran full force towards the enemy battalion, growling a throaty berserker roar. Suddenly, the bear skins on his back seemed to shimmer and grow until the shapeshifter had completely taken on the form of a twelve-foot tall Kodiak bear. Sara couldn't resist an astonished laugh as the monster leapt into the midst of the Underdwellers and rent them asunder with its massive claws. The were-bear mauled everything in its path, tearing through hogs and removing limbs with its powerful strikes.

Eon was next, floating to mid-air as her eyes turned solid white. She raised her arms to the heavens, like a living goddess. Her cape billowed in a self-made wind as the Super Power created some sort of field around her. Sara ducked from an attack by an orange-skinned, three-armed, Trigarian assassin and stabbed him dead in the gut. She turned back to Eon's enchanting display and watched as those targets caught in her blast slowed in their movements, the flow of Time around them growing thick like molasses.

"Let's do this thing!" Slyder shouted. With the enemies in the blastwave temporarily immobilized, she jetted through on her lightblades, moving at incredible speed. The nimble woman slipped in and around the aliens, dispatching them with ease in Eon's temporal anomaly, smirking triumphantly the entire time.

The mastodon was back in the action, raising its head to roar. From its damaged belly, Sara saw something like thin hangars opening, and robotic scorpions the size of dogs tumbled out and began to skitter towards them.

"Incoming!"

Edward and Candice traded targets, focusing their efforts on the mastodon's brood. Light Sphere stalked their way, extending his gloves, palm out, and irradiating throngs of the scorpion-droids, vaporizing them in tiny explosions of sparks and superheated metal.

"We've *gotta* take down that thing!" Sara roared once more as the mastodon hurled its trunks, bursting through a next-door building and showering them in loose brick and soil.

Light Sphere acknowledged and raised his glowing gauntlets towards the beast, but he was tackled from the side by an Underdweller. Sara raced for him, blasting with her MagTech, but its rounds refused to perforate the Underdweller's tough, volcanic armor. The tribal warrior smashed his bony face against Light Sphere's, dazing the Super Power, then lifted a two-handed slab-sword high, ready to cleave the hero's head from his shoulders.

Sara hurled her chukrahas in a fit of desperation, slicing off one of the monster's hands. It howled and dropped the sword to the ground, but Sara did not slow. She kicked out with her legs and wrapped them tight around the Underdweller's neck, using her momentum to sling him off of Light Sphere. The two of them sprawled on the ground, and Sara gave a sharp twist of her knees, snapping the Underdweller's neck.

Light Sphere rose, disorientated and bleeding from a thin cut across his nose "Thanks," he huffed.

"No problem."

He collected her chukrahas and tossed it to her hand.

Together, they surveyed the hordes. The orcs were on foot now, but still just as deadly, swinging crude axes and hooks. Mechanical scorpions still swarmed, but the Underdweller ranks seemed to be thinning.

Johnny stomped forward, clumsy-looking in his Zeo-suit, only his chubby face visible in the helmet's cutout. Sweating profusely, he shrieked over the gunfire and explosions. "What do I do? How do I work this thing?"

Sara hefted up one of his bulky arms for him. "Zeo!" she commanded. "Cannons! Come on, help out here!"

"Yes, Mistress Sara," the suit chimed politely.

Johnny flinched in alarm as his round arms contorted into impressive twin chainguns. "Yeah!" he beamed.

She gave him a kick in his mechanical rear. "Shoot something! And don't hit the big bear out there! He's on our side!"

Her friend didn't need to be told twice. He whirled his cannons towards the rush of soldiers and let fly. Thousands of glowing rounds whistled from his chainguns, mowing through resistance with ease. Aliens and cyborgs were chewed into pulp as Johnny howled with maniacal laughter.

The Morrison brothers managed to carve out an opening, allowing Candice a moment to rush towards Sara. Wide eyes filled with fear, she panted, "Have you seen Michael? I lost him."

Sara's heart sank and she quickly searched the battlefield. "Michael!" she hollered.

"Watch out!" she heard him reply from some great distance, as the mastodon veered off-balance, its paw coming straight down over Candice. Light Sphere dove right, and Sara hurled herself forward, tackling Candice to safety just as the beast's foot punched a fresh crater in the street.

The women helped each other up and looked into the sky where, riding atop the mechanized mastodon, was Michael Morrison. "Wahoo!" he exclaimed in boy-like revelry, and Sara smiled at the wild figure, the sun casting a sort of holy glow about him.

"There he is," she sighed, a wave of wonderful memories washing over her in an instant.

Indeed, Michael stood tall and glorious above them, his thrilled laughter ringing true across the bloody battlefield. Just like the Leviathan on Ruggashosh or the Behemoth on Toby's world, he rode the giant monster even as it tried to buck him off. Sara glanced to the warzone and saw that only a few stragglers remained—which were quickly dispatched by Seth's expert marksmanship.

As the carnage settled to an odd quiet, the heroes one by one abandoned their posts and gathered about, watching as Michael continued to laugh and crow, riding his wild bronco.

Sara spied Candice watching her husband with fresh perspective. The young woman's face positively glowed with awe and excitement, and Sara warmed inside. *Good*, she thought. It was good that Candice got to see the legendary Michael Morrison at work. At least once before he retired for good.

Sara's gaze returned to her hero as he pounded his Arkonian Power Bands into the base of the mastodon's skull. One-two, one-two, the tiny human hammered, the impacts like sonic booms that took seconds to reach their ears. The beast gave a low groan and pitched forward, with Michael still pummeling it, riding it all the way down.

Sparks and flames belched from the top of the thing's head, but at last it teetered and crashed into the street, digging grooves into the concrete. Dust billowed from the wreck, but Sara saw Michael swatting away at the smoke as he merely hopped off the ransacked creature, his smudged Converse sneakers touching down.

Coughing just a bit, he still managed a smile that was undeniable and contagious. "That's that."

Sara shook her head and smirked. "Always the show-off."

He shrugged and winked, then received Candice into his arms. She clung to his jacket, breathless. "That was the craziest thing I have ever seen!" She kissed him hard on the mouth, and Sara blushed, then looked away, suddenly needing a distraction.

Her gaze found a new target easily enough. There, still huddled in the stairwell to the apartment, Wurgyl cowered. Sara approached, cocking an eyebrow. "Wurgyl, did you fire a single shot?"

He wagged a limp finger in her face. "I just sell the guns! I leave it to lunatics like you to shoot them!"

Eon majestically glided to the street to join the others, her tone cultured, "How did they know where we were?"

A horrible hiss answered her, carried on the gunmetal grey skies, "I sssseeee yooouuuu, Mootthheerrrr…"

"Look!" Edward shouted, pointing over their shoulders.

Everyone looked to the horizon, where fleets of alien ships blotted out the scant sunlight, darkening the East. And floating at the head of the wedge of battleships, suspended along the clouds by purple lightning—

"Toby," Sara said.

She shook her head in frustration as the others scattered for cover. Treads rattled the loose gravel along the surface of the road, and she saw one of those skull tank-men grinding their way, its red eyes glistening with artificial malice. More foot soldiers marched alongside it, a bizarre mix of aliens collected as trophies from Toby's multidimensional conquests.

"We're linked," she spat. "I'm not going to be able to get away from him."

Edward and Seth re-formed their firing line as the elder Morrison called to his troops. "We hold them off here."

"There's no way," Sara argued. "There's too many, and with Toby…" She flicked her eyes ahead and saw the Chevy still parked on the curb. The tarp had been half-burned away, and large chunks of concrete had dented in one corner of the roof, but it looked mostly in one piece.

Whipping to Michael—who was already flexing his fists, ready for another round—she said, "You have to get to the school."

"That wasn't the plan," he said. "We go together."

"Toby's changing the plan. You guys go. Take Johnny. Close the rift."

He frowned, flustered. "I guess it would be pointless to argue with you right now."

"Trust me."

"What about you?"

"I'll lead Toby away. Plus side is, if he's here with his friends, school should

313

be a lot easier to get inside."

Michael nodded, no doubt surmising as much. Sara hurried to Johnny, giving his back a solid whack. "Zeo, deactivate Protocol 7."

Before Johnny had a chance to ask what that meant, the suit split open and ejected the large man out into a heap. He yelped in surprised pain and sat up, rubbing his head. "What gives?"

"I need this," she said quickly, then spoke again to the 'tron, "Zeo, initiate Protocol 12."

The empty suit whirred and whined, pistons repositioning, parts twisting and converting until, at last, the 'tron transformed into a sled. Small twin turbines on the underside powered to life, emitting white-blue fire, and Sara hopped onto the sled on her stomach, feeling around for the controls.

"What are you doing?" Johnny protested.

"Getting out of here. I'll lead Toby away. You go with Michael to the school."

As she gave instruction, Michael was already guiding Candice towards the car and moving for Edward. "Come on."

Light Sphere turned to his troops and hefted a chin. "We'll keep them busy here."

"Thank you," Michael said, his words weighty.

Seth gripped his Longshot and climbed onto the rocket sled, much to Sara's surprise. "What are you—?"

"You fly," he said evenly. "I'll shoot. I work better from the high ground, anyway."

Edward took hold of the sled. "Seth, no. We just got you back, man."

"Don't worry," he said without a smile. "I'm not going anywhere."

Michael herded Johnny into the car as the tank-man released a simmering blast of red heat that cut through a nearby stone building. "Come on!"

Johnny seemed hesitant to leave Sara, but she urged him on, "Move it, stupid-head!"

He grimaced and shouted, "Don't die, ya dummy!"

She smiled and pulled on the throttle. Over her shoulder, she told Seth, "Hang on!"

The sled lifted off the ground, and Sara spared one last look to see the remaining Morrisons and Johnny piling into the Chevy and peeling away. Another laser from the tank-man sizzled beside her, and she banked hard to the right, barely avoiding death. Pivoting the sled around, she watched the flanks of alien vessels looming large, raining devastating fire. Eon rose in the air to meet them, hurling her strange time-slowing energy fields at them, pinning them in place as Light Sphere released waves of white-hot phosphorous beams, cutting through their hulls to explosive results.

On the ground below, Slyder did her lethal ballerina thing, skating around the tank-man to draw its fire, pirouetting with an outstretched leg, taking out three soldiers in a rapid arc. Grizzly, too, donned his Kodiak form and lunged full-on into the melee, a furry force of nature.

Behind her, Seth took aim and popped off rounds, splitting heads left and right. But Sara looked to the skies. To Toby.

And, he, in turn, watched only her, his unblinking eyes white against his night-colored flesh. "Mottheerrr…"

"Come on, then," she muttered. "Let's end this."

17

Edward was fast earning his stripes as one of the best wheel-men in L.A.

The Chevy slid through an intersection, dodging green fire that bombarded them from all sides. Wheels spun as the street shattered around them, showering the car with grit.

"Go! Go! Go!" Michael shouted, pounding the roof with the side of his fist.

"Shut up!" Edward snapped, hands wildly jerking the wheel. "Let me drive!"

FWOOM!

A fireball ballooned behind them, blowing out their back windshield. Johnny squealed louder than Candice, tucking his large frame into the floorboard. Candice kept her cool, using the barrel of her alien rifle to knock out the jagged remnants of the glass, then firing on their pursuers with the power of her mind. Small scouting hover-sleds zoomed overhead, their single standing pilots steering the small crafts over the narrow Los Angeles side streets.

Michael's trusty silver-paint rifle clattered at his feet as the Chevy veered to and fro, but his focus remained on the road ahead. The sleds turned brick to ash beside them, laying down a heavy suppressive fire. Edward ground his teeth, his shoulders arched high as he floored the gas. The car cleared an alley, scraping sparks and leaving a bit of paint behind, and catapulted across the street into the next alley, just as the road behind them was vaporized by green heat.

Candice plucked one skid from the sky and traded blasts with the other two. A dark shape landed hard on the hood and Edward hollered obscenities, nearly losing control of the car. Michael stared into the eyes of a large, armored, reptile man clutching the hood and bearing large fangs—it was the pilot of the downed hover-sled.

"Get it off!" Edward shrieked. "*Get it off!*"

Michael gripped his rifle and blasted, coating the windshield in silver fluorescent paint-like energy. The explosive paint detonated, blowing out the glass, but the croc-man swung wide, hanging on tight.

"Shoot the guy!" Edward roared and yanked the wheel, taking a ninety-degree turn on two wheels.

Michael aimed again, but the croc-man disappeared from sight, clambering onto the dented roof. Suddenly, a curved blade pierced through, shoving into the backseat, tearing a bloody line in Candice's forearm. She screamed, and Michael loosed one hand to push her back.

"Down! Down!"

She lay flat on her back and fumbled in the tight space to shoot holes in the roof. Michael did, too, until the weight dislodged, bounced off the trunk, and rolled in their wake, now just roadkill.

Michael checked his wife over, frantic. "Okay?"

She bit her lip, paling. "Just grazed me."

Edward swore, drawing Michael's attention to the front again. "What?"

But then he saw. Up ahead, the school and its Black Pillar waited…but coming straight for them, swimming on air, its enormous mouth opening wide, was the terrifying Great Xanawhales Hortex.

"Crap," Michael whispered.

Johnny finally poked up from his hiding place, shoving his fuzzy face into the cab. "What? What is it?"

He took one look at the widening jaws of the flying dragon whale, squeaked like he had a tail and someone had just stepped on it, and fainted.

"We're dead," Edward snorted.

Michael unbuckled his seatbelt and gathered his legs up beneath him. "Keep us steady. Aim right for it!"

"What are you doing?" Edward barked, but Michael ignored his brother, crawling out the side window and easing himself onto the hood. The wind tugged at his long hair and hooded coat, and he squinted against the force, but remained steady.

The Xanawhales filled his vision now, and his eyes narrowed on the blue scales, the bony exoskeleton, the dozen yellow eyes, and the rows of thousands of jagged shark teeth.

Michael flexed his fists, feeling the power bands tighten against them, and rose to a crouch on the roof.

"Come on, come on," he breathed.

The Xanawhales swooped forward, emitting a roar that rattled the buildings. But somehow Michael heard his brother shout, "What are you—?"

The Chevy hit a bump that Michael had anticipated, and he used the moment, springing forward off the car, right in the path of the Xanawhales' jaws. Twisting in mid-air, Michael reared back and swung, smashing the side of the animal's face, knocking it off-course, where it crashed sideways into a building, leveling three blocks of real estate.

Still airborne, Michael tucked into a clumsy roll and toppled to the street, tumbling into a ball. When at last he stopped, his clothes were torn, his knee banged up and stinging, but he'd lived. Breathing hard and feeling triumphant, he watched the smoking wreckage that marked the Xanawhales' final resting place.

The roar of an engine drew near as Edward slid the car into a fishtail and hopped out, pumping fists in the air. "Woo!"

Edward was on him in a second, punching his arm, hugging his neck, and taking firm hold of his face to kiss his cheek. "Dude!"

Michael laughed at the exuberant display, and then Candice was there, too, wrapping her arms around his shoulders and squealing in delight.

The three rejoiced at their victory, but soon Michael faced the school, grim.

"Come on," he said. "It's not over yet."

18

Sara juked to the side, skimming over another bolt of violet lightning. The rocketsled was smoking from previous attacks, but Zeo was hanging in there. Around her, the clouds turned charcoal, tainted by the presence of the Shape as it came closer.

"How're we doing?" she shouted to her companion.

Seth kept his balance, Zen-like, firing calmly on the Shape. "He won't go down."

She'd figured as much, but at the very least they had managed to put considerable distance between them and the forces back at the apartment. Faraway, the darkening sky continued to light up with beautiful colors as Light Sphere's Illuminknights fulfilled their end of the bargain, giving the invaders a run for their money. She worried for them, knowing that as strong as they were, there were only four of them. Still, she could not afford to dwell on their plight.

"Motherrr…" the Shape whispered, though the word rippled like thunder in the storm clouds.

"Why does he call you 'mother'?" Seth asked casually, then fired another blast that the Shape harmlessly absorbed in its sticky black flesh.

"Really long story," she replied.

The smiling Shape gained ground and exclaimed, "Ha!" A tendril of black slime exploded from its center mass, reaching out at a dizzying speed and impaling Seth right through the shoulder. The youth shouted in pain, dropping the rifle to the building tops below.

"Seth!" Sara cried, grabbing him lest he slip over the edge.

The Shape retracted its limb, leaving a gaping wound in Seth's shoulder that oozed blood. Sara pressed down on the wound for a moment, but quickly returned her slick-with-blood hands to the sled's controls. "Put pressure on it!"

He shivered and nodded, gripping the hole in his shoulder. "Hurts."

Behind them, the Shape grabbed at them again, thick obsidian vines twitching and flapping their way.

"Hang on!" Sara grit her teeth and pulled on the controls, slipping and weaving through the spindly tentacles that popped and snapped like tight elastic. Seth's eyes lolled from side to side, and she feared losing the boy who'd given her away at her wedding. "Don't die, Seth! Don't you die!"

Distracted by her friend's condition, she was ill-prepared for the whipping tendril that slapped the underside of the sled. Zeo's hull creaked and hissed thick black smoke, puttering as its engine died.

"Zeo!" She pounded on the small console.

"Sorry—zzz—Mistress—zz—"

"*Zeo!*"

Seth scooted to her side, panting, but alive. "What's happening?"

"We're gonna crash!" She made to shout, but never finished. Gooey strings wrapped taut around her wrists and plucked her from the ride. She watched in helpless horror as Zeo's ruined frame—with Seth on board—disappeared into the darkened cityscape below without her. "*Seth!*"

The Shape whirled her about, clutching her with many arms that protruded from its chest. It brought her close, smiling into her face with those terribly bright eyes and teeth. "Moootthheerrr…"

"Toby, stop!" she screamed. "You're still in control! Make him stop this!"

A venomous chuckle oozed from the thing's open mouth, reeling her in. She felt a bitter cold seeping into her flesh from the tendrils, permeating every thought, drowning out her hope, her love, her faith. "Toby!" she shrieked. "Don't!"

"Aaaattt lllaasssttt…"

A high-pitched whine split the Shape's merriment and it looked below. Sara did, too, and saw the rocketsled barreling towards her, Seth at the controls. The Shape hissed in surprise and released Sara a fraction of an instant before Zeo smashed right into its mass.

Sara plummeted fast, meeting Seth in mid-air. They dropped from the explosion that followed Zeo's crash into the Shape, their arms wrapping around each other. Together, they fell straight down, smacking hard against a high-rise roof and rolling twice to a painful stop.

Seth came up wheezing, gnashing his teeth in agony. Sara climbed to her knees, checking him over. "Dislocated—" he coughed, madly groping his useless arm.

Sara took hold of it and tugged, snapping it back in place. He gasped in relief and rested his head on the roof. "Better."

She sighed and looked to the sky, where the Shape had since vanished. "That won't take him out of the fight for long." She turned to her savior. "That was nuts, by the way, what you did."

Seth tottered to a stand and shrugged. "Figured you needed a little rescuing."

Sara helped him up and grinned, impressed. "You Morrison boys."

19

Michael shoved open the door to the cafeteria and pulled the trigger on his rifle, bathing a green Viking, with squid-like tentacles protruding from his face, in silver plasma. The Squid Viking dropped backwards, only to be replaced by three more of his kin. Michael fired twice more, while Candice ducked inside— a fresh bandage on her arm— picking off the last.

"Come on!" she barked.

Edward double-timed his steps, a defenseless Johnny in tow. The elder Morrison fired a volley of rounds back out in the hallway from where he'd come, hollering all the while. Once done, his rifle whistled as it cooled, and he gave a quick nod to his brother. "That cyber-raptor-mutant thing is finally down."

"Good," Michael breathed. "This way."

He led his troops across the cafeteria, bombarded by flashes of his miserable time spent in this school. "Boiler room's out here," he said over his shoulder, trying to forget the teasing and dirty looks he'd received in these very halls. "Rift's down there." At least, he thought it was. He remembered all too well the boom-boom-boom in his gut when the Rage had tried to draw him to the boiler room. It *had* to be down there.

They crossed the caf, and Michael prepared to bang on through into the hallway, when the door swung wide, a dark figure filling the frame. Without pause, Edward and Candice raised their guns, but Michael watched in surprise as a familiar figure stepped into the flickering fluorescent light.

Through his bristly mustache and beard, a yellow-stained smile spread. Dark beady eyes glistening, the fat, hairy brute chuckled, and the smell of sulfur wafted in Michael's direction. "Lookiee here," the figure said.

Michael glowered. "Charlie Bost."

Johnny stumbled forward, his eyes growing large. "Charlie?"

Clad only in a black burlap cloak, Sara's ex-husband sauntered in, glaring at Michael. "Got myself an extended leave from hell, just to come meet you," he said, slowly parting the hem of his robe to reveal his naked, hairy gut. "You're

319

gonna die, you little punk."

Michael frowned, confused, then balked as Charlie's fat split open to reveal a large mouth with giant fangs. A barbed tongue shot out as the troll bent backwards to crab-walk on his hands and feet.

"*What* the—?!" Johnny shouted, but Michael pushed him away.

"Get out!" he roared. "Get to the rift!"

Candice and Edward hooked arms with Johnny and hustled away. The Charlie-Thing snapped at them, but Michael pelted it with silver fluorescence, getting its attention. "Hey! I'm right here! Come on!"

The misshapen mutation slobbered and growled and galloped for Michael. He braced himself, tossing aside his gun, and popping his knuckles. The Thing leapt for him, tongue lashing wildly, and Michael punched it square in the snout, shooting it across the length of the cafeteria and through the wall.

Grimacing, he charged outside into the hall as the abomination scrambled to its feet, Charlie's face prominent from a large fleshy trunk that reached almost to the ceiling. The ogre's pudgy face sneered, missing a couple teeth now. "You're gonna have to do better than that!"

"Don't worry," Michael said, swinging again. "I'm going to."

Charlie bent under the assault as Michael mounted him, burrowing his fists into his supple flesh. "You shouldn't have bothered making the trip from hell, because I'm just going to send you right back."

20

Sara and Seth arrived at the entrance to the school, using each other for a crutch. Seth handled Sara's MagTech5 while she brandished her chukrahas, which had already seen much bloodshed in their trek to the school steps. Yet, now that they were here, Sara saw only a smoking hole in the side of the building and various alien corpses littering the overgrown lawn.

She smirked. "I think your brother's been here."

They staggered inside, parting from each other to ease down the halls. More bodies lay scattered about, and the walls were painted in blood and scorch marks—but there was no sign of their friends.

Then, from somewhere deep in the dark bowels of the school, Sara heard a wounded screech and death rattle. She shared a worried look with Seth and the two picked up the pace, rounding a corner to see Michael standing over a twisted mound of flesh, claws, and blood-slick tendrils wrapped in a burlap cloak. Michael's Arkonian Power Bands dripped with gore, and he heaved giant breaths. He nearly jumped when he saw Sara.

"What is that?" she asked, stepping closer, thinking she saw a bearded face—

"Don't," Michael said, barring her path. "Just…don't. Come on, we have to catch up with the others."

Sara considered looking anyway, but something told her that she didn't need to see whatever thing Michael had just killed. Instead, she followed him down the corridor to a door marked BOILER ROOM. As Michael opened the door, sickening psychedelic light suffused their world.

"This is it," he muttered, and crossed the threshold.

Sara and Seth were right behind him as they clanged down metal steps into the boiler room, already hearing a loud hum coming from somewhere in the brightly lit recesses. When at last they touched down, they saw it:

The Black Pillar, casting a strobing rainbow effect along the brick walls, grew out of the floor and disappeared through the ceiling. The wind created by its incessant churning tugged at Sara like a vacuum, but not nearly as powerfully as the vortex on Yur. The Pillar was in some sort of idle mode, turning and pumping obscene power into the room, but not yet drawing things into its Void.

Standing around the column of unspeakable power, Sara spotted Edward, Candice, and Johnny. The latter was on his knees, scrawling something along the rough concrete floor in chalk. She noticed that his hand was cut and bleeding, dotting his intricate patterns with crimson. He looked panicky—even more so than usual.

At the sight of Michael and Sara, Johnny stood and raced forward. "It's not working!"

Michael ran his bruised hands through his sweaty hair. "What? Why?"

Johnny stammered, his hand still bleeding. "I-I don't know! It's not like the one we opened back at the store. I mean, there's not a rift here."

Michael pushed him aside and stalked forward, gesturing in frustration at the pillar. "Hello? Rift."

"No, I know, but it's not coming from the In-Between. You're looking at the base of the thing. Below it is just floor. It's like it's been planted here."

Michael rubbed his pronounced brow and sighed.

Sara touched Johnny's arm, drawing his attention. "So how do we stop it?"

"Sara, I'm not, like, some expert in Malitivarian Magick, okay? I'm just telling you what's working and what's not. And I'm telling you that this beam is not coming from the In-Between. It's been generated separately—like a seedling. It's drawing strength, yeah, but not from the In-Between. There's another source fueling it."

Then it struck Sara. "Toby."

She looked to Michael and he firmed his mouth, grave. "*He's* the rift."

Thwip!

A black arm extended into the basement and encircled Sara's waist, yanking her back through the doorway. She gave a holler and tightened her fist around the chukrahas, but soon lost it when the tentacle mashed her against the wall in the hallway. It immediately released her, and she collapsed in a heap. She gazed up to see the Shape walking towards her, its coat removed and bent feelers reaching from its blasphemous mass to trail the walls like living shadows.

"Toby," she gasped, feeling a cracked rib.

Michael burst out of the boiler room door, weapons raised. "Sara!" he shouted, then ran at the monster, swinging his super-powered fists.

He delivered a powerhouse of a hook—producing vibrations that dented the flanking rows of lockers—but the Shape absorbed the impact without incident, not once blinking its eyes or ceasing to smile.

Michael gaped in horror, and the Shape swatted him with one hand, sending him pinwheeling down the hall. He tumbled past the rest of their crew, who had just emerged from below. Candice roared in rage and fired, with Edward joining in alongside Seth, who had taken up Michael's alien rifle. The three Morrisons fired, but the Shape merely watched them, slightly bemused.

"Run," Sara croaked. "G-Go."

Candice knelt to help her up. "We're not leaving you."

But Sara shrugged out of her grip. "He's going to kill you all. It's me he wants. *Go!*"

At last, Michael picked himself out of the crater in the wall where he'd landed, and stumbled forward, fists at the ready. He scooped Candice's elbow and faced her, his blue eyes hard. "You need to leave now. This is…this is what me and Sara came here to do."

Resolved, his wife frowned.

"I'll be right behind you," he said, his voice strong and sure. Whether Candice believed it or not, she showed no emotion, gave no last embrace. Just gripped her rifle and raced away.

Seth followed after her, but Edward and Johnny paused to join their friends.

Edward clapped a hand on his brother's shoulder. "I'll take care of her, man. Don't worry about a thing."

Then he ran to catch up to the others. Johnny and Sara faced each other, and the fuzzy giant looked terrified. "I-If you manage to close 'the rift'—however you do that—I-I don't know what's going to happen to the pillar. Without its source, it could just simply shut off or-or…the backlash could wipe out the block, the city…this dimension."

"In that case," Sara smirked, "You'd better stand back."

"Sure," he laughed nervously, then left.

Michael and Sara watched their friends disappear, then turned back to their wayward son. The Shape remained standing, patiently waiting, watching the entire exchange.

"We're here, Toby," Sara said. "You don't have to be alone anymore. We came back for you."

"Wwweee aarreee not the boooyyyy…" the Shape growled, its timbres cracking the ceiling.

"No," Michael said, "But he's in there with you. That's the only reason you're walking around. You're using him. You need him, which means he has power over you." Stepping closer, he shouted, "Do you hear me, Toby? You have power over It! Just take it off, like a coat. Come out of there. Come out, Toby!"

"No!" the Shape screamed in a wild, lunatic shrill, and a black trunk burst out of the goop, punching Michael in the chest. He spun to the ground, gasping for air, senses shattered.

Sara watched him fall, knowing he couldn't take another shot like that. "Toby, it's me! It's Sara! I'm so sorry I left you! I let you down, but I'm here now!"

The Shape raved, gesturing with its hands as tendrils licked the walls and floor, moving in on her. Sara backflipped out of shot and came down into a low crouch, ducking beneath more attacks. Finding her chukrahas on the floor, she deflected the Shape's flails, knowing her blade was utterly useless against the Rage's god-like powers. She was only buying time. "Toby!" she shouted, then sidestepped another jet of black sludge. "Stop!"

Michael entered the fray, his face drenched in blood, his body visibly weakened, and punched at the tentacles, fighting his way to Sara's side. "Sara," he wheezed. "You have to—"

Whack! Michael turned sharp and landed on the tile. Sara joined his side, hands roving over his broken frame. "Michael!"

He looked up at her, one eye filled with blood. Through an equally bloody mouth, he finished, "Sing to him."

"What?"

"When you left…he…he didn't have anyone to sing to him."

Sara blinked back tears and stood. Michael collapsed in fatigue, and Sara turned back to the twisting, whipping Shape. Why hadn't the monster made the killing blow? Why was it toying with them?

Toby, I know you're in there.

The Shape grew, filling the hallway, its blackness spreading to block out all light. Sara stared at the growing shadow and closed her eyes, shedding few tears. Then, with nothing to lose, she opened her mouth—

And sang.

"My darling sunshine, my little sunshine
You send the rainy clouds away

Don't ever leave me, my little sunshine
And make my world so sad and gray…"

Her voice was small and off-key, shaky and uncertain. But she sang the lullaby that she'd used to help Toby sleep when he was so little and frightened of the dark. The song her own father had sang. She sang, moving closer to the Shape, begging God to be here with her. To forgive her for creating this monster. Begging Toby to forgive her for being a terrible mother.

I meant to be so good to you, she wept. *But I wasn't ready for you. I wasn't good enough for you.*

Finding her voice, she filled it with all the pain and regret and sorrow she'd ever felt. All the times she'd wished her father would notice her. All the times she'd pleaded with Charlie to stop hitting her. All the hugs from Michael—the tender kisses, and the powerful ones, too—that she'd taken for granted. All the smiles that Toby, her son, had offered her that were never good enough for her. Not then. But now they were. Oh, she just wanted him to smile for her again. To look to her with surrender. To need her.

She sang and cried, defenseless and completely open. Whether the Shape killed her or spared her, it didn't matter. She only wanted to sing for her little boy. Her song. Aztaroth, that damnable Maestro, had meant for her Song to destroy the multiverse, but she prayed she could save it instead.

The Shape writhed and jerked, hissing. It slapped at the ground beside her, shattering tile and concrete, but Sara did not flinch. With trembling hands, she reached for the black blob, still singing, still crying.

"I'm here, Toby," she said. "I'm right here, baby."

The walls shook and broke apart. The beast flailed and squealed in hellish fury.

"Come out, baby," she wept. "Don't be afraid anymore."

Mouths opened up all over the beast, snapping and howling. More arms scratched and clawed at its own mass, at the lockers, the ceiling. The thing seemed ready to explode, and Sara braced for her death, but could not abandon her son. "Toby—"

She gasped and broke into fresh sobs as the muck parted and a pale, human hand emerged, quivering as it extended for her. "Toby!" she exclaimed, wrapping herself around the hand and pulling. "I've got you, baby!"

But the amorphous Shape pulled harder, trying to swallow the boy back into itself. It roared so loudly that Sara's ears popped, and she tasted coppery blood running from her nose, but she tugged all the harder, screaming. "Come on!"

Yet, she wasn't strong enough. The Shape slurped as more arms detached from it, trying to stuff the boy back inside.

"No!" she screamed, desperate. "Stop! He doesn't belong to you!"

Toby's hand was slowly reeled in, nearly submerged once more. Sara held with all her might, wailing uncontrollably for fear of losing Toby again, when suddenly two more strong hands took hold alongside hers, and pulled.

Michael's hands.

Her cries quieted, and the two of them looked to each other, all of time seeming to freeze.

"Together," he said, calm and serene, his one good eye tearing up.

She nodded, resolved, and the two pulled with their combined weight, straining against the dying Shape's might. Toby's hand reappeared, soon followed by his arm. His head.

Together, Michael and Sara brought their son into the world, pulling him free from the Shape's sticky clutches. Sara let out a yelp as the three of them fell backwards. Trembling, she looked to the Shape, its empty cavity opening and closing like a starved mouth looking for its last meal. Black tongues flicked down the corridor, and Sara cradled Toby's head against her breast, scurrying backwards.

"Leave us alone!" she shouted.

The Shape did not press the attack—in fact, it could not seem to move now. Instead it was caught in the hall, fat and bloated by its own power and uncompromising hate. Even its tendrils withered and shrunk back into the central mass, hissing as if they were deflating. The thing twitched, but only in death throes, completely incapacitated.

But it wasn't exactly dead. Why wasn't it dead?

"Sara?" an ancient voice addressed her from the floor.

She looked to the boy in her arms, but saw it wasn't a boy at all, but rather an old man, shriveled and pale. His skin was papery and clung to his skeletal frame. But those brown eyes—their shape, the light there.

"Toby?" she sobbed.

Michael was there with her, holding the elderly man in their arms together, and Sara instinctively took her husband's hand, squeezing hard lest she lose her sanity.

"Toby," Michael said gently, "you're okay, now."

"You came for me," the decrepit figure rasped and smiled a toothless, puckered grin.

"We did," Sara said, fighting revulsion. How long had Toby been inside the Shape? How many decades had that devil sucked him dry, bleeding him of his life, siphoning his youth? She touched her head to his and felt her eyes flood anew with bittersweet tears. "I'm so sorry, Toby."

"I fought him," Toby whispered, giggling like a boy. "W-We found the

Gateworld, but I-I wouldn't let him break it… Told him…convinced him he wanted to find you first."

Sara kissed his head, brushing back the loose grey strands, watching, heartsick, as they softly fell from his head. "That was smart, Toby. You saved the multiverse. You saved everybody."

"I did?" he said, perking up. "I did?"

"You were awesome, Toby," Michael said, his voice heavy with emotion. "A hero."

"I wanted to be," he said, the words slipping through his delicate lips. "Just like you guys… but… was so tired. Am so tired…"

Sara decorated his wrinkled brow with soft kisses, squeezing her eyes tight to dam the tears. "Just sleep, baby. You can sleep now. I won't leave you ever again. I'll just hold you, okay?"

"Will you sing to me?" he asked, sounding just like the boy she remembered. The boy she loved.

"Of course I will."

Michael could no longer hold back tears of his own and leaned over, kissing the top of Sara's head, somehow imparting the strength she needed. Cradling their son, Sara sang through her sobs. Her voice cracked, but she carried the tune as best she could. Michael remained with her, holding her hand, as she sang Toby's last lullaby.

After a moment, Michael quietly interrupted. "Sara."

She opened her eyes on Toby and saw that he had passed away. His eyes were closed peacefully, his aged face lax and finally at rest. A loud crumble alarmed her and she watched as the Shape dried out and cracked, dissolving to ash and charcoal. Dead, at last, its only tie to its physical manifestation severed. Holding Toby close, she watched the accursed thing fade, feeling sorrowful but satisfied.

But the nightmare wasn't over yet.

From the belly of the boiler room, the sound of a freight train grew closer. The rainbow-colored lights intensified, turning bright, blinding white, and the school shuddered in its gut.

"The Pillar," Michael said. "Without Toby to hold it together, it's breaking up. The blast—"

Michael stood, weak, and held a hand to Sara. "Come on, we have to run for it."

Carefully Sara lay Toby on the debris-covered floor, her heart swollen with love and pride. She paused long enough to grab her chukrahas off the ground, then took Michael's hand as the winds in the hallway stirred away the broken ash of the dead Shape. The storm picked up, and Sara felt a hungry pull in her belly, drawing her towards the boiler room.

"Oh no," she said. "What, is it going to implode? I can feel it, like on Yur."

"Come on!" Michael dragged her away as the train noise increased, but not before another, more familiar noise met them from the other end of the hall.

Chkchkchkchk!

Sara groaned, feeling despair set in. "No…not them. Not now."

Michael held his ground and readjusted his power bands. "We'll fight them off."

"We'll never make it in time." She shoved him. "Go. I'll hold them off."

"Sara—"

"Don't argue with me right now! You've got the family you always wanted. A baby… Please, go. Let me do this. For you."

Michael studied her, his face slackening, and Sara knew he wouldn't fight her on this. A part of her was saddened that he'd leave, but she knew that it was for the best. He had his brothers and a great wife and a real shot at just being normal after all this time. She struggled to smile for him. "Just tell your kid about his amazing Aunt Sara, okay?"

He nodded and chuckled through tears. "I don't know what to say."

"Then don't. Go. I'm gonna clean up here."

"You're one tough chick."

She punched his arm, half-hearted. "I had a good teacher."

He grinned, then raced away, ducking around a corner and out of sight. Behind her, the clicking of the grey devils coming to attend their fallen Master grew louder, and she turned to await their hordes. Their shadows were cast along the walls, and she imagined, if she were lucky, the Pillar would explode before they reached her. She just didn't have the fight in her anymore.

Too exhausted to care, she dropped the chukrahas blade to the ground and lifted her head, her world filling with the terrifying snarls and snaps of damned souls corrupted by the Rage. She supposed Jerry, Mai, Chris, and the Hooded Man were among them.

"Come on already," she mumbled, welcoming her fate. *Just be ready to catch me, God.*

She splayed her fingers, arms limp, surrendering herself to the end, ready to see the Man in the Stetson again. With any hope, Toby was waiting for her there, too, in that White Place.

Yeah. She liked the sound of that.

Suddenly, thin fingers interlocked with one of her outstretched hands, and she jolted, her eyes bolting open.

"No," her voice cracked, seeing Michael standing there, holding her hand. "You idiot," she sighed, but had never been happier to see anyone in all her life.

He smiled, cavalier as always. "It's you and me. 'Til the end, remember?"

She nodded, overcome, and hugged him. The devils' chattering echoed closer, but she savored the final moment of calm and whispered to him, "I love you."

"I love *you*."

She sobbed into his neck. "Do you think there's a Michael and Sara somewhere out there who got it right?"

He pulled from her, grinning. "In a multiverse of infinite possibilities…I'd say there's a good chance."

"I hope so."

"Me, too."

The first of the monsters rounded the hall, and Michael and Sara faced them. Wiping away tears, Sara growled and yanked the chukrahas blade from the floor, ready for the devils. Michael cracked his knuckles, sneering savagely.

"You ready for this?" she asked, light and carefree, shrugging off her fears.

He returned her smirk with one of his own. "As a team."

"Go!"

Michael and Sara met the devils head-on. The grey beasts galloped forward on their curled toes and curved spears, clacking in rage. Michael slugged one, then another, across the face, sending them to bowl over dozens more. Two devils climbed the walls to drop from the ceiling, and Sara twirled and chopped, cleaving one at the neck and the other in the chest. Once more, Michael and Sara fell into perfect battle synch, staying close, moving around each other, using each other for support as they ducked and dodged and turned and fought on.

Always fighting on.

Around them, the world bucked and popped as chunks of wall, floor—even reality itself—broke loose. Devils screeched and clawed, but were ripped from their feet, evaporating in the pillar as it tore itself apart. The roof cracked, split, and caved in, slipping into the void.

Sara shot Michael a worried look, but he showed no sign of slowing down. He lashed out, devils crawling around him like giant insects, and punched, punched, punched, splashing blackish blood everywhere. Sara swallowed hard, her heart thumping wildly, and hacked and slashed her perimeter, growing light on her feet.

This is it, she knew, and lost her footing, slipping upwards into zero gravity. "Michael!" She clawed for him, abandoning her weapon for good.

He mashed in a devil's featureless face, and whipped about to her. "Hold on!" With abandon, he planted a foot on the crumbling wall and pushed off, sailing through the high winds, grabbing her wrist. "I've got you!"

They locked eyes with one another as the world broke apart around them. They spun in vertical free fall, aimed right for the vortex. Sara thought there should be so much to say to this man, but in that moment, she couldn't think to form a single word. Just knew that she was relieved he was here with her, at the very end.

He must have sensed it, too. He looked terrified, but smiled nonetheless.

Grey devils flew past them, still clawing, but no longer a threat.

A kind of magic washed over her, then a strong presence. A warmth inside that banished her fears and brought the light of knowledge to her, and she knew. She knew!

"Wait!" she gasped, letting go with one hand to dig around in her pockets. "*Wait!*" Fumbling urgently, her shaking fingers wrapped around the cylinder in her pocket. "I—"

Then the world turned to white.

21

Michael slowly blinked sight back into his eyes, his surroundings sharpening to clarity. He was outside, the brilliant sun banishing away the dark clouds and warming his back and face. Beneath him, a patch of scorched earth, dead grass blown back as if by a mighty bomb.

In his hand, Sara's.

They lay there on their stomachs, facing each other in the middle of a deserted field. Her blue eyes were wide with excitement, a breathless smile stretched wide. He released her hand and rose, spotting the familiar sights of Los Angeles—or, rather, what the aliens had left of it, though the invaders were nowhere to be seen. Michael realized he stood outside the school, only there *was* no school. It was just…gone. Vaporized.

"It imploded," he commented, feeling dumb. Turning sharp to Sara, he stuttered, "W-What did you do? How did we survive?"

She brushed the dirt off her jeans, standing, and tossed a metal cylinder into the air, deftly catching it again. Looking quite impressed with herself, she said, "Ifod Paradox Generator. One-time use. Creates a pocket dimension. Removes you from the timestream for a split second before bringing you back. Handy to have when you're facing a head-on collision or a band of Gryffyr mercenaries you may or may not have double-crossed on a deal."

He laughed, bewildered.

"It just came to me," she said, marveling. Glancing to the beautiful skies, finally free of the cold pall, she sighed, "Guess someone up there likes us."

"Guess so," he said.

Shapes moved in his peripheral, and Michael spotted Light Sphere and the Illumiknights. They looked beaten and worn, victorious—but not without cost.

Draped across Light Sphere's muscular arms hung the still form of Eon. Michael frowned, saddened by the loss, but appreciative of their sacrifice.

Johnny pushed his way from behind the gargantuan Grizzly, hustling over to them. "You did it! I don't know how—but you did it! The aliens just vanished! They must've only been kept here by the power of the rift, because once you shut that down—poof! And, hey, bonus points for the imploding pillar thingie not wiping out the entire dimension!"

Before he'd even finished, the big guy wrapped meaty arms around Sara and lifted her off her feet, twirling her haphazardly about. She laughed through it all, finally squirming her arms free to return the hearty hug.

Michael grinned at the sight, then searched the vacant lot, eyes settling on the parked Chevy. Edward sat on the roof of the car, lighting a cigarette and taking a long pull, looking spent and ready for a week-long nap. Michael smirked. He supposed his brother had earned it. They all had. With the aliens gone, they could finally rebuild Los Angeles. Tear down the wall and rejoin the rest of the world.

Seth leaned against the car, too, his arm in a makeshift sling, but well enough to offer a small wave. Michael returned it, grateful to God that the Morrison brothers had another chance to make their family whole again. He—

His breath stopped short, his eyes brimming with thankful tears.

Candice emerged from behind the Chevy, smiling and crying. Michael wept, too, and stumbled closer, knees weak from the battle, but weakened by her beauty more. Candice raced for him, laughing and sobbing, and when she reached him, she leapt into his arms, wrapping her legs around his waist and kissing him like he'd never been kissed before. Even with their mouths pressed together, they wept aloud and laughed and whispered "I love yous" and tender reassurances. Michael spun around, the love of his life in his arms, staring into her face and not caring if he ever saw anything else ever again.

He had her. At last he had her.

Still half-laughing, half-crying, Michael lowered Candice to the ground, and she snuggled close to his chest. He breathed in her hair, stroking back the curls to caress her cheeks, her chin. "And you were worried," he joked.

She slapped him on the chest, rolling her eyes and drying her tears. He waited for her to calm, then touched her stomach. Gently she placed her hand over his and stared into his eyes.

"Let's go home," he said.

"Where's home?" She cocked an eyebrow.

He shrugged, realizing they now had a brand new world ahead of them. "Wherever we want to it to be. Let's start with Wyoming."

She nodded and he tipped her mouth to his. When they parted, he turned back to Sara, ready to... Ready to what, he didn't know. What could he say to her? The girl who'd rescued him from himself. The girl who'd made him want to be a better man. They'd spent a lot of their time together hurting each other, but the lessons she'd taught him, and the joys they'd shared… Such unspeakable joy. He was alive because of her, in all the ways that mattered, and a simple "thank you" would never be enough.

She was his Sara. How could he ever tell her good-bye?

The question remained unanswered, because he didn't have the chance. When he turned back, Sara was already some distance away from the scene, Johnny practically dancing about her, still gabbing about their impossible victory.

But Sara was watching Michael, smiling.

He faced her across the empty expanse and could do nothing more than raise a hand in farewell. He wasn't sure from this distance, but he thought she was blushing. Then she tucked her long bangs behind her ear, shrugged, turned, and walked out of his life forever.

Candice lightly tugged at his shirt. "You going to be okay?" she asked, her grey eyes full of understanding.

He watched as Sara faded from sight. "Yeah. I really am."

He gave Candice a soft peck on the lips, and wrapped his arm around his wife, ready to face the rest of his life.

22

Sara and Johnny walked down the thoroughfare, passing by the streets where they'd grown up together. Getting here had taken a while, since Sara had the only rift and was responsible for depositing everyone back where they belonged. Light Sphere had a friend to bury, sadly, but was glad to have been there for the final battle. Wurgyl was more than happy to return to Supernova and, in fact, waved Sara from any obligation she owed him, provided she never asked him for another favor as long as she lived. She agreed to his conditions. Not surprisingly Seth had decided to stay behind on Michael's world, getting to know his brothers again. She imagined that would be awkward, but in time, they would repair their bond.

As for Michael, he was with Candice now. Which was good. Sara still felt a hollowness inside, but Michael had more than earned his retirement and a happy future filled with picket fences and free from rift jumping. He'd already spent his entire childhood saving universes. It was about time he started living. Sara told herself she'd check in with them, especially after the baby was born. She fancied herself as The Amazing Aunt Sara, blowing in from the cosmic winds with stories to tell and alien baubles to impart. But already Sara wondered if she'd ever go through with it. Maybe it was better to keep it at a clean break. After everything she and Michael had been through, they could never be "friends". She'd miss him terribly but…it was for the best.

"Need help with that?" Johnny asked, dipping his chin to the large box in her hands, filled with what little remained of Zeo.

"Nah, I got it," she said.

"Sorry about your robot."

"No problem. I'll just swing by the twenty-seventh century and get 'im patched up. He'll be back to doing my laundry and killing primitives in no time."

Johnny scratched the back of his head. "Well, can't say that makes me feel any better." A comfortable silence passed, and he eyed her. "So what will you do now? You've got the last rift, right? You could go anywhere. Anywhen. And I guess you've still got the Gateworld out there. What's the next adventure?"

She shrugged, indifferent, and exhaled peacefully. "I think I'm all done with adventures for a while. Thinkin' about sticking around here for now. I could use a job, though."

He guffawed. "Forget it! Maya would *kill* me if you worked at the store."

She giggled. "You're probably right about that."

The friends approached the familiar storefront, the sign above the door reading SUPERNATURAL SURPLUS. "Home, sweet home," Johnny groaned, seeing the place was still in a mess after the Shape's attack.

The door chimed and Maya stormed out, hands on her curvaceous hips. Johnny spread his arms wide to embrace her, "Honey! I'm home!"

But she stopped short and slapped him hard across the face. Sara balked, and Johnny wobbled in a daze. Then the woman gripped both sides of his chubby face and kissed him passionately on the mouth. Once done, she smiled, gave him a light pat on his fuzzy cheek, and headed back inside.

Johnny gaped at Sara for a moment, then threw his hands up in surrender. "Women."

The big guy hurried inside, taking a broom and sweeping up debris alongside his girlfriend, business as usual. Sara smiled to herself and set the box with Zeo's parts down on the front stoop. She sat there beside it for a moment, catching her breath and admiring the town. After all that she'd seen, all that she'd done, she was right back where she started. The multiverse called to her, but she was prepared to let it wait for now. It was good to be home. There were lessons that waited for her here. Lessons she'd failed to learn the first time around, but she was ready now.

She'd told Johnny true. The time for adventuring was over. Now it was time to grow up. Time to make a life for herself, just as Michael had done.

Overcome by a bittersweet view of the future, she stood to her feet, preparing to head into the store to pick up her own broom and get to work cleaning up the mess she'd made, when a familiar voice interrupted her musings.

"Hey," he said, casual and bright.

She blushed, turning to behold his face—pure blue eyes, long blond hair, those pronounced cheekbones and oh-so-serious brow. Had he come back for her? How? Why?

Yet, the olive denim jacket—that he'd finally grown into—gave him away, and she laughed at herself, remembering him now as a boy from school so very long ago. They'd last seen each other right before she made some terrible decisions that set her life down a painful path. She'd run into him that day, by chance it seemed. Called him a "jerk".

And now he was here, today of all days, when her life was once more at a crossroads.

"Hey," she replied, not sure what to do next. Her hands tingled with excitement and a healthy kind of fear.

He glanced over her shoulder, surveying the store. "You—uh—work here?"

"*No*," she said definitely, chuckling at the thought of Maya's reaction.

"Oh. I heard there was some excitement last night."

"Yeah."

His clear eyes—not an ounce of Rage within them—drifted to hers, and he narrowed his gaze. "H-Have we met?"

"We went to school together."

"Yeah," he said, growing more confident. "I thought so."

"But we didn't talk," she quickly offered.

The handsome boy laughed, "It's probably for the best. I had a real chip on my shoulder back then. Moped around a lot. But you kinda just wake up one morning and think, you know, life's too short to walk around ticked off all the time."

"I know exactly what you mean."

"Look, I didn't mean to bother you. I just thought…" He stuffed his hands in his back jeans pockets and shifted about awkwardly. "This is going to sound really weird, but I had this *crazy* dream last night. I was in this city, like with real trees and no dome, you know? Like in the old books? And there was this giant robot elephant thing and some guy who looked like a comic book character who shot light out of these weird gloves. And…" He stared at her thoughtfully. "And you were totally there. And we…"

She smiled, sinuses stinging with tears.

He shook his head and ruffled his long hair. "Crazy, right?"

"A little bit," she teased. "But it sounds like it was a great ride."

"It was," he said with sincerity. "Best dream I ever had."

Sara studied his every feature, her heart imploring her to act. Across the street, by the store where Michael had once saved her from Charlie, Sara spotted the worn brim of a Stetson hat, and the Man who wore it. And beside him, a little ruddy boy with disheveled hair and beautiful brown eyes. Toby—young again and happy, as she'd always remember him—waved to her. She thought to cry and race to him, but the pair were gone in an eye-blink, leaving her. But not really, she realized. They'd always be there.

The handsome man before her took a breath, then said, somewhat forlorn, "Anyway, sorry again, to bother you. See you around—"

"Maybe we could go get a cup of coffee," Sara blurted, terrified he'd leave. When he didn't, she finished, "You can tell me more about your dream."

He smiled, playing it cool, but the tips of his ears flushed. "Yeah. We could do that."

"Cool."

"Cool." He suddenly fumbled and extended a strong hand. "Sorry, I'm being rude. I'm Michael."

She eyed the hand offered her. *Well*, she thought, *maybe one more adventure.*

Slipping her hand in his, she beamed as something like destiny stirred her heart.

"I'm Sara."

Experience the adventure from the beginning.

Read on for an exciting preview of:

A Multiverse Novel by Greg Mitchell

Now Available from

1

Tony Carlson had it coming.

Cold rain pelted him from above as he pulled his collar tighter, shielding himself from the raw chill of the city. But the icy grip that seized his body had nothing to do with the temperature, nor the rain outside. Death walked the streets this night, and Tony Carlson feared he was next in line to feel the sickle.

A seemingly endless line of sculpted bodies in tight-fitting designer clothes stretched in front of the club—The Electric Kitty. Even in this horrible storm, hundreds of swingers and would-be partygoers waited outside, praying for the bouncer's blessing to enter and have the time of their lives.

Tony had no time for the patrons as he crossed the street and forced his way through the line. He wasn't like them. He wasn't particularly handsome or well-kept, instead sporting shoulder-length slicked back hair, and an ensemble straight out of the 2130s. He was a hipster from another time, out of place with the trends of Now.

But at least he wasn't a sheep.

Ignoring the usual snickers and stares, Tony marched right up to the door and nodded to the bouncer.

"Go on in, Mr. Carlson." The bouncer returned the nod in grim affirmation before stepping aside to let Tony in, only to immediately reclaim his post with folded beefy arms.

Tony moved through the club, trying his best to dodge the dancing clusters of people. The club pitched back and forth like a ship at sea, as he was bombarded by multi-colored lights and a sound system that crashed against him like tumultuous waves. He recognized a few of the girls as he continued to push forward, but shunned frivolous thoughts of romance, never taking his mind off his destination.

"Hey, Tony. Wanna party?" A bouncy little pink-haired number named Cammy be-bopped her way over and clung to his arm. Her skin sparkled with Glitterslam—the new drug that was all the rage these days. Spritz some on your body, get wasted and look hot in the process. *Kids today.*

"Later." He pushed her aside.

She gaped at him. "Hey, you don't look so good."

He kept moving, leaving Cammy's bewildered stare behind. He worried his fear was all too evident in his eyes. The shadow of fate loomed large over him and, even inside, he felt that dulling cold that permeated the city's streets. Some animal part in his mind screamed "*Not safe!*" over and over, filling him with the uncontrollable urge to find somewhere to hide.

He needed help, and the only help he could think of was Salvatore "Sal" Frazetta, the owner of the West Side district. Tony ascended the metal steps, clanking his way to the top floor. Two dead-eyed guards stopped his approach.

"I gotta talk to Sal," he blurted nervously, glancing behind to make sure he wasn't followed.

The guards looked at each other as though communicating telepathically, then stood aside. Tony scurried to the large oak door at the end of the hallway. He knocked and waited for a response.

"Come in," someone said from inside, the voice muffled through the door.

Tony hurried into the private office, closing off the rest of the club. The room was dimly lit and patched in shadow. The blinds were drawn on the windows and the neon advertisements from the nudie joint across the street periodically painted the room in bright reds. A small lamp on the coffee table in front of the couch revealed a young twenty-something blonde girl, clumsily shooting up her arm with blue glow. She was one of the new girls. Some country bumpkin who had come to the big city to be a star. Sal was the kind of guy who had connections and actually could make a wide-eyed pretty girl's dreams come true, but his prospects usually ended up here in his club, instead, doped up. The city, with all its promises of pleasure, was exciting and overwhelming, and all too often these kids fell prey to the allure of the party culture. Whatever this girl might've been, now she was just another junkie hitting the blue glow. Tony flinched in revulsion at the sight; he'd never been one for the hard stuff.

"Sal?" he asked to the quiet blackness. He peered harder, until he found Sal, sitting in the shadows at his desk. Tony recognized the familiar stench of Sal's favorite brand of cigars and followed the trail of smoke to the furniture.

"Sal." Tony approached the desk and gave himself permission to sit down. "We got a problem, man."

Only the outline of Sal's face was evident in the shadows. "Why's that?"

"There's a new player in town." Tony waited to see Sal's response, but there seemed to be none in the near future. "I don't know who he is. Pete said he heard about a takedown in the South End, right? There was supposed to be some big shipment come in and Pete was sneaking over there to see what the Southers had coming. But he said when he got there, all he heard were screams coming from inside and gunfire. Pete said he got so scared he left. He said he had never heard a man scream like that."

Tony paused again, expecting Sal at any time to lose his cool. But, Salvatore Frazetta was known for his cool. "And, what's this got to do with me?"

Tony ventured, "Word around town has it that this guy took out East and North too. Now he's coming here. We already lost Sidney. I found him myself. All gutted. Like a fish." Tony shuddered at the memory. "Pete said Donovan was supposed to come by to go over the plans for the Watson operation, but Donovan never showed. Now, Pete's missing too."

Sal sat there in silence for a moment. The smoke from his cigar trailed in the air, causing Tony to choke it back, just a little.

"What are we going to do, Sal?"

"What does this guy look like?"

"Nobody knows. They say he's like a whirlwind, man. He just comes out of nowhere and once he's done, he just disappears. A real pro."

Sal was quiet. Thinking about their options, Tony assumed.

"Maybe we should leave town, Sal. Just the two of us until this whole thing blows over. Maybe this guy will leave."

His knees started shaking, and Tony chewed his nails as sweat pooled under his armpits. The smoke continued to curl through his nostrils, nearly gagging him. He looked down to Sal's cigar, wishing he would put the thing out. That's when he noticed that the cigar was burnt all the way down to Sal's fingers. But Sal remained unflinching, as if he didn't notice the heat brushing against his knuckles.

Then, the shape replied, "Can't leave until it's finished."

Tony's knees stopped shaking.

"S-Sal?"

In the quiet that followed, Tony looked deeper into the darkness, seeing the outline of Sal's body, and he went rigid as he stared, waiting—hoping to God that Sal would move.

Sal Frazetta fell face first on the desk, his throat cut and bleeding out.

Tony yelped and jumped back, knocking his chair over, just as the blinking neon advertisements bathed the room in harsh red light and revealed the awful truth. Standing behind Sal Frazetta was a man—no, a *kid*. Some punk teenager dressed in jeans, T-shirt, sneakers, and a worn leather jacket. He wore a blank expression and had pale blond hair, sallow skin, and the darkest eyes.

The eyes were the worst.

Without a cry, Tony Carlson rushed for the door. The shadowed figure moved faster and a cold, uncaring hand burst forth from the darkness and grabbed Tony by the scruff of the neck. The hand, more powerful than anything Tony had ever encountered, flung him across the room, sending him crashing over the chair in which he had just been sitting.

The shadows pulled back and revealed their dark occupant. He moved with determination in each step. A scary confidence that revealed no hint of fear or mercy. Tony shrank back against the wall, pulling himself into a near fetal position, desperately trying to keep his distance from this specter of death.

"Tony Carlson," the kid said, as if pronouncing sentence. "Time's up."

Tony screamed his throat raw.

The door burst open and the two guards from before came in, their guns drawn and killer intent painting their faces. After a quick look to their boss stone-cold dead on the table, they opened fire. Bullets exploded from their guns and dug deep into the kid's back with dull *thuds*.

However, the teenager was not fazed.

He paused in his pursuit of Tony Carlson and turned around. His eyes, those hollow dead eyes that he'd fixed Tony with, now set their sights on the guards. He started toward them. Their bullets only seemed to tear through the boy's jacket, and *that* only seemed to make him angrier.

The kid came right up on them and grabbed the gun hand of the guard on his right. Instantly, the gun crashed to the floor, while the guard's hand crackled under the pressure. The guard cried out. Still holding onto the hand, the kid with the dark eyes slapped the other guard's chest with the flat of his other hand, crushing his ribcage with a crisp crack and propelling the man backwards into the hall.

The boy took hold of the first guard and lifted him off the ground, raising him high before throwing him on top of his fallen partner. Then the kid slowly closed the door again.

And locked it.

Turning back, he focused his baleful glare on Tony and marched toward him, stalking him. Ready to strike.

Tony whimpered as he crawled up the wall, trying to avoid the boy. The boy walked right up to him, grabbed his face in his icy hands, and hoisted him up by the head.

"Please!" Tony blubbered. "Don't kill me! I'll give you whatever you want…*whatever it is!* Please! I'll change! I'm sorry! I'll change!"

The teenager, with an unforgiving blackness behind his eyes, spoke. "Sorry. Nothing personal."

2

With a flick of the wrist, Tony Carlson's neck snapped. Michael Morrison hurled the thug's lifeless body across the room and through the window. Glass shattered as Tony's body pushed through. Michael moved to the broken window and stared down at Tony Carlson lying motionless on a crumpled hot dog cart two stories below. Panicked passersby and clubbers alike scrambled and screamed. The sight gave Michael pause at what he'd done. Something pulled at him. Sympathy? Regret? No, Tony was a bad man. He deserved what he had coming to him.

Just like all the others on a thousand worlds in the multiverse that Michael had visited.

Suddenly, he sensed a sharp *whoosh* as a switchblade knife cut the air just past his ear and plunged hilt-deep into his shoulder. Snarling, he looked to see the knife still stuck in him, then turned further to see the blonde girl from the couch, backing away as her pouty lips parted in mounting terror. The rubber string was still tied to her arm, and pink rings circled her wide grey eyes.

Michael wrapped his hand around the knife and gave a jerk, wrenching it free, before tossing it aside. Growling, he surveyed the fresh tear in his ratty jacket. "Don't. Touch. The Jacket."

The girl whimpered and staggered behind the table where she'd concocted her blue narcotic. Enraged, Michael took an angry arm and smashed aside the equipment she had used, splashing fluorescent blue liquid all over the floor. He reached down and undid the strap on her arm, throwing it to the side, then grabbed her with both hands as he had done to the late Tony Carlson. He slammed the girl against the wall, suspending her bare feet off the floor so that she faced him at eye level.

In that moment, he felt the fear in her as her body shook uncontrollably, but she was too numb from the drugs to fight back any more. She was helpless. He could kill her. Snap her in two without any effort and all of her pain would go away. He'd be doing her a favor, ending her miserable life.

It would be easy.

He studied her, curious. The girl before him was weak, and he pitied her for it. There was something in her grey eyes, such surrender there. She'd given up. Somewhere inside, he knew how that felt.

"What's your name?" he grumbled.

"C-Candice," she wept.

"Where are you from?"

She scanned his eyes, as though unsure of the reason behind his question. "Wy-Wyoming."

Michael cooled and released a heavy sigh, then glanced to the table. He reached over and picked up one of the needles to hold it before her, making sure she got a good look at its glowing contents. "Go back there. And never do this again."

The girl nodded to the best of her ability. Then he let her go.

She fumbled with the lock of the large door and stumbled into the club. Michael watched after her, his bloodlust subsiding. He wasn't sure exactly why he'd spared the girl, but he was glad he did. It felt good to give someone a second chance. He just hoped she didn't blow it.

"Hold it! Don't move!" a gruff voice barked from the doorway as a swarm of men in heavy armor filed in, automatic rifles raised. "Police!" the leader cried.

Michael snickered and held up his hands half-heartedly. "Relax, guys. I just killed Sal Frazetta for you, as well as all the other turf lords in your city." He offered a slight arrogant bow. "You're welcome."

The men in armor surveyed the mess he'd made of the room, finally spotting the kingpin's body. Through their clear faceplates, they traded dumbfounded expressions. At last, their leader glanced to Michael.

"*You* did this?"

Michael shrugged. "Just doing my job."

The man leveled his aim, struggling to maintain authority. "We're detaining you until we sort all this out."

A dark chuckle escaped Michael's smirk. "You can try."

"Tase him!"

A shorter cop at the leader's side unclipped a squarish pistol and fired off a round of electricity. Michael shrugged off the voltage and bolted for the window.

"Fire, fire!" the squad leader barked.

The police unloaded bullets on him as he ran, the slugs finding their mark, but doing no damage, save for shredding his poor leather jacket—the one he'd taken from Rip.

Michael darted for the window and leaped through the air, exiting the same way Tony Carlson had. He fell two stories and landed on the hood of a parked hovercar below. The impact blew out the front windshield and sent the car's alarm system into a tizzy. The retreating patrons yelped in shock.

Michael stood and hopped down from the car, onto the solid ground. The police lined up at the window, stunned into inaction as Michael offered a wave and crossed the street. High beams from a hovercar nearly blinded him. Repulsor engines groaned as they were thrown into full reverse, but the hovercar barreled forward along the slick pavement. Before it struck him, Michael stepped to the sheet of paper waiting for him and vanished in a flash of brilliant rainbow, ready to dish out more judgment on the enemies of the Light.